The Witch's Hat

ANDREW AABERG

Copyright © 2022 Andrew Aaberg
All rights reserved.

ISBN: 979-8-9861505-1-2 (Paperback)
ISBN: 979-8-9861505-2-9 (Hardcover)

Dedication

Dedicated to all the people who thought that I couldn't, in my brother's honor.

Contents

Acknowledgments ix
Foreword xi
Chapter 1: Torrent of the Spirits 1
Chapter 2: Rebellion 5
Chapter 3: Shrouded Star Spangled Sparks 10
Chapter 4: CPS 14
Chapter 5: STOP ahead 18
Chapter 6: Halt The Whore 24
Chapter 7: Reprogramming 28
Chapter 8: The Relapsing Puss 31
Chapter 9: Free Yet Oppressed 56
Chapter 10: Fine China 68
Chapter 11: The Mysterious Downfall 80
Chapter 12: Memento Mori 85
Chapter 13: The Media Swarm 92
Chapter 14: Change 98
Chapter 15: Cali 103
Chapter 16: Oofta 109
Chapter 17: No H8 113
Chapter 18: Aenema 116
Chapter 19: Progression 122
Chapter 20: The Journey 124
Chapter 21: Overkill 129
Chapter 22: The Pact 134
Chapter 23: Car Shopping 139

Chapter 24: New Years 144
Chapter 25: Work-Life 157
Chapter 26: Desperate Tweakers 166
Chapter 27: Home Invasion 172
Chapter 28: Sloppy Seconds 178
Chapter 29: Again? 188
Chapter 30: They Come and Go 200
Chapter 31: The Clash 206
Chapter 32: Homeless 211
Chapter 33: Rehab 219
Chapter 34: More Trouble 225
Chapter 35: The Real-Life 232
Chapter 36: The Medium 236
Chapter 37: The Beer Belly Man 240
Chapter 38: King of the Ring 252
Chapter 39: The Circus Retreat 256
Chapter 40: Surrender? 265
Chapter 41: Settling In 268
Chapter 42: The Mysterious Men 281
Chapter 43: The Warning 286
Chapter 44: The Folder 291
Chapter 45: Court Date 298
Chapter 46: The Watchtower 305
Chapter 47: The Inauguration 309
Chapter 48: Home Visitation 319
Chapter 49: Star Wars 323
Chapter 50: The Patriot 326
Chapter 51: Discharge 331
About the Author 335

"The wolfe also shall dwell with the lambe, and the leopard shall lie downe with the kid: and the calfe and the yong lion, and the fatling together, and a little child shall lead them."

-Isaiah 11:6 1611 KJV

Acknowledgments

This is the section where I would like to thank each and every person who has helped me achieve something that I consider to myself to be a success. First, I'd like to thank my wife for pulling me away from the hellish life I was living and helping me get straightened out. Next, I would like to thank my friend Dave for the initial push that I needed to get to rockin' and rolling along my writing endeavors.

A big shout out goes to the books editor, Samantha Wald for all her work making edits with her busy schedule. She was very eager to help and her expertise helped calm my nerves towards the end. Shawn was the book's cover illustrator who did a remarkable job. This book would not be what it is without his wonderful artwork.

I would like to thank all my supporters which may be teachers, office workers, county workers or any co-worker at both my jobs who showed an interest in my book and had to withstand me talking about its progress all the time. I appreciate you, you have helped keep the light burning along our path. For those of you that did the chapter illustrations, (Michelle, Jackie, Leah, Jordan, Cassie, my darling little sister, my beautiful wife and her coworker) you made this very special. I applaud you. Also, Mikaela, I would like to greatly thank you for your final walk through. Kelsey, I thank you for the green light. Lynn, I thank you for the final push. Finally, I can't forget "Cheeto-man" for the deep thinking. Thank you all!

Go Wolves!

If I forgot your name, just know I still greatly value your help and support.

Time to publish.

Foreword

Consider this a fantasy novel of a past life of a real person.

CHAPTER 1
Torrent of the Spirits

In June 1976 Strativarious was born. Strat was very talented. A prodigy. Even his birth caused the seismic implosion of the earth that caused Hurricane David at the end of August in 1979. His cool vibe wavelengths were slow to react to cause the devastation in the Caribbean. He had landed majestically like an angel, unlike Andrew who dropped like an atom bomb in May of '92 and rattled the earth like the devil below pounding to rise to the occasion setting off the chain of events that caused Hurricane Andrew a few months after. These two hurricanes would eventually meet years later as human tempests to stir things up, evoking magic through music.

In Andrew's early years he seemed to not fit in. Some may ask, "Why not? He's a white male." It didn't matter. He didn't talk much. There was too much going on. He was shy and wanted to keep to himself. He almost failed preschool for not speaking. Andrew didn't even want to be in the same vicinity as any of the other students. If the class was washing their hands after finger painting he would wait until everyone was done to wash his own to avoid any exchange of words.

He did however find solace with his imaginary friend. Andrew would talk to him on a daily basis. He and Teton did everything together. Teton was Andrew's outlet, but unfortunately, Teton never left the house. On the contrary, Andrew was also deathly afraid of his shadow. It would dance to its own drumbeat. For the most part, Teton protected Andrew from the shadow man but word went around of Andrew's fear.

"Boom, boom, shadow!" Chanted his uncle and father.

Andrew shuddered in panic when they did this. He would run away and hide. He wondered what the shadows did in the dark, but he didn't want to find out. He would sleep with the door open and keep his eyes peeled in case he had to run for his life. On some nights, when the lights went out and the moon shined through the window, Andrew would watch the shadows dance on the ceiling. On one of these particular nights, a shadow man reached out to grasp Andrew. Andrew wasn't in the mood for his soul to be manipulated. But it was too late. He was stained.

Andrew would scream with terror in the darkness of the night. He lived with his father's parents who were big alcoholics and would fight a good portion of their awakened time. His grandfather, Cornelius, was a Vietnam vet who was wounded and awarded the Purple Heart. Some may have referred to him as a "tunnel rat," which withheld the duty to clear out the underground tunnels in the communist state. He would come across the Vietcong and eliminate as many of them as he could.

Through the grandfather's journeys, he ended up getting shot in the ass. During his last days at warfare, he was ambushed and slid down a hill quickly and his gun shot him in the butt. This is not a story he would share with everybody. The medic gave him a blood transfusion and infected Cornelius with hepatitis C. After the war he settled into being a raging alcoholic. He would speak in Vietnamese in his bedroom all by his lonesome as he sipped from the bottle. Grandma was an alcoholic too. The two would throw things at each other and slam doors screaming in the process. Could it be possible negative entities were stirred up in this home?

Shortly rewind to March of 1995, almost 3 years after Andrew was born, and Andrew was blessed with a baby brother. The family ended up moving a few years after Josh entered the world to their very own home. They didn't move far and still lived in the big city of Minneapolis. It just so happened that when Josh got older he drew Andrew away from Teton and the two brothers became closer. Despite being best friends, Andrew had rage too. When Andrew was 6 he power slammed Josh onto a glass table and broke it. This he would never forget. Something possessive came over him. He was overcome with negative energy and beat the crap out of the poor kid.

"Take that!" Andrew yelled, "maybe next time you won't tell mom on me!"

Josh didn't think twice to run for the security of their mother. Andrew chased him.

"Get back here!" Andrew said in an angry voice.

Andrew shoved Josh to the ground. Josh scrambled to his feet and ran out of the living room through the kitchen and to their mom's bedroom. Tanya was on the phone like her usual self.

"Help me! Andrew sla-slammed me on the the t-table!" Lil J stuttered as he cried.

Tanya hurried to the kitchen where Andrew ended his chase and shouted, "Go to your room and leave him alone! We will see what your dad thinks of this when he gets home." Then she continued with her phone call discussing the incident that happened and blew it up, "I think he needs a trip to the psychiatrist. He won't talk in school. He is socially awkward. He's acting out! He needs to be put on some meds," she relayed through the phone line.

Andrew lay in his bed. He was full of anger. Time passed and he grew to regret the torment he caused his brother that day. It was a lesson learned but fortunately, it was the only time Andrew could remember harassing Josh. He didn't know what triggered his actions, but he had received a high tormenting him. He felt sick and knew that what he did was wrong.

When dad came home, mother told him all about what happened. Their father's name was Scott. He was ex-military and didn't have a problem imposing the same fear in Andrew that Andrew did within Josh. Scott grabbed Andrew by his ankles and held him upside down over the stairwell.

"Please don't!" Andrew's voice echoed through the stairwell in a piercing scream. "Let me go! Please!"

Scott started wiggling Andrew back and forth. He even loosened his grip and held Andrew with one arm. He pretended like he was gonna drop him.

"How do you like it?" Scott taunted.

"Please! Let me go!" Andrew screamed.

Andrew's dad set him down and Andrew raced to his room to hide out. Andrew had a fear of heights for the longest time after that day. He treated his brother kindly from then on out. He figured if you put out negative energy it finds a way right back to bite you in the ass. This was one of many lessons learned. Shortly thereafter, Andrew was placed on medication and attended therapy by his mother's will.

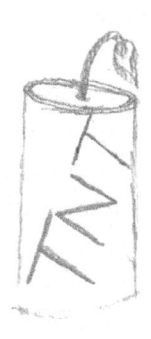

CHAPTER 2
Rebellion

It wasn't long until the family ended up moving out of the city and into the suburbs. Meanwhile, Andrew and Josh sprouted like Jack's beanstalk seeds. Before you knew it, Andrew was 11. The two brothers shared a bedroom and Andrew was now inching towards his teenage phase. He would get mouthy with his parents for good reason. Especially his mom. One day came along where Andrew called his mother a bitch. As soon as his father got home it was time for punishment.

Andrew was stripped to his boxers and was locked outside in the frigid Minnesota winter. It was windy which made it colder. He decided to bury himself in a snowbank to block the wind. The snow melted around his body and he became soaked. It was moments like this that toughened him up; as he lay in the snow he pretended as though nothing existed. Everything went blank and his brain processing was more extraordinary than ever. Eventually, his father opened the door to let him back in. Andrew hurried to his room and locked the door.

It turned out being prescribed medication made him revolt even more. So much it caused him serious problems. With Andrew starting to go through puberty, some of his actions were common among the crowd. Maybe some of his actions were justified by the out-of-control household. Or maybe not. Whether the case, Josh and Andrew felt like they were on the back burner. The parents started foster care when they had moved to this new home and the two would speak of how all their parents' attention was directed to the foster kids. Scott wasn't much to blame because he always worked, but all Tanya did was sit on the couch and yell at all the kids. She grew fatter by the day. Sure the siblings were spoiled and their mother bought them tons, but what they needed was more attention to level out some of the feelings of betrayal. They understood that what their mother was doing was her job and a good thing. They accepted it and made the best.

On the bright side, Andrew became good friends and was technically a brother to all the kids that came through. The boys would do boy stuff. They made leaf forts and would have slingshot wars with the neighbors across the street. Josh never attended. He was a gentle soul and he proved to make a smart decision not to partake because one of Andrew's friends got shot in the stomach with a nail.

After a while of doing foster care and cycling through an array of children, the parents decided on adopting. The little boy's name was Antonio. They took him in as an infant and by the time Andrew hit 13 years young, Antonio had become an official part of the family. He was ten years younger than Andrew and had anger issues growing up. Antonio would bang his head against things continually when he got mad. Now the mother of three, Tanya would take Antonio to see psychiatrists, therapists, and caseworkers. He was diagnosed with a multitude of issues. The more issues he had the more public assistance that mother got. This became a game for the longest time. Stories were brought up to doctors and were dramatized. By the time Antonio was 5, he was on a vast range of drugs, a human guinea pig to be exact.

It didn't take long to discover that Antonio liked to dress up as a girl. Scott didn't approve. Antonio loved the Wizard of Oz and even had the ruby red slippers to wear around the house. He would play dress-up for fun and owned tons of costumes. Everyone figured it would be something he would grow out of.

The Witch's Hat

But still, Andrew missed the days when he would play video games with his mom. When they would read together as a school assignment. But now she didn't have time for that. Or perhaps it wasn't the lack of time but the lack of effort. The only time it felt like she cared to spend with them was to discuss their mental health. She also put a lot of pressure on Andrew to find a job that made lots of money when he grew up. She wanted for him to use his knowledge for a bright future and to possibly maybe even make a few bucks off him. At the time, he got good grades. The parents were gracious enough to pay a little bit of cash for each letter. $5 for a C, $10 for a B, and $20 for an A. Andrew strived to learn but somehow it seemed like it was never good enough. He had some big shoes to fill.

They quit foster care after Antonio was adopted and the following year Andrew had started high school. Amid the stress of getting good grades and taking honors classes, Andrew slipped into illicit drugs. He started with drinking and smoking weed. He had a great time. This didn't go without any push back from his parents. They were clueless for the longest but shortly after graduating Freshman year Andrew was found out by them by smoking cigarettes and pot in his bedroom that summer.

His mom went to the gas station and bought a pack of Marlboro reds. She arrived back home and Andrew had both of his parents standing in front of him outside the front door of the house. She handed him the pack.

"If you like smoking so much why don't you smoke this whole pack at once and see how much you like smoking then?" she said.

Andrew wolfed down four smokes easy. As he got to his eighth his mother butted back in. "You are throwing your whole life away," Tanya claimed.

"I don't really care," replied Andrew.

"Are you stupid or something?" Scott asked angrily.

Andrew understood where his dad was coming from. His grandma had just passed away from cancer from smoking. She died in their house. The moment she passed she exploded diarrhea all over the wall.

It was a gruesome sight. Now Andrew was carrying on the tradition. At this point, he was experimenting. He was in his rebellion stage. Andrew got pissed off by the way his dad was talking to him and went inside and up the stairs...

"You are so dumb Andrew," his father said as he followed him inside.

Being the idiot Andrew was, standing at the top of the stairs, he told his dad to zip his mouth or else he'd get punched in his face. Yet his dad still egged him on.

"Do you want to fight?" Andrew petitioned.

"Go ahead and do it. I don't think you have the balls," Scott sneered.

Andrew stormed down the stairs and screamed in his father's face. "If you keep giving me shit I'm gonna kick your ass!"

"Do it!" shouted Scott.

Andrew stood inches away from his dad. "Fuck you!" he yelled. He was so close his father could smell the cigarettes on Andrew's breath.

A split second later his dad grabbed Andrew in a deathly bear hug. "Hurry! Tanya! Call the cops! He's making threats! Let's see if they can get some sense into him," he yelled.

Tanya was all over calling the cops. She needed something to gossip about with all her friends, siblings, and mother. Anyone who would listen. The cops ended up showing up and Andrew's dad released him. The cops were talking to Andrew, but Andrew was belligerent.

"We wouldn't argue if you guys took him to the juvenile center. Maybe he would learn his lesson," the parents said in agreement.

The officer cuffed Andrew and brought him to the police station for a mug shot and a collection of fingerprints. Afterward, they gave Andrew a ride straight to the juvenile center. Now he was in with the rough crowd. Andrew spent his time mostly in his cell. Every day they would do groups and discipline was enforced. If he didn't comply he was screamed at and degraded.

They called him names just like his dad did. Yes, he may have deserved it, but truth be told, the few-day hold at the facility didn't change Andrew much. They ended up charging him with a 5th-degree assault for making terroristic threats and sentenced him to 3 days. He was released from custody on July 3rd and his mother brought him home. He waited out front for his dad to arrive back from work. In his hand, Andrew clutched a baseball bat. When his father stepped out of the car Andrew darted after him and chased him around the yard with it. Yet still, his dad had the nerve to egg him on.

"Go ahead and do it bitch!" Scott shouted as he snaked his way away from Andrew. Tanya overheard the commotion from inside and opened the front door of the house. Scott saw her and shouted, "Tanya call the police! There's something wrong with this kid!"

Yet again Andrew was arrested. The cop never searched him before he was placed in the back of the police car. This time he wasn't cuffed either. Andrew had also been lighting firecrackers off in the yard before his dad arrived and had a few packs in his pocket. He managed to get a pack out along with a lighter. He stuffed the firecrackers through one of the holes of the cage leading into the front of the squad car and held it with just the fuse hanging towards him. He lit the fuse and dropped them. The firecrackers crackled and popped all over the place. They bounced off the computer and dash, leaving little burns on everything they touched. Andrew hated the police. This was his revenge. Andrew continued with his revolt trying to kick out the back seat windows without success.

Within a few seconds, the officer rushed to the car and tackled Andrew with the momentum of a football player, putting his forearm into Andrew's throat making him gag.

"You mother fucker!" the officer yelled.

"Fuck you piggy!" Andrew managed to gurgle back. He even added in a swine snort. The officer was super pissed. He didn't waste any time bringing Andrew back to juvie. Was it terrible for him to be locked up the very day he got out? Perhaps not in the aspect of retribution.

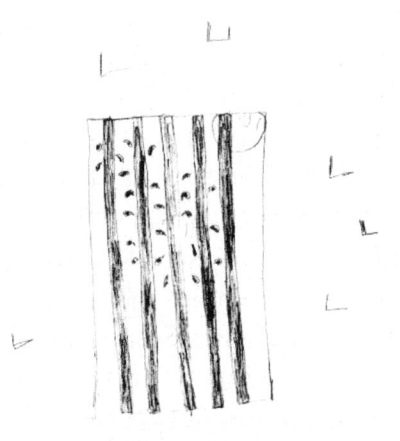

CHAPTER 3
Shrouded Star Spangled Sparks

THEY WENT TO the police station to pick up some more kids and took a 45-minute ride in a van to the correctional facility. Upon arrival, Andrew stepped out of the back of the van to his new home. On each side of him stood a correctional officer. Included in the bunch was the police officer that drove them. They uncuffed Andrew and more inmates followed to exit. One of the kids wouldn't get out of the van. He was maybe 12 at the oldest. He sat there silently and ignored the police officer's orders.

"Get out now," said the officer sternly.

Still, he sat there silently. As a result, the pig stepped into the van, hunched himself over, and grabbed the kid very aggressively. The kid tussled with him. This was Andrew's kind of dude, however, the power wasn't in their hands. This wasn't the time to revolt. What could they do? There were barbed wire fences around the perimeter. Escape was

The Witch's Hat

possible but what was the point? They would be right back where they started.

Another officer stepped in and they both pulled the kid out of the van violently and slammed him to the ground on his face. The kid cried out and blood was spilling onto the ground from his nose.

"You're gonna listen during your stay here. This isn't no game fucker!" fumed the correctional officer.

How stupid. Andrew looked at the shackled kid as the officers grabbed him from the ground. It was obvious that they had broken his nose. It was all crooked. Now what? He needed a hospital visit to fix his nose and guess who got away with smashing his face to the ground? There were similar qualities between the officers and the prisoners, they were both criminals, except the inmates were treated like garbage. No wonder why the kids aren't alright.

After getting yelled at, Andrew was brought inside. He was searched and given scrubs along with a pair of wool socks with grips on them. Andrew wanted to be secluded. They let him go to the bathroom quick as there weren't any in the cells then they locked him up. By this time it was evening and almost sunset time. Andrew had his very own room and just laid on the bed and fell asleep. No dreams that night.

The next day was the Fourth of July so no court. It would be the day of the freedoms which were taken from him. He was ready for celebrating the idea of true liberty. True liberty for everyone. Perhaps if Andrew had a dream that night he would have caught a glimmer. Instead, he slept dead until he awoke to a banging on his door bright and early. He could tell the energy was high that day.

The morning started with showers then summer school. The day consisted of normal groups plus the daily chores in the kitchen and dining room. He learned to keep his room tidy and his bed made from the previous visit to the detention center. He slipped up a few times and the asshole staff would scream at him. It was like a boot camp.

Many hours passed and it grew dark. Fireworks engulfed the heavens. The spirits of the inmates were as free as ever. They did whatever they could do to make noise. Shouting and banging echoed throughout the entire institution. They were going nuts. They felt as high as a kite while endorphins surged through their bodies to ignite the continuation of their rowdiness. Moments later they heard an angry voice on the intercom.

"Quit with all the racket! This is to all inmates. If you continue with the racket, each and every one of you will get a failed day!" snarled the drunken man through the speaker. The intensity grew. The inmates didn't care.

They began yelling and chanting, "Freedom! Freedom! Freedom! Freedom!"

They continued with extensive force. Andrew covered the window on the door with a blanket. Then he stared out the glazed window leading outside to gaze at the fireworks. What he could make out of them was amazing. Red white and blue filled up the sky with sparks. The embers were smiling as they glowed, falling toward the earth like raining rays of flickering sunlight. Andrew was chanting the "freedom" chant with all the others as he took in the great view. He pounded on the wall a beat that blended in with the slow but loud battle cry. It was powerful. Powerful at least until the intercom was triggered back to life again...

"We warned you! You have all failed your day! If you continue with the noise we have no problem adding on more," shouted the drunk through the sound system.

There was a mass shouting that quickly died down. The kids had a lot of energy and weren't willing to stop. Yet the noise came to a halt. They had realized that they weren't really free and that in this confinement their actions had consequences. Andrew discontinued as well. He didn't want to serve more days than he had to or any days at all. He decided to sleep it off until his court case the next day.

During the night, Andrew was woken by staff who came by for room checks. The C.O. unlocked his door. "You are not allowed to cover up your window. We consider that a hazard. If you keep this up degenerate, you will be here a long time!" the irritable man informed. He grabbed the blanket that was wedged in the crease on the top of the door and pulled it to the ground. What a dick. The bastard left the room and Andrew continued to lay his head to rest. He dreamt of emerald green rivers that night.

CHAPTER 4
CPS

THE NEXT DAY Andrew was transferred to the government center for court. He still didn't know much of how the judicial system worked. They ended up putting the fear of God into making him plead guilty, which was a shame. There are always at least two sides to every story and Andrew never got to tell his. This time he was sentenced to a 15/30 along with 6 months probation. The 15/30 signified 15 good days or up to 30 if he had bad/failed days. So he would yet again go back to being caged like a monkey at a zoo exhibit for the remainder of his time.

He attended the same old repetitive groups during his incarceration. This time he had had enough. He broke down and started crying. He felt so misunderstood and wanted to go home. The only correctional officer who was a lady approached him and asked him what was wrong. He scrambled for something to say and told her a story of when his dad had thrown him down the stairs as he sobbed. This was his attempt to get back at his parents. Play the victim. The next day a caseworker showed up at the parents' home and rang the doorbell.

The Witch's Hat

"Hello!" Greeted Tanya at the doorway, curious about who this thin lady wearing a suit was.

"Hi I'm Cindy from Child Protective Services, we had a complaint recently about some activity that has been going on in this house. Can I speak to you for a minute?"

"What? What's going on? Please! Please come in!" Tanya said with enthusiasm.

The caseworker entered and they both strode up the stairs to the dining room table and sat. Tanya was huffing and puffing due to being so out of shape.

"So the complaint was about Andrew's father, Scott was it?" Cindy began.

"Yes, that is my husband's name..." replied Tanya.

"Ok, so I'm here because we heard that Andrew had been thrown down the stairs by him, is that true?" asked Cindy going straight to the point.

"Oh my goodness really? Is that what Andrew said? Scott has never laid a hand on him. Darn that kid!" Tanya answered.

"So are you saying that Andrew is making this up?" Cindy asked.

"Of course! He is just doing this for attention. He's trying to play the victim. He's out of control!" said Tanya dramatically.

"Ok well, it's my job to look into these issues. If you don't mind, could I ask you a few more questions?" Cindy requested.

Tanya agreed and the two talked for almost an hour. Tanya denied any accusations towards Scott and instead went on about how Andrew had a mental illness and needed to be put on the right medications. She told countless stories to put a frown upon him. Eventually, Cindy had heard enough.

"Here, I'll leave you my card," Cindy said as she slapped her business card on the table. "Have Scott give me a call. There are a few questions I want to ask him personally as part of my investigation."

"Ok I'll make sure to let him know," responded Tanya.

"I'll give you more details on what the future holds once I talk to your husband. I appreciate your time." Cindy uttered as she got up from her seat and walked towards the front door. The two said their goodbyes and she was off.

Later on that day Scott came home from work. Tanya was waiting on the couch overlooking the entryway to the home. "Andrew told the workers at juvie that you have been abusing him," Tanya informed.

"What the fuck? We do everything for that kid and this is how he repays us?" Scott grumbled.

"Well, he's ungrateful. Anyway, you have to call this number and share your side of the story to the caseworker." Tanya held up a business card in one hand and the cordless phone in the other.

"You got to be kidding me," Scott fumed. His face was bright red. "Well, I suppose I better get it over with."

Scott grabbed the cordless home line from Tanya and dialed in the numbers. The phone rang maybe twice. Cindy answered fairly quickly and the two went on to greet each other.

Scott carried on pleading his case saying, "I've never laid a hand on my son. He is out of control and needs to be disciplined. I mean, he pulled a bat on me for Christ's sake! We just want the best for him! We need your help!"

Cindy was taken off guard. The conversation became more easygoing and they were even cracking jokes about how teenagers have a tendency to rebel. This was just an ordinary thing for her.

"I'm so sorry for taking up your time Scott. It seems to me like Andrew lives in a safe environment and that there is nothing to worry about here. Looks like he will be assigned a probation officer. If there is anyone that can get Andrew back in line it would be Brock. Your son will be under the county's supervision now. Hopefully, this is a step in the right direction and will reduce your stress. With that said I hope you have a good night and wish your family the best," Cindy concluded.

The phone call ended. Meanwhile, in juvie, Andrew was transferred to a locked room with a guy named Alex who was a hardcore drug addict. Alex's mom would sneak him in cocaine in bars of soap.

The Witch's Hat

What she did was carve into the bar to make a pocket. Then she would place a small baggie of cocaine into it and re-wrap it up. Andrew had never done any hard drugs and the kid never offered them to him anyway. Yet he was curious what effects would take place and wanted to experiment. In the back of his head, his conscience was yelling " No! Don't throw your life away!" while the rest of his mind was saying "One day.....One day..." Perhaps the street drugs would work better than the cocktail of prescriptions his mother threw onto him.

CHAPTER 5
STOP ahead

Near the end of Andrew's stay, he met his probation officer, Brock, who gave him the spiel of what he had to do to graduate from his probation.

"You have certain tasks you must accomplish. Your mother set you up for a treatment facility which we require for you to attend." Brock then thumbed through some paperwork on the conference room table. "It's called the STOP program and it's two weeks long. They will assess your mental health and you will have to follow any recommendations that they request."

Andrew shook his head in defiance. "This is ridiculous. What about my rights?"

"Unfortunately you broke the law and must suffer the consequences. You need to think about your actions. I will check in with you frequently. After you complete the program I will do random UA's so be prepared if I call you."

"Whatever!" Andrew snapped back, and that was that.

When his mom picked him up to drive him to the program, Andrew devised a plan. He was aware the place was located in Minneapolis at Fairview Riverside Medical Center near his mother's parents' house so

The Witch's Hat

he ended up asking her if he could have Taco Bell before he was put away as a treat for graduating juvie. His mom gave in and pulled into the Taco Bell parking lot in Northeast Minneapolis. They parked and went inside to dine. After they finished eating they headed towards the door to exit the restaurant. As Tanya was dumping the tray near the exit, Andrew took off. He was running for his life. He felt freedom course through his veins as he hit the streets full speed. He knew exactly where he wanted to go.

Andrew was close with his uncle Theo who was also similar in age and a major influence. The two partied together all the time shortly before Andrew was arrested. He was one of Tanya's 10 siblings who lived with Andrew's grandparents by the University of Minnesota. Andrew was used to taking the city bus or getting driven by his mom to get there for his multi-day party sessions. Now that he was on the run all he knew was that he had to head directly south. He looked at the sun in the sky to catch a sense of direction and continued sprinting. He ran down alleyways and zig-zagged from block to block until he was sure he had left his mother in the dust. He then slowed to a brisk walk, passing through all sorts of lively neighborhoods until he finally came upon a familiar area, the U of M campus.

In the distance, he saw the Witch's Hat, an old water tower designed by Frederick William Cappelen and constructed in the southeast portion of the city of Minneapolis in 1913 to help enhance firefighting efforts. It of course resembled a hat of a witch which rested atop a mostly hollow cylinder. Below the brim of the hat rested glassless openings with railings and pillars separating each. This area was used to observe the city from the deck. The tower had been stationed at one of the tallest natural land points in Minneapolis for maximum water pressure. In 1952 it was decommissioned. A few years after the tower ceased to function, the city talked of tearing it down and building a road through it. Andrew's grandparents lived just a few blocks away. His grandpa would tell stories of how there was a big thing back in the day with the city building a freeway in the vicinity. The neighborhood banded together and fought for the city not to tear down the tower as it was an incredible part of history. Instead, they ended up using eminent domain to take the land in front of Andrew's grandparents to build I-94. They took part of his grandparents' property which was his great grandparents' at the time, who had a house built on it around the same time as the tower. Luckily the grandparents' house was left untouched but the neighbors' houses next door were torn down. It is said that the basements still exist underground to this day. Long story short, the witch's hat was saved. They had it redone and it was made into a park. In 1997 it made the National Register of historic places in the U.S. and is quite an eerie place.

Andrew walked along University Avenue, exiting Dinkytown and entering Prospect Park. He cut through the neighborhood of the tower and arrived at his grandparents. He then connected with Theo and spent the next few weeks drinking and smoking herb with him and their friends at the tower. The group would freestyle raps at the sacred bench. Andrew would couch hop day to day through the hood and his uncle would sneak him food. On several occasions, Andrew did some covert missions to get into his grandparents late at night to sleep upstairs without them knowing. His probation officer had been in the area looking for him so Andrew wanted to play it safe. It came to the point where he used a rope of blankets to climb up and down to get in and out the second-story window undetected. One drunken night, Theo and Andrew took turns burning the initial of their first names on their upper arm. Theo put a deep letter "A" upon Andrew and Andrew did a light burn of a "T" upon Theo. They bit a book as they received the burns. This act cemented their relationship together.

One day shortly after, Andrew received another relentless voicemail on his phone from his P.O. stating that if he didn't turn himself in he was going to give him a probation violation and send him back to lock up. Andrew was to turn himself in and go to treatment at once. He waved the white flag and decided to do so because it was inevitable. He was at least able to enjoy about three weeks of freedom total. He called his mother and told her he would go to the Fairview Riverside STOP program but that his terms were that he would come home and take it easy for a night or two before he started it. He told them he wanted to spend time with family. They agreed that he could have a couple of

The Witch's Hat

nights to spend at home before he went in so he took the bus up to the nearest bus stop about a mile away and walked the rest of the distance.

When he got home he was greeted by them. Scott asked Andrew to go outside to throw some practice pitches with the cowhide pill out in the yard, which was strange. They went out and threw a couple. Moments later a squad car pulled up. Tanya came outside. She told the cops that Andrew needed to attend rehab and that she is afraid he would run again. The cop ended up zip-tying Andrew's wrists and threw him into the back of Tanya's car with the child safety locks on.

"Head to your destination and don't stop!" said the officer.

Tanya hopped in and started driving. Andrew made sure to thank her for betraying him and waited for his moment to escape again. After a half-hour, they exited off the freeway near the outskirts of East Downtown and immediately hit the Washington Avenue stoplight. Andrew instantly jumped over the center console into the front seat and sprung open the door. He took off down Washington towards his grandparents again and didn't even bother shutting it. As he was crossing the bridge overlapping the freeway he stumbled upon a couple of college students.

"Do you have scissors to cut these zip ties?" asked Andrew in a squirrelly manner.

"Sorry man," one of them laughed. "Best of luck to you though bro."

Andrew took off further down the street and cut into an alleyway between some businesses which led into a secluded area. Or at least he thought. When Andrew turned the corner around one of the buildings he came to a parking lot. He sprinted a few more steps and ran smack dab into a police officer who was slapping a ticket on someone's vehicle. It was a dead end. Andrew could have turned and ran but he was sick of running. It was obvious Andrew was a fugitive with his wrists cuffed so the officer grabbed him and placed him into the squad car. The man did an investigation, called Andrew's mother, and eventually escorted him to the STOP program himself.

Upon arrival, Andrew was processed and brought up to one of the hospital's upper levels. Again, right off the bat, he had to attend groups. They would discuss drug addiction and how bad your urge was to use them. They wanted to find the real problem behind the patients' drug use. They wanted to pin it on some kind of real-life experience. They never talked about how a person could just like getting high with an intrinsic value in itself. All Andrew could think of was that he used drugs to escape. This world didn't make sense to him. He didn't want any part of it.

One of the days during the beginning of this new experience, the staff gave Andrew a long packet that he had to fill out as his mental health assessment. He checked all the answers honestly. Did he hear voices in his head? Yes was what he circled. He heard voices. They were his thoughts. Did he talk to himself? Yeah, sometimes, especially when he was mad or frustrated. It may have made him sound crazy but maybe they would give Andrew some drugs that would make him feel on top of the world.

The next day the results came through. Turns out Andrew had severe depression and anxiety as well as a diagnosis of O.D.D. This acronym stands for oppositional defiant disorder. He could see himself maybe having that. He hated authority. He was anarchy all the way. A crappy skateboard punk. Soon after his diagnosis came all the medications. Andrew was made into a commodity. They had a drug for everything. He felt he was finally going to feel better.

At this treatment center, it was co-ed. He was placed with adolescent women and men. Since her arrival, this young woman would flirt with Andrew. Her name was Allison. She would purposely give him a good view of her ass when she would bend over. Her pink thong riding up drew in Andrew's eyes. She would steal a glance at him as she did her little bend. She told everyone during group that she was a sex addict and couldn't help herself. Andrew listened to her story of how she couldn't resist. When it was Andrew's turn to speak, he went on his usual tangent of how he didn't belong there. He had been taking all the prescribed pills for nearly a week and hadn't felt any better. He caught on to what was going on.

"All I do is smoke weed and drink. What is wrong with that? This is all some rigged money machine. Fuck this place!" shared Andrew to the class.

"Andrew, all you can do is make the best of your situation," said the lady running the group.

"I'm done with this. My meds don't even work!" Andrew shouted as he left the discussion room.

"Give it another week!" she called out back to him as he turned the corner and stormed to his room. He was done for the day.

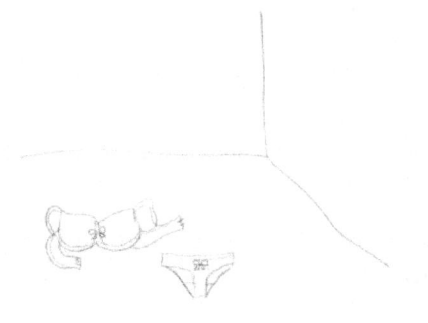

CHAPTER 6
Halt The Whore

Allison loved Andrew's bad boy attitude. She would find her way to walk past him in the hall and would smile at him. On one of these occasions, she used her pointer finger to draw him in closer. She whispered to him, "Meet me in my room in 5 minutes."

Holy shit, Andrew thought. It seemed like she wanted to get freaky. Andrew wasn't going to pass up this opportunity. He had 20 minutes before his next class which would be plenty of time to do the deed.

He crept down the hallway towards her room. He made it past the medication dispensing window and silently pussyfooted into Allison's domain. She was sitting on her bed. Andrew closed the door. This was it. He walked up and stood in front of her. Without hesitation, she pulled down Andrew's scrub pants and went at it like it was the best lollipop she had ever had.

One of the bearded staff workers walked down the hallway to the room. They heard a knock at the door. Andrew rushed to pull up his pants. He barely got them up when the middle-aged man had opened the door.

"What in the world are you guys doing? It's almost time for group. I'm thinking we need to discuss the rules again," he said.

He escorted them out of the bedroom and walked them towards the discussion room. On the way past the front desk, the man stopped and whispered to the lady at the computer, "I found these two alone in Allison's room. I believe they were about to have sex."

The lady put some notes in her files on the computer. Andrew figured this was going to be brought up in group and his counseling session but he didn't care. He did nothing wrong. He wasn't hurting anyone. What could they possibly do to him? In the meantime, he listened to the staff talk amongst themselves saying that they needed to leave out the incident.

"We could become a liability. We were supposed to watch them," said the same middle-aged man by the name of Ricky.

"Your right. We need to tighten things up on our surveillance of her. We will leave it out of the books. Sounds like they didn't even have sex anyway," responded the office lady.

"Sounds good! It never happened," Ricky agreed as the lady deleted what she had written in her notes.

Instead, the two trouble makers were lectured but this wasn't the last time Allison slept around. Andrew had seen and heard multiple young men go into her bedroom day to day from then on out. She and her new acquaintances were sneaky. They would wait until the staff switched shifts in the afternoon.

On one occasion, Andrew turned around during his walk down the hallway after watching another kid go into her room. He then went to his room to look out the window. He saw a ledge he could jump onto and he thought from there he could jump onto the ground. He would have to break the window. But what would that solve? They would just eventually find him and put him back in the same place or even somewhere worse than a treatment facility so he threw that thought away.

As he stared out the window he noticed the witch's tower in the distance atop the hill. He noticed trees surrounding it masking its lower body. It seemed like there was a hollow face below the brim of the hat watching your every move. Andrew imagined climbing one of

25

the trees near its proximity to the very top. He would climb through the whispering green leaves and maneuver through the branches. He visualized himself slipping along the way but saved himself from plummeting to the earth. He persevered until he made it to the point where he could jump through the empty window into the tower. He leaped to do a summersault landing then sprawled to his feet. His mission was now complete. He finally felt free. He would spend his future overlooking the horizons. Moments later, he realized he was daydreaming and snapped back into reality. He turned away from the window and made his way into the hallway to head to his next group.

As he walked down the hallway he heard someone call out to him. "Andrew! Your two weeks are up!"

Andrew gathered his belongings from his room and walked to the front desk to the staff fresh from shift change. The lady who called him continued, "We recommended that you spend only a month in outpatient treatment so you can concentrate on school. It's at a place in Blaine. You must follow up with a therapist as well as a psychiatrist. On top of that, we are suggesting that you attend AA meetings as well. Your probation officer gave me this sign-off sheet for each meeting you attend. Make sure to get the signees phone number." She then handed him a small 4x6 inch piece of paper. "Here, come with me and we can grab your belongings from the storage room."

Andrew followed her to the storage room which was to the left of the front desk. She opened up his bin and handed him a bag with all his clothes plus his flip phone and wallet.

After changing, Andrew sat and waited a few minutes until his mom entered the secured doors to pick him up. He waved goodbye to everyone. It was awkward saying bye to Allison. It was all good though. She made a motion with her hand going back and forth to her mouth, simulating a blow job. Oh geez, Andrew thought. She really must have sex on her mind all the time. She was good for a lay but Andrew wanted a queen who was loyal. He just smiled and walked out the exit after the staff had buzzed him out.

"What was that all about?" Tanya asked. "What was she doing with her hands?"

"Oh, that was nothing. It's her way of saying goodbye. It's an inside joke," Andrew replied.

"Oh ok. Are you excited for treatment?" she asked.

"Mom, you know I'm not. I wish you guys didn't fuckin call the cops all the time. You are fucking up my life."

"Andrew you need to understand that you are out of line. You need to straighten up. I have a psychiatrist appointment set up. I'll be coming with you to make sure they manage your meds correctly. Also, you start outpatient treatment tomorrow so be ready in the morning."

"Seriously? This is bullshit!" Andrew shouted. "Just take me home."

CHAPTER 7
Reprogramming

Upon arrival back at his pad, Andrew charged to his room to cool down. He was so happy to be in his bed. Unfortunately, he was still on paper so any fuck up wouldn't do him any good. No more partying. It was time to face reality head-on. His mind raced until he finally fell asleep.

The next morning Andrew woke up at 7 am. It was a few days from the last week in August. He hurriedly showered and got ready for the day. He didn't know why he was in such a rush. His anxiety took control and his palms began to sweat. He didn't want to meet new people again, yet he was driven by Tanya along the highways to hell. Little did Andrew know that he was already there and had started to reach its depths.

Time passed and they arrived at the rehab center maybe a half-hour after they left home. Andrew was at least fortunate that he only had to do outpatient. He didn't have to be deserted in another strange place. The treatment center he attended was also an inpatient center and he made a few acquaintances. He even started a little business. He would carefully sneak packs of cigarettes to the others for a fee.

"Hey man, you got my smokes?" asked some random fellow teenaged patient who Andrew barely knew as he entered the facility on one typical day.

The Witch's Hat

"Yeah, I threw them in the bushes outside. You got my money?"

"Yeah here is 15," said the dude as he slipped it to Andrew in a handshake.

They would all smoke in a porta-potty at the park when they had recess/gym time to keep hidden. Andrew started hiding the cigarette packs in the outhouse as the staff had found his spot in the bushes and took them one day. He didn't make very much but he made enough to afford his cigarette habit at the time. That was the only thing he could really indulge in because he got random urinalyses on a regular basis. The facility tested once weekly and they didn't make you aware of the day in advance. Andrew had to give up his pot-smoking which he had previously made into a ritual but was lucky his mother and a presently unknown child molester bought him tobacco.

When they weren't smoking during recess, they participated in class discussions indoors. They would of course talk about street drugs and how they affected various things such as the body and brain. They would share stories as well. The class group times were essentially education and networking courses. Andrew met a lot of addicts and learned a lot. This opened up doors for him. He collected phone numbers and held onto them for the future. He decided to keep chilling out on the drugs for the time being. The days passed by slowly and he learned more and more.

He started to attend his weekly AA meetings right away. He thought they resembled a cult, although others may say that description may be misleading. Continuing forward, he would share his stories during the meetings just like at any correctional institution and pretended like he wanted to clean himself up. Andrew was also due for his psychiatrist appointment. He started that right away too, his mother wasn't playing around. He wasn't too excited about the visits because he knew they wouldn't give him what he wanted. He wanted his hands on some Xanax. He wanted something that worked. He was told that he had something wrong with him. Would they help him?

He kept on going to his draining appointments regularly and what made things horrible was that he didn't have any privacy from his mom. What he had to do was get her on his side. She did a good job of dramatizing his issues. He was told he had anxiety so much that it manifested itself even greater. Any benzodiazepine or barbiturate would have been great at this point.

Tanya went on to explain Andrew's condition to Debbie, the psychiatrist. "He has crippling anxiety. He is socially awkward and has this thing where his palms sweat when he is out in public."

"Hmmm... Looks like a hint of agoraphobia. Anything else that I should know?" Debbie asked.

"He hasn't left his room much. He's in treatment right now. He's addicted to pot. He sits in his room and listens to music all day. He blares his gangster rap throughout the house which has swear words. I can't have that when I do foster care."

"I see. No, you can't. If he has trouble leaving his room, that could be a sign of depression. Depression and anxiety go hand in hand. How about I switch him from Lexapro to Celexa and let's see how that works. This will help out with both depression and his social anxiety. It's a whole new medication, so Andrew, please let me know how you feel next time."

Andrew agreed. It looked like his mom's help didn't get him the drugs he wanted. Instead, it got him another SSRI. This was a drug that would take a week or two to show effects and up to two months to achieve full potential. Never did Andrew feel much different.

CHAPTER 8
The Relapsing Puss

AFTER A FEW weeks in outpatient rehabilitation, Andrew was itching to try out some new street drugs because that is all they talked about. It caused his curiosity to grow. They talked of the horrors of drug abuse to deter the patients, but it did the opposite for him. A day after school started up again he dropped the program and refused to go. He wasn't having it. His probation officer luckily didn't punish him. He must have figured it was good enough for Andrew to attend his AA meetings along with his psychiatrist and therapy appointments.

Andrew still lived at home with his fam. Now that the rocky summer was over, he did his best to enjoy life while keeping up his grades during his sophomore year of high school. He took school very seriously for the most part and was proud to be in the top 10% of his class, but during passing time between classes, he slipped into hanging with his old friends. He was still tethered to the stoners from the year before.

Now and again he had to "call-in" to class for his appointments. It had been numerous times of seeing the psychiatrist and Andrew still didn't receive anything that would help him. To make things worse his parents were on the verge of losing the house to bankruptcy. He was stressed and had a habit of going out for cigarettes during lunch while at school. He would usually sneak out front to the parking lot. On this particular occasion due to a liaison officer, Andrew went out the back entrance by the gym. The wrestling coach spotted him and stood on the inside of the exterior steel door as Andrew smoked. He was surprised when he opened the door to reenter to be face to face with the brawny coach. He thought of running but didn't think his actions were a big deal. The coach scolded Andrew and walked him down to the principal's office. Andrew received a detention slip and had to find a new smoking area. In the future, he and his friends went behind the school into the woods. On another occasion, they were each smoking cigarettes and taking rips off a bowl. Before you know it the school police raced up out of the trees and through the prairie grass. The officer parked and quickly got out of the squad car.

"All of you! Come here!" he shouted.

Andrew's friend, another guy named Josh, threw the bowl and they extinguished their cigarettes. The officer found the bowl and loaded them into the back of the cop car. They took a ride to the main entrance of the school. When they got out he motioned for them to follow him. They weren't cuffed.

The officer called out, "What are your names?" as he took out his notepad.

"My name is Josh Anderson," said Andrew's friend.

"I'm Ray Cox," said the other friend.

As his two friends gave their real names, Andrew thought quickly and came up with the name of one of the other students at the school.

"My name is Drew Butler," blurted Andrew as he gave the name of a temporary alias.

The group then marched their way up to the entry doors to the mezzanine. When they pulled open the second row of doors, Andrew didn't think twice and took off down the large room with rows of lockers down the middle. He made it to the cafeteria which was a subsection

The Witch's Hat

of the mezzanine. When he reached the brink of the cafeteria he took a left down the hallway. The police officer was in hot pursuit.

"Hey stop him!" he yelled.

One foot in front of the other as quickly as they could go was Andrew's mission. He took another turn and ran past the gym while the officer was falling behind. He had at least a hundred feet on him. The distance grew as Andrew took the loop around the next perimeter hallway of the school and back through the mezzanine to go out the same entry door they had come in. As he passed through the mezzanine a track runner decided he would join the race. As Andrew exited, he was tired but kept pushing. The track runner was freaky fast and started closing in on him. They ran across the front lawn of the school. Andrew was aiming for the pedestrian bridge to cross a highway to get off of school property. It led to dirt paths behind a library. However, he didn't make it that far. The track runner dove and tackled him in front of a wall of windowed classrooms. The kids were pointing and laughing from inside.

"You fucking asshole!" shouted Andrew as he lay on the ground. The runner ignored him and faced the window flexing his arms to the students. What a douche, Andrew thought. At this moment, the cop was just exiting the front entrance and sprinted over to him and ripped him up from the dirt. He had grass stains all over his shirt and knees.

"You're in big trouble now," the officer instilled.

He grabbed Andrew tightly by the wrist and brought him directly to the principal's office. The principal was sitting in his chair. "Why did you run?" he asked, knowing Andrew's real identity.

"I didn't want to get in trouble. I'll go back to juvie," answered Andrew honestly.

"Why would you go to juvie?" said the big man.

"Because my probation officer will find out," Andrew mewled.

The principal then looked up Andrew's files on his computer. "Ah yes, it says here that his name is Mr. Brock Zsoldos. I actually know him. He checked in with me regarding you a few weeks ago. I'm sorry but I'll have to give him a call."

God damnit, thought Andrew to himself. Why did he tell him that? Either way he would have been in trouble because his parents would have said something to his P.O. anyhow.

"Hey is this Brock?" questioned the principal while holding his desk phone up to his ear.

There was a short pause, then the principal went on to say, "Yes, this is Ebenezer Fitzroy, the principal of A-NO-KA-TAN-HAN high school. I have Andrew here with me. He got into some mischief today at school. I'm just calling to notify you."

There was another pause.

"Yeah, he was smoking tobacco and possibly marijuana with his friends," Fitzroy said. Then another pause.

"Ok sounds good. I'll see you in a bit," Fitzroy again responded as he hung up the phone. He turned to Andrew and said, "Well, he's on his way."

Within ten minutes Brock was at the school and joined them in the office. "The question is what are we going to do to discipline you?" he asked hypothetically as he glared at Andrew. Andrew just shrugged his shoulders. He thought he was in deep shit.

"Well, you for sure are receiving a few days suspension," said the principal who took it upon himself to answer for him. "Mr. Zsoldos can decide what to do with you from there."

"For right now I'm not going to do anything. I'll tell you what. I'm going to give you a UA and if you fail it, I will decide what to do from there," said Brock while clicking a pen in his hand.

Andrew now knew he was an idiot for smoking. The stuff stays in the system for up to 30 days. He was fucked. Super fucked. He went to the staff bathroom in the office and was ordered to piss in a cup. Brock stood behind him to make sure there were no shenanigans. Andrew peed until the cup overflowed and it ran over the sides.

"Is that enough pee for ya?" asked Andrew with an attitude.

"How old are we? It should only be half full! Dump some out now and wipe the sides off!" Brock nagged.

The Witch's Hat

Reluctantly Andrew did as he was told. Funny thing was that Brock didn't even have to touch the cup. He told Andrew to put it directly in a plastic bag. Andrew's joke was a complete fail. Brock then of course called the wrongdoer's parents. The principal was unable to reach them earlier but Brock somehow managed to get through.

"Hey Tanya, it's Brock! Hope your day is going well," he addressed. Andrew then heard a muted voice from the other end of the phone line in response. He couldn't hear what his mother was saying. After she quit talking Brock resumed the convo, "I'm doing pretty well but I'm sorry to say I've got some bad news, unfortunately. I don't know if you got Mr. Fitzroy's message earlier but Andrew was caught smoking tobacco and possibly marijuana with his friends at school. As of right now he is suspended for three days and will await further disciplinary action. It will be based upon the results of his urinalysis."

"There he goes being out of control again," she loudly expressed over the phone.

"Yes, it's unfortunate... Is there any way you could pick Andrew up from school?" asked Brock. "If I have to, I can drop him off... Either way, he must leave school property."

"I'll be right there! He is grounded for sure!" she replied.

After a twenty-minute wait, Tanya arrived at the school. She, of course, lectured Andrew about smoking even though she bought him his cigarettes. But whatever, Andrew said nothing of it.

Tanya then looked at Brock and said, "he is only doing this because his medication is off balance. We can't seem to find something that works for him."

Here we go again, Andrew thought. It was clear he was just one big problem. He felt like he was made out to be mentally challenged or something. It had been planted in his brain that he needed medication to function to make it through life. So what difference is medicating with alcohol and marijuana versus various prescription medications? The difference was that the former actually worked.

Brock carried on, "we will continue with the psychiatrist appointments and hope we find a medication that works for him for the time being. I'll contact you to let you know what the future holds once the UA comes through."

"Sounds good. I look forward to hearing from you," Tanya excitedly responded.

"Well, you have a good day. I'll talk to you both later," replied Brock. He also looked over at Andrew sitting in the chair on the opposite side of the conference room table and said, "Bye Andrew."

Andrew nodded his head. Brock then turned to exit the room and Andrew followed out the door with his mother. Tanya waved at Brock once they reached the school's parking lot. She seemed ecstatic that Andrew kept digging his hole even deeper. Andrew knew exactly what she was gonna do when they got home.

It wasn't too long until they arrived. Immediately Tanya took to the cordless home phone and called anyone and everyone she knew. She shut the door to her bedroom and locked it as she gossiped. A couple of hours went by and Andrew's brother got off his middle school bus. He was a seventh-grader and was on his 2nd year of playing the cello. What a glory that was! With all his work and dedication, he was pretty fantastic. He would even make up his own songs. He seemed like a happy kid. He walked in the home entry and passed Andrew as they both took the stairs. There was a stairway going up and another going down from the entry platform. As Josh walked by, he gave a half-hearted smile and went on his way to his bedroom.

"Hey, J-man!" blurted Andrew while on his way to get munchies upstairs in the kitchen.

"Hey," Josh said shyly, resembling some sort of angelic innocence.

Josh went to his room in the basement. The two shared separate bedrooms since the family quit foster care and they hadn't talked much since Andrew began to go through all his problems. They had separate lives at this point. Josh went about his business as usual. He picked up the cello and started playing some strings. His notes were long and melancholy, but he made that used beat-up cello sound so lovely. The notes would chase each other up and down at different speeds as he free-styled. With a pluck of the string, the door slammed and their

The Witch's Hat

father was home from work. Boy was he irritated. His face was fuming red and did a mild blend into his brown but reddish-tinged beard. He saw Andrew upstairs looking into the fridge.

"What did you do now?" shouted Scott from the entryway. "What? You can't follow the rules? Smoking again? You're a dumbass!"

"Fuck the rules!" beamed Andrew from the kitchen counter with a container of eggs. "I'm old enough to make my own decisions. If I want to smoke cigarettes I can. Anything I put into my body is strictly my own business."

"Your such a fucking idiot!" Scott squawked as he stomped up the stairs.

There was an island wall separating the kitchen from the living room. To avoid being trapped in the kitchen corner, Andrew looped through the adjoining dining room and around the island wall to enter the living room from the opposite end of the stairway which would be his most suitable exit. He came face to face with his father, turned, and retreated. His dad pursued. The two played "Ring Around the Rosie" for only a semicircle, as he cut through the kitchen he saw his mother straight-ahead opening up her bedroom door to see what the commotion was about. She had a giddy smile upon her face with the phone still up to her ear. Andrew didn't hesitate to turn the corner of the island wall near the kitchen leading to the stairway. To his surprise his dad had turned around and was blocking it, trapping Andrew.

He stood by the living room couch where he had broken his foot as a kid wrestling with his dad by jumping from it. He then yelled, "Screw you! I don't know why you guys are always on my case. You're an asshole and mom's a bitch!"

"So you think you can call your mom a bitch, do you? You better take that back," Scott shouted at the top of his lungs. His army mentality began to set in.

Andrew ignored him for the moment as he listened to his brother's music echo up the stairwell. He drew near Scott for an escape attempt. Josh's music began to grow in intensity. Andrew took off towards his father and the notes grew faster and faster. The echo of the cello strings

37

caused a distortion. Andrew paused and turned around. He saw his mother still on the phone and plainly said, "You are a bitch! Gossiping still?"

Just then Andrew's dad grabbed him in a bear hug and started squeezing. He felt the air seeping from his lungs. Josh's music started turning into short staccato notes. He was shredding the cello with his musical depth. It only grew in intensity. Andrew tried the best he could to scream. All that came out was a light exhale of carbon dioxide. Scott picked him up and slammed him to the ground. Josh's notes suddenly slowed down as Andrew fought to breathe under his father's weight.

Within the drama, Andrew was allowed back up to his feet. Scott then picked him back up and whipped him back and forth. Andrew was in a daze. He thought he was about to be thrown down the stairs again. To his surprise, his dad used a sweeping motion of his foot to slam him to the ground once more. Josh did a sliding motion down to the base of his cello. Then he started playing fast with the vibrato adding a colorful nature to the dynamics of his music. The song was winding down past the climax.

"Get out of my sight!" Andrew's dad yelled as he lifted his weight off of him but pushed him to the floor as he tried to rise to his feet. "Don't worry you will get what you deserve."

Andrew managed to scramble to his feet and regained his breath. Then he ran down the stairs to the home's entry platform. The music had now leveled out. He looked back up the stairway and saw his mother. She was still on the phone. "Seriously?" Andrew said rolling his eyes. "Fuck off!"

His dad took a plunge down the stairwell and was hot on his heels. Andrew didn't think twice to run down to his bedroom. His brother strings plucked as both of Andrew's feet met each step of the lower stairway. He reached the bottom and there was one last stroke of the finger to bring an end to the rendition as Andrew grasped the doorknob to his bedroom.

He stubbed his big toe as he nearly walked into the door. He stumbled into his room and tossed it closed, locked it and that was

The Witch's Hat

it. He just wanted to be secluded. There was no use in trying. He was doomed yet again. Andrew's dad may have had his way with him but it was his probation officer's turn next. He couldn't stop thinking about his upcoming failure of a UA. He just wanted to forget about his problems.

He got off his ass and went to the window and opened it all the way to let the refreshing fall breeze in. Then he pivoted to the opposite side of the room and sat on the couch. He then took out his bong from his hiding space alongside it near the wall. The bong was an old 1-liter pop bottle with a hollow disassembled metal pen sticking through the side at a 45-degree angle into the bong water. Attached to the outer end of the pen was a handmade tin foil bowl. The lower end of the pen rested just about an inch from the bottom of the bottle. The water made a great filter. Andrew looked at the empty bowl. It still needed to be packed.

He lifted a seat cushion from the couch and reached in a slit he carved into the lining beneath. He thought he was so clever when he created this stash spot, although this was an absurd observation. He took his stash out of the couch and began to open it. However, his shaky hands fumbled with the bag of dope and he ended up dropping the baggy on the carpet.

"Goddamnit," he muttered.

His hands diced up the spilled buds and put them back into the baggy. The damn things probably had dog hair on them. Oh well, he thought. It all burns. He finally managed to pack his bowl and he definitely packed it full at that. He sparked up the bud and was taking big rips. His lungs clouded with smoke as he inhaled. So much that he started coughing. The room had become very hazy and amidst his lounging time, a pounding came at the door. "Andrew, what are you doing in there? I smell smoke!" yawped Scott.

Andrew sat in silence.

Bang! Bang! Bang! "Open the door now or else I'm busting this lock off!" Scott bellowed.

"Nah, I'm good," Andrew answered.

"Open it now!" Scott yelled in his grizzly voice.

"I just want to be left alone," Andrew replied.

"I guess we are calling the police then," Scott shouted. He then turned towards the stairs and gave them the third degree as well, "Tanya call 9-1-1!"

Tanya got up from her bed and wobbled her large body down the stairs. "What is that skunky smell?"

"He's smoking in the house again," Scott said in a normal tone as she was right behind him. Andrew could hear them talking outside of his room.

"Why is he smoking in the house? I'm going to call but we have to let his probation officer know too," responded Tanya.

"That's all we can really do," Scott replied before turning to face the locked door. "Andrew, you are just getting yourself in bigger trouble! You're really digging yourself a hole!"

Tanya already had her cell phone dialed up to the emergency hotline. She spoke rapidly. You could hear the excitement in her voice. "Hello? Yeah, my son is out of control. He is acting out and doing drugs in his bedroom. We need someone to assist in getting him out of his room. It's locked."

"I will notify dispatch immediately and an officer will be on their way," said the operator.

"Thank you so much!" Tanya returned. The expression on her face transitioned from a big smile to a joyous smirk as she bit her lip to cool her excitement. It seemed like a normal routine to get the local police involved in every situation. Andrew was sick of it. Didn't they see that none of this was working? Andrew had a flare inside of him and he didn't want it to fade away. They were just fucking up his childhood.

Since the police were already on their way Andrew threw in the towel. He got off his ass and reluctantly unlocked the door. His dad took a step in and said, "You're not getting out of here. The police will be here any minute." Scott had the doorway blocked to exit the room. His arms extended from each side to grasp Andrew in case he tried to slide on by.

The Witch's Hat

Andrew had an overwhelming urge to run. He had to get away. He was sure his mom was posted at the front door waiting for the Nazi force to come. What was he going to do? He knew the officer had arrived when he heard Tanya and him talking as they walked down the stairs into the basement. Thump! Thump! Thump! They were urgent steps over something so stupid. They turned the corner and made it to the bedroom doorway. The police officer took about 5 steps in and was about a few feet away from his father. They were crowded by the door. Andrew was trapped.

"It's Andrew, correct?" asked the sturdy officer.

"Yes," Andrew replied fearfully. He was scared he was going to go away again.

"I heard from your parents you are having trouble obeying orders. I advise you to listen up and follow through with what they say or you are going to have a really tough life!" the officer said with a serious look.

"I'm grown! I don't have to listen to them. This is bullshit."

"Well, we either have two choices. I can take you in or your parents will call your probation officer tomorrow morning and see what he wants to do."

"What the hell is going on? Can't a guy just live his life? People need to mind their own business. There would be way less drama that way. Some of you just thrive on it! I'm just so sick of you all!" Andrew said with intensity.

"Well with that attitude it looks like I gotta take you in," the officer responded.

Andrew was not about to go back to juvie or treatment or wherever they planned to send him. A light flickered in his head. He had remembered he left the window open. It was open enough that he could fit through it. His bed was just below it and would serve as a platform to make a leaping dive. The window dropped about four feet to the ground outside the split-level home and would make for a rough landing but Andrew was all for it.

He looked the officer dead in the eyes and shouted, "you will have to catch me first!"

Andrew stuck up both middle fingers with each hand at the three bystanders. He held them up for a brief second until the officer went to reach for his arm. Andrew was swift and pulled away. He did a turnaround and jumped on the bed. He quickly took a couple of springy steps then planted both feet together as he landed for his final contact with the mattress. The bounce from the impact gave him the momentum he needed to launch himself into a dive. While mid-air in his Superman dive, Andrew's palms hit the window screen followed by his face. The window screen broke free and he continued to soar through and out the window into the darkness of the night.

Andrew hit his face onto the rocky grass and landed on his right cheek with his body following in pursuit. With a couple of thuds and a sliding motion on the turf, he came to a halt. The screen he jumped through had flipped over his head and landed on his back. Scrambling to his feet he looked over his shoulder to see the officer and his father looking dumbfounded out the empty window. Andrew laughed and took off into the woods.

He broke into a clearing and ran as fast as he could through the prairie towards the next street. Once he reached it he noticed a set of headlights circling the block. Andrew scurried into the bushes. He laid there silently waiting for the car to pass in case it was a cop. The car pulled directly alongside him and made a dead halt. A beam of light spewed from near the side-view mirror. The light shimmered through the bushes to reveal Andrew's hiding spot. He was hunkered down as low as he could go. How did they find him?

Little did he know that they had just upgraded to some new equipment and could pick up the heat a body radiates through some sort of goggles. Andrew was the first person they had used them on. Lucky him.

Next came a muffled sound through the megaphone. "Andrew! It's time to give up! We are taking you in."

Now that it was apparent that they had found him and hadn't mistaken him for an animal it was time to start running again. This time he wasn't stopping for a break. Andrew rolled from underneath the bushes. He managed to scrape his arms up pretty bad from the

The Witch's Hat

foliage but that didn't slow him down much. He did a cyclone spin to his feet which morphed from his ground roll and was back at it again with leaves trickling down his back.

Andrew knew the area pretty well so he was able to navigate in the veil of night. He made sure to switch up his direction as he ran through the suburban neighborhoods. He zigzagged from block to block and avoided running on roads unless to cross them. He just kept going. This time he ran over 5 times further than the first run totaling well over a mile distance.

He stopped at a crowd of bushy pine trees at a not-so-busy intersection. He figured he could take cover. He knelt under the pine branches and plopped to the ground. He lay down in a daze staring up at the pine needles. Once he caught his breath, he rolled onto his side and stared at the horizon of stars in the sky. He looked for something peculiar but found nothing but airplanes. He was always curious about what was located, circling or flying in the heavens. He always felt like he was being watched.

He took one last look and located something very small that resembled a faint star. He traced it through the sky and found it ran in a continuous line and was fairly quick compared to everything else he saw. He learned from a friend that this was most likely a satellite. What do these objects do? Andrew learned in his meteorology class that these particular devices are used to study the earth and other planets as well as black holes. Some contribute by helping track hurricanes or predicting the weather, while others such as the growing group of navigational satellites that orbit earth donate to your real location through a transponder. Most smartphones as you know have GPS receivers which have been an outstanding service to many around the world. Better yet, some of these satellites communicate information such as phone calls and T.V. channels. Many rely on this every day to get information about what's going on in the world and to communicate with friends and family which is such an amazing feat that we take for granted.

However, there are many who would agree they would rather go back to a simpler world without phones. Andrew would agree that phones and computers were starting to take over people's lives at this point in his life. MySpace was huge and the masses were just starting to transfer over to Facebook. Andrew was guilty of this himself, trying to put the most positive things of your life out there to make it seem like you are so much happier than you really are.

During his stargazing, he began growing more and more sleepy. He gently laid his head down. His face rested on his extended upper right arm. An entanglement of mysterious plants surfaced from beneath and around his arm grazing his face. It tickled. He then used his left hand to rest below his chin to cover some of the plants from his face. Other than that he was comfy.

Every now and again a car would pass by along the road. It seemed like every time he was near his slumber this would happen. He was hoping that the police wouldn't drive by with their heat vision goggles but he was pretty sure he had shaken them. He laid there for a few hours tossing and turning. He couldn't sleep. The cars were loud and it looked like it was going to rain.

It was around 1 a.m. when he began hearing raindrops lightly sprinkle his surroundings. He felt a droplet of water drip from the pine branches onto his face. It was time to go. He crawled from under the trees and began walking along the ditch of the road. He decided to make the trek to his friend Ray's house. It had been 3 hours since he left home and he was pretty sure the police had given up but he wasn't going to take any chances. Every time he saw headlights he would drop to the ground along the ditch and become one with the earth. He had a long ways to go yet.

He kept up this routine for about 3 miles. His buddy's house was pretty much a straightaway from where he departed. Along the way, Andrew began to itch his face and the portions below his elbows on both arms. He had laid in something that had caused him an adverse reaction. It must have been the plants he sprawled across under those pines. It took him an hour and a half of obsessive itching to finally reach his friend's backyard. It was a fine middle-class suburban home with about a quarter-acre lot. The neighbor on one side had a privacy fence while the neighbor on the other side was separated by a row of bushes. Ray's yard was wide open so Andrew crossed over the top of a small slope that marked the border of his backyard and entered the property. He was soaked from all the rain.

He knew Ray kept his window unlocked at night but this time it was completely left open. There was no screen on it as it was used as an entryway to his room. His mom was pretty cool but Ray got into a lot of trouble. He would get grounded but his single mother couldn't enforce it. It seemed like she wanted him to go in the right direction but had to look the other way. Andrew and Ray shared the trait of being out of control teenagers. They could not yet be tamed.

Andrew crossed into Ray's backyard and made it to the window. He heard groaning and human whimpering coming from inside. What the hell was going on? Andrew looked into the dark room but saw nothing but blackness and a few dimly illuminated electronics. Suddenly he heard another moan. It was super loud this time and kind of provocative sounding. Andrew had to do something. He was sick of being outside. Plus he was still itchy and wet. He needed warmth. He didn't hesitate to call out into the darkness, "Ray! You there?"

"Ahhh! Holy shit!" shrieked Ray while a woman screamed. It took Andrew a second but he was able to focus on what was going on. The moonlight coming through the window revealed them. Mariah, who was Ray's girlfriend was on her elbows and knees with her ass up in the air. Ray had her mounted from behind and had paused his intercourse session with his shaft still inside her. Suddenly you could hear Mariah sigh as he pulled out.

"Who is it?" asked Ray.

"It's Andrew. I need a place to crash."

"Give me a few minutes and I'll be right out," Ray said in a chill manner with a hint of irritation.

Andrew took a few steps around the corner of the house and sat down on the wet lawn.

"Give it to me bad boy!" hollered Mariah in the background.

Andrew heard about 15 seconds of womanly whimpers and two loud groans to finally complete the innuendo. Moments later Andrew heard the sliding door bustle open along its rails and heard a voice say, "Hey! Where you at?"

"Over here! Give me a second. I'll be right there," Andrew replied as he bustled to his feet and fleeted around the corner to his friend. He rushed himself inside through the glass door entryway to shelter from the storm.

"Woah, man. You're all wet. What's going on?" Ray questioned.

"I ran away. I have nowhere to go," Andrew quivered through his chattering teeth.

"I got my girlfriend over but I guess you can sleep on my bedroom couch. Here I'll get you some dry clothes to wear."

Andrew followed him to his cracked bedroom door. "Hey babe! Andrew is staying the night. Can you get some clothes on?"

Andrew waited patiently around the side of the door against the wall as Mariah shuffled under the sheets for her panties and pajama pants. Once that was taken care of she slipped on one of Ray's shirts.

"Ok, I'm done," she said.

Andrew veered around the corner into the bedroom to meet both Ray and Mariah sitting on the bed. Ray reached into his closet which was beside his bed and grabbed some clothes. He turned to Andrew and said, "Here you go! Here are some pants, a t-shirt, and some socks. Hopefully, your underwear is ok. I gotta get up for school in a few hours so I'm gonna crash. You can sleep on the couch right there." He pointed to the couch beside the bed on the opposite side of the closet against the wall and facing the T.V. He then yawned.

"Thanks for the clothes man. I'm not going to school tomorrow. I got my probation officer after me," informed Andrew as he sat down on the couch.

"That's fucked up! Fuck probation! Looks like you're gonna have to chill by the fort until I get home tomorrow then. This is only temporary. They will find you eventually," responded Ray.

"Yeah, I know. Just trying to buy some time," Andrew replied.

"Well, I'm gonna turn on some T.V. and some tunes to fall asleep to. Goodnight man." Ray then used the remote to turn on the T.V. and then the speaker system. He played the movie *Half Baked* and had a death metal band called Cannibal Corpse on.

Andrew placed his feet up on the couch and kicked back. He tilted his head towards the muted movie playing. Ray had a subwoofer located under the couch cushions so Andrew felt the rumble of the music from the stereo. It was kind of like a high-intensity massage. Amongst the chaos, he managed to fall asleep. Everything in his mind turned pitch black as he tossed and turned back and forth. He felt like he was suffocating and there was nowhere to escape. It was like he was trapped in his head. One of his biggest fears was dying from lack of oxygen. What made it worse was that it seemed never-ending. There was no sense of time until he felt a nudge on his shoulder. He looked behind him but no one was there. It was still black and he was still suffocating.

"Andrew, wake up! It's time to get ready," a voice muscled in.

Andrew ultimately awoke as his body was being jostled. He gasped for air. "What? What's going on?" Andrew asked. He was kind of disoriented from the dream as he snapped back into the real world.

"It's time to go," said Ray.

"What? Where am I?" probed Andrew.

"Seriously? You're at my house. Mariah and I have to leave for school soon."

"Oh ok. Let me get ready then," Andrew stated with hesitation. He was still in a daze.

"Are you ok man? You there?" Ray asked.

Andrew snapped out of it and was alternating eye contact with Ray and looking around the room. "Yeah, I'm ok."

"Well, be ready in 10 minutes," Ray added to finalize the conversation as he left the room and headed for the shower.

Andrew didn't have to do much but grab the belongings that were left on the table which he had taken out of his pocket for a more comfortable rest. Then after about 10 minutes Andrew's friend and girlfriend stepped out of the shower, dressed themselves and walked into the bedroom. Mariah plopped a seat on the bed. Ray quickly turned off the tunes and grabbed a few belongings such as his keys, phone, cigs, lighter, etcetera. Andrew was sitting on the couch rubbing his eyes and slowly still coming to from his slumber.

"Hey man, where am I going? I can't go to the school."

"Just chill at the fort for a few hours," responded Ray.

"God damnit! That's gonna be boring," chimed Andrew.

"I'm sorry man but my mom is home today and she has been on my case all week," said Ray.

Andrew knew this wasn't the real reason. Ray's mom was somewhat trying to enforce rules but was somewhat an enabler at the same time. She just wanted to know she was trying to get Ray on the right track. Anyhow, Andrew knew she didn't care. The real reason why Ray didn't want him hanging in his room was that he was worried that Andrew would steal his pot. He had about a quarter pound of bud sitting below his couch. The same way Andrew had his. It wasn't locked up or anything so it would have been easily accessible. The trust just wasn't there.

Ray didn't bother grabbing a backpack. Who knows if even had one. He didn't do much of any homework. He always had friends over and would copy off of other students to barely pass his classes. Anyway, it was still the beginning of the school year and Andrew figured he was going to have to drop out. He waited until Ray was all set. Once done, he approached Andrew.

"You ready?" he blurted.

"Yeah I guess," Andrew returned.

Andrew followed Ray to the door which he slid open. Mariah and Andrew stepped out. Ray stayed inside, closed the door, and locked it. He then went up the basement stairs and out the front door to secure the house. Ray then met back up with the other two in the backyard. The three of them cut through the lawn and up and over the slope until they made it to the gravel road that led to the radio tower. The tower stood about 150 feet tall on the right side of the road. Andrew remembered the day they had climbed it and were in the local newspaper. What a day that was. On the opposite side of the road was the little fort hang-out. This was where Andrew was supposed to wait until Ray arrived back home from school so he cut off the dirt road and headed towards it. The fort was essentially a stack of logs in a triangle for privacy. There were wooden planks in the corners about waist-high wedged in between the stacks of logs to sit on.

"See you guys later!" shouted Andrew as he entered the tree line.

"See ya!" called back the couple in unison.

Andrew maneuvered his way through the woods to his destination. He sat down on one of the planks inside the fort and leaned back against the stacked logs. He closed his eyes and went into a meditative state. He thought of how he had gotten his first blow job in this very spot and then went on daydreaming of his future. He pictured living his life the way he wanted. At this point, his future had seemed so bleak. Although in his defense, he was only 15 and still had plenty of time to play with. He just wanted to party but he had no weed or alcohol at the moment so he grew very bored.

In the meantime, Ray and Mariah had almost a two-mile walk to the school. A half-hour had passed and Andrew had figured that they had arrived by then. Andrew may not have enjoyed going to school but he had goals. He feared his grades would go downhill because he didn't know how long he was gonna be on the run for. Was this the point when he would throw everything away? He didn't know. He was a rolling rock that hit bumps along the way. He let the winds and his intuition guide him on his path.

A few hours went by and Andrew began to get restless. He was sick and tired of sitting around. He stepped out of the fort to which lay even larger logs that surrounded the fire pit. He laid down on his back on one of these long logs to calm his nerves as he stared up at the tree branch-covered sky. The leaves were a fall color and provided only a little coverage from the sun which played hide and seek. He then saw a squirrel jump from branch to branch with a mouthful of acorns. The squirrel sprung herself across the opening from one flimsy limb to the other with success. The limbs sunk down upon her landings and rebounded back upward as she dashed to reach her nest. Andrew had imagined a family of baby squirrels inside. As the mother made her rounds, he kept staring through the decorated cobwebbed branches that embraced the sky and noticed that it had gotten dark. The clouds were a grayish black. He sensed yet another storm coming. He could sense the static in the air and heard the clatter of the Greek and Egyptian Gods bowling in the distance.

A thought came to Andrew's mind. Maybe Ray's window was still unlocked. Andrew needed to seek shelter so he didn't get all wet again. He had just gotten drenched the day before and was luckily relinquished with Ray's dry clothes. He didn't think it was the most comfortable walking around in wet clothes so he got up. He then stretched his sore body from laying on the log. He itched his poison ivy face which made it redder than it already was. His head looked like a patchy tomato. He marched out of the woods and onto the dirt path. As he was walking up the slope to get to Ray's house he heard a distressed sound coming from the other side. It sounded like whatever it was, was in pain. Andrew ignored it as he put one foot in front of the other to make it to Ray's window. He tried to slide it open but of course, it was locked and the storm was moving in.

"Meeeeooooow!" is what Andrew heard from beyond the bushes to the neighbor's house. What the hell was going on? It almost sounded like a cat. What a nasty harrowing sound it was. Andrew grew curious and wanted to find out what was going on. He strode back up the small hill which was also the barrier to the neighbors' backyard as well. Andrew walked along it to see if he could find out what the raucous was. He stood at the outside corner of the neighbor's property and peeked around the bushes that separated the homes.

As he peeked around the bushes he saw a naked man standing on his patio. In the man's hands, he held a cat. The man was making back and forth thrusting motions towards and away from the rear of the feline. The legs of the cat were zip-tied. Andrew guessed this was to prevent the cat from scratching the man as he raped it. The puss also had a cone on its head to prevent her from biting. How did this man get his pecker inside of this cat? How small would his member have to be to get inside of her?

The Witch's Hat

Andrew took a closer look at the guy. The fellow was skinny and looked like he did drugs. Meth maybe? His face had acne-like sores on it with a bunch of craters. This observation solved the question. The man must have had "meth dick" which shrinks it to a childlike state. He probably didn't have enough girth to pleasure a real-life woman so he got his satisfaction from an innocent animal. He was probably too ugly to even get a woman in the first place with all his drug use deteriorating his body.

And yet still the blood-curdling cries continued from the feline. Andrew was disgusted. He began to pull his head back from beyond the bushes and hit the road when the cat man saw him. The man became startled and kind of flinched a little bit. He stood in a pause until his instincts took hold. The man then dropped the cat on the ground and began chasing Andrew. Andrew turned completely around and ran down the hill. The bastard was on his heels. He was fast. Andrew kicked his legs forward as quickly as he could. His goal was to achieve sanctuary at a nearby gas station.

He ran down the dirt road past his fort. The dirt road ended and Andrew took a left down a paved street. He now only had a few hundred more feet until he made it to the highway. When he reached the highway he took a right and jaywalked across it. Then he continued sprinting towards the gas station. He was within reach of it when he turned around to see that the naked cat man had given up.

Andrew slowed down to a brisk walk. His stomach grew hungry. He needed something to eat but had no money. He had a plan. Fucked up situations called for desperate measures. He walked into the store and flung the door open for the person behind him. Then he scouted out the food. He grabbed a bag of chips, snickers, and a 5-pack of donuts and shoved them into his pants along his belt line. He did his best to cover it up with his shirt. He then proceeded to exit the store and noticed the clerk eying him closely. He opened his mouth as if to say something but hesitated and looked the other way. Andrew sensed the clerk had suspected him of a five-finger discount but Andrew looked rough and maybe the clerk had a sense of compassion for him. He then stepped out the door into the pouring rain and grew paranoid because he did something wrong. He acted as if the police were called and were going to be after him again as if the clerk betrayed him. But Andrew had nothing to worry about. The heat from the night before along with the cat man situation had receded.

Andrew trekked back to the opposite side of the highway where he originated from and heard the tornado sirens go off. His next mission was to make it to the school so he turned to the left and went the opposite way from Ray's house along the sidewalk of the busy street. The school was about a mile and a half away from this point. He couldn't be on the run forever. He didn't want to live like this anymore. He started feeling like he wanted to throw in the towel again.

He pulled out his phone and called his mom. "Hey, mom! I'm just calling to say I apologize. I'd like to come home and make things better. Please don't call the cops on me right away like last time. I want to enjoy some time before I get put away. Do you understand?"

On the other end, Tanya agreed she wouldn't call the cops but told Andrew that he would have to contact his probation officer to figure out what he wanted to do with him. Andrew agreed that that was something he could do. He felt like he had no choice but to trust his mother and her word. After the conversation, he hung up the phone and he was now approaching the school. It was nearing the end of the school day and the buses were waiting to bring home the students. Andrew progressed up the incline that was adjacent to the school with the school being on the right-hand side. Once he made it to the top he turned and walked through a small gravel parking lot and continued along a cement sidewalk leading to the senior high. The sirens were still blaring and he was getting pounded with rain. The wind gusts almost took him off his feet. Finally, he made it to the nearest entryway to which he opened the door and walked in. To the left, down the hallway, all the students were sitting on the ground with their legs bent into pretzels.

Andrew knew he came in looking like a bum. He had mud all over his shoes and was swamped with water. He got plenty of stares as people eyed up his poison ivy face. No one said anything about it to him. They just observed and whispered to each other. Soon enough,

Andrew spotted in the intersection of the halls sitting alongside one another was Ray, Mariah, and a few other friends. Among them was Nathan. He was a giant and had the biggest gauges in the school. His gauges and long hair distinguished him from the crowd. He was a friendly giant but an enforcer at the same time.

"Hey, guys!" Andrew called out.

"Hey, what's up man? What are you doing here?" Ray asked.

"Well, I wasn't going to stand out in the storm..." replied Andrew. He briefly thought about sharing his story about the kitty fucker but decided to keep it to himself.

"I'm sorry man," Ray laughed. "Now that you are here, you are stuck. They aren't allowing anyone to leave."

"It's whatever," said Andrew. "I'm just happy to be out of the rain."

"You ok man?" Nathan asked.

"Yeah, I'm better now. Thanks for asking."

Ray had a toothpick hanging out of his mouth clenched by a gap in his bite. "We are heading to my house once they say we can go. Are you coming?"

"No, I think I've had enough. I'm gonna take the bus home and talk to my parents," stated the pretender.

Approximately 20-30 minutes went by and the principal's voice crackled over the intercom saying it was ok to go home. The storm had passed. Andrew got up and said goodbye to his friends then headed outside towards his school bus. He boarded the bus and avoided any eye contact as he proceeded to the back seat. The seats were already taken so he plopped himself down 3 rows from the rear and leaned his head against the window. It was a bumpy ride as the bus took off. Andrew's head bounced off the glass. Stop after stop after stop went by. Finally, he had reached his destination which was the street corner along his family's yard. He stepped off of the bus and was walking to his front door when the police rolled up.

"Ah, fuck," Andrew mumbled.

His parents had betrayed him yet again! He just wanted a couple of normal days to relax. Tanya stood at the doorway of the home while a squad car pulled into the driveway. Andrew's nerves shivered in his body. He thought he was ready to turn himself in but his mind and body weren't having it quite yet. He turned his back to his mom and reeled in the situation. Just then another officer pulled up and parked along the curb. The one officer who pulled into the driveway opened up his car door.

"That's him right there!" Tanya squealed, pointing in Andrew's direction.

"Fuck this shit!" Andrew muttered as he took off across the front yard. There was a nature trail across the street. He was gonna hide in the woods. He ran down the hill of the trail where it separated into a fork of two directions. He went to the left. He was gonna cut left again through a small field of grass to get to his neighbor's treehouse. However, out of the wooded area came one of the officers with a taser.

"Stop! Or I'll tase you! Stop right now!" the officer screamed.

Andrew turned back towards the trailhead to see officer number two rolling down the path in his cruiser. Andrew darted past the vehicle and onto the opposite trail. Now he had both the officers on his ass.

"Stop now!" the initial officer roared.

Andrew kept going. He started running in zig-zags in order not to get tased. Then his mind went wandering again. Why was he running and where would he go this time? He had to serve his sentence eventually. With the officer definitely in range to shoot him, he decided to give up. The officer spared Andrew the voltage. He just didn't have what it took that day.

"Get to the ground and put your hands behind your back!" growled the officer.

Andrew did just that. The officer knelt on his back and cuffed him. Then he was escorted up the trail to the police car and was placed in it. He was scared of what his fate would be. He felt like he was gonna be locked up forever. His uneasiness never settled but he had no choice but to be ready for the aftermath of his actions. The panda car took off

The Witch's Hat

from the nature trail and they pulled up to Andrew's parents' house. The officer got out and approached Tanya.

"His probation officer said to take him back to the STOP program," she vocalized. "He is on his way to pick up Andrew right now."

Within minutes Brock showed up. They added shackles to Andrew's ankles and transferred him into the back of Brock's car.

"Can you tell them to make sure his meds get adjusted and that he actually takes them? He has a serious mental illness. We need him on the right meds before he can come back to live with us," Tanya told him.

Again with the meds. Just the mere fact that Tanya was showing concern didn't mean that she was sad about the situation. If you knew her you could tell that she was certainly quite happy and loved whatever attention she could get at the expense of her child. This led Andrew to believe there was something wrong with his mother, but at the same time, he thought it was normal. Was every parent so willing to turn their kids over? Was medication always the solution? Was all this a ploy for conformity? These were the thoughts that were going through Andrew's head during his city-paid ride to the medical center.

They ended up hopping off the freeway in Minneapolis and a few short blocks later they arrived at the hospital for Andrew to do the same boring shit again. Long story short, he did his two weeks a second time and was released. This time they still had Andrew do the exact same thing. It was a close call. He had to beg to not get put into an inpatient treatment center and used school as an excuse to be released back home. The only difference was that the outpatient treatment center he had to attend was a different place. With his treatment plan in order paired with his new meds, Andrew was free to go home.

CHAPTER 9
Free Yet Oppressed

"Only a few months left of probation. I wish they would extend it. I still don't think you are stable. I have another appointment with Deb tomorrow for you to attend," Tanya stated on the ride home from the hospital.

"God damnit!" Andrew said angrily. "Ok just send me to the pill pusher again..."

The two arrived home safely and life continued. Andrew attended his psychiatrist and therapy appointments for the following weeks. He had skipped out on outpatient treatment and Brock never came about to punish him. New Years came and went and Andrew spent it sober. It wasn't too long afterward when Andrew had finished with probation. He started partying again. He met a girl named Sage at one of the parties and they started dating. Andrew had his permit from the previous year in high school and his mom had just begun letting him drive since he had given the impression he was still sober. She was completely oblivious. The first night Andrew had his girlfriend at his parents' house, they got drunk. Andrew wanted to be Mr. Macho and drive drunk with his mom in the passenger seat during the middle of winter

The Witch's Hat

for some reason to bring Sage home. That winter night Andrew was swerving on and off of the road. Tanya called him out on his drinking but let him continue driving until they made it to Sage's house. Tanya bickered to him, then she exited the car with Sage and proceeded to the front door of the home. She ratted Andrew out to Sage's mother. This was not a good impression he made of himself. Andrew didn't know why if it was such a big deal driving drunk that Tanya let him continue to drive. The important part was that they didn't die but now Andrew had to rebuild his reputation.

After this incident, Tanya scheduled Andrew with a new therapist. The counselor man told him it was ok to be upset and to want to rebel. He said that when Andrew got his license in the coming months that if he wanted to speed to go for it. The man caught on to Tanya's character and took Andrew's side. Tanya didn't like this and made Andrew switch counselors again. He discontinued therapy altogether as he was now off paper. This was the time when he really needed it. The family had foreclosed on their home and they moved to a new home about 20 minutes away. Even without the counseling, he still continued with his psychiatrist. He thought if he could play out his anxiety issues a little longer he could get those good pills he had been drooling over. Tanya had grown very frustrated with Andrew.

"I knew you would start skipping out on your appointments!" she snobbishly whined after Andrew skipped his first up-to-date therapy session.

"At least I'm seeing the psychiatrist!" Andrew pointed out. "That's all you seem to really care about anyway so please stop bugging me!"

Andrew never did get the good meds he wanted so he had the bright idea to straight-up raid his parents' medicine cabinet. He did his research on every drug he could find and took note of the good ones. With the guidance of his friends, he began popping Percocet. He would consistently sneak pills from his mother's stockpile on a regular basis. Months went by of this and spring rolled around. Andrew's 16th birthday came to be and his parents rewarded him with a car. The main purpose they had intended it for was to get him to and from school. The new house wasn't on the bus route for his high school and he was also starting PSEO the following year so he needed transportation. On top of that, he also had to commute to work.

To the disapproval of his parents, in Andrew's free time he would drive to hang out with his druggy friends. Eventually, before you know it, his drug addiction had escalated. He was now taking methadone, fentanyl patches, and OxyContin. He took every last working antidote his mother had. He even found a secret stash in her wardrobe closet in a drawer with a missing knob. He took all of that as well. He flushed her clean dry.

Andrew absolutely loved doing opioids. They just so happened to give him this nice fuzzy warm feeling where nothing else mattered. Any stress he had was minuscule now. It wasn't like he didn't care because he did. He just learned to take life as it came without worries.

Summer eventually came. Andrew and Josh would spend time together writing music at their new house in Andrew's bedroom. Josh would make a melody on the keyboard then Andrew and his best friend whose name was also Josh came up with the lyrics. Andrew's brother proved himself to be a creative artist and had tons of potential.

Once the summer fulfilled with music therapy had passed, Andrew's junior year of high school began. He was attending the community college while his brother Josh was in middle school dealing with constant bullying. Josh was in 8th grade and was regularly dropped off by his mom at some random bus stop a few miles away. He was called out for being gay on his bus rides. All his friends were mostly girls growing up and the bullies had caught onto his secret at the school. It must have slipped by word of mouth because it didn't seem quite apparent that he was. No one else at home even knew.

Names were called. They would call him "fag" and "homo". He would get bumped into in the halls. Josh finally summed up the courage to come out of the closet to Tanya. She welcomed him and did what she thought was right to comfort him but it wasn't good enough. If she cared she wouldn't have told the whole world about it.

During Tanya's phone call with her mom, she stated she was worried about Josh getting treated differently in school. She said all this in a rousing voice with another smirk on her face. Drama. Drama. Drama. Then their grandma went on to tell the whole family. Now Josh was being treated differently by almost everybody. Sadly Josh never came out to say anything about himself being bullied, he just dealt with it. He was embarrassed and told his mom everything was going fine.

Andrew found out the news later on and was surprised just like their father. However, Andrew didn't treat Josh any differently like Scott did. Scott was very upset.

"How could he like boys? He's supposed to like girls," he said cold and thunderously over to Tanya from the kitchen. Josh was in his room listening to music. No doubt he heard what his dad said. It would take a little getting used to for Scott. Hopefully, his overall words didn't have too much of a negative effect.

Andrew's pills ran out from his mother's stash. She eventually found out after Andrew had already emptied all the bottles. It seemed as if she was just storing them for some purpose and must have only used them sparingly. She didn't catch on until Andrew took every last one. He solved this problem by buying pills off of his friends. Andrew would sit in his room at night and snort one oxycodone after another. He snorted as many as he felt for the day. They were expensive. He felt like he was half there, half not. He was numb. Why was he doing this to himself? He grew accustomed to melancholy. He wanted to be a rockstar but knew he would never amount to anything.

As Andrew stayed up late at night he would browse through social media on his desktop computer in his bedroom. On many scattered days, he would somewhat pass out with his head on his desk but was still coherent. He was hibernating in his mental hole. He listened as Josh would play The Fray on the stereo in the room above him. Such a beautiful blue song. The song was "How to Save a Life". He ran it on repeat and Andrew thought nothing of his brother crying out for help. He ignored reality. He only did what he had to for school and drug scavenging. He was a garbage disposal of pills.

Since Andrew needed money he would hang out after school with his friend Conrad and sell pot. They even would sell pills at a hefty price they could profit on. With the couple hundred bucks each day, they were able to get mostly whatever drug they wanted. Andrew had tried a multitude of them at this point but hadn't gotten into the heavy stuff yet. His habits consisted of weed, booze, and OxyContin. All usually at the same time. Andrew would drive his car around all fucked up but he was able to handle it and managed to get around town. He was smart and careful.

Andrew would get home around 10 or later during most school nights. Nearly every day when he came home a little earlier than that, Josh would be jamming songs on his cello or playing music on his stereo. The parents would sometimes get mad. Tanya would whine during her phone calls with everyone in the whole world about what she referred to as a nuisance. Luckily Josh had a lot of friends he spent his day with to keep him in high spirits but when he came home his nights were full of solitude and pain. Josh's cello was basically his drug. He enjoyed his fix as he played on immersed in emotion. Andrew didn't know what it was about the music but he enjoyed it. The cello playing would emit a lot of energy at moments but would descend into deep somberness. In other cases, it was still just deep sadness. This was Josh's outlet. Andrew never did know that something was seriously wrong. He would listen through the ceiling to the room above and drown in Josh's misery which would take him to a dark place that he endured. The two brothers spent the nights suffering together in different but similar ways.

On one spring day the following calendar year of the same fiscal school year, Josh was violated. Minding his own business, he walked down the tunnel leading to the cafeteria of the middle school with his best friend who was a girl. The tunnel was a secluded place with nothing but a few cameras protecting him from bullies. There were corners of the tunnel that were in blind spots. This made an unsafe location for Andrew's brother. Josh reached a point where it sort of turned a corner. Little did he know, one of the students walking ahead of him had stopped in the hallway and was hiding behind the corner he was turning. The kid had Josh locked in as his target and as soon as he turned the corner the kid sprung onto him and grabbed his groin.

The Witch's Hat

With a ridged squeeze of Josh's testicles, he leaned into his ear and whispered, "You like that don't you?"

"Get off of him!" shouted Kathy, Josh's friend.

"Fuck you bitch! What are you gonna do?" the bully said as he released Josh's genitalia and shoved him to the ground. "You faggot!" the tormenter snapped. He spat on him and went on his way.

Josh was hunched on his side in the fetal position. His face was red from embarrassment and tears ran down his cheeks. Kathy knelt to him and rubbed his back. "I'm gonna do something about this. I'll find someone to help you!" she said.

"No! Don't!" Josh sputtered. The duo squabbled in disagreement as Kathy pulled him to his feet. They continued arguing all the way to the lunchroom. Once they arrived, Kathy called out to a teacher to help them out.

"Kathy don't! It's fine!" Cried Josh.

The teacher was a male who stepped up in front of the two. "What's going on?" he muttered.

"My friend here was just assaulted in the tunnel," said Kathy with concern in her voice.

"Why is that?" asked the teacher.

"We believe it is because he is gay. This kid has been picking on Josh the whole school year!" replied Kathy with frustration.

The teacher turned to Josh. "Well is it true? Are you gay?"

Josh shrugged his shoulders. Kathy stepped in and spoke for him, "Yes he is and there is nothing wrong with that!"

The teacher's eyes narrowed and he looked angry. "Well if you are gay you are sort of asking for this kind of treatment, don't you think?"

Josh shrugged his shoulders again.

"That's not true!" said Kathy sternly.

"Well, from the way I see it there is nothing that I can do. My suggestion for you is to not tell people you are gay and you won't have these problems. Please don't bother me with this again!" said the teacher as he turned and walked away.

Little did the guy know that Josh had never told anyone but his girlfriends that he was gay but somehow the other students had figured it out. Josh just wanted each day at school to pass without any ridicule or problems. He wanted to fight this battle alone. Or did he? Perhaps he was just too scared and embarrassed to ask for help. If he could confide in his mom privately maybe he would have. But just as Andrew knew, Josh knew as well that that was near impossible. You would be in for a rude awakening because everything you disclose with her would end up on social media, and who wants that?

Luckily Kathy had Josh's back. Without Josh's approval, Kathy went to the principal's office and told Sargent Whangbottom of the ordeal that had just occurred. She told him that she believed Josh was receiving constant negativity from certain groups of people based on his sexual orientation. She also said that the teacher they had reported the incident to had done nothing to help the situation and essentially blamed the whole ordeal on the fact that Josh was gay.

Being a vet with a missing hand, Sargent Whangbottom had little compassion. He was the same guy who suspended Andrew back in the day for something so stupid. He finally chimed, "There is nothing I can do unless Josh comes and files a complaint in person. The fact that he is gay makes these things kind of tricky. I can see where the teacher is coming from. I'll request Josh down here to the main office and see what he says."

A trustee was sent to Josh's classroom to deliver a salmon-colored slip. The teacher received it and handed it to J-Dawg. This was his calling to stand up for himself. But what would he do or say when he arrived at the principal's office? On his walk, Josh decided to blow it off like it was nothing. This remained on his consciousness even as he passed through the doorway of the principal's headquarters.

Upon entry, Sargent Whangbottom pounced on Josh. "Is it true you were assaulted down in the tunnel earlier this afternoon?"

"No, nothing happened at all. It wasn't a big deal. I'm ok," Josh replied.

The Witch's Hat

"Well if anything ever occurs and you feel threatened you must let me know or else there is nothing I can do," said the principal.

"Ok," Josh said quietly.

"That's all I needed. You aren't in trouble. Have a good rest of your day," Sergeant Whangbottom hastily said.

"Thank you. You too," Josh replied in a gentle whisper.

J-dawg was ashamed. The principal didn't even take the time to alert his parents of what was going on. Josh came home that night and didn't say a word about anything that happened. He went to his room and started playing his time-worn cello. The chords vibrated through the house. Hours went by and he was still playing. You can tell that he was progressing at his artistry. His songs seemed to flow very well.

Little did Andrew know as he listened sprawled out on his bed below, that Josh was playing in the shadowy darkness. He was saddened. Andrew didn't recognize that Josh's music reflected his feelings. He figured it was just music. It had become Josh's great escape. Words can't express how low and alone Josh was feeling. He was strong in his own way. Bullies couldn't break him when it came to pouring out his soul into his notes. However, Josh was losing hope for the future. Would everyone he came across treat him differently because he was gay? Josh thought so. So where was the hope? In short, the hope was stolen from him.

He played and played and played. He would play to the very minute he fell asleep. Tanya would get on him time after time about playing too late. She would get annoyed. She also must not have enjoyed attending orchestra concerts either. Andrew couldn't remember a time when she came to his own when he had played violin in middle school. He doubted she went to many of Josh's either. Andrew himself was too preoccupied with getting high to show his support. He wasn't aware of much of anything going on in the household. It was a terrible situation. No one should ever feel so isolated. Josh knew his mom was talking about him because the family would treat him weirdly. This was all fairly new terrain for them. Andrew believed they still loved him but perhaps they didn't understand. No one really reached out to try to understand.

Josh sunk into depression and was put on antidepressants for a short while. He took them for a few weeks and quit. He told his mom that he wasn't taking them anymore because they didn't work. To Tanya's disappointment, he wasn't willing to try any new meds or even attend therapy at that. Tanya constantly pushed it but Josh was smart enough to not fall for her trickery. He didn't need some lady coming to his appointments telling the doctor what medication she suggested for him to be on after a couple of Google searches every few weeks. Josh took no part in it.

Meanwhile, Andrew would hang with his newly acquainted girlfriend. This was his first true and intimate relationship. Sage was Costa Rican. Her father was a drug runner for the cartel. They owned a marvelous mansion down in Costa Rica and were loaded with tons of money. Andrew never sacrificed his pride to ask for any favors. What threw a wrench into the equation was that her brothers did a lot of drugs themselves but despised Andrew for doing the same. In fact, the whole family despised Andrew for that reason. Their overall goal was to sabotage the relationship of the couple, yet the two young lovers ignored it.

When the pair wasn't together Andrew took trips to his birthplace in Minneapolis. He would linger in and around his mother's parents' property. His purpose was to do drugs and find a way to come up with the money to get them. Uncle Theo along with Andrew rummaged through the house for DVDs and anything of worth that would hopefully not be missed too much. On one occasion they packed a few things they were gonna sell in Andrew's subwoofer-stocked car. Andrew went into the house quickly to grab a soda. He happened to run into his other uncle named Malcolm at the entryway of the home. Malcolm was descending the stairs from the second floor heading towards the front door. He was only two years younger than Andrew. Notably, Malcolm was very ambitious. He was just getting over dark times and vented through basketball.

"Hey Andrew!" he said while spin juggling a basketball in his hands.

The Witch's Hat

"Sup?" Andrew said in a chill manner.

"So how do you feel about Josh being gay?" he asked as he chuckled.

"Honestly it doesn't really bother me. It's my dad that is irritated," Andrew responded with concern.

"Damn man, that's harsh. It's Josh's choice if he likes guys," Malcolm voiced. "I personally don't care either. I just don't want a gay guy to come onto me."

"Yeah, that's kinda how I feel. It's their choice but I don't want to join the club myself," Andrew laughed. "I'm worried he might get shit in school. I know the gay kids get picked on in high school and he starts senior high next year which will be a little different. I haven't heard anything from him saying he has been being tormented so he must be alright."

"Well, that's good," stated Malcolm. "I better get outta here man. I gotta hit the court."

"Alright man! Later! Have fun!" Andrew said back to him.

"Thanks bro!" responded Malcolm bringing an end to the conversation as he walked out the front door.

Andrew followed him out the door and did the usual by hopping in his car accompanied by Theo and making his trip to pick up a friend who was 18 to head to the pawnshop with the stolen goods. He knew he always got ripped off but he did it for easy money and didn't care too much about it. He was super happy to score his drugs shortly after. Timbo, the dealer, had a Lamborghini parked in his driveway which had been impounded twice previously when he had to serve jail time for writing fake prescriptions. He had a good lawyer but still had two strikes against himself. Andrew grabbed the cellophane from a cigarette pack containing the tablets from Timbo through the window of his damaged chevy cavalier. Andrew was sitting in it at the boat launch across from Timbo's house. Twilight had just begun and the spring air smelt like rotten fish as the dealer was quick to leave the scene just as Andrew was quick to snort the OxyContin he just picked up. Theo snorted half of his share as well. After that Andrew drove approximately 20 miles to drop Theo off and another 22 miles to get home.

He arrived home around 9:00 p.m. He exited his car and walked through the starry night towards the front door of the casa. He had the vibe that the stars were calling down to earth. Who were they summoning? Andrew opened the door to the home and heard arguing. It sounded like Josh and Scott. Andrew walked by Josh's bedroom to see him holding a knife to his stomach with his hands trembling. His face was crimson as well as wet from sobbing. The littlest brother Antonio along with Tanya was standing at the doorway watching while their dad stood a few feet away from J-man.

"Go ahead and do it bitch! I doubt you will!" shouted Scott.

That very second Josh pulled the knife about a foot away from his body. Stab! Stab! Stab! The punctures went straight into his abdomen. He had just jabbed the knife into himself 3 times! Just then, Tanya came walking into the room with a phone in her hand. She had just ended a phone call.

"Oh my god! What did you do to yourself?" she blurted as she saw blood sponging up Josh's shirt.

"He fucking stabbed himself Tanya!" Scott shouted. "Call the ambulance!"

Tanya called in the first responders as Andrew stood there starstruck. What in the hell had happened? What was the argument about? Why did his dad tell Josh to stab himself? Did he not care? Andrew knew what this meant. This meant Josh was going to be locked up with the crazies. Within a few moments, the ambulance came and Josh was transported to the emergency room to get stitched up. He didn't have any serious internal injuries and was placed in the psychiatric ward for a few days.

Andrew kept wondering when his brother would come home. Was he wrong for not stepping in? He felt guilty for not doing anything. But this was his parents doing this to them. The negativity reverberated through the house and stood still in his body as if it had no escape. This must have been how life was for all kids growing up, he thought. Maybe if Andrew would have done something to try and prevent the occurrence, then maybe Josh would have felt like he had an ally at home. The whole situation haunted him.

But what about Antonio? He was only 6 years old and saw the whole thing. Just another kid taken from the system and put into a fucked up household. And what for? Was it just for the money? The parents, however, did collect a paycheck every month for adopting him... This was to make it possible for Tanya to not have to work at a full-time job and to sit on her ass at home talking shit. It seemed as if the malady from the words spoken was spreading.

On the 3rd day after the scenario with Josh, he was able to come home with his freshly mended stomach. If it was up to Tanya he would have been kept longer. Andrew supposed they didn't keep him because this was his first incident. Josh desperately needed someone to come forth and talk to him. He sure as hell wasn't going to reach out to anyone on his own. He needed someone he trusted. Andrew could have been that person for him. So could have Tanya along with Scott. But those two were already ruined. They were programmed to show tough love in an ever-changing world with so many things to keep the mind, not at ease. They probably didn't understand. They didn't.

CHAPTER 10
Fine China

A YEAR WENT BY and Josh was still bullied while Andrew was spiraling out of control. The family had yet again moved to another home. Andrew was now 17 and on the verge of graduating. He was still enrolled at the community college which gave him the freedom to snort pills in the parking lot before class. Josh was just beginning his freshman year at the high school and was still dropped off at a bus stop so he didn't have to switch to another district. The two brothers never saw each other for the most part. They went to separate schools and possessed separate lives. The majority of the pair's connection was through Josh's nighttime cello playing. They each shared different pieces of reality through the same channel at that given time frame. Plato says, "Reality is created by the mind, we can change our reality by changing our mind." Andrew's mind wanted to change, but couldn't, so he drowned it out. Josh's music gave Andrew feeling again.

Since Josh was so fantastic with his music, when he tested for his orchestra classification before departing from the middle school, he was rewarded with the best bracket. As a freshman, he would be playing

The Witch's Hat

concert orchestra. He would be playing with the best at the school. Most of the classmates would be seniors and he would be one of the youngest. But he was just as good.

Josh felt very accepted in his orchestra class. The kids were way more open to who he was. He was a young teenage boy who happened to be gay but there was so much more to him. The orchestra classroom was in the same area as the theatre students. There was a couple of gay students who roamed the area and Josh would come to know them. Most of Josh's friends weren't gay but he did have gay allies. They had to stick together. They battled homophobic slurs and harassment almost every day.

On one occasion Josh went to his locker after class. He was awaited by a kid with curly red hair and freckles. The kid was posted around the corner of the lockers in the school's mezzanine. He ducked below the height of the locker compartments and peeked over at Josh. The kid was quite chunky and tall. He looked like he was a grown-up. When Josh finished grabbing his belongings for his next class, he departed and approached Mr. Freckles. The giant kid blocked Josh's lane.

"Hey homo, I saw you play at the concert last night. You suck," spewed Mr. Freckles.

"Yeah I know..." is what Josh said as he stared down at the ground. It was so sad he thought so low of himself and believed the negative poison pouring from people's mouths who despised him. Josh didn't understand that this kid may have been jealous of his accomplishments and his group of girlfriends. Josh just wanted to remain on the down-low. Unfortunately, the word was out that he was Uranian. With all the young pre-adults in school, it seemed a difficult matter to blend in when you are crucified daily for being different. We all bleed the same. It just came down to the bad apples.

"You need more practice! Actually, you know what? You should stop playing altogether because you will never be good!" the chunky kid said to Josh as he pushed his hands into Josh's chest to make him fall to the ground. "Have a nice day fag!" the kid said as he grinned and went on his way.

It seemed apparent that these incidents were some of the causes of Josh's depression. No matter what compliments he got he would take the negativity to heart. Most people cherished his music but he didn't feel that way. Andrew adored Josh's music as well but perhaps he didn't take enough time to tell Josh that. Their mom, however, may not have felt the same way. As stated previously, she would fret behind Josh's back but would show support to his face. All that practice he participated in was what Andrew thought was grounds for Josh's growing talent. He just lacked the appreciation.

Time ticked by with nothing much changing. Josh kept his mouth shut about his chronic bullying and Andrew continued to do drugs. The only difference was that Andrew stepped up the ladder on what drugs he was engulfed in. The main reasoning that pushed him to go to college was that it gave him freedom from being that kid who was steered around like a sheep. It gave him the freedom to smoke his cigarettes without getting in trouble and to skip class when he felt like it. Most importantly he could go to class high without being worried about being pulled aside. It was easy enough. He could snort his pills in the car located in the parking lot. He felt like an adult. He didn't have to worry about security stopping him as he went to his car to do so. Well, he kinda did but they left him alone and didn't cruise by too much.

He would rip a line or two and head back to class only to doze out at the desk. When he was consciously in the moment, he conquered and climbed his high and grew interested in some of the courses. He strived to be out of his mind but present at the same time. He could shed off some of the downer sensations with strong mental concentration. Certain classes, he did very well in for that reason. The classes he thought were boring or a waste of time he would drop out of or not do his homework and get a barely passing grade. His average grades went from an A down to a C since his attendance was lacking at the college. He didn't care as much and just wanted to skate by. He didn't have any big plans and wasn't too excited about any career path. So he just did what he had to do while partying all the time.

After school on a cloudy winter day, Andrew went to his friend

The Witch's Hat

Conrad's house. Conrad was one of Andrew's partners in crime. They were always looking for drug money and were trying to keep up with their habit. The pills were getting too expensive and they were running out of people to steal from. So on this particular day Conrad's brother, Ralph, came back to their home and had a tied-up baggy with some brownish-white powder in it. He held it out in front of himself up to Andrew's face.

"Guess what this is," he said with excitement.

"What is it?" Andrew and Conrad both asked.

"It's China white. Wanna try some? It's basically crushed up OxyContin but stronger and cheaper," Ralph replied.

Andrew didn't mind trying new drugs. He called out to Ralph, "Yeah I'll do some."

"I haven't done any yet," Ralph chuckled. "You need a needle to inject it." He pulled out a bag of 1 cc needles from his hoody pocket and set it on the nightstand.

"Wait, is this heroin?" Andrew asked.

Ralph laughed. "Maybe..."

"Well is it?" Andrew asked with concern.

"Yeah, it is," Ralph said with his dumb dopey laugh.

Andrew's heart started racing. He knew this stuff was bad. He also had the knowledge that it could lead to overdose, especially by injecting it. But Andrew was chasing the highest of highs. His body started to quiver.

"Shit man. I never injected anything. I'm kinda nervous," Andrew said strongly. "You said you haven't done it yourself?"

"No, I haven't. I just wanted to see someone else do it before I did," Ralph answered.

So basically Andrew became the Guinea pig and was succumbing to peer pressure. Don't forget the stuff was free and Andrew was always in for a fix. Maybe if this stuff was good he would save money in the long run to buy other drugs. It was worth a try. Hopefully, it wouldn't cause him to die. Andrew rubbed that thought out from his mind. He was determined to do it.

Andrew grabbed a syringe from the bedside nightstand. There was a spoon laying next to it. He took off the caps to the syringe and set them down. "So how do I do this?" asked Andrew.

"I watched a YouTube video. Here, I'll be right back," said Ralph as he grabbed the plunger cap and went to the bathroom faucet.

Less than a minute later, Ralph came back with water in the cap. They then grabbed the paraphernalia and moved it to the desk on the opposite side of the room next to the Sid Vicious poster. On the desk was a lamp to illuminate their taboo activity. Ralph instructed Andrew to put the tip of the needle into the water-filled cap and drawback to the 40 unit mark imprinted on the side of the needle. This was almost half the syringe's full capacity. Andrew did so.

Ralph then dumped a fair amount of the brownish powder onto the upside bowl portion of the laying spoon. Then he told Andrew to squeeze the water from the syringe into the curvature of the spoon by pushing the trigger on the tool. The trigger consisted of a rubber stopper connected to a plastic stick that you could pull in and out of the hollow cylinder of the syringe. It was inserted into the opposite end of the needle. To pull was to draw water or blood. To push was to expel the contents.

Andrew shakily squeezed the trigger to squirt the water onto the spoon. His heartbeat was galloping while he grew butterflies in his belly. The next step was to mix the concoction together. Andrew used the remaining orange needle cap to mix it up. He was gonna do it. Obviously, Andrew knew the next step. But wait, Ralph dropped a piece of cotton from a Q-tip into the remedy.

"What? Is that supposed to be a filter?" Andrew questioned.

"Yeah, stick the needle into it!" Ralph eagerly demanded.

"Alright man! Chill! I got this!" responded Andrew.

He stuck the needle into the filter puddled with the dirty dopey water. He slowly filled the syringe up by drawing back the trigger. It

The Witch's Hat

looked like dark urine. As the syringe filled up, it just so happened that it ended up getting filled with bubbles.

"Flick the needle to get the bubbles out. The guy on the video said they can kill you if that air gets into your bloodstream," Ralph said without a worry. He was slowly nodding in and out from his Oxy's.

Andrew looked at Ralph with wide eyes. "Jesus Christ!" he muttered with uneasiness.

Andrew licked the remainder of the liquid from the spoon and made a sour almost disgusted face. It was a strongly bitter and twisted taste. He knew this stuff was gonna be good. He then did what Ralph told him. He flicked the needle to settle the mixture and slowly pushed the trigger with the syringe upright to get the air out. The bubbles disappeared. He pushed the trigger just a tad more to make a hair of the heroin potion drip out. It was now all ready.

"Now what?" Andrew asked anxiously.

Ralph walked over to his closet and grabbed a belt for Andrew. "Here. Wrap this tightly around your upper arm."

Andrew did so. "Ok..." he chirped back.

"Make sure it's tight then open and close your hand like you're squeezing a stress ball. Once you do that you should be able to find a decent vein."

Andrew had pulled the belt tight and squeezed it under his armpit with enough pressure so it wouldn't come loose. He began looking for veins. From what he could see he didn't have much to choose from. All Andrew noticed were faint blue lines that were scarcely detectable under his skin. None of them protruded or stood out for him to use.

"Ralph! I don't know where to go!" Andrew said with exasperation.

"Looks like you have baby veins. You will just have to choose one and hope it works," Ralph responded.

Andrew grabbed the needle and held it up to his cubital fossa to a vein he was gonna try his luck at. He was beginning to have second thoughts. He never knew of any heroin addicts but he assumed that most of them either died of an overdose or went to jail. Did he want that fate? Why of course not but he was gonna roll the dice. He rejected the cubital fossa and went to a baby vein of his choice near his left wrist. All he had to do was shoot the needle into the bullseye.

His hands were shaky and his nerves were jostling. The butterflies in his stomach were flapping their wings rapidly at this point. He looked at Ralph and said sternly, "If I overdose you better call the ambulance and get me to the hospital."

"Don't worry about it. Nothing will happen," Ralph replied with a brainless laugh.

Andrew immediately summoned the courage to slowly break the skin with the tip of the needle. He then pushed straight down instead of at an angle. "Now what?" he asked.

"Now you pull back the plunger to see if blood draws. If it does you hit the vein and can inject it," he answered.

Andrew pulled back the plunger but didn't get a single spurt of blood. It just didn't want to pull back.

"You missed," Ralph asserted. "Keep searching."

Andrew decided to push the needle a little deeper. The needle struck a nerve and hit something hard. He felt a sharp pain go up his arm. He quickly pulled the needle from his skin.

"Fuck man!" Andrew shouted. He set the needle down on the desk and cupped his wrist with his freed hand to prevent the blood from making a mess. "I'm pretty sure I hit my fuckin bone!"

"You've got to go in more of at an angle," Ralph informed.

Andrew was determined to get this over with. He picked up the needle. This time he poked into his flesh just a hair atop the same vein. Then he angled it at 20 degrees and continued inserting the needle ever so slightly. He reached a point where he thought he hit the bullseye so he drew back the plunger slowly and it majestically filled with a mushroom cloud of blood.

"I got it!" Andrew blurted with anticipation.

"Now just slowly inject it," Ralph instructed.

As Andrew went to inject the remedy his hand was jostled out of

The Witch's Hat

place. He was also squeezing the plunger at a faster pace than he should have been. He instantly noticed a bubble appear amongst his skin along the surrounding area. By the time his brain had registered what had happened, he had already injected the remnants of the needle. The concoction was now under his corium looking as if it wanted to burst.

The bubble was maybe an inch and a half in diameter formulating a circular shape on his lower forearm towards his wrist. It looked like a fat pussy blister. It withheld a whitish-yellow color and itched. It started to spread up his forearm in smaller yellowish bubbly blotches. Andrew itched it rapidly and his arm turned discolored. Red scratches covered the surface in lines that quilted the bubbles. The drug was being absorbed through Andrew's bodily cells creating a chemical reaction. He felt a slight buzz. It felt fantastic. Andrew only imagined if he had hit the vein how he would have felt.

"Looks like that went to waste," sighed Andrew.

"It's ok. You have time to learn," Ralph vocalized with disappointment.

Conrad was laughing. "Dang man! That sucks! You missed!"

"I hope these bubbles go away..." Andrew said nonchalantly but with internal anxiety.

"They should. You will be fine," Ralph commented.

"Well, I hope so. I think I'm gonna head out now," Andrew announced.

"Alright man," Ralph said.

"See ya man!" Conrad added.

"Bye!" Andrew said, bringing the convo to a conclusion as he headed out the bedroom door to leave.

He took his car home. It was just another ordinary night. In fact, the next few months were pretty ordinary. Music. Music. Music. The rhythm traveled through the home to bring a small glimmer of hope in a negative world granted through the trailblazing instrument Josh handled.

Weeks and weeks went by. It was springtime and nearing Andrew's birthday. During the duration of time, he had mastered the art of banging (shooting up). It was the same routine over and over. Meanwhile, Josh was still struggling through his agonizing freshman escapade. He maintained being strong as well as social but in reality, he felt he was alone. Josh knew Andrew's drug habit was out of control. "A-dawg" had pawned off the ps2 the two used to play together as kids. They embraced many hours playing co-op on *Medal of Honor* on that bad boy. On top of that, Andrew also kept taking from Josh's change jar. Amongst some other things he pawned were his dad's power tools. He even went as far as to pawn his great grandpa's accordion his grandpa had passed down as an heirloom. Andrew made a pawn shop run almost every day.

A few days after his birthday, Andrew completed his college semester thus graduating high school. His reward was that he could now buy his own cigarettes and not have to depend on his mother bootlegging them for him. On a negative note, Andrew and his girlfriend broke up shortly after he earned his degree. She was seeing a different guy in Wisconsin so they grew apart. She stopped coming around which began a long period of depression for Andrew. But since he was done with school he had more time to sidetrack his mind to something else by delving into more drugs. The pain was buried but still lingered.

The past few weeks for Josh were terrible as well. The students at the high school knew school was going to end soon so they were more reckless with their bullying and name-calling. In contrast with Andrew, Josh had begun seeing a guy his last week of school. His boyfriend never came out as a homosexual. Only a select few knew. Josh himself still rode with his feelings to himself through the rest of the school year and completed the 9th-grade thanks to his friends. Josh continued talking to his boyfriend through the beginning of summer. It was the first significant other he had ever had. Josh's heart was of fragile gold. There was no telling what would happen if his heart was broken. He already had too much on his plate.

When it wasn't in school, it was on the internet. Josh was cyber-bullied through a new website called Facebook. This was Josh's main means to talk to his boyfriend. They didn't have much face-to-face

The Witch's Hat

contact. They didn't so much know each other very well either. They began the summer talking every day over the internet on messenger. This lasted maybe three weeks until the last week of June. During this week the boy began to ignore Josh's messages. Josh began to get worried about what happened. Had he done something to upset his partner? No, he hadn't. In retrospect, the runaway was just struggling with his own issues at identifying as gay.

That weekend Josh and Andrew went out of town with their parents for a festival called Waterama. This was located in the area where the family name had immigrated from Norway. It was a getaway. The festival was packed but not overwhelmingly. The parents sat on lawn chairs beside a lake that bordered the city and watched fireworks launch from the dock. It was amazing. Andrew and Josh were on the grass near the beach on a blanket. Andrew laid gazing at the sky taking in the artistry of gunpowder. E.T.'s raced through his brain after a plane flew by. It reminded him of a time when he saw a reddish light surrounded by a triangular set of white lights far up in the sky hovering over him. The lights intertwined and pulsated. Then in a blink of an eye, it disappeared. He reflected on what aliens were like and what their objective was. Meanwhile, Josh was sitting pretzel-legged hunched over fixated on his phone.

Josh texted his ex, "Hey Tyler, how is it going? Why are you ignoring me?"

At the present moment, Tyler couldn't resist and was talking to numerous other guys. "Leave me alone!" is what he replied. Then nothing. Not a single word.

"What did I do?" Josh typed back.

Still nothing. Josh went back and forth from staring at his phone to burying his face in his hands with his back slumped over. Something was going on in his mind and he was feeling very low. He must not have been good enough for a real devoted relationship. Besides, he was gay and shy. So how would he meet his true best friend? It seemed so difficult. Josh was experiencing the puppy dog blues but to the extreme. He carried on moping as the grand finale of the fireworks lit up the sky.

At that very moment, his phone blew up from multiple people. His hand wielding the phone was getting a massage. Josh checked his messages. It was Tyler as well as some of Josh's 3 closest girlfriends. Even his biggest tormentor, another closeted gay guy named Genesis, somehow got word and was talking shit. All 5 were ganging up on him, saying derogatory comments, and making fun of him. Josh was feeling like a burden as his world fell apart.

After the fireworks concluded the brothers headed back to their dad's father's house on the other side of the lake. Upon arrival, Andrew hurried to the loo with a spoon and a needle that he concealed in his sock. Within 7 minutes he had injected the potion and was fading in and out, but he was ready to party. Coincidentally, there was a country fest going on just a few blocks away. Andrew was entirely down to go and was ready to float his body down the street. He left the bathroom and walked up to his brother who he found on the computer in the dining room.

"Hey Josh, wanna come with me to the country fest down the road?" asked Andrew. "We can walk."

"No thanks," he answered.

Andrew was bummed out. He wanted to do something with his brother. He missed hanging out with him like in the olden days. "Come on! Come with! There will be guys there!"

Andrew was serious about Josh cruising for other guys. He just probably couldn't pursue a relationship because being gay wasn't yet part of the norm. Plus Andrew didn't suspect many gay guys at a country fest in the boonies. Andrew wished he could cheer his brother up. He didn't know what was wrong. After Andrew tried to push his brother to come a few more times he gave up and ended up going to the country fest alone.

Andrew walked down a few blocks to get to the gig. The lights to the merry-go-rounds and rides were overwhelming. The mind-boggling feeling was mostly overtaken with excitement. Then loneliness set in. Andrew was single himself at the time but he didn't have the courage to seek a new mate. He needed a wingman. He thought about why his brother didn't come. Josh was spiraling into deep sorrow but the family figured it was normal and that it was something he would work himself out of. It was just the way of life for the 3 siblings. What Andrew wondered was what the cause of Josh's misery was and why life had to be this way.

Andrew kept wandering alone and ended up finding himself in the way back of the crowd facing the bandstand. He saw tons of cute girls but still didn't bother to pursue them with a smooth intro. His palms were sweaty with slight distress which wasn't unusual. The drugs seemed to be for the nonce moment to slightly debilitate himself and calm his nerves a little bit. Again, the times he was told he had crippling anxiety made him believe that he actually did and so his body acted in that manner. It had seemed like a learned behavior. Street drugs were needed to combat this. Maybe in time, he would find the cure. Maybe it was just all in his head. Alas, the truth was that at this juncture he was absent of the cure in its entirety. He only had the cure to make the worry more abatable and to get through the day without getting sick. It was well known that he just couldn't get enough. In a sense, it was a whole lot of trickery.

Andrew couldn't take the flashing lights flooding his eyes so he decided to leave to ride his high horse. Andrew arrived at the home to see that Josh was still on the computer. He was arched over typing away. Who was he talking to? It just so happened that he had another gay friend in Brazil whom he had befriended and would vent to. Maybe they had a thing for each other or maybe they didn't. Either way, Josh was still hung up over Tyler.

Andrew did his routine in the bathroom with just a small dose to briefly engulf him in substantial euphoria. He exited the lavatory and noticed that Josh was nowhere to be found. He must have gone to bed. Andrew along with his two uncles and father pulled out a game of Risk and began playing. Andrew was going to conquer the world.

CHAPTER 11
The Mysterious Downfall

ABOUT A WEEK had come to pass since the trip to Waterama. It was now the Fourth of July as well as gram gram's birthday. The family headed to the grandparents on Tanya's side this time for a celebration. Andrew brought his mini fireworks which included bottle rockets and firecrackers. When they arrived, Andrew circled the street in front of the house looking for things to blow up. He found a dead squirrel on the road and began to unstring a strand of firecrackers so he could isolate and use just a single one.

"Let's blow this thing up!" said Andrew. "It's dead anyhow."

"Yeah, let's do it bro!" voiced Theo who was standing beside him.

Due to their proximity in age, the two called each other cousins but felt more like brothers. Anyhow, Andrew then grabbed a lone firecracker and put it in the squirrel's mouth. "You ready?"

"Yeah! Let's do it up!" replied Theo.

Andrew lit the fuse...

Boom!!!

The squirrel's jaw blew halfway off! A splattered stain of lineage possessing blood wet the hot summer pavement. It wasn't too gushy but the jaw was hanging only by a strand on one side. The other side was completely and utterly dismantled. Mr. Squirrelly looked violated and disgraced.

"Let's shove one up its ass!" shouted Theo.

"Ok, let's see what happens," laughed Andrew.

Andrew had a harder time getting the pyro article into the squirrel's ass than he did with its mouth, but he managed to get it in. He had to wiggle it back and forth then push with some might. The firecracker went so far inside that only the fuse was protruding from it.

"Ok, I'm gonna light it!" Andrew remarked as he held the lighter up to the green fuse.

Andrew then flicked the bic for the creature's second afterlife execution. The fuse sizzled as it approached its fate into the arsehole. As soon as the sparkle via the sparks of the lit fuse disappeared there was another loud explosion! Bam!! The anus blew open and the intestines were exposed. A couple of small chunks of meat went moderately airborne and landed on the pavement. The detonation had left a crater where the ass used to be. Andrew felt like a murderer even though the squirrel's physical body was already still and lifeless. He got over it and moved on to the next thing. It was time to get high again.

The pair walked to the front door of the home. Andrew noticed Josh sitting on the nose of the front steps glued to his phone all by himself. Poor kid. He was missing out on the present moment with his family and the real world. "Andyboy Gorilla Beast," as was Andrew's stoner name, didn't pay much mind to it at all. He walked up the front stairway and passed through the home's entryway. Then, with Theo tagging along, they went up to the second floor to enter the bat cave.

Next, they each injected a shot of heroin apiece. This time they did black tar. It was a little cheaper than china white. They got it from the Mexican cartel. It came packaged inside empty tied-up balloons only containing the dope in which the cartel members would store in their mouths. They would spit them out when you made a purchase. In order to stray away from being detained, if they were ever stopped by the cops, they would swallow them. Thereafter they would puke them up if within the one-hour time frame of ingestion, otherwise, they would search their excreted feces later on. Most of them were illegal immigrants. Luckily for them, Minneapolis is a sanctuary city which means the local municipalities do little to enforce the national government's immigration law. On a note, Andrew also noticed that this particular dope had an aroma that resembled the smell of vinegar. It was also a lot darker than the fine china product. After the injection, Theo and Andrew felt another spike in elation. They stashed the paraphernalia and subsequently took flight from the bat cave and continued back down the stairs in a cool sedated swag. They then freely made their way to the dining room to eat.

The food was sprawled over the table. Andrew grabbed a hamburger as well as a hot dog. He stocked up on potato and taco salad. He didn't fill his plate with dessert quite yet unless you consider fruit salad one… After succeeding in equipping his plate with food, Andrew walked to the living room past his brother who was waiting in line. Malcolm was waiting as well right behind him.

"So… You're gay Josh?" Malcolm asked.

Josh bobbed his head up and down like a bobblehead.

"Man, that's crazy! I would have never guessed. I'm proud of you for coming out. That must be tough," Malcolm assuredly told him.

Josh hadn't heard words like this in a very long time. It lifted his confidence for a short while but it didn't cover up the fact that he still felt like an outsider. Josh's focus was on the negative and he had let it take control. He just smiled as his only reaction to Malcolm's words.

About 15 minutes went by, during which time Andrew got pie and more fruit salad. He sat back down on the couch in the living room and overheard his mom telling everyone about his drug use. Andrew got pissed off. He did what his instincts told him to do. He grabbed his plate of goods and threw it at his mother. The plate got stuck on her canary face. Batman and Robin then took off towards the door to go pawn shit. Out of nowhere, Andrew was tackled to the floor.

"You think you can do that to your mom, bitch?" Scott shouted within the commotion.

"Get off me! You're crushing me!" forced Andrew from his lungs.

The Witch's Hat

The family watched as Scott lay on Andrew for the next 15 seconds yelling at him. He got off Andrew and Andrew took off out the front door.

"C'mon Theo! Let's go!" said the red-faced loser. Just then they did a walk-run to the car and left on a mission.

The 4th of July party simmered down a few hours later. Tanya, Scott, Antonio, and Josh all left in a separate vehicle but towards home. Along the car ride, Tanya turned her head to the backseat and went on to say to Josh, "I saw a cool chinchilla online that we can pick up this Friday. You should come with me."

Chinchillas were Tanya and Josh's thing. It was the biggest way for Josh to connect with his mother and have a normal relationship. He poured all of his love into the chinchillas. Josh's eyes lit up as he looked to the front passenger seat at his mom, he was super excited. "Yes, I'll go!" he said.

"I'll wake you up Friday morning to get ready," Tanya disclosed as they exited off the freeway.

They ended up getting home at about 7 p.m. Josh rocked out on the cello for another while. Two hours later, Andrew arrived home alone with a 60 bag of China. The pawnshop was closed so Andrew and Theo did yard work for the grandparents' neighbors. They managed to scrounge up enough money for a half gram each. Luckily, grandma was a diabetic so Andrew took a few used needles out of the garbage can when he dropped Theo off. Andrew tangoed with one of these needles to medicate himself in his bedroom; however, this time he got really sick. He had managed to give himself cotton fever. His body was being invaded by bacteria growing on his reused filters and he was burning up in temp but felt chilly. His skin was sweating beads and his body painfully ached. He became nauseous and ran to the bathroom to vomit. After, he grabbed a bucket and went to his bed to try to sleep it off. He puked a few times throughout the night and by the time morning came he woke up drenched in a pool of sweat. This didn't deter him from rising from the bed like a vampire from a coffin and doing more. He took it somewhat easy the next few days and made sure to use new clean cigarette filters to purify his dope to avoid another serious illness.

About five days came and went by since Independence Day and Andrew needed something to do. He continued to entrench himself in misery from the thoughts that were trapped in his head. Negative energy flowed through the family's home, but since it was a nice summer thirsty Thursday night, Andrew ended up texting his neighbor to come over for a relaxing bonfire so he could get out of the thick overwhelming air in the family's quarters. The two friends smoked bud then went into Andrew's room to do a line of heroin. In addition, Colton had brought a bottle of vodka. The two partied until about 2 in the morning when they put out the fire and wrapped up the night. The night was concluded or so Andrew thought. He passed out in his bed thinking about life.

A few minutes later Andrew was awakened by a sliding noise along the floor above him. Josh must have been rearranging his room. He never played his cello that night which was strange. It was silenced just like they wanted. Just shut up, they say. You have no bounds to speak. Just do as you're told in this warlike society and deal with it. Therefore Josh dealt with it. During the passing time, Andrew listened and was lulled to sleep by a faint pattern of notes spiraling from the edge of a cornerstone and containing the lyrics from the song "How to Save a Life" by the Fray. Andrew surely wasn't prepared for what the next day would bring about.

CHAPTER 12
Memento Mori

"Josh! It's time to get ready!" called Tanya as she knocked on Josh's bedroom door.

Only silence answered.

Knock. Knock. Knock. "Josh! Let's go. I told them 11:30. We gotta go!"

Still nothing but silence.

"Ok, I'm gonna go to the gas station and get gas and when I get back I expect you to be ready," she shouted.

Still silence.

Tanya went to Target and then the gas station with Antonio to fill up her gas tank. When she came back she knocked on Josh's door again and still no answer.

Andrew heard the commotion and awakened. It wasn't unusual for him to lie in bed late on the weekends or any day to be exact. Andrew was dope sick and starting to get clammy yet he was still functional. He rubbed his eyes then rose to his feet and opened the door.

"What's wrong?" Andrew shouted up from the basement up to the main floor of the split-level home.

"Josh won't answer his door! It's locked and I can't wake him up. Can you get it open?" mother asked frantically.

"Yeah, I can! I bet he snuck out last night! Just let me grab a screwdriver!" Andrew yelled languidly.

Andrew turned his sluggishness to a man on a mission. He hurried up the stairs to the platform entry and out to the garage to grab one of the screwdrivers. He re-entered the house and continued up another set of stairs towards Josh's bedroom door. During this set of motions, he pondered how Josh could sneak out of the home by being on the upper level. It sure was possible but it probably wouldn't be the easiest. You would need a rope or a blanket sheet to climb to the ground. Maybe he left and couldn't climb back up, getting himself locked out of the house. Perhaps he stayed the night with a friend.

As Andrew approached the door, Antonio and Tanya parted like the Red Sea. Andrew then stuck the Phillips screwdriver into the fastener of the doorknob and started turning. The other two were standing behind him. Andrew was curious about what was going on. He turned and turned. The screwdriver slipped a few times but he adjusted it and would continue turning. Finally, the screws were loose enough to turn with his fingers. The speed picked up and the screws were now free from the threads. Andrew pulled the doorknob off. On the other side of the door, the other half of the knob fell to the floor. Andrew stuck the screwdriver through the hole in the door into the cam drive units of the remaining latch assembly. He fidgeted with the driver until he found a position where he could twist to release the latch. Once he did this the door opened and what he saw burnt a hole in his heart for infinity.

Josh was hanging near the window by a belt he had wrapped around his neck. He had the fabric belt tied up to the top of a futon frame he had positioned upright. His back was to the sun which had well risen from the east. His feet dangled just an inch from the floor. The putrid smell of the room filled Andrew's nose. It was the smell of rigor mortis. He had never felt this kind of pain before.

"No! Josh! No! No! No!" screamed Tanya.

The Witch's Hat

Andrew's 8-year-old brother was standing in the doorway watching as Andrew fell to his knees in disbelief. Was he dreaming? Was he even alive? Was this for real? Andrew soaked in the vision of Josh's blue face attached to a stretched-out neck hanging from the noose. Josh had a waterfall of drool slowly dribbling from his mouth down to his chin and even further. The saliva was hanging about 6 inches towards the ground. It must have been thick and goopy. It reminded Andrew of kids' slime when you stretch it out and dangle it to the base of the earth. It was horrifying.

Tanya ran away to grab her cell phone to call the authorities. She left Andrew and Antonio in the bedroom staring at Josh's corpse. Andrew noticed a bunch of crumpled-up papers below his feet. He wondered if there was anything written in them. He never managed to get near Josh's feet to see. Instead, Andrew was frozen in incredulity as he gazed at his face. He noticed scratches along his neck and lower chin area. Had he tried to free himself? Did he have a change in heart? Andrew had the sudden urge to cut him down from the noose but Tanya walked back into the bedroom's doorway and discouraged him from doing so.

"They said to not touch the body! They have to do an investigation," Tanya cried with the phone up to her ear to Andrew. Then she directed her energy back to the phone call. "He's dead! He's dead! Please hurry! Oh my God!"

Andrew remained on his knees thinking that maybe his brother could come back to life. Maybe if he cut him down he would take a huge gasp of air and be ok. Andrew would never know. The police and EMTs had arrived and Andrew was told to leave the room. They asked the mother if they could go through Josh's cell phone and told her to leave as well. She let them grab the phone from his pants pocket. They also found his driver's permit identification freely resting in his other pocket. At this point, they were conducting their investigation.

One of the officers followed Andrew down to the basement living room to question him.

"So did you have any last words with your brother? You guys didn't have an argument did you?" quizzed the blue coat.

"No, we were just fine. I haven't even talked to him in a few days," replied Andrew nervously.

Andrew's idea of talking was plainly saying "hi" to Josh and getting a "hey" back. Was Andrew responsible for Josh's death? It had been nearly a few weeks since the two of them had a prolonged conversation during the Waterama weekend but even that was brief. Andrew couldn't even convince him to try to have a good bonding time. Maybe he didn't try hard enough. Currently, Andrew felt like this conversation was gonna turn into an interrogation from the way it began. Andrew felt like he was guilty and was gonna be led to jail, especially if they searched his room and found syringes or the bag of dope in his wallet.

"It appears he has taken his life. Do you have any idea why he would have done so?" asked the man conducting the investigation.

Now the explanation had veered off of Andrew and was now directed directly at Josh. Andrew felt a little more relief. He answered, "I have no clue. I thought he was fine. He didn't talk much about himself."

"Ok, that's all I needed to know. I'm sorry for your loss," the fuzz man fed back with cordiality written on his face as well as in his voice.

After about 45 minutes Andrew heard voices coming down the stairs to the entryway. They had Josh's body in a human remains pouch and were carrying him to the coroner's vehicle. This was it. He was classified as another statistic. Another poor soul sacrificed for the progression of a cold society. All his suffering had ended.

Andrew went up to Josh's bedroom to check out what was written on the discarded papers but they were all gone. Tanya hadn't received Josh's phone back and would never see it again. There was no way for the family to find physical evidence of why Josh would have done what he had done during the final moments of his life. Why did they take the phone? Andrew's heart had sunk to his stomach and would remain there for quite some time. His mind went stir crazy from not knowing what had happened but it was mostly cluttered with an overwhelming amount of disbelief and pain.

The futon was left in place standing straight up and down. Andrew

The Witch's Hat

could remember trading that futon to Josh in exchange for a bed. Now it was used as a tool for suicide. Andrew wished he had never given it to him but maybe Josh would have ended his life either way. Andrew felt guilty. He should have been arrested.

The family gave away the futon to try to forget the horrible memory. After about 5 and a half days, it was time for Josh's funeral visitation. The family was the first ones there. Then tons more people showed up. It was lovely to see all the people who took the time from their day to visit Josh one last time. It was their final farewell.

Andrew sat on the curb outside the funeral home and smoked a square as he watched people pass by. He got a few greetings and condolences from some of the visitors. After he extinguished the coffin nail, he went inside to see Josh once again. J-dawg laid motionless in his coffin. He was dressed up, looking snazzy in the suit that he used for his concert orchestra gigs. His collar, however, didn't go high enough to cover his neck. Surrounding his neck you could see a circular ring wrapped around the collum where the belt had been. It was a saddening scene. Even if you never knew anything about his death you could probably take a guess at what had happened by looking at the part of his body between his head and shoulders. Andrew's mother had wished they could have covered up the noose marks. As did Andrew. This made it for a distasteful last visit. At least they had used makeup to cover up the scratches, Andrew thought.

Moments later, Andrew and his mother each gifted a eulogy in Josh's honor. Andrew went with the Lord's Prayer. He read it shakily and teary-eyed. Tanya straight-up bawled on the stand. She made a decent speech but she would stray away and make it about herself.

"What will I do without you," she cried. She would glance around the audience to see who was watching. She loved the attention. Who knows if she actually cared as much as she made it seem.

A couple of other speeches from the lost one's friends came afterward and then the funeral commenced. The casket was closed. Being the pallbearer, Andrew was one of 6 friends and kin to carry Josh to the jet black hearse which would carry him westward. After Josh was placed into the hearse the crowd started to disperse. Upon departure,

Andrew crossed paths with an old neighbor and his girlfriend. Andrew was sitting on the curb, just the same, smoking another fag, and didn't see them. The neighbor's name was Enoch. His lover's name was Journey. Andrew wasn't aware of her name at the time. As said, he never even laid eyes on her. Even if he would have seen them, he wasn't into sizing up other men's women. Anyway, he was sidetracked with staring at the ground contemplating. Little did he know, as his oblivious mind fast-tracked like a distorted slideshow animation, that this young woman would play a key role in his life.

The next day, after a 3-hour trek by car to the motherland (Starbuck), the pallbearers carried and staged the coffin above the gravesite pit on a set of virgin webbed straps. The group of attendees was small due to the distance they traveled, yet the service was still flooding with tears. The town seemed like a nice quiet place for a final refuge as not too much went on in these parts. Andrew's frail paternal grandfather was at the funeral as well. While they were standing around the dark hole molded into the somewhat flat tree baron terrain, Andrew felt his grandfather's arm rest on his shoulder. This was unusual. Andrew's grandpa rarely talked. He had managed to pull himself from his seclusion and was without a bottle. Andrew felt as if his grandpa really cared behind that masked tough guy veil. Even though Cornelius's arm was around Andrew for only a couple of seconds, it made them feel better, but Andrew still struggled to hold back tears as Josh was lowered into the earth's deathly crust. The wind began to howl.

Josh was positioned in the same spot as his favorite grandmother at the cemetery. The two always baked cookies during J's younger years. Those were the good old days when they visited the grandparents frequently or even when they lived with them. They worried less. Sure there was fighting going on but turn on a VHS tape of the *Woody Woodpecker* or *Barney* and things were dandy. Grandma June was a pillar of the family but she smoked and stumbled upon the fat c-word and you know the rest. Andrew could remember the day she died when he was 12. June moved into the family's home to be taken care of and Andrew could recall helping her with her amputated stump leg. It would bounce around sporadically and uncontrollably. On bad days when it flopped around, Andrew would hold it down for her. It was a tough time and became the children's most tangible observation of impending death up to that point. The day she departed she spewed diarrhea all over the wall through her gown sometime after screaming for Cornelius and then taking her last breath. That recollection lingered deep within Andrew's mind the older he got.

June's ashes were taken from beneath the turf and were now inside Josh's casket to be put back underground again. Josh would have been very proud to know he was resting next to her and his family. His body would now lay to rot and decay in an enclosed box under the plains. Andrew just hoped he was at peace in the afterlife and that his soul wasn't lost in some sort of turmoil searching for what he needed most. Love.

CHAPTER 13
The Media Swarm

During all the commotion from Andrew's brother dying, a bunch of stories surfaced about Josh being bullied in school. This was all news to the family. The talk went on about it in the following months. Within that time frame, they held a fundraising event for Josh's headstone bench. Anti-bullying advocates met at a local VFW for the occasion. About a hundred people showed up and the talk spread about Josh's suicide being the result of gay-bashing, whether it took place in school or online. He had passed away in July so he couldn't have presently been dealing with in-school bullying, although it could have been something that added to Josh's loss of hope. Andrew had suspected the bullying Josh endured had chipped away at his self-esteem around moments of the ticking clock which led Josh through a dark tunnel in which he tried to escape. The only way to reach the light was to kill himself.

The school district had encountered multiple suicides amongst the gay community that year before Josh's death and even more had followed. The casualties were broadening. This became a subject of analytical speculation. The media contacted the family along with close friends of Josh to investigate. One of the news crews ended up showing

The Witch's Hat

up at the fundraising event and asked Tanya critical questions. She began her crying with her poor me attitude. Albeit, she did do her best to speak up against bullying which resulted in admiration among folks. Andrew was proud that she was speaking out about this chronic issue. She did get her point across and was the perfect pawn for the tragic matter arising in the community.

The newswoman continued with her questions, "Josh was perceived as gay, right?"

Tanya had tears falling from her baggy eyes. "Yes, he was. He had just recently came out."

"I see. Was he ever bullied in school?" the lady inquired.

"We just found out that yes, he was!" Tanya sobbed into the mic. "It had been going on for a number of years. We had no clue until recently."

"Do you think his bullying had anything to do with him being gay?"

"Absolutely! From the stories I heard from his friends… I absolutely think he was bullied for that very reason. Some of the stories made me feel sick."

"Do you think any action could be done to resolve this issue?" prodded the newshound.

"Yes of course! We need to get these policies fixed within the school district to protect these kids. The bullies need to be held accountable," Tanya asserted. "I also want to add that we are starting an organization called "Josh's Gift" to give support to all the local LGBT kids in the region. We believe this will be a step in the right direction."

"Sounds fantastic! Do you think this issue could be totally eradicated?"

"Yes absolutely! It will be tough but with lots of teamwork and perseverance, we can make it happen. The first step is to get these policies changed…"

"I hope you are right Tanya. Thank you so much for your time," said the reporter with a smile on her face. Then the lady turned to

James who was a local teacher who had also attended the fundraiser. He was kind of like one of Tanya's first sidekicks during this troubling era.

The newswoman opened her mouth and asked, "So James, what do you know about the bullying going on in the school district being on the frontlines as a teacher?"

"I witness it all the time. Especially those who are different. Gays are especially targeted the most," he replied with concern. "I'm gay myself and know how petrifying it can be attending school on a daily basis knowing that you are not fully welcomed at all. You constantly have to be aware of your safety and deal with constant bigotry on a regular basis. I feel sorry for these kids. I've been there. Something needs to change."

"Nicely put! I must ask, have you taken the initiative and done anything personally to protect these kids?" the lady lightly pried.

"Yes, whenever I see it I step in. That isn't always the same for other teachers," James answered.

"Ah, I see… Let me say that being gay yourself as well as being a teacher here in the locality, I believe you make a great spokesperson. Same goes for you Tanya, for your current situation. I would like to thank you both for rising to the occasion and speaking out."

"Yes! Thank you! This issue is very important to me. It breaks my heart that these kids have to die in order to be heard. We will without a doubt be attending the school board meetings to see if we can do something to resolve this," the school teacher informed.

"Absolutely!" Tanya added. "We will make it our mission to get through to them and won't stop until we do!"

"Sounds great! I wish you guys the best!" the news commentator delivered back. The camera was still rolling and turned back to focus on James.

"I might add that we will be dedicating a lot of our time to this organization as we are getting up and going," he stated with a determined look upon his face.

"That's great! Looks like you have a lot of support behind you. We believe in you! However, I regret to say that we are running short

The Witch's Hat

on time so I must conclude the interview. Thank you guys so much and Tanya, my condolences for your loss again. Best regards on establishing your life-changing organization. It really is a gift to society." The dolled-up lady flipped her hair. "If anyone is interested in finding out more info, please visit our webpage and it will be available for you. Thank you everyone for listening. Have a wonderful day!"

The interview was brought to an end. The newsgroup mentioned something about staying in contact and they all said their goodbyes. The overall meeting for the relief effort concluded a few hours later as well. Later on, they counted up the proceeds from the event and it turned out that they had raised the perfect amount of money to buy Josh a beautiful bench for his burial plot. It was ordered right away.

The days continued and Josh's death was brought up over and over. Andrew had trouble sleeping at night. He had the same recurring dream of Josh digging himself up from beneath a tree at the old home. Andrew overlooked his brother's decaying flesh and felt a mixture of a frightened peace until his mind out tricked itself and Andrew realized the reality of the situation. He would wake up in cold sweats. He just could not get the situation off his mind. His drug use carried on. He was mixing his dope up stronger than usual to try to keep himself out of mind.

As time passed, to Andrew's dismay, Tanya would see strangers in public and tell her story to them as if being on the news wasn't enough. "Yeah, my son committed suicide. He was bullied to death for being gay," she would say randomly out of the blue. It was nonstop. She soaked up the limelight with her seemingly staged tears.

People would stand there and try to comfort her but really didn't know what to do. She craved sympathy and wanted the recognition by using the method of making people feel bad for her. She would drop the bomb and it worked. The stochastic strangers gave her all the attention that she could soak up.

While all this was happening Andrew had reached out to his most recent ex-girlfriend for comfort. She felt bad for him and they started dating again thereafter. They mostly spent their time having coitus in the family's new home. The household had to get away from the wretched memories of the other one. The pair seemed more like a lust relation at this point. During those moments Tanya craved and craved as Andrew sat on the sidelines and watched the show.

The boys' mother was so busy keeping up with things that she even got a manager. This guy was another helping hand and did it free of charge. His name was Jace. He would speak out at interviews as well. He would tell stories of when he was bullied as a kid just like James and Josh. He was gay himself and dealt with similar issues so this topic was very important to him. He withheld the necessary passion to trudge through the workload which brought forth progression. Bluntly speaking, Jace was about 8 years older than Andrew and the two formed a well-built relationship.

"You are the perfect prospect for speaking out. You are a straight white male with a gay brother and you were supportive of your brother's identity. You have a story to tell. People will actually listen to you," Jace enlightened upon Andrew. They sat in the dining room shooting the shit at the unfortunate family's new run-down home.

"Yeah maybe. But I doubt it. I'm not very good with words."

"You are better than you think. You can tell you mean what you say and you're empathetic."

"O.K. Well, maybe I'll make a video for practice."

"I'll take you up to my place sometime. My sister loves throwing parties. I think you'd really like her. I'll hook you guys up. Her boyfriend is a douchebag. I've been trying to break them up forever!" Jace disclosed. "Then sometime after, we can record a YouTube video."

Andrew's curiosity sparked but he had second thoughts. "Sounds good, but I have a girlfriend already."

"Yeah, a girl that left you a few months ago for another guy..." Jace pointed out.

"Well, I guess I'll come check it out!" Andrew said with a delayed response.

"Sounds like a plan. Keep in touch man. I gotta head home," Jace tiredly announced. He had been working long hours. He caught an uptick and managed rapidly saying, "I'll reach out to you when I have a date. Everything is so crazy right now!"

"Sounds good!" Andrew acknowledged. "I'll see ya later man. Get home safe!"

"Thanks! I'll catch ya later!"

It was nearly midnight when the friend left and as a result Andrew immediately jolted down the stairs to his room. He went hard with his hands-on needle fixation. In everyone else's eyes, he had quit using after his brother died but he obviously hadn't. Since he was a functional addict he wouldn't let his lie squander. Presently he was out of brand new sharps so he had trouble finding his vein with the dull needle he had. He pricked, pricked, and pricked. He wiggled the tip under his skin hoping to find a flow of blood. It felt like a PVC pipe swallowing his derma. He had no luck.

CHAPTER 14
Change

Tanya kept her word and went to her first school board meeting near the end of August. It was the usual speech. The only difference this time was that Andrew made a speech as well. This was the first time he had ever spoken out. He pointed out in the meeting that church needed to be separate from state. Who knows if they actually listened?

With all that, things really began to pick up pace. Jace was taking incoming calls from all over the place. Mostly for interviews. However, he did end up scheduling a spot at the local HRC Gala in Minneapolis for networking. Shortly after that, Jace got another call to take an all-expense-paid trip to Los Angeles for an organization by the name of GLSEN. The approaching future was going to be busy.

During this time, Andrew had started another year at the community college but post-high school this time. He had loans stacking up. He would borrow about 2,000 dollars cash each semester to supply his drug runs. It was a small poor man's fortune to play with. It was all pissed away pretty quick just like his graduation money. Even so, he still made sure he was stocked up for all these media outlet events. He wanted to be numb but appear happy.

It was the midst of September when the "It Gets Better" project was brushed over by the local Human Rights Campaign. Josh's friends and family drove to downtown Minneapolis to arrive at their destination at a place called The Depot. This was where prom was held a few months prior to Josh's death. Both of the brothers had attended. They didn't spend any time together at prom sadly enough, but at least they had gotten pictures with each other before they departed from home to get there. Andrew's girlfriend, Sage, was along for the ride on both occasions as well.

The posse was greeted by many upon arrival. People crowded around them to talk and give their political viewpoints as well as stories. The swarming mob was very sympathetic. Josh's clan connected with Kristin Johnston from *Third Rock From the Sun* who was also there and who gave a speech. She thanked the family for everything they had done before she was called up to the stage and granted an ally award. She spoke some heartfelt words of what the award meant to her and how proud she was of it before she exited the idolized podium.

Surprisingly, Tanya wasn't called to speak. Instead, she shared her story with more bystanders. "I don't know what I am gonna do without him. What I do know is that he did not die in vain," she cried.

It seemed as if she made a lot of her talk into a show to make herself look like some sort of hero to others so she could prize herself with intrinsic pleasure. However, she did make some great points about bullying. Overall she did an ample job sharing Josh's story which guided people through her broken-hearted radiation of energy. She had the right amount of fight in her tear-dripping eyes and looked quite sad yet ambitious as she took in the spotlight which she paved for herself.

Meanwhile, Andrew was plumped down in his leather cushioned chair at the same table with his mother and late brother's companions. Sage was sitting nearby to Andrew's left. The rusty love birds had ceased showing each other much of any affection. Andrew was disgusted by Sage's new tattoo of herself with angel wings on her back. It looked like a fairy. How could anyone be so full of themselves? The distance between the two definitely showed. It seemed like Sage was back in Andrew's life to briefly comfort him through tough times. He didn't want the pity. He knew she felt bad and that's why she was there. Life had torn them apart.

Josh's clan, as well as many others, stared and listened as Tanya talked to the surrounding crowd. To Andrew, it seemed like this gala was meant for only the prestigious to attend or for those who actually had the money to get in the door. How could they exploit such large amounts of charitable funds into such big expensive galas like this? All this classy food and needless swag bags to put on a show for the people? All that currency could have gone somewhere more meaningful. So basically people are donating to continue to do these events, spreading the word through high-end social gatherings. Didn't seem like much action was going on within the school as it just remained stagnant. Something good had better come of this because Andrew felt like a puppet.

The next weekend after the gala, Andrew went up with Jace to his sister's house. It was the night of one of her parties. Andrew walked in the door and was introduced to her. She looked sharp and kind of reminded Andrew of Amy Lee from Evanescence. Her name was Nadine. Andrew made it his duty to stay by her side. They went along flirting and making small talk. She knew Andrew's brother had just recently passed so she felt bad for him. Something about Andrew had attracted her attention. Was it his good looks tagged with charming nature? Or was it just like the Sage situation to be pitied upon again? Either way, Andrew was enjoying himself and looked beyond this thought he had rendered through his mind.

They sat on the couch and Andrew had his arm around her. They took shot after shot until they were out of their minds. They definitely had the hots for each other, that's for sure. Andrew also had the hots for Nadine's best friend who was also present. He was trying to figure out which of the two would make a prime selection for the thunder down under.

Andrew got up to get another drink and crossed paths with Nadine's friend Madison. The two talked. They giggled and laughed towards each other. Nadine got jealous and got up from her seat to take Andrew's hand and pull him back to the couch. She then laid her lips upon his. She shoved her tongue in Andrew's mouth. Andrew could tell she was a freak.

The Witch's Hat

After maybe a few minutes they pulled away from each other and headed to the bedroom. To their surprise, Madison was on the bed with another guy and they were kissing all over each other as well. There was a voice within Andrew that told him he shouldn't be screwing a woman who already had a man. Especially when he had a woman himself. Andrew brushed it off. He was gonna pursue what he wanted. Unfortunately today he didn't get to home base but it was probably best to save that for next time anyway.

Andrew left late that night after a stretch of cuddling and kissing. Jace had also tagged along for the ride to Andrew's house and stayed the night. Jace was the sober driver. The next morning came and Andrew called his girlfriend to come over.

Jace was also up and at 'em. Andrew advanced towards him and asked, "What do I do about my relationship?"

"You have to end it. Obviously, you guys don't have what you used to have when it began," he replied.

Andrew knew Jace had no idea what they had at the beginning. But they did have something. Now it was torn apart with hardship and Andrew's wandering eyes. Just then, a knock came upon the family's front door. She had arrived.

"I guess I'll get right to it then!" Andrew said with composure. He walked to the door to let his girlfriend in, then led her through the kitchen and then the living room to the arcadia doorway leading to the backyard. They sat on the stoop just outside the sliding glass doors. Andrew swiveled his head after popping a squat, looked her dead in the eyes, and flat out said, "We aren't going to work out anymore."

Sage's eyes grew a little shiny but she didn't seem too hurt. Maybe more irritated. "Okay… What did I do? I've been doing everything I can to be by your side and help you with the pain you are feeling. It isn't working?" she asked in a defensive manner.

Andrew ignored the question and softly spoke, "It's not your fault. I just feel like it isn't the same anymore. I still feel betrayed by you leaving to Wisconsin for that dude. It doesn't feel right now. I want to see other women."

Sage's face was completely disgusted. She got to her feet and swung her purse over her shoulder. "Well, it was nice knowing you I guess."

She made her way back into the home and retraced her steps with intense energy to exit the front entryway. Andrew followed and closed the door behind her. The relationship was now annulled.

"Congratulations! You did it!" said a voice from the living room. Jace was sitting on the couch on his laptop keeping up with connections and research.

"Yes, I did. Wasn't too bad. It almost seemed mutual. It's sad but at least she will always be my first love," Andrew replied somberly. His words flowed through the kitchen via the open space above the kitchen counter towards Jace in the living room.

"Good Job! Now you and my sister can start dating and she can get rid of that d-bag she is with," Jace excitedly proposed.

"Yeah… We will see," Andrew said as he turned directly around and went down the stairs to his bedroom. His bedroom consisted of over half the basement. It was huge. He had a mattress, an office area, fireplace, couch, and a table. Even with all that, he still had tons of space. He entered the roomy room and went straight to a table to open the drawer underneath. Next off, he grabbed his drug paraphernalia. He just got a new bag of needles so he was fairly happy. He didn't have to prick up his arm this time. He ended up finding a vein right away. He was now a pro at this. He pulled the belt from his arm and passed out on the couch for the day to wake up that night and smoke a pip of meth.

As the days passed, Andrew and Nadine began to hang out every day. She split from her boyfriend and moved out and into her parents' home. This made the pair's relationship more convenient. Andrew would have her over at his place as well. He even brought her to his meth dealer's house. She never asked questions. Andrew would sneak to the bathroom to get lit. His pip broke so he had to use a light bulb. Nadine was oblivious. She was too amused with all the media stuff going on that she might not have cared anyhow, but for the time being everyone still thought Andrew was sober.

CHAPTER 15
Cali

In Andrew's free time, he continued robbing people by selling fake heroin. The raisins in the water balloons really seemed to pass as black tar smack until the customer tried to mix it up. Andrew was running out of customers to choose from. He was broke and had spent the school semester's loan money. One day he and some friends came across a guy selling mushrooms. They had bought some and ate them and felt light effects if any. They had a hunch that they may have been fake so they set up another deal.

The guy hopped in the front passenger seat of the car and withdrew the bag of mushrooms from his hoody. Andrew's partners in crime were sitting in the back passenger seat of the truck directly behind the guy whom we will call Tucker. Andrew locked the doors as Tucker was about to hand over the mushrooms. Andrew withdrew the cash and halfway extended it to him. Just then a spun-up twisted bed sheet that served almost as a rope was wrapped around Tucker's neck and pulled tight around the headrest of the seat. Tucker sat there choking struggling for breath. He reached his arms to the blanket sheet to relieve some of the strain but it didn't help much.

"Hand over the shrooms, and your phone while you're at it nigga!" shouted Andrew's friend Sylvester from the back seat. "Oh and your wallet too!"

The victim handed over all the items requested to Andrew in the seat of authority behind the wheel. After Andrew retrieved the items he unlocked the door and his friend released the sheet from around Tucker's neck. "Get out nigga!" Sylvester demanded.

Tucker sprinted away. They used his cash to secure more drugs. It was an ongoing cycle. They sold the mushrooms and bought some scag they had picked up thereafter. Andrew's drug rate was rampant. It was the only way to settle his nerves still. All this time being told he had a problem had a placebo effect upon him. It had only gotten worse since his brother died and was getting even further out of hand. Yet he was still functional. Drugs, drugs, and more drugs are what he desired to achieve his warm fuzzy place which was getting harder and harder to chase down. The dragon was flying away.

The first few days of October came and Andrew needed some dope for the upcoming trips they had planned. The next trip event was just in a week. Andrew ended up stealing some more of his dad's power tools to pawn. He pawned a few other things and ended up coming out with $150!

He texted one of his few dealers to get a gram of black tar heroin for $120. Andrew and Tim met up with their middleman dealer named Chet and he hopped in the car. They were to meet the Mexican cartel on one of the side streets in Minneapolis. Andrew pulled out the cash and gave it to Chet when they reached the location.

"I'll be right back," Chet told them.

Chet hopped out of the car and into a van packed full of Mexicans. They had parked in front of the 3 hoodlums on the side of the street in a quiet neighborhood. The van drove off and Andrew noticed an hour had passed. Andrew texted Chet but never heard back from him. Andrew was getting worried and dope sick. Another half-hour passed until Andrew realized he had been a victim of fraud of an illicit activity. Now he had to go back to square one. Time was running out. Damn low-life drug addicts.

They had 30 bucks left which wasn't enough to supply Theo for the day as well as Andrew for his trip. They didn't have any more people to rob and obviously, karma had come back to bite them in the ass. Now what was he supposed to do? The answer popped into Andrew's head. He had remembered his grandpa had given him an accordion which had been Andrew's great grandfathers. Grandpa told him to keep it in the family. It was immaculate. It looked in pristine condition. Andrew had reached one of his low points and he felt he had no other choice but to bring it to an antique shop. He explained to them that it was at least 50 years old and only asked for 100 bucks. He just wanted them to bite. They didn't even hesitate to jump on that deal as Andrew opened the case to show it to them. Andrew and Theo retrieved the money and went to go score some more goodies. Andrew gave Theo twenty bucks worth of dope and kept 5 twenty bags for himself as well as the remaining $10 for gas. He planned to have one baggy of China White for each day on his trip if he could manage that. He didn't know how long he would be gone. He drove home and packed for his upcoming journey.

With the end of the first full calendar week in October approaching, the family ended up waking at 3 a.m. one morning to load the car for their trip and grabbed any odds and ends they could think of. They had to pick up another member of the family to drive them to the airport so they didn't have to leave their car there. The person just so happened to be grandpa. Andrew said nothing of the accordion to him. Gramps dropped the family off and now Andrew had to make it past the airport security. He had the heroin in his butt cheeks. He saw a dog walking up and down the aisles sniffing out drugs. He saw the dog slowly making his way towards him. His heart started racing. Would this dog sniff out the heroin he had stashed? Andrew remained still as he didn't want to attract any attention. The dog passed several people and was about 20 feet away when the K-9 stopped and started barking at the foot of a man with a large duffle bag. The dog was sniffing hard at it. The officer asked him to please step aside. He asked if he had any drugs and the man said no. The officer led the man to a back room of the airport where Andrew assumed he was searched and possibly booked. Andrew was extremely lucky he wasn't in that man's position.

Instead, Andrew safely made it past security with his needles in his check-in bag. The plane took off and the ride took about four hours until they touched down. They were picked up by an Uber and were driven to a hotel to drop off their stuff. Then they were driven once more to the Beverly Hills Hotel where they arrived for the GLSEN event right on time. Yet again, it was the same meet and greet. They got to meet some actors from the show *Modern Family* which Andrew thought was interesting. On the contrary, Antonio didn't have any interest in the child actor who tried to conversate with him. However, when he found out the kid was an actor they began playing together.

Then began another meal among activists while they announced the respect awards. Other than that, nothing too interesting happened. Andrew was just excited to be in California. He loved the sight of palm trees and the smell of salt from the ocean. He felt alive again. It was always wonderful to have a break from the cruel real world and enjoy life. After the meal, Andrew wandered around to chit-chat with people. He met a lot of gay and straight persons who were actively pushing for gay rights. He also talked to men and women who were transgender. The family met an upbeat lady who had made a full transition. She explained her life story and the process she went through to become a woman. She said it was the best decision she had ever made.

"I'm the happiest I have ever been!" the lady said confidently.

Antonio stood there in awe. He was inspired. He was always dressing up in girl clothes since he was a toddler. He just needed the right role model to mold herself into the woman she dreamed to be. Antonio had never mentioned anything about becoming a girl up to this point and wouldn't act upon it seriously for a few years. He was only 8 at the time and still had a while to go before transition.

This opened up a new world for Andrew. In his earlier days, he may have been on guard and kind of fearful about trans people. He gained an open mind during this political process and was able to understand that no one at all should be told who they should be. Andrew learned trans people are just like everyone else and he was proud to be a part of this crusade.

They had left the GLSEN gathering and went to the beach. The

The Witch's Hat

family roamed the sand during which Antonio approached Tanya privately and exclaimed, "Mom, I really want to be a girl!"

Mother was excited. She had a straight son, a deceased gay son and now she has a child who wants to be transgender. She would represent the whole rainbow. This would make her stand out from everyone else and would show how accepting she was. Scott didn't yet know about Antonio's plans which were probably for the best in order to keep things chill. There is no telling how open-minded he would be.

Andrew overheard the conversation as he treaded through the water in his baggy cargo shorts. The shorts barely fit as he had lost weight in the previous months. His belt was too loose from him pulling it tight around his arm. Even his shirt was too big for him. He was up to his thighs in water. He watched as the waves crashed into himself. About a half-hour went by when he stepped on a sharp rock and slipped, submerging himself below the water. He regained composure and ran back to shore to sit on a boulder facing the sea.

In the meantime, Antonio was playing with dead sea creatures along the shoreline. Tanya talked about him and the trans situation with Jace near the parking lot up the slope behind Andrew while Scott roamed the beach for shells. After Tanya finished catching him up to speed, she turned to the family. "Alright, guys! Are you ready to go? We have an important dinner to get to!" she shouted.

Antonio came running from the beach with a dead crab in his hands. "Look mom, I found a crab," he blurted.

"Eww, that's gross! Put that down! We have to go!" Tanya enforced.

Andrew got up from his resting space and noticed something was amiss. He felt that his shorts were a little lighter than usual but detected his front pockets were full of the normal stuff. He checked his rear pocket and recognized it was empty. He was missing his wallet. He had just withdrawn the last of his emergency gas money funds from the ATM minutes before arriving at the beach. Andrew was now getting butterflies in his stomach. His I.D. His social security card. All that was missing.

Tanya hollered from the hilltop, "C'mon guys! Let's go!"

"I can't," Andrew said. "I can't find my wallet."

"You better find it or you will be stuck here!" Tanya replied.

Andrew pointed to everyone to where he had been and they all began searching. Maybe 10 or 15 minutes after sifting through the ocean and exploring the beach they discontinued their search empty-handed.

"We have to go to this dinner! It's important!" Tanya said frantically. "You're gonna have a tough time getting home but we will figure it out. Are you sure you had it with you?"

"Yeah, I had it. I remember putting it in my pocket when we were at the bank!" Andrew said back in offense.

"Well, we checked everywhere!" Tanya said with frustration. "My guess is that it is in the ocean. Run along the shoreline to see if it washed up. If you don't see it, oh well. You're going to have fun with TSA," she then laughed with irritability as she rolled her eyes. She would never be late for such an important dinner date.

With no avail, Andrew gave up looking for his stupid wallet. At least he had his cigarettes, he thought, as the group hopped in a taxi and took off to a restaurant. Andrew tried to push his worries to the back of his mind but he could not. Would it really be so bad if he got stuck in Cali? He loved it here but the thought of being all alone scared him.

It was about 15 minutes to some Asian hibachi place. They dined with a couple of the key drivers behind the LGBT movement. The hosts laid out the family's next move. They mentioned another HRC Gala in D.C. and the leaders really wanted them to attend. All expenses paid for yet again. The plane was supposed to depart the very next morning. It wasn't much of a notice but they took it. Andrew remembered one of the men mentioning that the presidential advisor would be there and even thought he heard one of them say the president would show up as well. Andrew was super excited! What an honor it would be to meet the president. You couldn't meet a person more powerful and important than the president of the United States.

CHAPTER 16
Oofta

ARRIVING AT THE airport was a hassle. The crowds of people standing in line to get searched was irritating. Andrew was nervous about his lost ID. He remembered the twin towers years earlier and wondered how strict they would be on letting him slide on through. Andrew didn't have a second copy of his papers and kept his fingers crossed hoping they could look him up in their system somehow.

The family took their place in line and waited their turn. Andrew didn't notice any drug-sniffing dogs this time. This relinquished some of his anxiety but overall he was still paranoid he wasn't going to make it through. After a good minute they made it up to the front of the line and Andrew put his belongings on the conveyor belt. He took off his shoes and did the same with those as well.

"Do you have your ID?" asked the machismo TSA worker. "You're supposed to have it to pass through."

"I'm sorry sir, I lost it in the ocean when I was at the beach yesterday. I don't have any form of identification. Is there a way you can look me up without it? I promise I'm not a terrorist," Andrew answered apprehensively.

The TSA worker's bald head glimmered in the overhead lighting as he asked Andrew his name and his social security number. The man then plugged away at his computer. A picture popped up and he looked at Andrew to match his likeness. "Looks like I found you. I don't believe you would fake your identity and I clearly see you here on the computer screen," the guard said coolly. "You're clear to pass through."

The man stamped Andrew's ticket and let him go through the metal detector which due to Andrew's bad luck went off. Now what? Andrew thought. It had turned out that with a wave of a wand it was just his belt buckle. The man gave Andrew the thumbs up and at last, he was allowed through. He began to think that maybe if he was middle eastern or even had darker skin, this process would have been much more difficult to pass this standard checkpoint. It was too bad racial profiling existed but Andrew was glad he was white. It wasn't always what it was cracked up to be though. Andrew had been punished just like anyone else who was caught in the act but perhaps more leniency was given to his wrongdoings. He wouldn't deny that these so-called "ism's" did in fact exist every and another day minus two at the beginning of the beginning of the end.

The group separated after clearing security. Scott and Antonio took the flight back home to Minnesota whereas Tanya, Jace, and Andrew took the flight to Washington D.C. After about five hours the group of three landed at the nation's capital. They taxied through the city to a hotel that looked ritzy. It was splendid. The Human Rights Campaign was very generous, which gave Andrew second thoughts again of their money spending. He figured the galas were necessary to promote the movements and a nice hotel is the least they could provide as Andrew wasn't getting paid for his time being put on blast during grievance. He was getting seriously behind in school. What was important was that he did all this out of love for his family and most of all his brother.

After dropping their luggage off in their rooms, the threesome walked to the nearby Holocaust Museum. They saw all the heavily worn Jewish children's shoes in a massive pile in an exhibit as well as much else. After finishing their visit, they continued their walk to arrive at the Washington Monument then proceeded to the White House.

The Witch's Hat

Once they got to the White House a homeless black man showed them a colostomy bag he had hanging from his stomach and was begging for change. Andrew told the man he had lost his wallet and the group walked away. Shortly afterward, they called an Uber and were picked up then transported to the location where the HRC event would take place. Upon arrival, they ate an extravagant meal. After that, they did another meet and greet. They got to meet the artist Pink who was fierce yet caring and genuine in nature.

The triad also met with Valerie Jarrett who was Barack Obama's presidential advisor. They had a heartfelt conversation about Josh in addition to the related topic at hand. She seemed like she really cared and wanted to make things better. Even though it was cool to meet the presidential advisor, Andrew was bummed the president wasn't there. He would have loved to meet one of the most powerful figures in the country. Andrew had possibly misconstrued what the men in Cali had said when they invited them. Or perhaps Obama had something more important to take care of. He just heard the word "president" as they spoke in Cali and just assumed the commander in chief would be there. Maybe Andrew was not as important as he thought. He felt like a piece of dust floating through time. Why would the president take his time out of his day to sympathize with his family? Maybe instead of sympathizing he could have contributed to fixing the problem at hand. It had mostly become the people's job to create change through the masses at this point.

Andrew was still sad but there wasn't much he could do but drown in heartache. He pulled himself aside and went to the bathroom. He snorted a couple rails of Xanax off a toilet seat to numb his brain then began thinking that none of this was real again. All this traveling was fun but it wasn't worth it to him. He wanted to go home. After the event came to an end, Andrew was slightly relieved but his sweaty palms still hadn't ceded the whole trip. He was nervous for whatever reason even after the pills. They made him feel better but the spell of the anxiety curse his mom bestowed upon him was still in control of his autonomously functioning programmed nervous system. By and by, the time had come where the threesome said their goodbyes to everyone and retreated to settle into their hotel rooms for the night.

The next morning they took the flight back to Minnesota. Andrew was to catch up on his coursework from his dwindling grades. His mom continued with her "Josh's Gift" organization which was still in its infancy. During this time Andrew took a step away from the scene. That said, Tanya would hold an event every Saturday at a local church to provide help, information, and interaction among the attending LGBTQ youth. Andrew would only maybe attend if there was a big holiday celebration occurring but otherwise not so much. He just didn't want to be zonked around the children.

CHAPTER 17
No H8

The year's end holidays had concluded and Andrew skipped out on all the previous "Josh's Gift" events. He hadn't attended a single one. On the other hand, his relationship with Nadine was on a roll. Eventually, February of 2011 came around and the couple had been dating for months now. The time had eventually come when Tanya asked Andrew to do an activism photo shoot. He was totally fine with doing the shoot. It was part of the "No Hate" campaign. The idea of it was that people suffered in silence. Particularly those who are beaten down by others throughout life for the reason of being LGBTQ. Imagine those who are silent and never come out of the closet for fear of being ridiculed. A requisite prior to the photograph was that the subjects cover their mouth with duct tape while wearing plain white shirts. The duct tape resembled silence while the signature white shirts brought everyone together as no different from one another. The purpose of the campaign is to promote LGBTQ rights across the world. They promoted gay marriage and gender equality education among other things. The movement was important to spread concerns through the protest of images while raising awareness.

Andrew's family along with Nadine were all interested in participating. They went to downtown Minneapolis to the Foshay Tower to get their photos taken. Andrew considered it a nice building. It had an upscale steakhouse and was pretty classy. He liked the atmosphere and purple ambiance that filled the entryway. They proceeded up the stairs upon arrival and were told to budge to the front of the line. They talked to the guys who owned the non-profit organization. They were super open and nice. Andrew felt important for once in his life. He didn't even have to waste his time in a line. He felt like a movie star.

After they finished their short chit-chat with the leaders of the campaign, the family started with a family photo while Nadine stood aside. Due to the depressing situation, they all looked pretty doleful during the shoot. The sadness stemmed from the constant talk of Andrew's brother. The point was to not let him die in vain. He would be a cornerstone of what would be the outcome for gay rights for places around the country and especially in Minnesota.

Minutes passed and the family had finished the photos. At the time they weren't able to see them. But later on, when Andrew received them through the World Wide Web he noticed the effect the duct tape had on the eyes of each person. It really brought out the person's soul and enunciated their emotion. This had to be a common observation. Andrew felt that each person carried a burden with them that entrenched the mind with sadness, pain, and anger. He contributed this to society. He understood there were good and bad things about today's civilizations. He also understood that money was bad and life wasn't fair. He wanted everyone to be happy. A place where no one felt pain. A place where everyone was always kind and lending a helping hand. Was this only his figment of heaven? Was reaching this utopia possible? People shouldn't have to die for someone to realize that this world has issues that need to be resolved, and quickly.

Nadine and Andrew took a photo as well. You could see them standing in front of the white sheet while Nadine covered Andrew's duct-taped mouth with her finger to symbolize his silence even more. While looking at this photo Andrew noticed that he looked grief-stricken while his new girlfriend looked fierce. Maybe she had a flaring

The Witch's Hat

soul as a result of any suffering she endured through life's journeys which motivated her to stay strong. She didn't look the least bit sad. In compearison, she didn't just lose a family member. She also wasn't programmed to be nurturing. Their relationship was even more lustful than the relationship with Sage. She only wanted Andrew because he was hot shit at the moment and it looked like he had a bright future. She probably pitied him too. All Andrew cared about is that she was down to have sex any time of the day. They would do it over three times a day sometimes. Andrew never knew a woman who liked it so rough. She encouraged Andrew to choke her and slap her on the face as well as her ass. Was this what it was like to be a man?

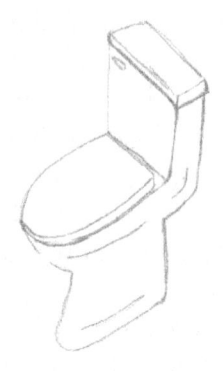

CHAPTER 18
Aenema

Andrew was informed that spring by Jace that he had scheduled another event in D.C. on May 13th, a couple days after the date of Andrew's 19th birthday. Andrew's mother was to speak at the Anti-Defamation League. Andrew along with his mother, Jace, and cousin all joined along for the ride while Scott stayed home with Antonio again. Fortunately, Andrew had just finished up the spring semester at the college so he didn't have to take off school this time. Instead, he was being led around like a sheep by the media as an object to use Josh's death as a tool for their agenda. But still, he felt special.

Through the passage of time, they had arrived in D.C. by commercial airline. Andrew had his drugs like usual. They arrived at the hotel and Andrew did his deed, then they toured around the city. The event was being hosted at the John F. Kennedy Center for the Performing Arts. They had arrived a little early. They did the usual visiting with members of the gathering along with a couple of advocates from the television series called *Glee*. Andrew felt like he had finally reached stardom. He had to sacrifice his brother to be there. No matter what happened or who he met he would've rather had his brother back but Andrew believed everything happened for a reason.

Once the ceremony commenced there were a few speakers who

The Witch's Hat

continued talking about the theme of the event and what it was about. They explained the tragedies that bullying caused around the country and that the goal was to put an end to the devastation. They explained that Tanya was the mother of a victim of suicide as a result of torment from a select few peers. They motioned Tanya from her table and up to the stand after about midway through the occasion.

Tanya was eager to be a hero. She explained her story and how she suspected Josh's death was a result of bullying to which his friends had pointed out. "I'm doing this for all the kids that are perceived as LGBTQ and everybody else getting picked on for who they are as a person," she proclaimed.

Tanya may have wanted the best for the kids but her lust for attention and fame was greater. She was doing the right thing but may have had the wrong intentions. She had loved Josh but what her kids needed weren't gifts but something broader and more sophisticated. Or plain and simple. Carrying on, it certainly is not doses of meds giving the impression that you are defective. Andrew was definitely worried she would push this philosophy upon the public. She wanted to be the next Judy Shepherd in her own crazy way.

Andrew's mother had succeeded with her part of the ceremony and got a good portion of the attention that she ever so craved momentarily satisfied. She connected with a lot of new people during this voyage, as did Andrew. At the table they sat at were a group of lawyers and Andrew told them he was going for his political science degree. They chatted on what Andrew's goals were and they decided to offer him an internship at either the state or national capital. This was interesting and gave Andrew something to think about.

After the event ended the group dilly-dallied around the city before making the flight back home. It was now time to tend to Josh's Gift. James and Tanya spent their time having gatherings at the local church. They and the kids, amongst a handful of dedicated volunteers, would all eat and play games. On special days like the upcoming prom, they would even have a DJ. It was considered an LBGTQ prom, an everyone prom. To supply food and pay for things such as DJ fees, the organization collected donations from the community. Tanya had all the say of where the money was spent. She did a good job of pouring the money back into the operation to keep it afloat. It was a non-profit and nobody was making money. Their time was spent volunteering.

During the meetings with the children, Tanya struggled to not make every conversation about herself, but luckily she would steer back into the teenagers' problems and tell them things were going to change. She wouldn't stop until they did. Her plan was to consistently pester the school board until the day they would make a set of guidelines to protect the gay kids. The school district wasn't too fond of the LGBTQ students at this time and didn't want to give an invitation for gays to flourish in their community so they would hold off on any policy changes for the time being. In the meantime, a lawsuit was filed against the school by one of the several other victims of similar circumstances in the district. Tanya told the students to report any type of bullying and to let her know if anything was done about it. Tanya wanted to be involved as much as possible. She felt like the sun and that people were orbiting around her with admiration. This was her niche.

What James and Jace did was help to run Josh's Gift by doing planning and set up. Since James was a school teacher, he had really close bonds with the children. They all liked him. Jace did his part by trying to come up with new ideas to do things. It came to a point that his ideas began to upset Tanya. She wanted to do things her way. Andrew had heard that Jace had told Tanya to calm down on the crying during interviews. That would have definitely made Jace her enemy. She felt like she didn't need him anymore so Jace was discarded.

It was kind of awkward with Jace out of the picture while Andrew dated his sister. He saw him all the time when he visited their parents' house where he lived. Jace enjoyed talking shit about Tanya and how demented she was. Thereafter, Andrew and Nadine took the next step and moved out together into an apartment in St. Paul. It was Andrew's first home on his own. They split the rent four ways between the couple, Nadine's brother Chase and her friend Madison who was the same best friend from the party. Sure the group had some good times at the new home but Andrew gained a bad reputation. He didn't pay his share of the rent. He always flushed his money into his veins. His relationships with his roommates began to get rocky. Even so, no one said much to him. They would mention his drug use behind his back but not to his face. Andrew still denied he did any chemicals and tried to continue to play it off like he was sober.

One day when Andrew was home shortly after he had quit his job making cookies, Chase called. Chase said his friend had relapsed on cocaine. He wanted Andrew to run to the friend's house and coach him to drop the habit he had picked back up since Chase was busy at work. Andrew agreed to do so and arrived at the friend's house who went by the name of Adam. Adam had dark hair and you could tell he lifted weights. He was ex-military and was Chase's boyfriend at the time. As you can see, Nadine had two gay brothers. Maybe the trait ran in the gene pool.

Andrew snatched the bag of cocaine from on top of the mini-fridge where Adam was snorting it. "I'm going to flush this down the toilet, OK Adam?"

"I don't know if I want you to. I want more but it's probably for the best!" Adam said in a rapid voice. "Goddamnit, I fucked up! Thanks for being a good friend."

Adam was flailing his arms in the air pacing around the house. He was cussing up a storm and was very ashamed. Meanwhile, while Adam was pacing, Andrew sneaked into the bathroom and quickly whipped out his wallet to grab his I.D. to draw up a line. He snorted a fat line and flushed the toilet. He then walked through the doorway in a jittery fashion. "I flushed it," Andrew said.

Andrew brought the strung-out Adam with him back to where he lived, so he could get Adam out of his drug use abode. Hypocritically he went straight to the bathroom to bang. He drew out his needle, mixed the concoction and put it in his arm. Andrew didn't know Chase had gotten home and was standing outside the door. Andrew opened it to see Chase at the entry eavesdropping. Chase knew what Andrew was doing and even caught a glimpse of his bloody hand that was swollen like a golf ball. Andrew had missed with his dull needle so he wasted the cocaine. The only effect he had was a very small rush for a second and a completely numb hand where he inserted the rig.

The atmosphere started to get unpleasant at the groups' apartment. The roommates were fed up with the jobless Andrew not paying his share of the rent. After the short-term lease was done they all disbanded except Nadine and Andrew. They decided to take the plunge and move to their own condo afterward. Andrew still used drugs. Chase had told Nadine about his bloody hand and they both made assumptions. Nadine was not oblivious anymore. She was on Andrew's ass for it. She saw him slowly falling apart.

Almost every day while Nadine was working, Andrew went to his grandparents like usual. Andrew would hang out with Theo from the early afternoon when he woke up all the way until the evening. On this particular day, Andrew had to take a watery shit from coming down. He did, however, have a bag of dope he mixed up on the sink countertop as he was sitting down on the throne. He felt the rush of the injection and passed out. Who knows how long went by until Andrew was discovered by his grandpa. By that point, he was hunched over with his blue face almost touching his knees.

An ambulance had shown up. Somehow Nadine found out about the situation as well and turned up too. How did she get there so quickly? She must have come to check up on him just at the right moment. She followed the EMTs up the stairs to the bathroom and they grabbed Andrew and laid him down on the hallway floor. The medical team gave him a shot of Narcan which sedated the effects of the heroin. Andrew came to with his pants down to his ankles and his dong catching a breeze as he laid on the ground half-naked. He saw Nadine standing above him. She didn't seem as worried as one would suspect. He began to get up drowsily from the ground and the ambulance personnel pushed him back down. They said that he had to visit the hospital to get a check-up. Andrew thought it was bullshit and told them he didn't want to go. After being grilled on the topic, he eventually agreed to do so as they were pretty adamant. He went on the ride in the meat-wagon as Nadine followed in her car. Andrew basically got his vitals checked and sat for a few minutes upon his way to the E.R.

He knew something would have to change if he wanted to stay

The Witch's Hat

alive. He lay in the hospital room staring up at the blinding lights. He wanted to be sucked into the illumination and reflectivity dispersed throughout the universe, free traveling anywhere he wanted as an electromagnetic wavelength. He promised himself there and then that he would clean up from heroin. But did he really want to live?

The doctors had recommended that Andrew be put on the methadone program. Upon being discharged, he contacted Theo to see if he was interested in joining with him. Methadone is a synthetic opiate used to get users off of opiates like heroin, Percocet, Oxys, and a bunch of other pills. Andrew explained this to Theo to which he agreed to go and the next day they arrived together at the clinic. They went through a long admission process and were given physicals. Once an hour or two went by they were ready to receive their government-funded drugs that were completely legal to use in the state of Minnesota. How crazy is that? They started them off at a dose of 30mg. Each day they hiked it up. Theo and Andrew learned that if you complain of withdrawals to the dispenser lady on a daily basis, they would increase your dose. They got up to a dose of about 160 mg apiece. What an awesome deal. Free drugs were the way to go!

They were pretty much maxed out on their doses. They ended up being able to take home a week's worth of the red liquid after a few months of starting. In order to get any more, they would need an approval from the doctor from now on. Andrew would complain of anxiety to the therapist and to his luck she talked to the clinic's psychiatrist. As a result, he ended up getting put on Klonopin. They must have trusted him because Klonopin is very lethal when mixed with opiates, synthetic or not. They gave him a warning then let him go to enjoy his plunder.

Andrew would only take a half a dose of methadone a day and snort a few benzos. When he needed money he sold some. He was always trying to get refills as soon as he could on all his prescriptions. He saved up plenty of doses of methadone and would trade for pot. He was living the dream.

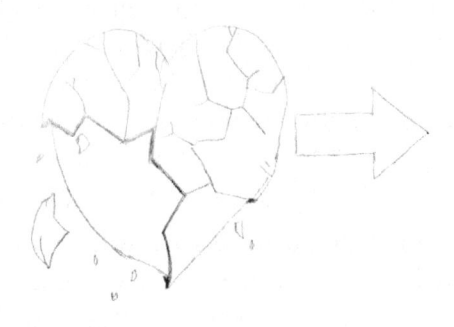

CHAPTER 19
Progression

THE YEAR HAD come to an end with nothing too crazy happening. It was in the middle of winter and Nadine had grown angry with Andrew's mother. Jace was still upset with her as well, for other spider-webbed reasons. The basis for why Nadine was mad was because Andrew was taken out to eat by his parents but when they dropped him back off at his condo he didn't have a key. It was extremely cold outside. The parents left him. They didn't care too much that Andrew had to wait in the Minnesota frigidness. Andrew called Nadine who was over a half-hour away located at her nanny job. After what seemed like forever, she had arrived to save the day. Andrew's hands were numb and he went inside to warm up. Nadine was so sick of Tanya and the family by this point. Perhaps they weren't the people she thought they were.

May it also be revealed that Andrew wasn't the person she thought he was either. It wasn't good enough that he tried and failed to be sober. His methadone and Klonopin use turned into lazy chaos. He still couldn't hold a job. He just was not able to. In addition, he wasn't in the limelight anymore and didn't even have a running car. His short-lived fame and admirable sublimity were running dry. He felt useless. At this point in time, Nadine was so fed up that she kicked Andrew out of his living space. He begged and begged to stay but failed to succeed

The Witch's Hat

with his attempts of persuasion. It was now back to square one. He had to move back to his parents.

Andrew moved in with his rents and brought a couple of his favorite pets from the condo. They were two rats. His parents had moved again. They seemed like vagrants. Currently, Andrew hung out in his new room strung out on methadone letting his rats run around as they pleased. He only did this when he wasn't out getting into mischief. Still and all, he hadn't gotten caught with doing any crimes, yet.

Shortly after Nadine and Andrew broke up, Andrew hit a new achievement, a milestone of his existence. The previous year in 2011 a young college student named Justin had started filming about a Michigan kid who had struggled with bullying in school but lived to tell his stories. Presently, it was still the early part of the year in 2012 when Justin flew to Minnesota to meet Andrew's family and talk about possible participation in the film. On the voyage of the flight, Justin came across an article in the *Rolling Stone* magazine about them. He grew more excited to bring forth the full picture of what was going on. He talked to the family upon arrival and they agreed to take part in the motion picture. This was a big move.

It wasn't too long thereafter when interviews were conducted for the documentary. During Andrew's cross-examination, he tried to be as real as possible. He shared what he could. He didn't really hold any secrets. The recording took place in Andrew's room with his stinky rats polluting the air. It seemed to go very well aside from the small nasal inconvenience and once the canvas was painted into the motion picture, the group of the three producers smoked a bowl of ganja to chill out. They were now Hollywood bound, and for the right reasons.

CHAPTER 20
The Journey

Justin and the crew had interviewed a few more key members of the school district and surrounding community then headed home to do their editing. Andrew felt important again, like a rockstar. In the meantime, he became close with one of the sons of a parent that helped out with Josh's Gift. His name was Tavin and was also a troublemaker too. He smoked pot but wasn't into the hard stuff at the time. The two adolescents would chill and Nate-Dog it up inside Andrew's car. On one occasion when Andrew was visiting Tavin's house, Tavin's mother invited a girl over to meet Andrew. Her name was Journey. She walked into the home from the garage entry leading into the house and looked absolutely amazing. Andrew chit-chatted with her a little bit and even got her number. She was beautiful. Andrew thought he would never have a chance with her. She had also brought along her friend named Kayla who was a redhead. Andrew had never been with a redhead before and his penis thought she would be an easier target to get with.

The two girls would come over and hang out with Andrew at his parents' house. They would all play with the rats. Well, it wasn't so much but the rats roaming the room. The gals may have actually

The Witch's Hat

thought they were disgusting but they played along. Journey sat on the bed and eyed up the rodents as they maneuvered around the empty methadone bottles scattered over the floor.

"What's this?" Journey asked as she picked up a bottle with pink residue inside.

"It's my medication. I'm getting clean off heroin," Andrew replied coolly. He couldn't so much say he was sober but Andrew wasn't going to display himself that way. Andrew hoped he wouldn't scare them away because he was a loser. He was just being honest but not telling more than he needed to.

Journey didn't seem too bothered by it but Kayla seemed a little setback. The trio then left the privacy of his bedroom and went to the living room to watch T.V. Andrew sat next to Journey and Kayla was hanging out with Antonio playing with toys. Eventually, Antonio and Kayla took over the T.V. to play Wii. Andrew got to know Journey and found out she had just recently got a boyfriend. She had been single when they first met and had waited for Andrew to ask her out but Andrew didn't show much of any interest. His idea of pursuing her completely diminished and besides, Andrew was curious about tallying off a redhead from his checklist. So Andrew's mind went from wandering from Journey to Kayla who was kinda a bitch. She was very slim and copied everything Journey did. Kayla would even buy the same clothes and chase the same men. The men they chased all typically liked Journey. Journey was an original trendsetter and Andrew could temporarily settle for a fire crotch who mimicked her. In all honesty, Kayla tried to seem nice but she really wasn't. In contrast, Journ was the sweetest person Andrew ever met. The three wrapped up the night and Andrew's mind began to plot ways to have at least a friend with benefits. It had been months now since he had been with a woman and he felt like a double loser after they both went home.

Andrew however did get Kayla's number off of Facebook. He began hitting it off with her and she came over. They watched a movie then went to Andrew's bedroom to play with the rats. As they were laying on the bed Andrew thought it was the right time to make a move. He rolled onto his side as she was on her back and grabbed at her boob and tried to kiss her. She pushed him away.

"I'm not ready for that!" she said, revoltingly disgusted.

"Oh ok, sorry," Andrew said in skin sparkling shock. He ended up getting up from the bed and put the rats away. She ended up leaving and told all her friends that Andrew had tried to rape her. Some women don't know what rape is. What a cunt. Now Andrew was a low-life rapist.

Andrew ended up drifting away from hanging out with the both of them for a long while until he got a message from Journey asking to hang out later that year during the summer. He went to her apartment and the bitch Kayla was there. Andrew's mind was on Journey now. She was way more pretty. Her boyfriend was in the next room of the home. He looked like a fat piece of work, just as much of a bum as Andrew so maybe he had a chance. One of Andrew's childhood friends was hanging at Journey's apartment as well. His name was Johnny. He was now Kayla's boyfriend. Looks like she got around.

Johnny was big into BMX biking and tricking on his skateboard. He had both a bike and board with him and asked Andrew to go on a cruise. Andrew wanted to show Johnny he still had the skills from years ago. On the downside, he wasn't as athletic and was about 30 pounds heavier than before. All the chocolate chip sugared oatmeal from when he lived with Nadine and the dope seemed to do that. But that didn't stop Andrew from resting one foot on the board and pushing with his left. Johnny liked to ride very loose. His board was really wobbly as Andrew tried to keep up with him cruising on his bike. Andrew ended up hitting a rock and fell backward on his ankle. He heard his bones crack. His ankle was twisted almost completely backward.

"Ahhhh, God damnit!" Andrew yelled.

"You ok?" Johnny said as he rushed to Andrew's aid.

"Fuck no! I'm pretty sure I just broke my ankle!" Andrew shouted with pain.

Johnny helped Andrew to his feet and gave him the support he needed to hop into Johnny's car. They got in and sped off.

The Witch's Hat

"Fuck man, those trucks are too fuckin' loose!" Andrew whined.

"You're not going to sue me are you?" asked Johnny worriedly as he stepped on the gas.

"No, you don't have to worry. I'm more concerned about if I will be able to walk again bro!" replied Andrew hastily. He was in deep shock.

A few minutes later they pulled into the E.R. drive-thru at the local hospital and Andrew was zoomed inside on a wheelchair. After an X-ray, the doc said he broke his ankle in three places. They wrapped it up and sent him home to prep for surgery for a few days to allow the swelling to go down. Bright and early the morning of the procedure, Andrew met with his surgeon at an orthopedics center. Members of the clinic put him under anesthesia and puzzled together his ankle with screws, plates, and pins. Then they stapled him up.

When Andrew awoke from the anesthesia he kept pressing the morphine button. It was on a timer limit and he was out. He complained to the surgeon as he lay on the gurney. The surgeon ordered the nurse to give Andrew a Dilaudid injection and left the room. Andrew hadn't been prescribed pain meds yet and he wanted to go home. He received the injection and was still in pain. Andrew made sure to let the nurse know that he was prescribed to methadone and that he took more milligrams of that than what he weighed. He explained he would need a hefty dosage due to his tolerance. To his surprise, the nurse urged that Andrew take one to two 8mg tablets of Dilaudid as needed for pain every 4-6 hours, which was quite the dose. She left to consult the doctor. Andrew was happy for a good twenty minutes until the nurse reentered and switched his dose to only one to two 4mg tabs every 4-6 hours. The doctor probably didn't want to be responsible for an overdose, which was smart.

Andrew had on a temporary cast with bloodstains slightly seeping through. He was directed to come back to get the real one on when the swelling went down again and he did just that. Now Andrew was basically immobilized.

Andrew stopped taking his methadone from the clinic and suspended his visits. He had no way to drive himself to the weekly appointments. In his free time, which was all the time, he snorted pills to feel better. He was in a ton of pain and they didn't work as well as they used to. His tolerance was shit. He watched T.V. all day and got used to his crutches. He had no help from his family. He basically starved himself because it hurt so bad to get up the stairs to the kitchen to get food.

It wasn't long until Andrew finished his pills. He did a month's worth of tablets within a week. He complained to the doctor and got another script then went back to snorting his crushed candy. His skin was crawling from not moving. His body had so much energy to burn as it had been weeks since he got decent exercise. Andrew's parents began to get very upset with him just sitting around at home. They told him he had to go to school or get a job. If he didn't do what they wanted he would have to find another place to live.

Andrew was mad. How was he going to work or go to school on crutches? His parents were assholes. "Fine, I'm moving out so I don't have to listen to you bitch! Drop me off at grandmas then!" Andrew bellowed during an argument.

Just like that, they dropped him off. It was now time for turmoil. This was where the trouble multiplied. Andrew and uncle Theo fed off of each other. They were a team of deadheads as granddaddy referred. There were no obligations to fill at Andrew's mother's folks' house, all he had to do was just take up space and breathe.

Andrew received yet another script. This time for Percocet to come off the Dilaudid. This would be the final prescription his surgeon would give. Andrew sold them for stronger narcotics. He then decided to use his broken ankle as an excuse to get more painkillers from another clinic. No car, so Andrew took the 3-mile hike from his grandparents on his crutches to get there.

His arms grew very tired along the walk and he got a bunch of weird looks along University Avenue. He stopped to rest here and there but kept going. He forced himself along until he finally reached his destination and was almost immediately denied any kind of painkiller. He was told to consult his surgeon. Andrew was out of luck.

CHAPTER 21
Overkill

Andrew now had to solely deal with his pain aside from the methadone his clinic offered. He resumed his treatment at the same dose he left off on. They even gave him a refill on his Klonopin prescription which he hastily filled. This was warranted due to Andrew's supposed "crippling" anxiety yet again. Andrew knew in reality these drugs weren't helping him develop his true self.

After getting back to his grandparents from getting the meds, he gave Theo some, then sat down on the couch on the porch and took 12 mg of Klonopin which he washed down with 320 mg of methadone along with some water. Andrew ended up passing out on the couch hunched over with his head laying on his left arm. His blood flow was slowing down and his face turned a grayish-blue.

Andrew had an unconscious vision that he was falling from the sky. He was in a free fall. He kept dropping from the clouds through the clear fake blue atmosphere. About halfway he noticed he was gonna die. What happened? Did he jump out of an airplane? It seemed to feel like forever until he would finally reach the ground. It looked like black asphalt. The space was closing in between him and what will be the barrier to the center of the earth.

When he hit the pavement there was a loud bang. Andrew felt like he was being absorbed as the barrier stretched like an upside-down bell curve. Finally, he reached the end of the curve and it started to bend in the opposite direction as Andrew was vaulted back into the sky. The ground cracked open and there were flames surfacing from it. As he looked behind him he could see a silhouette as he was bound back up to the heavens. Andrew had noticed the shadow wasn't his. It had glowing red eyes and grew bigger as it crept towards him. The sky had darkened and you could see the faint shadow transform into a scary monster. Andrew could see the trees burning from below adding a little more light to the darkness. It looked like hell. The beast began to reach towards him. Its red eyes were captivating, drawing Andrew in. He felt anger take over his body.

Andrew felt like the demon was trying to bring him to the depths of hell. Its arms were stretched out before him in a choking manner. He got so close that the detail of the figure had become more apparent. It had a goat face and horns. The goat creature had wings that compelled the air to lift him higher and higher toward Andrew. Andrew noticed the creature had a marking burnt into its chest as well. The insignia was in the shape of a pentagram. It just so happened that this was the symbol of the Sigil of Baphomet which had been advertised by the Church of Satan in recent years.

The demon didn't get close enough to choke Andrew but he did grab a hold of his leg. When he did this he stopped flapping his wings and began dragging Andrew downward. Upon touch, Andrew could see his life flash before his eyes. Every memory he had, distant and future overcame him. He became very overwhelmed. What was he supposed to do? Join forces with the devil? Maybe it wasn't such a bad idea since at the moment he wanted everything to burn. But he wouldn't let that happen.

Andrew kicked his feet but couldn't break free. He did, however, propel his foot to the demon's mouth. It didn't have much effect. There was heavy death metal music playing in the background which overtook

The Witch's Hat

him. The demon bared his sharp fucked up teeth and hissed. Then the fanged demon started pulling Andrew still rapidly down towards the flames. Andrew struggled as he was tugged. The flames began to devour him and everything went blank.

Andrew woke up with perspiration. Or at least he thought he woke up. In a split second his soul left his body in a haze, his view changed. His vision now tunneled down from the ceiling and he saw that his real material body wasn't roused. He was motionless and limp. Andrew also spied that his grandfather was giving him CPR to keep him alive. What the hell was going on? This present scenario was short-lived as a heavy strum of chords manifested Andrew right back into the depths of the flames. The demon had never let go.

Now he was in his face shaking his head as if saying "no" with his Gene Simmons-like tongue flickering up and down. The beast had gotten a grip around Andrew's torso but Andrew's arms were still free. He used both hands to clutch the djinns tongue and then he pulled as hard as he could. Something had given out from the tension of the tongue. It felt lifeless but was still dangling from the demon's mouth. Andrew had ripped it out of place. The demon then let go of Andrew's waist and next grabbed him by his clutched hand trying to break free. Andrew did not let go and from the extra momentum of the beast's tug, the tongue was torn out with strands of muscle hanging from the departed end. The demon was silenced.

A brief moment later a beam of light had shown through the night, a bright cylinder piercing the sky. It connected with Andrew's immortal soul and his apparent visible flesh. The demon's grasp on Andrew was demolished as he was vaporized by the radiated luminosity of the gleaming light.

Andrew was being carried up through the shining light. Up. Up. Up. His eyes focused above to see where he was going as he was slowly being drawn to a full moon-looking circle up in the sky. But it wasn't a moon. It was a portal into what Andrew thought of as the unknown. Andrew's eyes fixated on a motionless figure that was lending a hand to him. As he was drawn in closer he noticed that the figure was his brother Josh. What was going on? How did he get here? Andrew was in the reality of his dreams as he reached for his brother's hand. Josh had clenched it tightly and pulled him in.

"I've been waiting for you," Josh said in an infinitesimal echo.

Andrew was momentarily blinded by the light before it faded to a spectrum that was visible to the naked eye. He looked around and saw all his family members. His deceased grandma was there along with a bunch of other people with whom Andrew felt connected. Andrew knew this was his bloodline. It made sense that Josh was right by their grandma's side because he loved her so much.

"What's going on? Where are we?" Andrew asked.

Josh gave a somber look. He looked sad but still had that sparkle in his eyes. "I'm sorry Andrew. I didn't mean to do it. I'm sorry," is what Josh replied.

Just then Andrew woke up. He gasped for a deep breath of air to restore his depleted lungs. As he looked up from the ground he saw that the paramedics, his grandparents, and two uncles had surrounded him. He saw one paramedic with a small 3 pronged pitch fork-shaped object. It just so happened that it was nasal spray. The spray contained Narcan which was used to bring Andrew to a life-like presence again. Andrew felt a little dazed but he definitely felt soberer.

With an extended arm from the Narcan man, Andrew was pulled to his feet with his one useful foot. Andrew came face to face with the medic and realized his name was Josh by looking at his badge. What a coincidence Andrew thought. He was a little disoriented but he was all there. They handed him his crutches and he balanced himself upright.

"If your grandpa hadn't found you, you very well could have died," voiced the medic with concern.

"Holy shit!" Andrew said as he scratched his arm. "Man, that's crazy!"

Andrew had the feeling that someone was watching over him. It frightened him a little but he almost didn't care if he died and at the same time he felt invincible. Andrew wasn't done playing his own prescribed doctor. He was ready to rock.

"You need to quit doing that stuff, it is bad for you," chimed the

The Witch's Hat

medic. "Now we have to take you to the hospital to make sure you are ok."

"I don't need to go! I'm fine!" answered Andrew as he maneuvered through the crowd of people to try and escape.

"Dude, you ok?" asked Theo as Andrew passed by. Theo had a sedated look on his face and his eyes were pinpoint.

"Yeah, I'm fine. They can't make me go to the hospital though!" Andrew sternly announced.

"Andrew, if you go to the hospital they can help you," Gramps informed.

Andrew shook his head. He then got the third degree from most of the surrounding group. Eventually, they convinced him into going. They had threatened to get a police escort.

"Ok fine I'll go!" Andrew replied reluctantly.

The medics pulled the stretcher up the sidewalk of the house up to the front steps. Andrew walked down and laid on it. He thought this was all unnecessary. However, when he tried to move his wrist he realized he couldn't lift it. He told the medics and they replied that the overdose had messed with it and the hospital staff would check it out. They then wheeled Andrew into the ambulance and then left to go to the restorative institution. They quizzed him on his health and inserted an I.V. along the ride. Shortly later, they arrived at a Minneapolis hospital. The stay was only a couple hours. They checked his vitals and offered a drug treatment plan but Andrew denied it. He did however take the number to a therapy clinic to fix his wrist.

When Andrew met with the occupational therapist, he was diagnosed with wrist drop. The therapist constructed a device to fit Andrew's arm. It was a splint that went halfway up to his elbow with rubber bands connected from the top extending to each individual finger to lift his wrist. It kinda reminded Andrew of Spider-Man. Even after all this, he would not steer away from future dope use… He continued his regimen without much of any fear.

CHAPTER 22
The Pact

It was fall and it had been 3 months since Andrew had his cast put on. During that time he would roll around the projects of Southeast Minneapolis in a wheelchair or on a bike and always was down for a party, especially at the Witch's Hat. He gained respect. It was good times but now it was time for the cast to be removed. He was now able to walk again but with a boot on his foot. He spent his time fixing up his walking game. His days around that time consisted of methadone and sleep. Before you know it winter had rolled around and Andrew was able to completely walk without the boot. On a side note, his wrist was repaired as well. He was able to move it. The numbness in his hand had subsided and he could sense his nerves again. Andrew was done being a bionic man.

Andrew hadn't talked to his parents since before the overdose and for some strange reason, he went to visit them. He wasn't on the best terms with them but figured he hadn't talked to them since he almost died and it's what his brother would have wanted. He walked right into the house without knocking. He was greeted by his father who trampled down the stairs towards the entryway.

"Oh no! Look who it is? You here to steal more stuff?" Scott jeered.

"No, I'm just here to visit," Andrew replied.

The Witch's Hat

In the background, you could hear Tanya excitedly yell as she waddled up the stairs, "Andrew! I heard you went to the hospital!?"

"Yeah, I overdosed," he replied.

"You have to be more careful with those medications," Tanya said with a twinkle in her smile. She was happy Andrew was struggling. Her sly grin told it all.

"He obviously didn't learn his lesson! Look at his eyes right now, he's high!" shouted Scott. "Get the fuck out of here Andrew!"

Andrew could have pointed the blame on his mother for promoting pills during his lifetime but he didn't want to deter her from ever giving him any of her own stash in the future. Instead, he turned to his parents and said, "I wish the overdose would have killed me, I'll just shoot myself instead!"

It wasn't a surprise that Tanya had the cops on speed dial. They pulled up to the house with guns drawn because of the content of the phone call. Tanya never made it clear to the 9-1-1 operator that Andrew never actually owned a gun or even had one on his person. The officers walked up to Andrew and guided him to sit down on the front steps of the house before drilling him with questions. The red, white, and blue lights were flashing as the next-door neighbors were outside gaping at the scene. Andrew didn't deny to the officers what he had said about shooting himself but claimed it was no big deal because he didn't actually even own a gun. Apparently, you don't have the freedom to kill yourself these days so Andrew was directed into an ambulance that had arrived on the scene. He was to be placed on a 3-day psychiatric hold at some sort of hospital.

Due to bed availability and Andrew's risk of fleeing, he was brought to Fargo, North Dakota. This was the longest ambulance ride Andrew had ever taken. A total of 3.5 hours. Andrew would never forget his time at this facility because the bastards didn't supply him with his methadone. They said they didn't give it to their patients so he spent Easter of 2013 in a single bedroom which was basically a prison cell. He spent the holiday curled in a ball between spurts of vomiting into a trash bag. He puked so much that he had nothing left to puke up. He would heave up yellow stomach acid amidst burps of air.

"Give me my fucking medication!" he yelled as he pounded on his cell door.

No one paid any mind. They had quarantined him in his room for being sick and getting out of hand with his demand for drugs. He spent the remainder of the three days mostly rolling back and forth in the fetal position on the cold floor, throwing up until the day they released him. He was drenched in sweat and starving. His body was trembling. This was the longest Andrew had been clean for a while, and he had done it the old-fashioned way. He would never, ever suggest coming off such a high dose of methadone by going cold turkey, but he was proof it was possible. To Andrew, it didn't make sense that he threatened to take his own life; only to be put in a situation where he was forced into a life-threatening withdrawal. Nothing ever quite made sense to him. He was just thankful to be alive and was released to immediately puff on a delicious cigarette. He had a long bus ride back home; it seemed like he was locked up for months in what seemed like the slammer but was still ready to get his party on. It was the day after April Fool's day and his 21st birthday was only weeks away.

May 9th rolled around and Andrew met up with his mother at a Mexican restaurant for his first legal drink. As to why Andrew still desired a link with them was beyond him. Very deep down he just appreciated having been raised by them and given a decent life even though they had their differences. On the contrary, Andrew left himself open to sabotage being around them. He just had to think positive and not give them anything to use against him. They fed off of him doing bad but his birthday was a day of privilege. He was coming of age in his own way. He was becoming his own man. The legality of drinking would now become a normal thing for him and a floaty in the water on his journey.

When they arrived at the restaurant Andrew took a picture with a cutout of the Dos Equis man. His mother snapped the shot and they went to sit down. Out of all the drinks Andrew could have had, he chose a margarita. He wondered what it would be like to live in Mexico.

The Witch's Hat

Would life be easier and freer? Or would it just be more dangerous? He pondered this as he guzzled his drink. He imagined himself on a beach in Mexico on some type of island with no one to bother him and a place to call his home.

"Andrew, you there?" questioned Tanya.

"Yeah, sorry. I wanna let you know that I would not be sitting here drinking this drink if I was still on methadone. I guess that is one good thing about going to that Fargo hospital. I really wish you guys wouldn't do that shit though," Andrew said in an inclining pissy mood.

"All we do is care. We want the best for you," Tanya said in an almost fake and dishonest way.

"It just always seems like you go through drastic measures instead of just talking to me on a one-to-one basis. You don't always have to call 9-1-1," Andrew said in desperation.

"I've lost a kid already and I don't want to lose you too!" she pleaded. Andrew understood where she was coming from. It was insensitive of him to threaten his own life given the history of his brother. "Let's make a pact," she said. "Pinky promise that neither one of us will ever commit suicide"

Oh wow, Andrew thought. This was crazy but fair enough. He held out his pinky to his mother and interlocked it with hers. They both had one less thing to worry about from now on.

"Oh my God, Andrew, I have something to tell you. It's about Josh," Tanya blurted.

"What is it?" Andrew inquired.

"You remember the house Josh passed away in right?" she asked, seeking for validation.

"Yeah..." Andrew replied.

"I found out from your dad's cousin that her friend had moved into the house and her kid is having a bad experience there. The kid said there is someone hiding in the closet. A bad man..." she responded with curiosity.

"No way. So what does that mean?" Andrew implored.

"I don't know. But the kid is deathly afraid of his room and has been sleeping with his parents. It makes me wonder…" she said, going off on a limb.

It made Andrew wonder too. He had toyed around with Ouija boards before his brother's death. He did it with Sage in high school and it sparked his interest. The first Ouija board experience gave answers from a spirit guide of some sort who was in contact with his grandmother who had passed a few years prior during that measure of time. The board was answering questions that his partner was unaware of. This gave motive to Andrew to buy his own board.

A few months before Josh passed Andrew took his board to the cemetery. It was just him and the same friend whose name also happened to be Josh with whom he made music with. They asked questions like "what is your name?" and got the answer "666". The friends got a little spooked. The grand final question asked was if they were communicating with a demon. When the answer went to yes the pair of friends both decided to leave. Andrew hoped and hoped he didn't bring something home with him that night which may have interfered with the energies that led to his brother's death. This definitely was something for him to think about. Andrew got up out of his seat, he was finished with his margarita and his delicious chimichangas.

"Where are you going?" Tanya asked.

"I'm going to get drunk," Andrew boasted as he weaved through the tables and walked out the restaurant door.

CHAPTER 23
Car Shopping

Andrew hung out in a rough neighborhood near his grandparents where he was the minority. He had gotten a call from his mother that she tried to overdose herself on medication but the dog wiped its wet nose upon her to wake her up. The story goes that she reflected upon her life and took action to call the ambulance. She said she consumed a whole bottle of sleeping medication which may have been true. The question is if she wanted to sleep forever or if she wanted something to post about on Facebook. It was unknown exactly how much she took but they had to have her stomach pumped.

Andrew was plainly bummed. In the meantime, he felt like he was always taken advantage of because of his skin color. He felt like he was an outsider. He slowly bonded with some close-knit friends who were of Native and African American descent that helped him blend in a little better. Andrew wanted to think he had somewhat of a street rep because he broke his ankle cruising on a skateboard but really he was just a dumb white boy. He had no idea how to skateboard but he could ollie and cruise down the street. However, he did prove his toughness by playing football with the boys. On one occasion in the parking lot "football field", Andrew dove for an overthrown ball during one of the games and busted his chin on the ground. Blood was all over the place and a few of his molars were chipped but he was too drunk to care.

It was moments like this that earned Andrew and his uncle Theo the title of the crazy white boys as they were always wandering around like a pair of crackheads. They were fiends, except now Andrew's biggest problem was alcoholism. Theo didn't come around much to chill with the gang because he didn't like to ingest alcohol on his methadone. However, he did come around from time to time to smoke herb.

One day during a usual night of drinking Andrew had the idea to go car shopping because they were short on money. Andrew was on welfare and couldn't afford to supply all the good times every day with his own cash so they needed moolah. A group of five, which included Theo, Marcel, Sylvester, Niccolo, and of course Andrew walked down the street. They were split between each side of the road. It was past 2 am so there wasn't much going on on this side of the twin cities. Of the two on each side of the street, one was assigned to each side of the car. They proceeded down the roadway in four columns with the one extra person playing catch up. Every seven or so cars you would find one unlocked. At that moment they all swarmed the vehicle looking for goodies. They would take anything of worth and throw it in a backpack. They would take CDs, change, money, drugs, liquor, guns, army gear, etc. Andrew thought some of these people were idiots for not locking their cars in the big city. He figured they were more to blame than he was.

It was about 2:30 am and they were about halfway down the street when they came to a red sedan. Andrew opened the door and saw a camouflage marine corps hat and left it. A few brief seconds later he saw a glimmer of light flash from between the front seats. The street lamps had revealed a large knife. He grabbed it and walked quickly to the next car. The group then proceeded to follow him.

"Hey! What are you doing? Get back here!" shouted an angry man's voice.

The boys took off running. They cut around the corner of the block

The Witch's Hat

to the left and then veered to the right down an alleyway. Andrew saw a black cat dart in front of him and cross his path. He continued to pump his legs in retreat. Near the end of the alley was a pedestrian bridge that crossed the I-94 freeway system. The group went up the stairs to the top and started jogging across. From the few cars on the freeway, they must have looked like silhouettes dancing in the moonlight in some ghetto horror film. They were just missing purge-like Halloween masks which would have put them out of place as it was only June.

After they crossed the bridge they followed the railroad tracks back to the opposite side of the neighborhood; from there they trekked alley by alley to Prospect Park to the sanctum of the Witch's Hat. The old water tower was Andrew's central hangout spot for whenever he needed to lay low. The group sat and overlooked the Twin Cities. Today it gives an eerie feeling to know that they were sitting on the same bench where Bob Dylan would sit and write his music during the time he attended school at the U of M. This info has long led Andrew to believe that Dylan's song "All Along the Watchtower" which became popular from the recorded version by Jimi Hendrix was based on this very landmark.

It is an understatement to say this place was sacred to Andrew. It gave him a feeling of history being written in an almost fatalistic way through the channel of Dylan's Devine vision. If you were to ask Dylan how he came up with the lyrics to his music his answer would be along the lines of "God made me do it". At this point, it was too early for Andrew to know how much this song would resonate with the most terrifying moment of his life. He had no clue who Bob Dylan even was at the time, but what he did know was that "Watchtower" song...

Aside from all that, the night of burglarizing cars was put to a halt. Theo went home and the rest of the group blared the night air with music as Andrew pondered his life as well as his future. There was bound to be a point where he would get caught for the bad deeds he has done and have to pay the fortune of the price whether it be karma or so-called justice from the courts. He had to change but there was no sense of urgency. He basically had it easy living with his grandparents only having to pay $200 in EBT for groceries every month. He didn't have to work for anything but at the same time, he wasn't getting anywhere. What was to happen when his grandparents died? Where would he live? Why was he even considering only himself over his grandparents' passing anyway? He felt guilty. There had to be a better way.

"Yo whaddup?" shouted a mysterious voice from the woods.

"Ayyyy!!! It's Nasty Nate!" shouted Sylvester as he greeted his Native cousin with a G shake.

Sylvester, Niccolo, and Nate were all Lakota who valued honesty, humility, and respect which in return Andrew respected. How could he scorn them? They seemed more real than anyone else Andrew affiliated with at the time. Andrew's race had stolen their land and he felt like he had to show there was some good in the white man. They may have even had the same enemies. They all greeted each other, then moved over to the picnic bench to sit. They sat down and Andrew was still the official D.J. As a matter of fact, he may have been the only one with a cell phone to even play music. He had grown so accustomed to the gangster rap music of his everyday life that he had to switch it up.

"Hey guys I'm gonna play some Kurt Cobain," said Andrew, as he envisioned his past heroin endeavors.

"Aight!! Some Kirko Bangz! Let's do it!" replied Nate.

"Aight then," Andrew said as he played Nirvana from his cell while staring off at the horizon of the city.

"This isn't Kirko Bangz!" said Nasty.

"Kurt go bangs? What is that? A rapper? No, this is Nirvana!" Andrew retorted in confusion.

"Ohhhhh.... Kurt Cobain. Shit, my bad dude. Nirvana's the shit bro!" said the drunken Nate.

It wasn't just Nate who was drunk, they were all intoxicated. "Something in the Way" spilled over the speaker as Andrew tried to determine his life, as well as reminisce his past. Sylvester knew who Nirvana was. The band was bestowed upon him by Andrew on his heroin-crazed car rides. The present had shown that Sylvester had held a great appreciation for Nirvana as he sported their tees. Andrew hoped he could promote the same rock lifestyle onto others as well but he

The Witch's Hat

mostly listened because of his own emotions and turmoil. His search for his own meaning within the depressed anger-stricken lyrics grew.

The song finished and Andrew resurfaced to the new age of rap and played some little-known Kirko Bangz. It wasn't bad at all. Andrew was always in the mood for new music because it altered his reality and made an imprint on who he was. There were different types of music for different situations. Songs essentially became tools in Andrew's life and better yet, all the music was available in the palm of the hand on smartphones. It was still 2013 and cellphones had come a long way since when Andrew was introduced to his prepaid Nokia for emergencies as a kid. To many, music is classified as almost a necessity to get the wheels spinning, it's just deciding what to play.

Before long the night came to an end as the energy died down. They left the tower and parted ways after they made it to the bottom of the hill. Andrew then staggered back home to his grandparents in search of some much-needed direction in life.

CHAPTER 24
New Years

Andrew was still living in the big city. He didn't have a car and relied on city buses to get from place to place. He drank a lot. He had a habit of supplying himself and his friends a bottle of booze every day. They would all pitch in what they could but it was mostly Andrew paying for everything. He worked hard doing yard work each day that summer for the neighbors to provide.

Fall passed and winter began. New Year's Eve crept up and Andrew had gotten into a drinking frenzy, even more than most typical days. He was drinking away his worries at his grandparents' with a bottle of tequila which was a first for him. Andrew's friends weren't there but he did share some with his uncle Topher who was now 18. Topher was one of the smartest, most empathic persons that Andrew knew. The doctors classified him as autistic which meant he had superpowers. This was Topher's first time drinking and he did very well. Andrew poured him a shot and Topher drank half of it.

"Eww, this is nasty!" Topher said with a disgusted look on his face.

"It is, ain't it?" Andrew replied.

The Witch's Hat

Topher tilted his head back and poured the remainder of the shot glass into his mouth.

"Ahhhhh, it burns!" Topher said while exhaling deeply.

"I know! Here, take a sip of this Pepsi. I'm going to pour you another shot," insisted Andrew.

Topher took another shot and stammered, " I can't take anymore. I think I feel it. My head is fuzzy."

Should Andrew have felt bad for giving his autistic uncle tequila? It felt like others would judge upon this but equality entails that Topher should have just the same rights as everyone else. If he's 18 and wants to try it out, let him do so. Andrew never shoved it down his throat anyhow. Topher was smart enough to know if he liked it or not and it turned out that he didn't.

"Woah! I'm getting dizzy. I don't think I like this," Topher indicated. "It's kinda we-awd"

"You don't have to drink anymore but I'm gonna have a couple more shots myself," Andrew added.

As Andrew was filling the shot glass his aunt Jada came down from upstairs. Andrew was cool with her but he would suggest others not to get on her bad side. She had even more screws loose than Andrew did!

"Hey Andrew! Pour me a shot 'muh-fucka!" Jada commanded with her hands up in a "Y" shape like she was nailed to a cross. "Let's get our drink on! It's New Years!"

Andrew filled another shot glass apiece and they took turns washing down the liquor. "One! Two! Three!" Jada pronounced as the two tilted their heads back and swigged. Jada made a disgusted face after each and every one.

"Eww! That's strong and tastes kinda nasty," she stated with a slightly sick, agonized face.

"Yeah, but it does the job!" Andrew said with a smirk.

As Jada was just getting started, Andrew had had about 6 shots all within an hour and his gut was already stuffed with beer from earlier that day. The tequila was strong! Some straight-up Mexican bottle of rage. Andrew began feeling a little edgier. He seemed to act in an autopilot sorta way like a robot where he didn't think before he acted. Andrew was well underway and they still had an hour before the ball drop.

The clocks ticked down and the drinks ticked up. Andrew and Jada were about two more shots in when his grandpa came down to the chill spot in the basement.

"15 minutes until midnight," he said as he placed himself into his office chair in the center of the underground room and swiveled it towards the T.V. which was set to the news channel. The countdown had reached 10 minutes and Andrew had just finished his last shot. He was swaying from side to side trying to focus his dizzy eyes on the television. Andrew bumped his leg into the table and almost fell to the ground.

"You should chill out on the drinking, Andrew. You look like a mess!" said his grandpa who sat a few feet away.

Andrew turned red for some reason or another and took a step forward. He extended his arm and swiped a stack of papers off his grandpa's desk. "Fuck you, bitch!" shouted Andrew.

His grandpa swiveled 180 degrees around towards Andrew. "Goddamnit! What are you doing?" Gramps yelled. A few strands of oily black hair fell over his face as he tried to get to his feet.

Andrew didn't know what came over him. He was filled with rage and wasn't completely there. When he saw his grandfather try to get to his feet he pushed him back onto the seat and swung a fist at him. Andrew missed and in the process, he stumbled backward and fell on his ass.

"Gertrude!" Andrew's grandfather shrieked up the stairs to grandmother. "Gertrude! Andrew is out of control! We might need to get the police out here!"

An inaudible voice followed from the floor above as Andrew shimmied back to his feet. He began to pace back and forth at the bottom of the stairs for a good minute hollering and screaming. Little did he know that the police were on their way. As Andrew was

The Witch's Hat

distracted, his grandpa rose from his chair and snuck up the stairs with tears in his eyes.

About midway up he turned down to Andrew and in a tough voice said, "You might want to calm down. The cops are gonna be here shortly."

Andrew heard what his grandpa had said and turned in pursuit. He stomped his way up the stairs to the first floor and saw the American flag colors flashing through the front porch windows. Here we go again, Andrew thought.

Gramps answered the door. A total of 4 officers stepped in and woke Theo up from his methadone doze upon the couch. He sat and watched as Andrew stood nearby. The scene gave Andrew the impression of a Nazi brigade that meant business.

"What's exactly going on here? We got a call about a disturbance," conveyed a bald-headed sergeant. He had on a furry winter trooper cap and seemed like he had a chill personality.

In the meantime, Andrew stood swaying to and fro in the living room with his eyes half-closed. "Everthin okie," he assured in a terrible slur.

The sergeant gave Andrew a pitiful look then grandpa piped in saying, "He was out of control throwing my papers around downstairs and destroying things. He took a swing at me. I figured we would call you guys out here to make sure he doesn't hurt anybody." He seemed as if he was devastated. He didn't know what else to do.

All of a sudden Gertrude butted in saying, "All I heard was a bunch of yelling and arguing coming from downstairs." she said, reminding Andrew of his mother with her excitement.

"Ok, well it looks like he has calmed down a bit. Seems as if New Years got the best of him. What do you say if we put him in a bedroom to sleep it off?" asked the skin-headed sergeant.

"Yes upstairs, at the end of the hallway," said grandpa.

The sergeant stepped towards Andrew and put his hand lightly on his shoulder to lead him up the stairs. Andrew jerked away so another one of the officers grabbed his arm forcibly and the two policemen guided him up the steps.

"This is stupid! I'm not gonna go to sleep!" Andrew asserted with a disorientated fashion.

Regardless of Andrew's vocals, a few moments went by and the group made it to the top of the stairs. They then veered to the right straight into the bedchamber. Andrew then repeated his intention of not sleeping.

"Well, you are going to have to, son. The other option is that you go to jail and I bet you don't want that," said the more militant officer.

Andrew couldn't make out the words his badge said for his name. He was going in and out of consciousness. The next thing he remembered was laying down in the bed and the door being closed behind him. It seemed like a blink of an eye but apparently, a few minutes had gone by and Andrew started screaming. He was in the dark alone and getting the spins.

He growled as he sprung to his feet and flung the door open. He saw 3 officers standing at the top of the stairs.

"Hey! Get back in there!" commanded the sergeant.

Andrew said nothing but instead made another growling noise and darted down the hallway leading to the stairwell. He used all his might to try and plow through the small crowd of officers with no avail. Instead of clearing a path, he fell right into the bear hug of one of the leader's soldiers. Andrew felt a jolt of energy flow through him and he broke his right arm free then punched the officer square in the cheek. It landed with a thud. It wasn't a loud thud but it was definitely a solid hit to where it drew his comrades' attention. Within a split second, Andrew was on the ground in a hog pile with knees on his back as well as his neck as the group rustled to get his hands cuffed behind his body.

"Looks like we have no choice but to bring you in now. We gave you a chance..." said the top dog.

They violently pulled Andrew to his feet and held him firmly by his upper arms down the stairway. Andrew felt like he was being somewhat carried and pushed at the same time to where his feet just barely grazed each step.

Ultimately they reached the bottom and the head guy called to Andrew's grandparents, "Looks like we are going to have to book him. He just assaulted one of our officers. Punched him in the face."

The sergeant then held the front door open for Andrew to be escorted through. Upon departure a bone-chilling breeze took hold.

"Do we have a coat for him?" requested the sergeant.

Andrew's grandfather came over with his jacket and the officer took it to give to him to put on. Two-foot steps ahead was another staircase. This one was cement which led down to even more cement leading to the street. An officer nudged Andrew forward down the stairway. It happened to be the same one he had punched. About 4 stairs from the bottom Andrew slipped on a patch of ice and his body went forward. The officer holding him seemingly didn't have a tight enough grip and Andrew went head first towards the cement. His chin took on most of the impact as it bounced and slid along the pavement. He lay belly first on the ground for a mere second before the officer pulled him back to his feet. Andrew was dripping blood from his beard. He reopened the same wound he shredded up playing football. It didn't even phase him.

"Looks like we ought to take him to the hospital. He may have suffered a concussion," ordered the sergeant. "Either way he should sober up in detox. I think he learned his lesson." The hatted Mr. Clean then peeked his head into the house and hollered "Happy New Year" to the family as he closed the door. "Ok boys, let's take him to HCMC."

"Will do sir," said the man holding Andrew.

Meanwhile, inside the house, the New Years' ball was inching to the bottom of the pole-stand to its resting spot to signify a new year. Andrew could hear the countdown from inside. "Ten! Nine! Eight! Seven! Six! Five! Four! Three! Two! One! HAPPY NEW YEAR!!!"

Those words quivered in Andrew's head as the squad car door closed in his face and hit his knee. Great! He may have missed the ball drop but at least he existed until a new year. He was starting it out rough and in quite a unique fashion. To be honest, this was just another case day in Andrew's somewhat crazy life. He knows everyone has a story. The purpose Andrew would want to expel is to give people hope even though during this moment in time he had none. His destiny had landed him in detox this cold winter day. Now he just had to enjoy the ride.

Seven hours had passed when Andrew woke up in the hospital. It was a little past seven o clock. He saw white walls all around him and had an IV in his hand. He was laying on a gurney with his left hand cuffed to the bed. He had no clue how he got there. He thought what had happened previously that New Year's Eve was all a dream. After a short while of thought, he realized it was not a dream and that he was lucky to be at the health service center.

Andrew wasn't sure if he was able to leave or if he was going to be arrested but he ended up deciding to give his quest for liberation a try. He pushed on the call button laying in his lap.

Next, he hollered out, "Hey is anyone there? I'm ready to go home now!"

It felt like no time at all when the nurse got up from behind her computer and entered the drywall cage of a room. The nurse was an attractive lady with brown hair.

"Are you feeling better? Looks like you had a crazy night!" she said with a smile on her face.

"Yeah, it must have been pretty nuts. I don't remember much of it..." Andrew tiredly replied.

"I was here when the police brought you in late last night. You didn't seem very happy," she laughed.

"No, I probably wasn't. I don't like the police. They get to do whatever they want. They make their own laws," Andrew muttered.

"I'm sorry to hear that," she voiced. "But it looks as if you are coherent now. I'll have security come in here and uncuff you from the bed. We just have to make sure you can stand up and walk."

Andrew couldn't believe it. They were letting him go off the bat. He imagined that they were busy with all the crazy accidents that happen on New Years and was so happy he would be free in a few minutes. He

The Witch's Hat

had no appreciation for the favor the cops did for him. He had no idea he could be in jail for assaulting an officer. He was angry he was in the hospital but he showed a decent level of respect for the employees with a smooth flamboyancy.

The security officer came into the room and undid the iron from Andrew's wrist. Andrew saw that he had a red circle encompassing it. He glanced up to see the guard had moved to the doorway.

The nurse approached Andrew and said, "Now let's see if you can walk."

Andrew flung his legs over the side of the gurney. He still felt a buzz going on in his head but was determined to do his best. He got up and stood in place for a second near the bed to make sure he had balance. Then he took a few steps towards the door and turned around to walk towards the sink.

"Looks like you got it under control," the nurse reckoned. "You're free to go."

"Awesome," Andrew replied, "have a nice day!"

"You too! Be careful out there and don't forget your jacket. It's on the chair right there," the nurse said as she pointed to a loveseat against the wall a few feet from the doorway.

"Oh, thanks for reminding me. I'm sure it's freezing out there," Andrew said. "See ya!"

Andrew grabbed his jacket and slipped it on. He ventured through the hospital and searched for the exit signs. He was sure he was going to get lost but he found his way. There were two sets of sliding glass doors leading outside. He was speed walking so fast that he had to slow down to allow the door to open so he didn't walk into it. The temperature was negative 8 degrees so he definitely felt the chill of the breeze run up his legs and through his unzipped coat.

"Geez! It's freezing out here!" Andrew shouted to a cab driver standing, leaning against his taxi.

"It sho is," the cab driver responded.

Andrew nodded his head as he stood under the covering of the hospital entryway peering in each direction. He had to figure out where to go. He seemed a little lost. His cellphone was out of battery so he didn't have a GPS. He knew HCMC was downtown so he looked up to the sky which was still fairly darkened but couldn't decipher where the North Star was. He was trying to compose a plan to make his way back east towards his grandparents. So what now?

In the meantime, a lady came outside and blurted to the taxi driver, "I don't need a ride anymore, my sister is picking me up."

"Oh.... OK. Thanks for wasting my time!" said the cab driver. The two exchanged a few angry words before the cab driver turned to Andrew, "How about you? Do you need a ride?"

"No, I don't. I have no money. I'm just gonna walk home. Thank you though," Andrew replied. "But do you know which way the U of M is?"

The cab driver pushed away from the taxi to stand upright and pointed in the correct direction. "It's down that way, go up Chicago and take right at first turn past Bank Stadium. That take you there," said the cab driver in broken English.

"Thanks man! I appreciate it! Sorry about the lady ditching on you."

"You're welcome! Not your fault," said the cabby in almost a whisper.

"Take it easy," Andrew said as he began his trek.

He waltzed past the driver heading northeast. He made it to a cross-section with stoplights past the stadium and near the light rail. The streets were empty of pedestrians. He took a right and continued the frigid, brisk walk. He was now on 4th Street. He wasn't sure what that meant direction-wise but he kept walking down on the sidewalk on the outskirts of the right side of 4th Avenue and checked out all the street signs for the perpendicular streets to see if he could find something he was familiar with.

He finally stumbled upon a bridge that crossed the street he was walking on. He looked to see if there was a sign and there definitely was. It was Cedar Avenue! He had a good idea where he was now but

The Witch's Hat

he had to find a way up there. He noticed a ramp on the opposite side of the street. He crossed the road to climb it. He was now facing oncoming traffic. Once he got to the top he took a hard right down Cedar without crossing again and continued his quest. He was now about a half-hour into his walk from HCMC. His legs just kept on slogging along.

It gradually kept getting more and more familiar as he made his way down the road. He realized this street led to Franklin Avenue which he would take a left on to get to the side streets his lovely grandparents lived on. He was only two blocks from Franklin and still had a long way to go. He wasn't even halfway to the house from where his night initially began. The freezing wind was getting to Andrew so he pulled his arms into his coat like a turtle and continued down Cedar for another 5 minutes. Then, out of nowhere, kitty-corner from where he was walking, a three-story building exploded.

It was nearly 8 am when Andrew saw the windows being blown out from the impact of the combustion from within. Flames reached for the sky piercing through the window frames. Holy shit, Andrew thought. Did he have a duty to go in and save them? It would have been a cool story to tell but instead, Andrew ran into a Somalian restaurant which was strangely open early on the holiday. He raced inside in a panic.

At the counter was a man sitting patiently by the register watching the news. He had dyed red hair and dark skin.

"Hey! A building exploded just down the street!" Andrew said in a blurted shout.

The man gave Andrew a weird look.

"Look outside. We should call 9-1-1. We need the fire department!" Andrew pleaded impatiently.

The man briskly walked to the door, glanced outside, and ran back to the counter to the phone. He quickly called the authorities and reported the incident.

"They are on their way," he said after he hung up.

"Ok good. Do you have any water? I've been walking for miles! I had a crazy night!"

"You want a freeze slush?" the man countered, pointing at the slushy machine.

"Heck yeah! I'm thirsty! But I have no money..." Andrew politely responded.

"It's ok," said the man pleasingly. "You get for free."

"Wow! Thanks man! I really appreciate it. You're a lifesaver!"

Within a minute Andrew received his blue slushy and told the kind clerk he would be right back. Andrew headed towards the door to go outside and watch the devastation. The gentleman followed but never came completely out of the doorway. The door was cracked. He peeked through the wide slit. After gazing for a few seconds he went back inside to make some phone calls. It was a Somali community so Andrew wondered if he knew anybody that may be in danger in the dwellings.

Andrew was curious about what had started the fire. Minnesota has one of the larger Somali populations in the country. A lot of them are from the wild territory in Africa. There is little technology in that area. The cause could have been something simple such as having a gas leak and then lighting a cigarette. Or perhaps it was a New Years' drunken mistake that could have happened anywhere. Either way, the building was currently on fire and Andrew hoped that they had a sprinkler system. He snapped out of that thought then turned to the man with the door propped open again and asked if he could use the phone.

"Yes," said the man. The two of them went back to the counter where Andrew made a call to his dad to get picked up. Andrew gave him a sob story about his night and convinced his dad to reluctantly make the half-hour trip to get him. The call finished and Andrew rejoined the man at the storefront to examine the turmoil. They stood silently until the sound of sirens drilled into their eardrums.

It was fascinating how quickly the fire department responded. The sirens grew closer. The fire was out of control. Andrew was sure that people were still sleeping inside. On the other hand, there were people on the top floor struggling for life and gasping for air. Andrew couldn't imagine the strong feeling of fear that was sure to creep over them knowing any minute the fire would weaken the floor beneath their feet. Andrew knew they could die at any moment. He felt he owed a debt to those still sleeping as he could have possibly saved lives. He was a coward.

Minutes passed and Andrew witnessed two men jump from their apartment windows. Shortly after, a woman had jumped as well. He saw them struggling to get up from the ground. He was sure they had broken bones. By now the flames were shooting twenty feet out of the second and third-floor windows. Finally, the fire department had pulled up. They ran into the first floor to do room checks but were halted by the inferno blazing down the stairwell. They then collected what survivors they could, and retreated outside to tackle the flames, spraying thousands of gallons of water onto the fire. The water slid down the rubble turning to ice in the subzero temperatures, making for a slippery situation.

30 minutes passed and the flames were still ablaze by the time Andrew's dad arrived at the wreckage. His dad stopped in front of the Somali shop and Andrew hopped in the car. "Holy shit it's freezing! I'm freaking starving!"

"You look like shit! You gotta grow up Andrew. You need to take care of yourself," said Scott, ignoring Andrew's comment.

Andrew nodded his head in silence. Meanwhile, his dad pulled out from the curb and did a u-turn to avoid the chaos. They took a right on 4th Street/Riverside Avenue and headed towards DinkyTown to pick up some Mickey D's. Andrew ordered a couple of sausage egg burritos from the value menu and scarfed them down. He may have had resentments towards his family but on this particular occasion, they had had his back. He greatly appreciated the warmth of the car ride. While Scott was munching on a McMuffin, he pulled onto University Avenue towards the grandparents. They came up to their route's turn and you could see the Witch's Hat standing atop the hill staring at them. It was partly masked by empty tree branches but still visible. The eyes loomed into Andrew's soul. The tower had witnessed what Andrew did not do when the building exploded. Andrew was ashamed and turned away and focused back onto the road ahead. They took a few more turns and reached their destination. Andrew thanked his father for the ride and went inside to share his story with his grandparents. Maybe it would help relieve his headache. He needed to make some changes in his life and soon. If not, death or jail would entail.

CHAPTER 25
Work-Life

WINTER PASSED BY and Andrew was approached by his uncle Malcolm about a job after he had arrived home from work one spring day. He walked in the front door and proceeded to sit on the couch next to Andrew.

"Hey man, they have a new position open at my work. Are you interested?" Malcolm questioned. "I can get you the job!"

"Hell yeah, I need the money bad right now. I need to save for a car," Andrew responded. "What do you do?"

"It's a scale operator position. You basically just weigh shit that comes onto the scale. They will teach you. It's easy," Malcolm said, handing Andrew an application for the scrap yard he worked at. "Fill this out and give it back to me. I'll turn it in."

The conversation ended abruptly as Malcolm hustled up the stairs to shower. He was getting ready for yet another hot date.

Andrew filled it out right away and gave it to him before he left out the front door after his beauty cleanse.

"Actually you know what? Hold onto that. I'm just going to drive you to work with me," Malcolm said. "That way I can show you around."

"Sounds good," Andrew replied.

The two pounded fists and out the door, Malcolm went. Andrew kicked his feet up onto the couch and took a nap. He woke up hours later to Malcolm coming in the door laughing hysterically with a young lady pounding their way loudly up the stairway to heaven on the home's second floor. Malcolm was a lady's man. Tally another woman to the list. Andrew closed his eyes and went back into his slumber.

"Andrew, wake up, it's time to go!" a voice vociferated.

Andrew jumped up and headed straight for the shower and put on his best clothes. He wasn't playing around when it came to this money. Malcolm was already ready when Andrew exited the bathroom upstairs. Malcolm's bedroom was across the hall. The door had a big hole in it from someone's fist during an argument. Andrew knocked and shouted, "I'm ready, let's go!"

"Alright man. They might hire you on the spot. You should grab something to store piss in. You're gonna piss dirty bro. Gotta use mine. It's clean," commented Malcolm.

"OK. I'll grab one of Theo's methadone bottles," revealed Andrew.

"Sounds good. I have hand warmers to keep it body temp. Let's bounce!"

The two pounded down the stairs of the house to the exit. They entered Malcolm's car, started it up, and took off. The car ride was only about 5 minutes. They pulled up to the recycling station and walked into the office to meet Laura. She was a middle-aged blonde lady. Andrew introduced himself and presented his resume. The interview was very informal. She offered him the job on the spot. The only condition was to take a drug test.

Andrew and Malcolm were right on it. They immediately took a short trip down the road to the clinic to do his urine examination.

"Aight man, get out real quick. Give me a minute," said Malcolm.

Andrew stepped out of the car while Malcolm peed in the rinsed methadone bottle. Meanwhile, Andrew admired the parking lot. There was a light dusting of snow on the ground from a late spring snowstorm. It was quite chilly. Malcolm wrapped the bottle with a

The Witch's Hat

hand warmer and secured it with a rubber band. He then hollered for Andrew. Andrew hopped into the car and accepted the container of pee as his own. He would now stuff it into his sock.

"Hopefully this works!" Andrew said nervously as he opened the door to step out of the vehicle.

"Good luck!" Malcolm said with positivity.

Andrew shifted his weight to his feet and slammed the car door. His heart was racing as he walked through the clinic doors. He had never used someone else's pee before.

He checked in at the front desk in a fluttery voice. "My name is Andrew, I have a 9:45 appointment for a U.A." he relayed to the receptionist.

"Someone will be with you shortly," the reception lady said with a sunshine smile.

Andrew turned around and took a seat. He could feel the warmth of the pee bottle on his leg. Minute by minute went by and they still hadn't called his name. Finally, Andrew checked his phone. It was ten after ten. He had been waiting 25 minutes and grew more worrisome about the temperature of the piss bottle. Andrew was interrupted from his thinking by a nurse who called his name and motioned him to the single-stall bathroom near the lobby.

"Please empty your pockets of everything and wash your hands," the aged woman instructed.

"Sounds good," responded Andrew as casually as he could.

After Andrew had emptied both his pockets and washed his hands he was handed a cup. "Fill this to the black line right here," she said pointing to a black line marker. "Also don't run the sink or flush the toilet while you are in there," she added.

Andrew agreed to the stipulations and closed the bathroom door behind him. He reached for his container in his sock and nearly dropped it. He was trying to be as quick and quiet as possible. He didn't want to be found out. What did he have to lose at this point anyway? A job he didn't have? Andrew resumed dumping the lightly tinged yellow urine into the cup. It was only 3/4 of the way to the black line. Oh no, he thought. He really hoped this would be enough.

Andrew waited and counted to ten. He zipped the zipper on his pants down and up in case she was listening. Then he opened the door and handed the piss to the nurse.

"Sorry I couldn't really pee. I only made it to about 3/4's full," Andrew said.

"I think it will do but we have a problem. The temperature isn't in the proper spot. It is too low. I can't accept this test. You will have to reschedule to retake it," said the nurse sternly.

"Ok then… That's ridiculous! What a waste of my time," Andrew retorted. "Bye!"

Andrew stuck up the peace sign and exited the building. He told Malcolm the news and they took off back to the scrapyard where Andrew shared the news as well with Laura.

"It was inconclusive. They couldn't get a proper reading on my test," Andrew informed her.

"I'm not gonna worry about it," she replied in a relaxed tone but with a tad of excitement. "You got the job! I just need your shirt and pant size please."

"Awesome! I'm an extra-large shirt size and a 32/32 for pants," Andrew said feeling mighty.

Andrew began to work the next day and did a great job. He felt like he only had such a good chance of getting the job because Malcolm was well-liked. Andrew didn't want to make Malcolm look bad so he did the best he could. He was still struggling with money at the time and after a few days on the job, Andrew went home to try to scavenge some whiskey money. He couldn't find any.

He went out to find his friends in the projects and that night they went car shopping again. It was the same five people. Niccolo, Sylvester, Marcel, Theo, and Andrew. The friends had actually had the money to pitch in for a bottle so they had the juice to make their night. The group just needed more money and a way out.

The Witch's Hat

They made it past a few cars with no luck. The streets were bare and dimmed so they had easy cover. They finally came to a van that had unlocked doors. To Andrew's surprise, he found the key to the ignition in the cupholder. Boy was he lucky. He started the car and the boys hopped in. They decided to go for a little joy ride. They drove around the city of Murderapolis going through hoods trying to find someone who would trade the van for drugs. No one wanted to touch the car as it was hot.

While Andrew sped down the road, he saw a cop at the stoplight and slammed on his brakes before he passed by. Thankfully the cop didn't pursue. Andrew wasn't taking any chances and wasn't looking to go to jail. He decided to take the rest of the ride easy and made it back to the projects where his night began. He then parked the van in plain sight in the parking lot. He figured it would be just fine. He was excited to have his own ride to work and in the meantime, he took a couple more swigs of the bottle then called it a night. He did his handshakes and fist bumps with the boys then went on his way back home.

The next day after Andrew got ready for work he took the two-block walk to get the stolen car but to his surprise, it wasn't there. It was 11 o'clock in the morning and Malcolm had started work at 8 so now Andrew had to walk. The lady on the driver's license in the car must have searched for it or called the cops to do the work for her. They found it and now Andrew was bummed. He was just glad that he didn't suffer any repercussions for his guilty actions.

Andrew ended up walking the railroad tracks to get to work. He had to climb over a halted train in a docking yard. Up ahead a train was just departing and was chugging slowly down the needed track. Andrew waited and waved at the engineer. After the train had passed Andrew did his best to wobble through the rocks along the rails. He frequently tried to balance on the rails themselves to get a level footed hold. But this was all a game. After Andrew navigated his way to work he got right to it. He hopped into the little scale operator cubicle and relieved one of the workers to go home. He did his 6 hours and called it a day.

Andrew continued this routine for about a week. He still hadn't received his first paycheck. In the time being, he ended up getting connected and making relationships with the scrappers. He gained trust with them and devised a plan that would benefit both parties. He rigged the scales to pay them substantially more than what they should have gotten. Andrew agreed upon a 50/50 split among 4 frequently flying customers. If the scrapper made $200 extra, Andrew would get $100. With all the clients in cahoots coming through multiple times a day, the money flowed. They did handshakes to say farewell. During this moment they would transfer the stolen bills. There were even times when the customers wrapped the cash in a napkin and dropped it in the trash. This was sloppy. Andrew tried to be as inconspicuous as possible to collect it. He adopted the mentality of Hakuna Matata. He let his worries go. It didn't bother him to steal from a business that made millions in scrap metal. They could afford it.

Andrew's supervisor was fired by the owner due to fraud and was replaced with a new one. His old manager knew of his deeds but kept her mouth shut. The new manager's name was Bella. She was a nut about everything being done spectacularly. Andrew wasn't so worried because she had a major crush on him. She took heat from up above about the crunched numbers and the need for improvement but Andrew kept to his own business.

Andrew continued being a fraudulent scale operator for the remainder of his time employed with them. Now that Andrew was making 500 plus dollars a day on the side, he had money to party. It's hard to understand why he pursued so much partying. It didn't benefit him much but made him feel good. Andrew bumped into a friend of a friend he would kick back with and he brought his older brother over whose name was also Journey. The same name as the beautiful angel he ran into months prior. This was interesting.

Anyhow, Andrew connected with Journey and learned quickly he was a drug abuser as well. It was pretty welcomed among the group of friends although not everyone participated. Andrew was ready to get back into the drug scene. The marijuana wasn't doing it for him anymore and on this particular occasion this guy whipped out a small baggie with what looked like broken glass in it.

"What's that?" Andrew asked. "Is that meth?"

"Yeah, we refer to it as shit," Journey responded.

So now Andrew was reintroduced back to this substance called "shit" but this time it got out of control. All that gangster music was getting into Andrew's head. He wanted to be a flashy boss man who was treated with mad respect. This was Andrew's fantasy and his ego got the best of him.

He was spending roughly $100 a day supporting both himself and Theo's drug use; cheeba, meth, and then of course Andrew's alcohol fuel. Andrew was supporting the habits of everyone. It gave him a feeling of power. He was still able to save a lot of money on the side as well.

Andrew stayed up for days at a time and wore himself out. His mind was drained and he was barely present. Months went by at his job and he was able to save up enough to get a loan for a van. He planned out his own scheme to fill up the van with a small amount of scrap metal and rigged it to where the other scale operator paid Andrew for more precious metals like stainless steel 316 instead of the cheaper metals he brought in. This was another nifty inside job that added to Andrew's income.

More days passed. Andrew felt light-footed after injecting his daily dose of shards. It gave him a feeling of invincibility. He felt like a superhero with extra strength. He got a little careless with his job but still maintained himself enough to not get fired.

Just about every night or two when Andrew got home from work in the evening he would call up his new dealer Journey. Frequently Andrew would accidentally call the beautiful woman with the same name. She would answer the phone so excitedly. Andrew would apologize and end the call to take away her happiness. She developed a thing for him but Andrew was too far gone to realize it. Plus, he was unsure if she still had a boyfriend or not. He continued to call her and she would always get let down. It was a voltaic crossroads of which journey to take.

Andrew decided to stick with the choice of his new dealer Journey as he had gotten ripped off by meth-head hustlers. He was sold table salt and had injected that instead of the real stuff. Andrew tasted it after he had shot it up. It was not good. In years prior Andrew and Theo were doing the soapy-smelling injections of bath salts and it opened Theo up to his obsession with time travelers. The stuff was so strong it got Nadine high in the past just by sweating next to her in the same bed. The stuff was crazy and so was the meth, the current drug of choice.

The day finally came when after a 4-day binge on this so-called "shit" that Andrew made a huge mistake at work. Uncle Malcolm got a new job as a flight attendant and moved to L.A. He was going to pursue his dream of becoming a pilot. In the meantime, Andrew was dancing alone with the wolves. He was a walking zombie that day.

On this occasion, an unfamiliar scrapper had to weigh up a car whose fate was to be junked. Andrew grabbed the VIN scanner to scan the barcode on the car. He scanned it and noticed a bunch of garbage in the back seat. He set down the VIN scanner on the front passenger seat and moved a black garbage bag to see a group of 3 rubber tires. The man poked Andrew from behind.

"How much am I going to get for this?" the guy asked.

"Well, first off it all depends on if you have a title. You get paid more with a title. Second of all, you will get docked for all the garbage in the back seat unless you take it out," Andrew replied to the man impatiently.

"How much do you estimate without the title?" questioned the scrapper.

"Well, I'd say between $120 and $160 depending on if you take the garbage out or not," Andrew replied as he leaned against the open car door.

"Fuck that, I'm going somewhere else!" said the man.

"Ok, that's fine!" Andrew said, slamming the car door.

The man hopped in the pickup and went on his way. Andrew retreated back to his cubicle to erase the captured weight and collect the new one from another tow truck driver. After he did so, he went to

The Witch's Hat

grab the scanner which was nowhere to be found. He had left it in the junk car! The device was worth roughly 1 to 2 grand. With Andrew's poor job performance in recent times, along with adding to a loss of a piece of equipment, he was unsure if he would have a job. It didn't matter if the manager had a crush on him. It didn't mean he would get any special treatment from the owner. When Andrew finished up for the day, he deeply apologized to Bella before taking the train tracks home.

Andrew returned to work the next day. After about 5 minutes on the clock, he was called to the side by Bella. She took him outside and gave him the horrible news.

"This was none of my choosing and it's really hard for me to say, but I talked to the boss about getting a new VIN scanner to replace the old one and he was super pissed. I'm very sad that he told me to end your employment with us. As of this point, you are no longer an employee. I'm so sorry," Bella said unwillingly.

"Seriously! That's bullshit! It was an accident!" Andrew said in a manic state. "Whatever, I'm outta here!" He turned away from the scaling office and started walking away. Bella followed.

"Don't forget your walkie. I can put it away. If there is anything I can do to help let me know."

Andrew reached from his side and handed her the radio. "You could have helped by not fuckin firing me. Fuck this place! Peace out!" Andrew said in revolt.

He stuck up both middle fingers at the building and began his footslog back home amongst the tracks.

CHAPTER 26
Desperate Tweakers

It was nearing the beginning of fall and Andrew was jobless yet again. All his money was depleted into drugs. It was back to raking yards again. This time there was no car shopping. He and Theo were so twacked that it wasn't a big deal raking leaves for a few hours a day. The other remainder of the days was spent cruising in the van and scoring "shit". Andrew felt no need to pay for gas. On multiple instances he would swap out the plates on his vehicle from some he stole at an apartment complex nearby. He would fill her up at a gas station and simply drive off. Without the correct plate numbers, they had no way of tracking him. This helped as raking leaves wasn't raking in the money. He had to find another way to come about it.

On one speed-ridden night on the gak, Andrew noticed his grandpa put away one of his golden coins into his safe. To do so he had to open up a locked wooden cabinet with a key which opened to the sound of more jangling keys oscillating from hooks screwed into the inside of the door. The key to open the safe was among them. He took the key from within and inserted it into the orifice of the metal security box and turned. Bam! There on the top shelf was a stack of bills maybe 10 inches thick wrapped with a rubber band.

Among other things in the cabinet were mint antique coins along

The Witch's Hat

with medications. This was the holy grail! Andrew took note of this. He had to devise a way to get into this thingamajig to manage to slither out a couple of hundred dollar bills. He was gonna do it! Whether it meant pulling the wooden cabinet out from the wall and sawing a hole into the back to reach the key, he was going to get in.

Andrew mentioned the large sum of money he had spotted in the safe to Theo. "We can get into it. I know we can," said Andrew.

Theo laughed. "Yeah right! There's no way of getting into that thing."

Andrew was dead serious. He craved more and more. The fact that they were injecting the "shit" made it worse. Work was getting slow. They were clearly running out of people to rake for and Andrew didn't want to travel far to solicit door to door.

"We are getting into it one way or another," Andrew declared. "Grandpa will be going to bed in a lil bit and we can go downstairs to check it out."

"Ok broskie," replied Theo.

It was an hour to midnight when grandpa walked upstairs to the main floor. He entered the living room where the two seemingly brothers were chillaxing on the couch.

"Go to bed deadheads!" Gramps shouted as he rounded the home's interior and continued his way up the next stairwell.

"Goodnight!" Andrew shouted back.

Andrew listened to the creaking of the stairs groan back and forth as his grandpa pitter-pattered up them. Once he made it to the top you could hear hollow footsteps along the hardwood floor to the bedroom and then the screech of the bedroom door opening. His grandfather shuffled into the sleeping pad and then another squeal was heard as the door closed and latched itself.

Andrew along with Theo sat in silence. They could hear the twangs of the box spring as grandpa climbed into bed. They waited about ten seconds to be sure that there wasn't any more movement happening up above them. When they heard nothing, they felt safe enough to proceed down into the basement.

Theo and Andrew looked at each other. "How are we gonna get into this thing bro bro?" Andrew asked.

"I don't know man. It's your idea. You figure it out," Theo answered in a nervous manner.

Andrew took a closer look at everything. He looked at the back of the cabinet which was nestled against the side of the stairway. The angle at which the stairs went upward left part of the wooden cabinet exposed. Andrew thought about getting the buzz saw and going to town on the back of it. Although he couldn't because he realized that it would be too hard to hide the hole he left behind. The whole point was to achieve the money from the safe by leaving as little evidence as possible. That wouldn't be possible with a saw-toothed hole in it and not to mention the racket the saw would cause.

He took a few more minutes to completely study the situation. He noticed the cabinet hinges were on the exterior and resembled that of a regular door. From what he could remember as a kid working with his father was that you can pull the pin up and out of the tunnel of the hinge to literally remove the door. Andrew wondered if it was the same case with this as well.

Andrew went under the stairway to the toolbox. He came out with a pair of pliers. "I have an idea. Let's see if this works," he said to Theo who stood behind watching.

Andrew gripped the tip of the pinhead of the lower of the two hinges and pulled upwards. To his surprise, it moved about half an inch up. The pin was about 4 inches long so he had a ways yet to go. He repositioned the pliers to get a better grip and pulled again firmly. This time the pin came all the way out. The door stood still in place. He had one more to go.

"Looks like we might be in luck!" Andrew said as he stood up and worked at the top hinge. The pin came out like butter. The door didn't fall open or anything, it just sat there unanchored. Andrew tried wiggling the door by its handle and it came loose but not loose enough. He was afraid if he jostled it any more then he would bend something out of place. He pulled his attention back to the needle-nose pliers. He

The Witch's Hat

grabbed the hinge knuckles connected to the door up top and pulled the pliers towards his chest. This action separated the hinge leaves on the top portion but resulted in the bottom caving in a little bit. Andrew repeated the same step to the bottom hinge of the door and mission success. The right corner of the door fell and rested on the ground. Now the door could be swung open using the padlock as its makeshift hinge from the opposite side. Andrew felt like a genius for a brief moment but knew he wasn't in the clear yet.

He swung open the wooden door and scrambled to look for the safe key amidst the dangling mess. He glanced at what the safe keyhole looked like and saw that the shape of the key was cross-shaped. He fixed his eyes back on the closet of keys and was able to easily spot the only key in that particular shape. It rested behind another set of keys which he then removed to set on top of the cabinet. Next, he wiggled the key he needed from the hook and immediately placed it into the safe with a perfectly snug fit. This was yet another battle won.

He couldn't turn the key quick enough. The door swung open to stacks of coin books, jars of wheat pennies, bonds, and of course the stack of cash that Andrew had fixated on earlier that day. Andrew took note on how everything was placed then reached in for the band of cash.

"Question is, how much do we take?" Andrew inquired.

"Well, I wouldn't take too much. We don't want to get caught!" Theo replied.

Andrew guesstimated that there had to be well over $100,000 in the palm of his hands. He had never been in possession of so much money at once and never would have if his grandpa had believed in banks. This was his retirement fund so Andrew didn't want to go overboard. He managed to slip 3 bills through and out of the giant rubber bands for a total of $300 which he then stashed into his wallet.

"You want $100?" asked Andrew.

"No, I'm good," Theo said. He seemed reluctant in taking any money. He probably felt guilty. What Andrew was doing was wrong.

He let his jittery mind take control over his actions. This was not a proud moment for him.

Andrew put the stack of cash in the exact same spot or close to it. He had it faced with the long stretch of the bills perpendicular to him just as the way he had found it. He locked the safe and put the key back on the hook in the wooden cabinet. He also made sure to put the keys from on top of the cabinetry on the hook as well. Now it was on to the tricky part of lining up the knuckles of the hinge leaves to place the pins back.

Andrew struggled with lining up the knuckles and his anxiety took control. Was he even going to finish the final step before the morning came? He needed to keep a cool mind and complete the task so he wiggled the door back and forth until it was lined up evenly. He then grabbed the pins and pounded them in with the pliers making a couple minor adjustments. He was immersed with the feeling of relief once they were situated. Now the wait to see if he was found out the next day. He felt bad but was eased with a notion of accomplishment at the same time.

The two white boys made their run to Walmart to rack up some shards from their dealer which kept them up the rest of the night. When the morning came they heard nothing about the shenanigans from the night before. They had succeeded.

The heist they had partaken in had become a habit and they had developed a process. Every time they ran out of money they would go into grandpa's retirement stash. Theo lost his feelings of guilt and in turn, greed took control. The two bought new phones and Theo bought himself some clothes. It was getting out of control. A few months went by and there was never a day where they didn't have any dope. Andrew was in tweak mode. He went on a rampage cleaning his grandparents' house. He figured he would do something nice for them since they provided him shelter while he rid himself of the wrongfulness he held inside.

By this time they had shaved off about 2 inches of the 10-inch stack of hundreds. They had gone a little overboard and were getting lazy due to the free money. They didn't have to rake leaves anymore and could enjoy life. Andrew had estimated that they had taken about $20,000. Andrew pointed out that the stack was looking a little low so they switched over to taking coins to pawn. That worked for a while until the day they needed the quick cash and decided to pull from the stack of hundreds again. They put the stack away and eventually got to the point where they laid down on the couch for the night and rested their aching bones from days of no sleep or rest.

The next morning they heard a shriek from the basement. Gramps had woken up and noticed his items missing from the safe.

"Theo!!!!" Grandpa yelled. "Theo, God damnit!!"

Theo rolled in his slumber on the main floor couch. Grandpa came up the stairs with tears in his eyes. "Someone broke into my safe! My money is missing! THEO! WAKE UP!"

Theo had crashed from the binge and managed to peep his eyes open. Meanwhile, Andrew was sitting on the love seat watching the history channel. He heard everything that was going on but pretended not to.

"Damnit, Theo! Did you break into my safe?" Wallace cried out. His voice was rough but defeated. His eyes were red and his cheeks were wet. How could someone do this to him?

"I didn't break into that stupid safe," Theo groaned angrily. He knew they had been caught.

Andrew's grandpa yelled, aiming his anger at Theo again. Andrew was his grandson and it may be that for that reason Wallace cherished him. Maybe he didn't want to ruin their relationship so he disconnected. Plus it was easier to yell at his son who he'd been living with for years. Little did Grandpa know that it was Andrew's idea to break into it. Andrew deserved some kind of karmic retaliation. His dumb luck would run out sooner or later and he would pay for his deeds. Even through all this heartbreaking theft, Grandpa Wallace never had the heart to kick Andrew out of his house. He knew Andrew had nowhere to go.

CHAPTER 27
Home Invasion

GRANDPA PAINTED THE pins in the cabinet hinges white so it would scrape off if tampered with so Theo and Andrew were back to the struggle with money. It was coming up to winter in early November and the snow was starting to flow in. The two of them spent their days shoveling again. They would hit up the regulars whenever it trickled down from the sky. They sometimes would wait until the snowfall was complete, however, sometimes the person who hired them would let them do it twice for twice the money. They had made friendly connections with the whole neighborhood. They may have looked like crackheads but the neighbors themselves had no reason not to trust them. They were shown love.

Ultimately one day they took the time to wait until the snow slowed down from falling from the sky prior to making their rounds. It was close to 5 p.m. and it had grown pretty dark outside. They beat at the door of a few houses, shoveled, and then collected their money. They each got about twenty bucks per house. After finishing up a tidy job at a fellow neighbor's they went on to their next customer. They began

The Witch's Hat

the climb up a long stairway. It seemed like approximately 50 stairs. When they got to the top Andrew saw a few abandoned newspapers sitting below the home's stoop which was roughly covered in about an inch of snow.

They proceeded into the foyer and freely rang the buzzer with no answer. Next off, Theo knocked. Still, there wasn't an answer. Andrew put two and two together. If there were three bundles of papers sitting in front of the house, wouldn't that mean that the inhabitants weren't home? It was getting cold out. Maybe they had left out of town on a vacation or perhaps visiting family in another state.

This gave Andrew another faulty idea. His mind took control and bad thoughts flooded in. He was desperate. He was pondering being an idiot traitor to these neighbors. He was devising a plan to make trips to the pawnshop or to sell their things online. He had made up his mind. He was definitely going to break into this house. What a terrible mistake.

"Hey, Theo," Andrew whispered. "I have an idea."

"What's that?" Theo replied.

"It looks like these guys are out of town. I think I can find a way in," Andrew said. "Anything in this house could be ours…"

"I'm good on that man. I'm not trying to get caught up," Theo responded.

"C'mon! I'll drive the van into the back driveway. All we have to do is load it up. It's dark out here. I'm sure no one will even notice," Andrew retorted.

"Fuck it. I guess," Theo said reluctantly. "Let's go home quick and warm up. We can come back in a few hours."

"Sounds good! Let's head back then," agreed Andrew.

The two grabbed their shovels and proceeded down the alleyway across the street from the heist location. It led directly back home. They tramped through the light snow with just their shoes. To think upon, it was remarkable that they had never bought boots with all the money they had had. They were used to soggy feet.

Eventually, they made it back to headquarters and sat on the couch to warm up. They had a space heater blowing towards them to whisk away the chills within their body. Grandpa had made food so Andrew helped himself to a few servings. Gramps always made healthy food which may not have been the most appetizing but Andrew scarfed it down anyway. It wasn't all that bad. He just wasn't used to eating so many veggies. Theo withheld from the food as usual. He didn't like it. He survived off of candy, pop, and fast food.

Meanwhile, after Andrew finished his plate and put it into the kitchen sink, he returned to the living room with Theo. Time passed and it was around 9:30 p.m. "Looks like it has been a few hours. Are you ready to go?" Andrew asked with a mountain of energy. He had just done a shot of meth a few minutes prior and was hyped up. Theo did a dose as well. They were ready to go as most of their fear and panic had subsided. They were high out of their gourds.

"Let me get my black sweatshirt and pants on quick. Then I'll be ready," Theo said.

He walked to his closet by the front door and grabbed his clothes and swapped them out. In the meantime, Andrew went upstairs to get on his own black jeans and sweatshirt. They would soon be prepared for the crime but they had no blueprint. The plan was to go with the flow and keep a mellow mindset. That was Andrew's goal at least. Theo was still a tad bit nervous.

Once they were set, they left out the front door and into the tundra. They hustled their way down the driveway in back of the grandparents' house which connected to the alley. Andrew's minivan sat there covered in glittering snow. He opened the car door to grab his snow brush and slammed it shut again. He watched the snowfall to the ground from the sides of the vehicle. Next, he grabbed his brush and waved it around like a sorcerer brushing the remainder of the snow off. The car was mostly snow-free by this point so they hopped in to resume the mission.

Andrew started the car and backed out of the driveway. He pulled forward and went up the alley to take a right at the first intersecting street. They went about a fourth of the way around the circumference

The Witch's Hat

of the oval block then turned left down another alleyway. The alley went up at an incline to the top of a hill where the marked house rested. Andrew curved the car to the right and then put it in reverse to back into the powdery driveway. He looked around to make sure there were no witnesses. Neither of the two had on masks so if a neighbor spotted them they would be outed. Luckily the streets looked as if they were dead. Everyone was inside. The crank gave Andrew a keen sense of a lifted awareness. He didn't hesitate to get out of his car. Once done, he took another look around before beginning his walk towards the home.

Their shoes left snow prints so they had to be careful as they were committing a felony. It wouldn't be smart to leave tracks leading back to where they stayed. Even fresh tire tracks could give away the heist. Andrew didn't even bother checking to see if the doors were open. He had to be quick. Who would go out of town without locking their doors anyway?

After shortly examining the windows, Andrew realized the ones on the main floor started at about the height of his head. He didn't have a ladder nor the ambition to lift himself up that high. He glanced down and noticed a window within a window well below his feet. This was perfect. Andrew took another look around. Theo was standing a few feet away unsure of what to do. Andrew didn't spot anyone in the vicinity who could be watching so he quickly swung his foot and kicked in the window. He used his soggy shoe to swipe away all the glass shards pointing out like jagged knives from the edges.

Once he cleared out the majority of the glass he maneuvered his legs through the window up to his waist with his belly down. He then used his gloved hands and slid his stomach along the bottom of the window. Luckily he had a jacket on so none of the glass cut him. His feet came about a few inches from the ground inside the basement. He let go of his grip from the window frame and dropped the short distance to the floor. He looked around and saw 3 fancy bikes. There were two Trek bikes and one by the name of Pinarello. He had a little knowledge of Trek bikes and knew they were worth thousands of dollars. He came along a small gold mine.

He quickly grabbed one of the specialized Trek bikes and carried it up the flight of about 14 steps to the ground level floor. At the top landing, there was a door going outside of the house. He unlocked and walked out the door then turned to the right to roll the bike down the snow-covered sidewalk to the van in the backyard driveway. He had the seats taken out of the van so there was plenty of room for storage.

He found Theo outside and gave him the bike to stash into the car. He seemed very squirrelly.

"Hurry up man! We need to go!" Theo griped.

"Dude, chill out! Everything is fine. There are still two more bikes inside. They are worth a lot of money," Andrew said speedily. But Theo was right. They needed to be quick.

Andrew turned back to the house and made two more trips with the bikes in hand. Theo did the same routine for each and barely got all three to fit in the vehicle. Andrew went back inside to rummage some more. Meanwhile, Theo was outside on the lookout. They would be screwed if the police showed up. The alleyway was a dead end and the house they were at was at the end of it. They were trapped if anything happened. Would they run on foot? That wouldn't be a smart idea because they would trace Andrew's van back to his home and arrest him. There was no need to worry, Andrew told himself. The drugs made him feel invincible. He did a great job keeping a positive frame of mind, Hakuna Matata is what replayed in his head.

Andrew had noticed a medium flat screen T.V. in the living room which he managed to get his hands on. He almost tripped on the step of the doorway leading outside. He caught himself and handed the television set to Theo. Then again, Andrew did another hike back inside. This time he went to the second floor. He opened all the drawers in the master bedroom and dumped everything on the bed. He saw a backpack on the floor near the closet and started loading her up. He grabbed jewelry, keys and anything he thought was of worth. After he dumped out all the dresser drawers minus the ones with clothes he moved on to the closet.

The closet withheld a bunch of plastic bins on a shelf about a foot and a half from the ceiling. It was basically a wooden board spread across the width of the closet above. Andrew reached up for the bins and set one on the bed. He opened it and it revealed a bunch of coins. He quickly examined a few and saw they were from all over the world. Andrew didn't bother with sorting through the bin. He just dumped the whole contents into the backpack. He was on a come-up. He imagined all the money he was gonna make and had to snap out of his trance.

Andrew had figured he had had enough. He grabbed the backpack full of goodies and then proceeded down the stairs and out the door. "Alright, I'm done. Time to go," Andrew said in a low monotone voice to try to keep quiet.

Theo didn't hesitate to hop in the car. Andrew went to the back sliding door of the van and plopped the backpack beside the bikes. He jumped into the captain's seat then put the van in drive to pull out. They proceeded down the alley hill to the street. Once they got to the street, Andrew drove around the neighborhood a few times to make sure his tire tracks would be scrambled up along the road. This would make it more difficult to track back to his grandparents' house as the snow trail could be your downfall if you aren't smart about it.

Once Andrew circled around a few times he pulled onto the block leading to his mother's parents. They pulled into the driveway and parked. "We better bring this stuff inside in case someone looks into the van," Andrew said cautiously to Theo.

"Aight then, let's do it."

They both loaded the stuff into the house and up to Andrew's bedroom upstairs. The bikes were a little tough getting up the stairway but they managed to pull through. After they had crammed all the stuff into the tiny room, Theo and Andrew went to the bathroom to inject yet another fix. Afterward, they went down to the main floor family room to chill.

CHAPTER 28
Sloppy Seconds

Moments later during the same night, Andrew's balls started to burn. He had to come down from his high because it was apparent that he had a case of meth balls. His mind recollected that he had a bottle of Xanax that he had received from his mother due to his "crippling anxiety". This was her way of helping Andrew while still playing doctor. He couldn't blame her for what was about to take place.

The goal was to calm his nerves and relax. He had been up for three days with Theo by this point and was starting to feel a little edgy. Andrew was an idiot and was always pushing the level at which he could fry his brain cells by flying high. He dumped twenty 1 mg football-shaped Xanax into his hand and swiftly dropped them all onto his tongue. He dowsed the pills down his throat with a beer with a tilt-back of the head. A couple of them got lodged in his throat so he took another swig to wash them down.

After about 3 beers Andrew was getting antsy. Was there anything else in the neighbor's house to steal? He didn't want to miss a chance at more free stuff so he decided to call his dealer, Journey. He was a criminal as well. After a dumb mistaken first call to Miss Journey,

The Witch's Hat

he quickly apologized and hung her up to dry. He hadn't touched a woman in about a year and had no intention to. Sure he wanted a woman but he was too preoccupied. She could have been his savior but the timing hadn't been realized. After his rude erroneous call, he hit the end button on his cell phone and dialed up the other Journey. He answered and Andrew went on to share his tip-off about the vacant house and mentioned there might be more to plunder.

"I can come pick you up," Andrew told him. "I already took a bunch of shit. You can check it out and see if you want anything for yourself."

Journey agreed to the arrangement and Andrew left to go get him. It was about two in the morning and the Xanax was still fresh in his stomach. He traveled to the opposite side of the city to fetch Journey along with his meth head friend. On the way home, Andrew started feeling a little drowsy. He continued driving as the veils began closing over his eyes. The feeling didn't become more prominent until he got back home. Once they arrived, they went inside to huddle and smoke some crystal. Andrew woke up a tiny bit but he felt like he was losing control.

The group of four devised a plan which wasn't really a plan. They would plainly show up and rob the neighbor blind again. This time Andrew pulled up to the larceny location and decided to wait in the car with Theo. At the present moment, he felt like he had taken enough. He let the two visitors indulge in what they pleased. Why was Andrew being so nice? What was the point of calling someone to take the leftovers of a house he had already robbed? He only did this out of kindness and the satisfaction of seeming cool. He was called "white boy" a lot but he wanted to be a gangster. This was his way of proving that he was an outlaw.

Andrew waited and waited for the two hoodlums to return from the unattended house. About ten minutes went by and still nothing. There's no way it should've taken this long. Where had they gone? Andrew decided to go inside the home and snoop for them. He peered into the cellar from the side entrance of the home and saw no one. He then took off on a sprint around a loop from the main floor and up to the second. He rapidly searched every room in the abode and yet again, nobody was found. Andrew's stomach cringed. He had a very bad feeling. He raced outside to his car, started her up, and hit the road. The streets contained enough tire tracks by this point that he wasn't too worried about being traced so he zoomed straight to his grandparents with Theo riding shotgun.

When they got there Andrew pulled the van up along the side of the road and quickly parked. He raced inside. The lights were on like usual. Andrew took a quick look around and noticed things missing out of the house. He searched for his laptop which he had booted from the U of M. It was gone. He went downstairs and Topher's laptop and Nintendo DS were missing along with the flat screen T.V. What else was taken? Andrew grew infuriated. He was trying to help someone out and was betrayed, just as he had done to the neighbors. Karma was a bitch.

Andrew pulled out his phone and sent one final text message to his mother. "I'm gonna kill these motherfuckers," is what he thumbed. Next, he ran up the stairs 3 steps at a time and then wrapped around the home to the front door. Through the window on the door, Andrew noticed the two meth head robbers walking up the walkway to come inside for more loot. Andrew was so drowsy by this point that he was barely coherent. He was in the spirit world and it was a bad trip.

Andrew opened the door and was face to face with Journey and his tweaker friend. "What the fuck is going on? Why aren't you at the house down the block? I'm not fuckin stupid."

Journey was silent. His friend reached to his waist which withheld a butcher knife. He put his hand on it and looked Andrew square in the eyes. "We need a ride, NOW!" he pressed.

Andrew's face was red with anger. He was so mad that he was shaking as his nerves were on edge. He really did want to put an end to these guys' lives but he was too much of a coward. He knew he had been beaten. Everything was in slow motion. He felt like his speech was even dragged. There was nothing to do but drive the two home. They must have thought Andrew was dumb. For sure, and he was.

The Witch's Hat

Andrew went inside and grabbed Theo. "They are outside right now. The assholes robbed us. Let's kick their ass. The one has got a knife," he informed. His mind was bouncing back and forth.

"Let's do it!" said Theo. Then he had a moment of hesitation. "Actually I'm good. I'm not trying to get stabbed by a crackhead today," he chimed. He didn't have anything of value which was stolen so it didn't matter to him.

Andrew came back with a delayed comment. "Well, I guess our only option is to drive them home. I don't know what else to do," he said with his eyes barely open. Andrew had gone way overboard on the drugs today and it really fucked up his game. He wasn't a violent person at all but hated, just like anyone else, to be taken advantage of. Following their discussion, the two decided to wrongly swallow their lost pride and head outside.

They met the piece of shit "homies" outdoors and they all strode to the car. Andrew started it up and went on his way to drive them home. He was curious as to where they had stashed all his family's belongings. Maybe if he got back soon enough he could search around the outside of the house. Perhaps they had already had one of their crackhead friends pull up in their hooptie and swoop it away already. It could have all been long gone.

Amongst the worries in Andrew's head was the fact that Journey's sketchy friend had a knife ready to be pulled at any time. What if he were to extend it from the back of the seatless car to Andrew's throat? This would put Andrew in a position of getting his car stolen and tossed out to the side of the road. He wouldn't have even known what hit him. He was on the brink of numbness as he zoned in and out. He hopped on the freeway system to get to their destination and felt like he was in a living dream. It was not a very clear dream either. Maybe some folks would even consider it a mild nightmare. Overall within his stupor, he remarkably arrived at the drop-off spot.

After Journey and his friend exited the car, Andrew should have pulled over and parked on the side of the road to take a nap. Instead, he continued to back out of Journey's driveway and hit the road again. His eyes were shutting for longer and longer periods of time. He wasn't in control anymore. At one point when he woke up from his drug-induced insensibility he realized he was swerving off of the freeway. He straightened himself out but his consciousness was like a strobe light. He exited the freeway ramp near the U of M from highway 280 and was almost to his grandparents.

It was now early morning and the sun was just peeking its head as Andrew crossed University Avenue then took his first right onto Franklin. By this point, he was just about paralyzed. It was almost like he let Jesus take the wheel. But God wouldn't allow a good outcome today. The Hindu God of Vishnu pushed Andrew's imaginary monotheistic God out of the way and enforced his dose of evil karma upon Andrew to even the score. Maybe Andrew's uncertainty in the belief in God had its repercussions.

Anyway, Andrew passed out in the driver's seat. The van veered into oncoming traffic. It crossed the width of the road, then hit and jumped the curb. While the van was in mid-air it collided with a street lamp. He trampled over the street light and it seemed like the car did a 50-50 skateboard grind along the length of the light post until it hit the part where the light fixture was. The car deflected itself from the fixture and turned to the right towards the street, plowed through a snowbank, and hit a street sign where the van came to a complete stop.

A lady was walking down the street and had witnessed the whole thing. She scrambled for her cell phone and called 9-1-1. Theo, being awake, decided to flee the scene. He grabbed the meth from the center console and took off. In the meantime, Andrew's head rested on the steering wheel. He felt the impact of the crash so he must have been partly aware of what was going on. He lifted his head from the steering wheel after about 30 seconds. Everything truly seemed so foggy to him. In the distance, he could see Theo running back home. Andrew sat and rested in the seat totally in shock. He wobbled out of the car and looked at the scene he had created. A few moments later a police woman showed up from the U of M campus. They must not have been too far away. Andrew knew he was screwed. He should have run and just reported the car stolen. He could have even set up Journey to

The Witch's Hat

get charged to get his share of karma. That would have required some thinking which Andrew wasn't doing much at the moment.

The fat lady in uniform got out of her cruiser and began walking over to Andrew to question him. "What happened?" she shouted as she was crossing the street.

"I crashed my car," Andrew said with his eyes half-open.

"Are you high or something?" she asked.

"No," Andrew said in a slow slurred voice.

"I can obviously tell you are high. I'm going to have to take you in. I'll need you to put your hands behind your back," she said sternly.

It sounded like she was speaking a different language as she cuffed Andrew and grabbed him by his arm. She didn't even bother giving him a sobriety test. Instead, she pulled him across the street to her vehicle. She opened the door and directed Andrew into the machine.

"Watch your head," she muttered as Andrew slid himself into place.

She closed the door and they took off to the hospital to get his vitals checked as well as a blood test to search for drug use. Upon arrival, they cuffed him to the bed and hooked up little stickers to his body with wires leading to a machine. The machine was used to monitor him. He also had an I.V. pumping him full of fluids. Andrew was waking up a little but still fairly drowsy.

It wasn't long before the police lady entered the room with a nurse. "We have to get blood work from you," she told Andrew.

"Why? Fuck that! I'm not doing blood work! My blood is none of your business!" reamed Andrew angrily.

"This is required from you. If you don't do the blood test you will get charged with refusal," said the officer.

"That's fine! You're not getting my blood! I'm not taking a piss test either! This is bullshit!" Andrew shouted.

"Well, you're not leaving here until you get your blood drawn," the lady enforced.

"Well, looks like we will be waiting a long time then," Andrew replied.

The officer lady disappeared for a couple hours and came back with the doctor. "OK, time for your blood draw," the pig asserted.

"No! Step towards me and I will freak out!" Andrew insisted.

The lady gave up and left the room with the doc and Andrew overheard her lingering outside of the bedroom quarters talking about him. "Looks like we have a refusal. I'm going to bring him downtown to book him," she informed the doctor beside her.

"Do what needs to be done," the doctor replied. "The patient's vitals seem fine so he should be good to go."

"Thanks doc, I appreciate your help!" the cop lady voiced as she turned to reenter the room to retrieve Andrew. Andrew knew her goal wasn't to bring him to the hospital to see if he was all right. Her plan was to get him to fail a drug test. Andrew wouldn't let it happen. She looked at him and said, "Are you ready for the big house?"

Andrew turned away and ignored her as she uncuffed him from the rail of the bed. The two left the room and meandered through the halls to a secret garage that held all the squad cars. They got in one then departed into the streets of Minneapolis. A few moments later they arrived at another garage. This one was connected to the jail. Andrew was still in a daze at this point and would have no way to recall certain details.

What he could remember however was being questioned and having to do a strip search upon entry. He took off all his clothes and bent over to cough, which was humiliating. They took all his belongings including his cell phone. He now had to rely on the jail phones which charged collect. He didn't know of too many people who would accept that charge.

Afterward, he was placed into a holding tank for a long period of time before they called him up for his mugshot. With how angry Andrew was he sure did his best to remain chipper. He took his mugshot with a smile on his face.

"Sir, you can't do that. You aren't allowed to smile!" the armed photographer said. He snapped the next photo in which Andrew held an expressionless face. Next, he proceeded to sit on the bench

The Witch's Hat

to await the next step. One of the officers who was behind the desk nearby recognized Andrew's last name. He got up from his seat and approached him. "Hey, are you at all related to Josh?" he asked kindly.

"Yes, he was my brother," Andrew announced back to him.

"I'm sorry about what happened man. You seem like a nice guy. You don't seem like you belong here," the public servant said as he walked Andrew to the fingerprinting station. The next officer took each finger individually and rolled it back and forth on the scanner to get a nice full print to upload into the database. The friendly officer bid Andrew a nice day and turned around to go back to his station. The man continued to roll Andrew's fingers on the scanner. He got a little angry as Andrew's fingers were a little resistant and smudgy from sweaty palms.

"Please allow me to control your fingers," the man said in an irritated voice.

"Okay, sorry," Andrew came back. He was kinda excited to be going to jail. But on the downside, his record was looking like it was going to be tarnished forever. Andrew seemed to do a good job masking his frustration from the previous night and was actually doing alright.

Once the man finished scanning Andrew's fingers he placed him back into the holding tank. Andrew waited about 45 minutes while the room filled up with about 4 more people. They looked rough. Three of the four were of African descent. It was already looking unproportional. Of the 5 people in the room, there were 60% that were black. The total number of African Americans in the United States is approximately 13.4%. The number of blacks behind bars at this time was at least 34% of the prison population. Given he wasn't in prison, it still seemed as if things were looking a little sketchy.

Since the waiting time was over, a pair of guards unlocked the door to the holding cell and then escorted the group through a maze of locked doors and then up an elevator to another room. They entered a room full of about 15 more people and were locked into the decent size enclosure.

The room was full of several bunk beds. Maybe twenty. Think of it as a 6 car garage with bunks all along the walls with tables to eat in the inner area. It was a dirty place. It probably wasn't disinfected too much throughout the time that passed. Andrew decided to go to the bathroom which was completely trashed with toilet paper all over the floor and a turd in the toilet. The walls were covered with smeared feces. Andrew had noticed the stalls had graffiti on them too. He was now part of the poor man's club.

Andrew lay in his bed for most of the time. He had the top bunk. He stared at the ceiling for the longest time. Eventually, he got up and played a game of spades with a dark group. They taught Andrew how to play. Andrew did his best to catch on so he didn't upset anyone. He actually didn't do too bad. Halfway through the game the door opened and a food cart was wheeled in. It was now time for dinner.

Andrew agreed that the food wasn't necessarily gourmet, but it was free. Jail hadn't seemed too bad at this point. Although, he figured he still ran the risk of going to prison. That would be a whole tougher ball game from where he was at right now. At the moment he was fixated on what was going on outside of the walls he was locked in. What was Theo doing? That bastard left him to face the storm all alone. This could have all been avoided. Andrew learned that the trick to jail is to take your mind off of what was going on in the outer world. If you think too much about it then it will drive your brain a little nutty and make you miserable. Andrew tried his best to focus on the moment. It proved difficult. His court case was the next day and he was anticipating getting released.

They ate their soggy Salisbury steaks, mashed potatoes, and fruit cocktail. Andrew took it upon himself to chug his milk. He placed his tray back on the cart and laid down again. He just laid there thinking. He was trying to enclose himself from the rest of the world with all the chaos and emotional storytelling amongst the prisoners. Eventually, a few hours went by and a voice on the ceiling speaker wailed, "Ten minutes till lights out! Get ready for bed!"

Minutes flew by and the lights were suddenly slightly dimmed. There was still a bunch of chit-chatting echoing from wall to wall. Andrew wondered when it would stop. It wasn't all THAT bad. It was just an inconvenience that disrupted his comfortability. Eventually, he tuned them out and fell asleep. It was November 16th of 2014 and the day was now winding down to an end.

CHAPTER 29
Again?

Andrew woke up the next morning to the clatter of keys at the cell entrance. An officer with a crew cut opened the door. He called out the names of 6 people and Andrew was included. It was about 8:30 in the morning. The group was ordered to line up in a single file line and were then escorted through the labyrinth of hallways with locked doors. They went down the same lift as before to the basement. They were now located in a dimly lit tunnel leading to the justice center.

Although the tunnel was hazy, the white walls illuminated the pathway. They were on the way to meet their fate. As they advanced through the underpass a single light flickered on and off. It manifested an eerie feeling. At this moment Andrew felt like his decree would be life in prison or the death penalty. He was growing more and more anxious. Even with these thoughts in mind he also had high hopes of being released. He had to remind himself that he wouldn't be sentenced quite yet as it was still his first court appearance. Overall, he just wanted his freedom back. Technically he was still somewhat free but it had its

The Witch's Hat

limits. He was free in his head but what he craved was a space to call his own, preferably not in jail or prison.

In the meantime, the shepherded posse was led into another holding room with a group of about 10 people. Everyone was in their orange jumpsuits. Andrew looked around and noticed the coloring was yet again disproportionate. He entered the room, sat down, and was silent as he listened to the "blackies" talk.

"Damn nigga! They got me caught up for something I didn't even do ma nigga! On chief bro!" said one of the prisoners with straggly black dreads.

Another bigger, darker fella responded saying, "I'm innocent too, G! They say they had me on a camera robbing somebody. They got me in here on some bullshit!"

Andrew understood that there was a gray area with upholding the law and claiming innocence. Sometimes circumstances can alter into a tricky situation. If you are involved with people who bring you down, that can likely be one of your downfalls. This may have been relevant to many of the other prisoners as well. In Andrew's case, he would have gotten away with his money-grubbing deeds if the crackheads never flashed the knife to him. The accident may not have been fully his fault but he did break the law by burglarizing a home, even though that wasn't what he was booked for.

In retrospect, everyone is guilty of something, whether it's speeding or breaking some old-time law passed by legislation long ago. A lot of the folks in the jail had charges related to drugs which Andrew knew was a hard thing to break away from. A lot of drugs motivate a person to commit crimes and uppers seemed to be one of the main issues among the crowd. Such drugs as cocaine and meth. Andrew had wondered if jail or prison time would be considered the answer to this problem. Perhaps so. Or maybe it would be better to send the druggies straight to rehab. Luckily in Minnesota, they have pretty good accessibility to sobriety programs. Andrew figured he should have gone to drug court but was glad he didn't have to have that on his record. It would have messed with his job interviews. On this particular day, he was readily destined for his first appearance in traffic court.

Time passed and they called his name. The inmates wished him luck. He was brought to the courtroom and was seated in a cubicle that was surrounded by glass windows overlooking the vicinity. He wouldn't have doubted if the glass was bulletproof to protect the inmates from retaliation from their victims. There were five of them including Andrew seated in a row. The judge sat on her throne to dictate the future of each of the persons incarcerated.

Eventually, the ball started rolling. Two African American defendants were told their jail stay was extended for the next court date unless they paid a tremendous bail amount. They were at risk of fleeing. One had kidnapped his son and fled the state. He was charged with a felony. Why he was in traffic court was beyond Andrew. The third defendant that followed after the previous two was told he could be released on his own recognizance. He had a multitude of traffic violations with unpaid fees. He made a promise to pay the fees and appear at the next court date. He was ecstatic to be released.

Finally, Andrew's name was called. It was his time to face his determination. He got up and stepped to the glass. The judge proceeded to inform Andrew he was entitled to an attorney and one would be appointed to him if he hadn't the money. Andrew told her he needed one. She then continued explaining what he was being charged with and what the maximum penalty could be.

"Do you understand what the charge is?" asked the judge. Her name was Judge Barrett. She seemed nice enough. She had blonde hair up in a bun and was still relatively young. Maybe around 40 years of age.

"Yes, I understand what I'm being charged with your honor. A DUI," Andrew politely returned.

"Fantastic!" she said in a giddy voice. "It looks like this is your first charge as an adult so I will make this quick. You will be released on your own recognizance but you must, I repeat, you must come to your next court appearance."

"I will, your honor!" Andrew replied.

"Your public defender will set you up with a date and time," the

The Witch's Hat

judge said. "Make good choices," she added. Then with the sound of the gavel, his court appearance was adjourned.

Andrew took a seat back on the bench within the glass box enclosure and waited. There was one more defendant left. Andrew paid no heed to the court's discussion. His mind was back to getting out and continuing on his old path. He heard another sound of the gavel and looked at the crying defendant. It appeared that things didn't go too well for him.

A moment later, two officers came to the door. One of them called the names of those being released and led them like ducklings through the tunnel to yet another holding cell. The other officer took the remainder of the prisoners and went on his own route to lead them back to a community jailhouse with individual cells.

Hours went by and finally, the public defender showed up. She was some old lady who had too much on her plate and was used to seeing people get slaughtered. She called Andrew into the room across the hall which was a small area with just enough room for two chairs on opposite sides of a laminated table. Andrew sat down on the side closest to the door. Next, the lady put a bunch of papers in front of him.

"Your next court date is December 3rd at 10:00 a.m. Understand you MUST attend the court session. Sign here to confirm you understand what I just said," she ignited towards Andrew.

"Sure, can I leave now?" requested Andrew after signing the document.

"Just a few initials and that is all I will need for today," she said.

Andrew initialed where she had motioned for him to do so and they shook hands and said their goodbyes. Andrew was then brought back to the holding cell where he waited another couple hours. 3 o'clock rolled around and he was summoned again. He was taken to the inmate's personal belongings inventory to grab his stuff. Everything was placed in a bin which was slid underneath an opening of a caged room along the counter by a guard. Andrew noticed right away that all his cards from his billfold had been pulled out from where they had been stored. He felt seriously violated. First, they take his belongings into their possession then have the nerve to rummage and displace every damn thing about? What business did they have?

Next, he went into a stall around the corner to change his clothes. He set the bin on the bench. He cherry-picked from the stack of clothes to put on, starting with the boxers and ending with his winter jacket, hastily shimmying them all onto his body. Andrew then grabbed his wallet and started putting all the cards quickly back into place as he was ecstatic to leave. Only his cell phone, lighter, and cigarettes remained. A thought had fluttered in his head and he soon realized that he was missing his cash. They had stolen his cash.

Andrew crammed the remainder of his property into his pocket and stormed out of the locker room. He was met by an officer at the room entrance. They walked by the inventory office and Andrew shouted to the man in the cage. "Where the fuck is my money? You fucking took it didn't you?" directed Andrew towards the inventory keeper.

"If it wasn't in the bin then you didn't come with any," jeered the officer.

"What the fuck? I know you fuckin took it!" Andrew roared. He looked to the leading officer beside him and bellowed, "Fuck you both! Get me the fuck out of here!"

The officer beside him didn't hesitate to escort Andrew down the hallway, around a corner, and through a secure door. The doorway led to an enclosed hallway maybe twenty feet long with another secure door at the end. The deputy buzzed Andrew through the final doorway and said, "Good luck! Don't come back!"

Andrew took his first step back to freedom. He was in the lobby of the jailhouse. To the left sat a lady at a desk on the corner of an intersection to another hallway. Straight ahead was the main entrance. Andrew had no intention of changing his ways but this definitely was a wake-up call. He had to be more careful.

He ignored the officer's words and took a brisk walk towards the entry doors. He hurled his body weight using his hands through the

The Witch's Hat

door and it flung open so hard that it sprung back towards him. He absorbed the impact with his palms and proceeded outside.

The wintry wind hit his face like a brick as he gazed at the government plaza. He made out the light rail system right away. The tracks went along the street in front of him. To get to the station he had to cross. He heard the toll of an incoming train and sprinted. He didn't even bother with purchasing a ticket because he didn't have any money. Instead, he ran straight to the front of the platform and stood behind a large group of folks. He was just in time for it to slide into a complete stop. Andrew boarded and seated himself in the middle of the car. He was joined by many others. With a smooth jerk, it took off in motion.

Andrew shared his story with a passenger to pass the time. They came upon two more stops at a couple of stations before a pair of transit police boarded. They began checking tickets for validity. Andrew began to panic as he hadn't paid for one. They were about three rows in front of him and would be hot on his tail in a minute. Andrew got up from his seat and walked to the back of the railcar to the doorway.

"Looks like this is my stop! Have a good one man!" he said to the guy he was chatting with. The light rail started screeching to a halt. Andrew peered out the window. Inching closer was the Witch's Hat illuminating through the dimly lit sky. Its view was partially hidden from the groves of shadowy trees.

The doors glided open and Andrew stepped out. The two officers followed him as he departed.

"Hey you! We need to see your ticket!" lipped one of the officers.

Andrew didn't think twice before skedaddling. He didn't even look behind to see if anyone was following either, he just ran and ran in the direction of the tower. Eventually, the view of the tower disappeared from the tree cover but Andrew continued to kick his feet. He zoomed past the street of the house he had robbed a few nights prior and then around the block that led to his grandparents. He slowed to a walk once he made it to his grandparents' sidewalk. He looked over his shoulder and noticed no one had followed him. He left the pigs in the dust.

He was going at a turtle's pace up the front steps of the home.

193

He didn't know what to expect when he walked in. He turned the doorknob and it was locked so he pounded on the door. Couple seconds later Theo's head pops up in the door window. Theo fidgeted with the lock and opened it.

"What the fuck are you doing here?" Theo said in a rapid voice. He looked like he hadn't slept in days and seemed very tense.

"I just got out of jail bro. What do you mean what am I doing here?" Andrew replied, sounding irked.

Theo gave Andrew a dirty look. "You should still be in jail you retard. You could have killed me!"

"Seriously? I'm the one who doesn't have a car anymore. You fucking left me there!" Andrew said distinctly.

"You better get your shit and go! They know of all the shit you took upstairs!" said Theo in his scary crackhead voice. He was trying to do anything to pin the full blame on Andrew but Andrew didn't move a muscle. Theo then quickly ran upstairs and began throwing a tantrum. "I said get your shit and go!" he yelled down to Andrew at the bottom of the stairway.

Andrew began hearing things being thrown around. He heard a clang of a wooden dowel crash to the floor. Andrew used all his might to run up the stairs to find Theo in his closet. Andrew's clothes were scattered all over the floor and Theo was stomping on them. Andrew was infuriated and felt madly disrespected. He charged with all his weight towards Theo. He ran all the way down the hallway about twenty feet and collided with his uncle. Andrew used his arms to pivot Theo from his closet and into the doorway of the nearby bedroom containing all the stuff they had stolen.

He picked Theo up and tried slamming him to the ground but Theo's feet kept breaking the fall. Andrew dropped Theo and started hitting him in the stomach with his right hand while holding him with his left.

"Mom! Dad! Call 9-1-1! Andrew is going crazy!" Theo pleaded.

Theo took a couple swings himself. A couple of shots landed into Andrew's gut. Andrew then wrapped both of his arms around Theo and

The Witch's Hat

squeezed. He gave Theo a mighty bear hug to keep him from moving. This would have been a good time for Andrew to release and run which he did. He pushed Theo, grabbed the stolen bike, and made a ruckus going down the stairs. He took off down the street but had trouble making it through the snow. He had no plan on where to go so he turned around about halfway down the block and went back to gram and gramps's house to face his fate. He didn't feel like he was in the wrong. He went back up the stairs of the home and gave Theo an evil glare. He was done fighting.

Minutes later two police showed up. They stomped up the stairs with tasers drawn. Andrew's grandpa followed as tears fell from his eyes. Andrew just froze in place.

"Arrest him. This loser just got out of jail. He belongs back in there. He got out and assaulted me," said Theo acting like a child.

The police inched down the hall. They had the red dot from the taser laser aimed at Andrew's thigh.

"Get to the ground now!" shouted the officers in an offset unison. "Hands behind your back!"

Andrew rested his belly on the dirty floor that probably hadn't been mopped in ten years. His chin rested on the sticky-ness with his hands placed behind himself. Both cops leaped onto him and dug their knees into his back. They tightened the cuffs to his wrists and lifted him from the ground.

"Why are you arresting me?" questioned Andrew somberly. "He was destroying my stuff!"

The cops ignored Andrew and walked him out to the squad car. They placed him in the back seat. Andrew sat in the dark as they went back in to discuss more with the family over what was going on. Ten minutes later the officers came out. One of them opened up the back door on the opposite side Andrew was on.

"Looks like we will be bringing you in for a domestic assault charge. Also, your brother in there said you robbed a house down the street. He showed us all the belongings in the bedroom upstairs. Is he telling the truth?" the young officer asked.

"He's not my brother," Andrew said in disgust. "I don't even want to talk to him again. As for the shit upstairs, I know nothing about it."

"Well, just so you know we will be returning the belongings back to the owner and they will decide if they want to press charges or not."

Andrew sat there in silence. He knew he was probably going to be locked up for a while now. He didn't understand why he was arrested while Theo got off scot-free. He felt like an idiot. The officers then closed the car door and the three of them took off to the Hennepin County Public Safety Facility. As soon as they arrived Andrew went through the same process as the day before. During the booking procedure, Andrew bumped into the same kind officer he met previously.

"Hey, you're back! What are you doing here again?" he asked.

"I got into a little tangle with my uncle. He was frickin destroying my stuff so I tried to stop him," Andrew replied with embarrassment.

"Oh no! I'm telling you man, you don't belong here. Your calling is somewhere else," said the sympathetic man.

"Hey, thanks dude! Just out of curiosity, do you know my other uncles, Eddie and Mario?" Andrew asked.

"Yeah, I actually do. They come in quite often for being drunk and disorderly in public," the officer responded.

"Wow! That's kinda funny. Those guys are always getting into trouble," chuckled Andrew as he was brought to the holding cell. "Well, wish me luck. Hopefully I'm not here too long..."

Just a few minutes later Andrew was pulled from the tank. He had already turned in all his goods and was dressed in his jumpsuit. A bald man took him to the camera screen with the same plain white backdrop. Andrew didn't bother smiling this time. He had on an angry face. He was more frustrated than the day before because he knew he was fucked. Although, he still kept his cool.

He had his picture taken which was printed out as a wristband. The officer put the band on Andrew's wrist. Andrew glanced at it while the man escorted him to the holding cell to grab the other prisoners to bring to the jailhouse. He noticed that his hair looked black in the photo. Why was that? Andrew figured the meth he had gotten from

The Witch's Hat

Journey was cut with something that changed his hair into a darker color. Who knows what was coursing through Andrew's veins. He was even starting to feel a little sick coming off the shit.

Moments later another officer joined the bald man and took the group of 6 to the large room with all the bunk beds. It was basically the same as before except Andrew had difficulty falling asleep. He was sweating profusely. He only slept for two hours and was feeling almost fully drained.

The next morning Andrew's name was called for court for another go around. He knew it looked bad getting arrested two days in a row. To make it worse the guy who would be deciding his pending kismet was named Judge Dredd which Andrew was unaware of at the time. His body, mind, and soul were filled with anxiety. He tried to pull out some kind of hope from within. He ended up coming to the decision that he was gonna focus on asking to be released on his own recognizance again. He absolutely didn't want to do time, especially in his condition.

Again with the escort to the holding cell where they awaited for court. It was the same exact process as before. In the meantime, a bunch of angry voices filled the room with cuss words. The inmates shared stories to pass the time as usual. Andrew was kinda paranoid to talk about his deeds. There were speakers with microphones in the room. He wasn't sure if they were live recorded like the phones in the facility so he planned on not talking too much. He didn't want to incriminate himself. The way Andrew looked at it was that he was a guilty victim. He sat quietly and pondered as he waited.

A good while later, Andrew was called out of confinement and directed straight to the courtroom. When he entered he noticed Judge Dredd sitting at his throne in a black silk gown. He was a mean-looking older man with dark silvery hair. On his cheek was a brown mole that was undeniably noticeable. It was about the size of a pea. As Andrew was checking out the blemish, the judge spoke up and explained what Andrew was being charged with. Afterward, Andrew pleaded to be released.

The judge then peered up from his glasses to look Andrew directly in his eyes. "I cannot release you. Being as you were just in court yesterday, I wouldn't know if you would leave and commit another crime. I will, however, set your bail amount to $2,000. We will combine this charge on the same court date as your other. Your public defender will touch base with you. That will conclude this session," the judge voiced as he pounded his gavel. "Next!"

They pulled Andrew out of the courtroom and into the holding area to await pod placement. Inmate after inmate were dumped in the room and joined him in the waiting game. Finally, they were all called at once from the room and lined up like school children in a row. Andrew was at the front of the line. This was typical in his life due to reasons other than his choosing. It made him anxious but prepared. They were then handed a bag lunch to eat and went on their way.

The line was led by a stubby guard and followed up by a tall skinny one. The stubby guy guided them down a series of hallways and into the tunnel with the same flickering light bulb. They made it to the other side and the stocky man led them to an elevator and went up one floor. They exited and went a short way down the hallway when the officer buzzed the door to a jailhouse to alert his team in the surveillance room to unlatch it. It unlatched and the stubster opened the door. The room revealed a flood of angry sounds of inmates yelling and taunting each other. This was considered the violent offender section.

"Don't make me come in there!" said the leading officer as he shouted into the room of immured individuals waiting for their sentence. He then guided half of the group into the pod. The batch of remaining prisoners along with the authorities continued through the bright hallway until they reached the elevator again. They all boarded and went up to another floor. Two of the ducks got off and were escorted by the thin man. After that moment, Andrew went up yet another floor. He was the only one left. The bell dinged, the doors opened and the man directed him out to the right where there was a crate with a bunch of sleeping mats. On the opposite wall of the elevator was Andrew's new home. The officer buzzed it and it opened.

"Hurry! Grab a mat and go to your assigned cell. Your cell number is 11 which is straight ahead and to the right..."

The Witch's Hat

Along the two of the sides of the pod of which were parallel from each other situated a line of seven cells along the lower level. The cells were paired within a foot of each other with another 12 feet to the next cell pair and so on with one lone wolf cell at the end. Above each of the previous cells was a balcony. The balcony contained another 7 cells. Keep in mind the cells were concrete walls with a solid steel door containing a square window overlooking the rest of the pod. The top tier consisted of single inmate compartments and the bottom tier was composed of bunks. Unfortunately, Andrew was on the bottom level.

He had walked into the pod nonchalantly. He held a stern face because he was upset from his predicament. He entered his cell and an old man was laying on the bottom bunk. He had short messy silver hair with a matching goatee. He seemed a little oily. Andrew introduced himself and it turned out this guy was in for a DUI as well. Andrew settled his mat on the top bunk and made his bedding. He lay on his bed and ate his food then crashed early for the day. The old man slept as well and was not a bother at all. This was the beginning of Andrew's somewhat long-term jail experience.

CHAPTER 30
They Come and Go

THE NEXT DAY Andrew woke up to the sound of his celly flushing the toilet. Andrew laid there staring at the wall. The majority of the day he mostly lingered around in his cell except to get chow. But even then he ate in his room. The day that was to follow was when Andrew roamed out into the pod during rec time. He didn't want people to think he was a punk by always hiding away.

He began the second morning in the new jail pad when he heard the intercom ordering them to get up for roll call around 6:30 a.m. Shortly afterward they were called by cell numbers to line up for breakfast. Andrew's group was called last. Evidently, he wasn't first all the time. Next, he retrieved his food and went to eat with the group. The tables were in the center of the pod. He went to one of the tables with four seats. Two of the seats were taken. He was respectful and asked if anyone else was sitting there.

"Yeah these spots are taken," one of the men said. He then shouted over to one of the nearby tables. "Hey Cowboy! You guys have an open spot over there?"

The Witch's Hat

"Yeah, we do. He can sit over here," responded an inmate at the adjacent table. Apparently, he went by the name Cowboy. Andrew walked over to him, sat down, and introduced himself. Other than that Andrew didn't initiate much of any conversation, however, he was bombarded with questions. Andrew provided a credible answer to all of the grilling the inmates had brought forth. They wanted to know his background. Why was he there? Did he do drugs? Could they trust him? After the chit-chat, Andrew felt like he was willfully accepted. He felt thankful.

They had about a half-hour to eat and then were locked in their cages again. The old man went back to sleep. Andrew took a piss and laid down as well. It seemed like a blink of an eye and it was already lunchtime.

Andrew sat alone on this occasion in front of a blank T.V. There were 3 rows of chairs and he plopped himself right in the middle. A guy who looked like he was from India was sitting behind him. After Andrew finished his meal and put his tray away he asked the Indian guy how he was doing as he looked very down. The two spoke for a few minutes until the inmates had to yet again go back to their cells.

They were allowed out of the cells again after a few hours when rec time started. During this time Andrew was pulled aside by Cowboy. "You know that fucker you were talking to earlier is a chomo right?" he said with a dirty look on his face. "I would stay away from him if I was you."

"No shit? He told me he was in for fraud," replied Andrew. "I'll stay clear."

All Andrew needed was to be put on the shit list for talking to a child molester. In a sense, he felt bad for the Indian guy because he was bullied all day every day. However, Andrew absolutely did not condone sexual abuse among children. He was to avoid all chomos. Unfortunately, he was put in the pod with the most chomos and mentally ill people in the whole institution.

Next, Cowboy had Andrew follow him to a kiosk and proceeded to show him how to order commissary on a computer screen. Andrew had money in his wallet on a card but it wasn't in his account. Plus his wallet was locked up. He tried to call his mom but the voice reader on the phone for verification didn't recognize his name so he screamed it at the top of his lungs. Everyone turned to stare at him as the room was pretty quiet. His bellow through the phone had luckily worked. His mom answered the phone call and Andrew begged to get bailed out. They argued. She said he had to learn his lesson so she wouldn't pay the $200 bond to free him. Instead, she put $20 on his books. Andrew called multiple bail bondsmen to see if they could work a deal out but had no luck. He got off the phone and tried to order canteen but the money wasn't available yet. He turned around and sat in front of the T.V. to watch *Gotham* to pass time.

The next day Andrew's roommate departed in the early morning so Andrew confiscated the bottom bunk. Later on that day he had gotten a new roommate also by the name Andrew. He was a methhead as well. The two druggies got along splendidly. They spent the day telling war stories. The new Andrew, who we will call Grimes, shared all the scams he would do at corporate stores. Andrew learned some criminal-minded information from him and in return fronted his new roommate a tray of cookies to be nice but never did again. He realized Grimes had a serious gambling problem. It didn't take long for him to rack up a substantial amount of debt with the others.

On this very day during rec, Andrew decided to shower. He had watched *American History X* and remembered Derek getting raped by the Aryan Brotherhood. This jail didn't seem like the scenery for that but you never know, it could happen if you had a crooked guard or if it was hidden in your cell by your bunkmate. Andrew wasn't too worried about it as he didn't have any enemies and nonetheless there was always a guard on duty as if they were babysat so things would hopefully be resolved quickly. He actually felt fairly safe. It was a nice place to be if you didn't want any responsibilities.

Andrew waited until there wasn't a soul in the shower room and took to it. He turned the water on and the shit was freezing. He waited and waited. It never warmed up so Andrew had to dodge back and forth through the water to keep from getting a brain freeze. He made

The Witch's Hat

the choice that he was gonna go a long time without taking a shower from that point on. This began the cycle of only showering every other week or two. He never shaved his face either. He never heard anything of it being mandatory.

Also on his schedule was the routine of taking books from the book cart to read them for many many hours. It was very peaceful to keep his mind off his frustrations, especially the ones with Theo that were boiling inside. On an average day, Andrew would get through a book or a full magazine front to back even if he wasn't interested in the article. Sometimes he read biographies. Sometimes he read novels. He kept a list of everything he read.

One night while he was reading in his cell he saw his bunkmate slip a kite through the door. The lights were always left on so it was obvious. Was he snitching? Who knows? Andrew lay there until an officer came and told his celly to grab his stuff to roll out. Grimes had just purposefully called upon himself to get expelled from the pod. The next day Andrew found it was because he had owed so much money to all the gamblers they resided with. He was very well in debt. All Andrew lost out of the deal was a tray of cookies. He wasn't petty about it. It was just a tray of cookies.

The next day the pod was loud with all the upset inmates. Meanwhile, a new prison mate entered the cell named Brad. He was a tall sturdy guy who had tics. He scratched his neck a lot and was a meth user as well. He had frequented the jail just as the previous roommate had. This guy was different in the fact that he had been to so many institutions that he would sleep on the floor next to the toilet. He claimed it was more comfy and he liked the coolness of the concrete. He was booked for multiple warrants in different counties. He would joke that "the best celly is the one who sleeps on his belly." Andrew didn't like that. Andrew had to sleep on his belly to avoid the fucking light that was on all day and night. In addition, the new dude actually had a lot of respect amongst the inmates as he had done prison time. He made fake I.D.s and committed robberies. Two weeks flew by and at that point, he was transferred.

The day Brad left was over halfway done when dinner time came upon them. Andrew noticed two inmates walking into the pod. One, a short scrawny black man with missing teeth named Marvin. The other was a Russian guy who spoke with a very deep accent in broken sentences named Igor. Turned out that the latter was another new cellmate and Marvin was the one who was placed in the room next door.

Andrew asked Igor what he was charged with and the reply was "Living the American dream." He never said what he was in for so Andrew just labeled him as the white Russian. This guy didn't give a fuck about stinking up the room any day of the week with his nasty ass shits only when Andrew was in the cage with him. Igor would also snore very loudly in his sleep every night. Obnoxiously loud. Also, his shit smelled so bad that it was an inspiration for a song that Andrew wrote as a spin-off copycatting "Folsom Prison Blues."

It went like this:

Hello, I'm Andy Ward.

(Applause)

(Music begins)

I hear the light rail coming

It's rolling round downtown

Every time I hear it

I bow my head down and I frown

I'm stuck in Hennepin County

And time keeps dragging on

But that light rail keeps a movin

All the way down

To the UNI-YAWN

When I was just a baby

My momma told me, "Son

Always be a good boy

Don't ever play with guns"

But I shot a guy in Murderapolis

The Witch's Hat

Just to watch him die
When I hear that light rail coming
I hear my freedom bell cry
(Instrumental)
In front of me my roommate
He takes a great big shit
Made myself a calendar
But dare not look at it
Yeah I'm stuck in Hennepin County
And time keeps dragging on
This world is just so fucked up
And now I may be a con…

The remainder of the words got lost within the sands of time. Andrew had a lot of fun piecing it together. It sucked him away from his negative thoughts for a moment. It was meditation.

CHAPTER 31
The Clash

Andrew roamed in front of the T.V. one day during rec time. He met another new inmate. He was an Afro-American who had served in the military as a medic. Very smart. He sat in front of the television with Starvin Marvin. Marvin had referred to the war vet as Spiderman so that is what we called him. Spidey would talk about how he wanted to make movies. He was on a directly set path and would use his tunnel vision for success. Andrew thought it was amazing what jail can do to your ambition. It will either make you or break you.

All in all, Andrew was more of a Batman guy but he believed Spidey could fulfill his own dream. In fact, Peter Parker was in jail for something he didn't even do. He just got caught in the wrong situation with the wrong female. Anyway, these guys all hung out on a regular basis and would watch Gotham. Bruce Wayne along with Tony Stark were both Andrew's heroes, among others.

The Witch's Hat

As time went by Andrew couldn't take the severe annoyance of his roommate snoring. He flew a kite through the slot in the door and asked for a new room. To his surprise, he got one. Not only that, but he got his own single cell up on the second tier.

Andrew settled into his new cell. It was nice and peaceful and he didn't have to deal with any roommate stench. Within his own sanctuary, Andrew got addicted to jacking off. It was one of the only ways to bring about dreamy pleasure in a place with such an immense sum of boredom. One of the nights a guard caught him jerking it. Maybe the cell wasn't as private as he thought.

Aside from that, Andrew had been in jail for quite some time. Eventually, his arraignment date came to be. He went to court and had Mr. Dredd again for a judge. Andrew pleaded not guilty but still wasn't allowed to be released. This judge was definitely a tough nut to crack.

When Andrew came back to the pod he began watching T.V. like usual and connected with a thug. Andrew told him how he wanted to break his uncle's knee caps with a bat when he got out. He was pissed off. He plotted it out in his head. He could hide in the bushes by the house until Theo left to get his daily snacks from the gas station, hopefully sometime after twilight. As soon as Andrew would see him he would take a shortcut through a park on an obscure trail and meet Theo near a street lamp. Andrew would be wearing a mask and possibly some black clothes. He would break his knees then run and forget the whole thing happened. The Georgia thug Andrew was conversing with was enthused by what Andrew said. He had mentioned they thought alike. Andrew tried to put the idea aside but couldn't. He even considered hiring a hired gun but it never got to that point.

Christmas went by with no presents or visits. At least they had a decent meal. They spent time watching reruns of *Breaking Bad* and *Burn Notice* on the T.V. The show *Burn Notice* was interesting because it was about a CIA spy who was banned from the agency. Keep in mind burn notices are used to discredit or announce the dismissal of agents. The main character, Michael, is in pursuit of the person who burned him. Andrew would have never known what a burn notice was if it weren't for jail.

As Andrew was watching the show a guard called his name. He had gotten a letter. It was from a man named Dave (A.K.A. Strativarious). This was the moment where the two hurricanes collided, spawning a Fujiwhara effect. The two storms merged into one and created one of a much larger magnitude. They would have a tremendous effect upon the world. A positive effect for sure. Instead of destroying, they did the opposite and created.

In the letter, Dave informed Andrew that he had worked on the film *Either Which Way* with Justin. Andrew had no clue who this guy was but he was intrigued. Strat said that he had worked intensively on one of Josh's songs and had developed it into something he was very proud of. He had gone to college at Julliard as well as Harvard. He was very prestigious. Strat also performed with the likes of Sheryl Crow, Phillip Phillips, Coldplay, and Evanescence. He was very plugged in.

He then went on to share stuff about his life that was very personal. They shared the same circumstances in which they had both lost a sibling. They also both had suffered some sort of abuse but to different extents. Also, *Either Which Way* meant a lot to Strat as he had been bullied himself as a kid. It may seem as if Andrew and Strativarious were two peas in the same pod. Andrew treasured the letter and would go back to read it several times. He didn't get too much mail in jail so it was a fine gesture.

New Year's Eve crept up and Andrew needed something to celebrate. He went through a whole month and a half without any sort of drug but he was gonna score some that day. He knew the guys who were prescribed pills in lockup so he decided to trade his New Years' dinner for a small oxycodone pill along with some Valium. The dude he got it from was part of the native mob and was very open for business.

When the night came to an end and they were contained again, Andrew took and crushed both pills. With a rolled-up piece of paper, he did a bump a piece. He looked out the prison cell door window and made hand signals to the native inmate across the pod. The guard, some guy from Africa, started laughing. He was a cool cat. He knew what was up. Andrew threw up his hands in a "rock on" signal and stuck out his tongue like a crazy person. The C.O. just smirked and

The Witch's Hat

shook his head. Andrew then went ahead with some workouts. He read for about an hour then went to bed.

The next day Andrew was reminded of the crazy Ferguson riots from the previous weeks. It was all over the news. What happened was a black man was killed in Missouri by a white police officer without facing any charges. This was a big topic in the jail. Andrew felt like he had been in there for an eternity but a joyous feeling came over him when he heard BLM protesters outside. Andrew was hoping they would engage in total anarchy upon the correctional center so he could be released. He imagined an artillery shell blowing a hole in the side of the building so he could jump out using his bedsheets as a rope. It was definitely a mesmerizing fantasy.

Day in and day out Andrew would listen to a fuzzy megaphone roaring with demands outside the walls. He tried looking out there but the window was glazed with a foggy residue. His tympanic membranes became swamped with a bunch of clanging and pounding of drums. As time went on Andrew was less and less excited about being broken free. He realized it probably wasn't gonna happen.

Finally, the third week of January came to be and it was a Thursday. Andrew was called upon to court for his trial. Disastrously, his much-needed counsel was on vacation. His new public defender tried negotiating but Andrew wouldn't budge. She would go back and forth meeting with the prosecutor then come back with more lenient deals. The system probably had nothing on him but Andrew chose to plead guilty for two misdemeanors. They dropped the D.U.I. plaint to careless driving and the domestic assault to brawling/fighting. He was awarded a solid year of probation and to also complete a treatment program if need be. He would only have to go to treatment if he gave them evidence he was using drugs or alcohol. He wasn't quite ready to quit so he would game his way into the clear. To top it off, they slapped on a DANCO order as well. If Andrew contacted Theo he would go right back to the slammer.

After serving two months in jail you would have thought he would have had time served but both charges carried up to 90 days. They weren't lenient with him like Andrew thought. He knew Theo had probably not even shown up for court to even testify. However, Andrew's grandpa did. To think of his grandpa testifying against him would have been terrible. Andrew shall not regret the deal that he made because they were planning on placing 6 more charges on him if he denied it. Most of the 6 charges were from the past when the police were called for getting in a fight on numerous occasions with a guy they called Bummy D (Marcel) who would come over and steal things. Anyhow, Andrew gathered his things from his cell and the property room after court and was released to the streets.

CHAPTER 32
Homeless

AFTER ANDREW WAS released he had nowhere to go. He found a mattress he could sleep on that rested outside. He cleared off the snow. He was near Theo's home. He ended up finding him when he left the house one day. Andrew never did break his kneecaps. He was still very angry but he needed the sleeping bag that was stored in the house to survive in the wintry urban wilderness. Andrew received the sleeping bag and boogied on back to his chill spot.

It was five below with the windchill. Andrew laid on the mattress and watched the cars go by on the freeway. He was on the side of a wall nearest the interstate that separated the neighborhood from the busy road. He lit up a fire to keep warm. Eventually, he succumbed to the frigid weather and called his mom. He asked her to pick him up and bring him home. She said no and said again that he had to learn his lesson. In the meantime, his mother was more interested in what diagnosis she could come up with for his brother Antonio who was in his puberty stage, and talking seriously about transitioning into a girl. He would now be referred to as a she with her new name being Stella. She grew her hair out, started wearing makeup, and was put on estrogen. Andrew had just lost and gained a sibling at the same time.

Also, Andrew's newish foster sister, Sabrina, was taken from Stella's birth mom as well about a year and a half prior and left in Tanya's care. This concerned Andrew. The two children were put into the system coming from the same birth mother but different fathers at different points in time as they were different ages, only to be put in a home with a person with Munchausen syndrome by proxy to administer cocktails of medication. Stella had so many pills prescribed that the multitude gave her liver toxicity. Sabrina was only about 2 years old herself and was just being introduced to meds at such an early age. Andrew had no clue of this and the phone call ended abruptly as he was upset with Tanya for not being a good mom to help out her only existing son. Andrew wasn't going to ask anyone else for help at this point because he felt like a burden.

Tanya called back and had mentioned that Andrew's sisters' mother agreed he could stay at her boyfriend's house and her boyfriend would move in with her. Romeo was his name. He was an ex-navy seal who dressed up in leather clothes and who had a brain injury. He was not the guy to mess with.

Andrew spent almost a month at Romeo's apartment. Andrew was offered pot from his sister's mother but he denied it. He didn't want to fail his U.A. He was on the color system. Each day you would call the government center after they gave you a color. If your color was drawn you had to have a piss test. Andrew knew they would test for alcohol as well. But that only stayed in your system for two days tops. He decided he would take his chances and drink after his color had been called with the chance it may not be drawn again soon. This went by the whole duration living at the new home. It was pretty nice. He would smoke cigarettes in the living room and it was quite great to not have any responsibilities still.

Eventually, after about three weeks, the color showed up two days in a row. Andrew drank tons of water and went in to try to piss clean.

The Witch's Hat

Turned out he had failed. He had gotten scheduled to go to drug court in a few days due to this scenario. He still had a little more time to party.

Romeo had called Andrew and told him of a program that he had participated in at the Union Gospel Mission in St. Paul. Romeo worked his way up and got government assistance for his apartment and paid next to nothing. He also got social security somewhere down the line. They even gave him a car. Andrew was very interested in this organization and was going to look into it. Romeo had mentioned that Andrew should bring it up to the judge. It would have been a good move because it really did sound great given Andrew's position but the downfall was that they still didn't allow drinking. It was a program to get yourself on your feet without the use of drugs even though half of the homeless that were there did so anyway. They paid close attention to the ones who did good and rewarded them for their good behavior. Andrew did some thinking and eventually came to the conclusion that he would pursue the homeless shelter over treatment. He was convinced that this program would be better for his future.

It was a day before court came. Andrew decided to punch himself in the eye several times until it was black and blue. It was his way to make the judge feel sorry for him. When the court date came the following day Andrew stepped up to the stand. He was a little buzzed from the beer he had drunk earlier but managed to smooth talk his way into attending the Union Gospel Mission. He was relieved.

He had a couple days before he had to check into the Christian mission. He went back to the apartment and hung out by himself when a car came to a screeching halt outside. The sliding glass door in the living room opened shortly afterward. It was Rachel, his siblings' mother. She came in wondering if Romeo was there as they had gotten into a fight. She told Andrew to leave immediately with her so he did. He hadn't a clue what was going on but in retrospect, he didn't have much else to do. He was just drinking alone like usual.

They arrived at her house which was more of a duplex. It was in the heart of St. Paul. She mixed him up a drink and Andrew didn't remember much more after that. He blacked in and out. One second she was pulling him into the bedroom then everything went black. He snapped back and she was lying in bed without clothes. She had on some netting and high heels. Her legs were wide open and Andrew could see a tear in her vagina from giving birth. Then everything went blank again. Next thing you know Andrew was banging her. He had just fucked his siblings' mother. There wasn't much recollection of what happened and Andrew almost believed he was drugged. He was brought over just for that reason.

The next morning Andrew woke up and Rachel was nowhere to be found. He threw on his clothes and sat in the living room. He heard a pounding at the door. He peered out to spot a police officer.

"Open the door!" the man shouted.

For some reason, Andrew did.

"Where is Rachel? We want Rachel!" the officer said aggressively.

"I don't know. She's not here. I don't live here," replied Andrew.

"I have a warrant. I'm going to check this place out whether you like it or not," the officer said as he and his squad slid past Andrew. They all proceeded to search the whole second floor of the duplex as Andrew watched. Out of nowhere, two of the officers pulled their guns on Andrew and told him to get to the floor. They walked into the corner of the den where there was a replica AK47. They discovered it was only a BB gun. They let Andrew get to his feet and they left the BB gun behind. They took off in their cruisers down and away. In truth, they had never had a search warrant in the first place.

Shortly later, Rachel came back freaking out. She had run over Romeo with the car. Her windshield was totally shattered. The two of them immediately left for Romeo's apartment in the damaged car. They entered the apartment and all Andrew's shit was gone. Romeo had thrown it in the dumpster. All Andrew's clothes, everything. Romeo was high off his ass when he was run over that morning. Rachel said he had sold Andrew's empty safe for drugs. That was the reason for him being hit.

The two of them decided to hang out in the vehicle along the street until Romeo got home from the hospital. As soon as he got back he grabbed Andrew by his collar and pulled him close through the open car window. "You better not be fucking my woman you little fuck!" he roared.

Andrew denied any accusations. Romeo pulled Andrew out of the car and took his spot. He and Rachel argued all the way back to her duplex. Andrew was left behind. That night he slept alone on the couch in the apartment. All in all, Romeo had the assumption that Andrew had screwed his baby's mother but he didn't exactly know.

The next day all three of them met up at Romeo's place. Romeo apologized for what he had done and Andrew kept his secret. It was time to visit the mission. Andrew had to take the initiative to go to the homeless shelter and prove to his probation officer he was trying. Romeo was more than happy for Andrew to leave. He wouldn't have to worry about Rachel being promiscuous with him anymore.

Andrew was dropped off at the mission by the couple and began his first night sleeping in a large gym-type room with something like 100 or more people lined up in rows. Andrew kept all his belongings nearby, especially his cell phone. He didn't go far when he had to charge it. It was his link to the world around him. At night Andrew would use his backpack as a pillow instead of placing it under his cot. There were many cases where things ended up missing from and by the dwellers.

The following few days Andrew would drink by a fire under a bridge in a grassy knoll in the big city. He hung out with a black guy named Steve. They went everywhere together. They would join a stingy old homeless man sitting on 5-gallon pails around burning logs as the weed smoke filled the air. Andrew tried to snag the old man's bottle one day but the man released his fury upon him. He told him to get his own bottle so Steve and Andrew hiked to the LQ. They bought a cheap container of vodka with the last of Andrew's government aid and came back. It was very cold outside but the fire and the liquor did their job to keep them somewhat warm.

After getting drunk for the day the pair went back to the mission and had gotten kicked out for being belligerent. They left and took the light rail to Andrew's grandparents' neighborhood. They almost missed the train stop so Andrew pulled the emergency lever to stop the train and jerked open the door. They got off and Andrew took Steve to his mattress hideout where the two spent a few nights in the frigid cold huddled together for warmth to survive. Don't get the impression there was any freaky business going on, it was just extremely cold out.

One day after getting inebriated and roaming the streets with Steve, Andrew hit up his friend, Niccolo. They were invited to his cousin's house with Nasty Nate and his brother Samson. This would be their home for the next few weeks. Steve and Andrew made sure to let them know the stay was only temporary. They would sooner or later move on to find another shelter within life's mess.

They now lived with a whole family of drinkers, plus two. Steve and Andrew made their fair share of contributions with booze. Every day they came back with a bottle. They were all a bunch of alcoholics. In order to get the liquor, they would have to wander into the liquor store and slip a bottle of hooch into their waistband. One day Andrew was found out so he took off running. He ran outside and took to the streets of north Minneapolis to meet with his homeboys. They were standing in the parking lot, so Andrew stopped running as he wasn't being chased.

Next thing you know some white boy who was totally out of place that dark winter night whipped out his camera and started snapping photos. The four of them including Steve, Samson, and Nasty Nate posed for the camera and gave the kid the finger. Then they took off running from the security guard who decided all of a sudden to take pursuit. They got away easily. They did this liquor run routine for a few weeks and were somewhat mobile with a stolen hoopty for a very short while for their getaways until they abandoned it.

During their stolen, drunken binges they used their massive amount of free time to play football outside in the snow. Andrew played barefoot. On one occasion the whole neighborhood was watching. The boys were tough and weren't taking it lightly. Andrew had great traction with his feet, but they started turning blue. They heard sirens coming down the road and a fire truck stopped in front of the house. Someone had called the fire department. The gang got sketched out and went inside.

The Witch's Hat

Then there was a knock at the door. The sister of the two brothers' answered it. Andrew stood at the top of the stairs in front of the entryway. The firefighter came in wielding an ax.

"I heard someone had frostbite. I brought the ax in case we need to do an amputation," he said.

Andrew didn't know if he was joking or serious. His face dropped and he took off and hid in the basement near the back door. They weren't going to amputate his fucking feet. They were just fine. The sister luckily told the fireman that Andrew was perfectly OK and they left. Back to drinking they went.

On the dull side, they had no more liquor stores to steal from. The employees had the kids' faces locked into their memory. Now the vagabonds were unable to provide the home with booze. They were flat out of cash to pay for the food the mother served them too! It wasn't agreed upon to pay any sort of rent but doing so would make Andrew feel better, but he had nothing. Meanwhile, it ended up that Steve found a place at the Salvation Army while Andrew still lingered around. The mother of the house ended up supplying the booze the next few days until she snaked out on Andrew and told him to leave during the night.

Andrew had no choice but to go back to his luxury mattress and sleeping bag by the freeway. On his walk to his camping location, he got really cold and decided to seek shelter in a dumpster. He was glad that the garbage man didn't come the following morning because he had fallen asleep. He could have gotten pretty messed up.

He resumed his walk after he awoke. It was a couple days after Valentine's Day and Andrew hadn't a partner to celebrate with. Instead, he wandered from store to store to keep warm that morning along his journey. He took his time putzing around. He couldn't sleep at any of the stores so once evening rolled around he was placed with the dangerous task of surviving a night in 30 below weather. He slept outside at the royal mattress with a bottle in his hand that he snagged from an LQ that didn't recognize him. This night he fell asleep so close to the fire that his sleeping bag along with his lower pant leg started ablaze. Andrew woke up startled and patted out the flames.

Unfortunately, when he slapped his hand against the sleeping bag, the melted plastic stuck to it and burned him wickedly. For the moment the front and back of his hand were covered with hot goop that was slowly congealing. It was terrible. He peeled off the remains of the sleeping bag from his hand and some of his skin went with it. He moved a little further away from the fire and stayed awake for the rest of the night so he knew he wouldn't freeze to death.

During the dead of night, he heard sirens. He knew it was the fire brigade by the sound of the horn. They were very near so Andrew kicked out the fire then sat and waited. It seemed as if they had vanished so Andrew got up and trudged the streets with his arms pulled inside his coat like a turtle. Then he used his breath to warm up his hands and body as an entirety.

As the sun started surfacing the horizon, Andrew arrived at Fairview Riverside Hospital. What he wanted was just to warm up. He brought in the liter of vodka he had and was hitting it excessively hard in the waiting room until, in the end, a security guard showed up. Andrew got up to leave but the security guard followed him outside and took his bottle. He gave Andrew an ultimatum, either he attend detox at Fairview or he would call the cops. Andrew didn't have the strength to run so he made the decision to check himself in. This stay would prove to help Andrew with his struggle to survive and was a very smart decision.

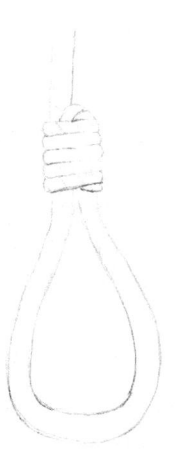

CHAPTER 33
Rehab

ANDREW WAS QUICKLY admitted to the building's detox center and was prescribed Gabapentin and Wellbutrin. Andrew somehow got ahold of the bottles and would take a massive amount of Gabbies to get high. He would drink tons of coffee to keep hyped as well. Then he just lounged around and took in information from the people in there. He talked to a treatment advisor and she told him that he had to be transferred to a long-term treatment center. They knew Andrew was on probation so they didn't release him. He had to do a treatment program this time around or else go back to jail and serve the rest of his sentence which was 90 days or 60 for good behavior.

Andrew even looked like a straight-up bum with his long hair, beard, and burnt clothes. Luckily his native friends shaved the sides of his head bald about midway from the top of his ear and the top of his head so he may have looked more like a rolling stone with perceived style. Whether a bum or a rolling stone, he only wanted to move up in the world.

With this in mind, he began one afternoon asking the staff if he could be transferred to Hazelden. They didn't oppose his suggestion. Andrew knew Hazelden was a place where celebrities have gone. It was a luxury treatment center. Andrew needed a soul-cleansing vacation. He figured that one of his insurances would cover it. He had insurance through his dad's work as well as medical assistance through the state from when he hurt his ankle. Most of the time he got hospital visits for free but unfortunately, neither insurance would cover this legendary rehab.

They searched for days for a different treatment center. Andrew called around to several places and finally found an opening at Twin Town. He told them he was ready to do intake as soon as possible. He was sick of being trapped in the stuffy hospital but damn sure appreciated the boiler. Two days later a van picked him up. The driver's name was Ku. He was a short Asian man in his late twenties. He was super cool.

The duo arrived at Twin Town around 10 o'clock p.m and Andrew did intake. He was brought to another man inside an office. He was asked if he carried a phone and Andrew said no, but in reality, his phone was sitting nice and snug in his pocket. The fat man finished piecing Andrew's info together and escorted him to a room where he introduced himself to his native roommate. Andrew's mom had ended up dropping off clothes and a native folklore book he had stashed at his old home. He planned to educate himself about one of his favorite cultures. It was a wonderful experience.

The day after check-in Andrew was thrown into the weekly routine. The occupants had to attend group which were on and off all day long. It was all about discussing core values and ways to stay sober by keeping busy and finding hobbies. They also did a lot of reflection. Andrew enjoyed listening and sharing stories for some time but eventually got sick of going to groups.

Out of view from others between the scheduled meetings, Andrew would text people and post pictures on Facebook. He shared with people his struggles and how his day was going. He was still plugged into the world. He was kind and would borrow his roommates his

The Witch's Hat

phone late at night so they could talk to their peeps. There were two individuals per room and they would come and go. Andrew had to weigh out who he could trust and vibe with.

Time strolled and it was now about March and the snow was melting. The residents would play volleyball outside. Andrew was a volleyball star. Everyone wanted him on their team. He met a guy on the court who was also prescribed Wellbutrin. He said he cheeked them from the nurse and snorted them later on in the day. Andrew started this process as well. They both continued through treatment high off their gourds.

One day Andrew had paid an occupant to get him liquor. It never arrived so Andrew consulted someone to talk to him. As a result, it was figured that for some reason the middle-aged man bought PCP instead with Andrew's $20. Andrew was actually quite happy. He had never done PCP intentionally before. The guy called it sherm. It was taking a while to arrive from his homeboy so they all went upstairs that night after lights out to the top floor of the building to wait.

Eventually, it came but the doors to the building were being watched. A young buck from Chi-Town ended up jumping out of the window of his bedroom on the second floor. He climbed over the iron bars and reached down to receive the goods. He struggled to get back up but the guys pulled him in. Then they all went back up to the top floor. They sat back and smoked the sherm which was an awesome experience. Andrew enjoyed it. Ku walked into the room to check up on them, he gave them a nod and then eased his way out the door to go to the next room.

One thing Andrew will never forget was another middle-aged man with his own family. He was a middle-class white guy and looked as if he hadn't belonged there. He was very quiet in groups however he shared just a little. He struggled with alcoholism. He was obviously distressed. He was stuck in a situation he wanted out of. On one dreary night, the police and ambulance showed up at the treatment center. Andrew stared out the window and saw a body wheeled out the side door. The man had hung himself. The same way Andrew's brother decided to take his life as well. Andrew wished he would have talked to the man to get to know him. He imagined how alone he must have felt.

The next morning Andrew went to check his meds then went to the room of the guy who had had his back from the PCP ordeal the other day. He was a young white man who was studying the ways of Islam. He had just gotten out of prison. He was deeply involved in anything and everything. They talked about the man that had just passed. They were seriously concerned about the staff pretending as not a thing had happened. They assumed they didn't want anyone to know someone had committed suicide at their treatment facility.

The ex-con shared a story about how his life was almost taken. He showed Andrew a picture of a car wreck he had been involved in.

"Geez, that looks terrible!" Andrew said. "I can't believe you survived that!"

"Yeah, I was lucky," the guy humbly replied.

Andrew looked closer at the picture and noticed a figure in the window of the cracked glass. "Holy shit bro! There's something in the broken glass! It looks like the grim reaper!"

"WOW! HOLY FUCK DUDE!" said the convict. "That IS the Grim reaper! Clear as day!"

There definitely was a figure in the picture. It looked like a skull face wearing a garb. It was just staring. Its mouth consisted of a grin or maybe it just looked that way because it had no lips to cover its teeth. The grim reaper had, no shit, spared the fellow occupant's life. It may have all been an abstraction but it was crystal clear if you focused your eyes on the midst of the windshield. The young gentleman began to get creeped out but laughed it off. He got on the topic of speaking of Allah. Andrew was willing to learn. The dude gave Andrew a copy of the Quran then Andrew continued about his day.

Shortly after beginning his stay at the facility, Andrew reconnected with Journey. Not the dickhead that got him locked up but the sweet dazzling girl. Every day they talked. She came in to visit him without hesitation. She brought him anything he wanted. Hot Cheetos, tobacco, a cigarette roller, green tea, and cookies were just some of the

The Witch's Hat

things she supplied. Andrew ate like a king. He absolutely loved his hot Cheetos. He ate so many that he was shitting fire. She would always bring more.

On a visitor day, the staff told Andrew he could not have her visit because of some stupid reason. Some technicality. Andrew signed up for visits but somehow they said he hadn't. It was mandatory to sign up. It's like they saw him doing good and they had to take it away. He threw a huge fit. He was yelling at the top of his lungs, bitching at the staff. He wouldn't let up. He was about to kick some ass. Before long they came to their senses and let her visit. Journey entered and said that she could hear Andrew distinctly from outside. He wasn't going to let her slip away that easily.

Andrew skipped out on group the next day to sit in his room and talk to Journey on his cell. Sadly, he was caught in the act. A staff member had walked into the room and heard Andrew drop his phone to the side of the bed. He made Andrew get up from his resting place and slid the bed away from the wall. Lo and behold, Andrew's phone lay on the floor still plugged into the charger. The douchey man took it. He left the room and bragged to everyone in the building about his find.

Andrew sat down and laid his head in his hands. He was furious and devastated at the same time. No longer could he contact Journey at any time he pleased. On the darker side, the entire building only had two phones. One was free and the other was a payphone. Unfortunately, you could only get the free one during certain times and it was always overflowed with a line of recovering addicts. Andrew wasn't a peasant. He refused to waste his time and he wasn't going to be charged by the minute either. How did they expect him to succeed without a relationship with the outside world? Journey had become his main motivation to do better. It wasn't easy without connection and he still had two weeks left at the shit hole.

Days went by and Andrew walked the halls after getting his cheeked pill. He pulled the pill from his mouth and put it in his pocket. He saw the guy that took his phone. Andrew was pissed about the man's shit-talking.

"You fucking asshole! All high and mighty cause you found a fucking phone? Fuck you!" Andrew shouted. Luckily he only had two days left at Twin Town. He was heated for his last few days and needed something to calm him down. He would have more freedom at the next place he would be transferred to and would actually be able to leave the facility. Andrew was already making plans.

"Aren't you supposed to be in group?" the man replied with an attitude. Andrew ignored him and went right to his bedroom to lay down.

Finally, the day before he would be transferred came to be, and Andrew left for the liquor store between groups. To his dismay, the staff saw him leave the premises with his sidekick. When the two patients got back Andrew tucked the pint into his waistband. He hoped it didn't protrude too much but he took his chances hoping he could just sneak into the building and stash it in his room. What he should have done was place it behind the garage outside and grabbed it later.

He entered the building and they forced him to get searched. They lifted his shirt and found his vodka. They confiscated it and probably drank it themselves. Andrew immediately had to meet with his counselor. He had a transfer set up for the next step of his treatment program. They claimed he was set up for a nice place. It was a place called Juelz Fairbanks for people who took the program seriously. They said it was hard to get in supposedly. They threatened to withdraw the offer to the residential center and extend his stay. Andrew pleaded to leave. The next place allowed phones and he would love to talk to his girlfriend again. The staff said they would think about it.

The last day came around and they woke Andrew up and gave him his morning pills. They told him it was time for his transfer. Andrew was so happy. He packed up his room with his food, books, and clothes. He read a lot as it was a habit from jail. After that, he went downstairs and they gave him a brown paper bag with his pills in it. Andrew had an idea and planned to take advantage of this opportunity. He just had to wait for the right moment.

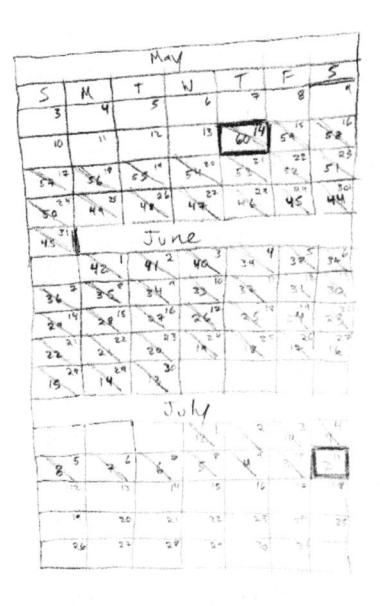

CHAPTER 34
More Trouble

Ku gave Andrew a complimentary ride in the van. Andrew was the only other one in the car. They drove about a mile and a half away. It was definitely walking distance if he wanted to visit his buddies at the old rehab. There were some good candy connections over there with a lot of street dealers lingering around. He kept that instilled in the back of his mind in case he would ever venture back to that area.

To continue on, they arrived at Juelz and Andrew checked in. Afterward, they brought him up to his room upstairs. His new roommate wasn't present as he was in group. The lady that walked Andrew up left him alone for a second so he went to the bathroom with his backpack. He still had his pills. He dumped out about 20 of them and put them into his pocket for later. He kept out two to crush on the bathroom counter and began to peel off the film so his nose didn't get too clogged. After it turned to a lumpy powder Andrew snorted it with a dollar bill from his cigarette sales. He wiped the powder from his upper lip when he heard a knock at the door.

"What are you doing?" asked the staff lady.

"I had to throw some water on my face to wake up," Andrew said as a white chunk of powder fell from his nose. She didn't say anything about it but Andrew was sure that she suspected what was going on. She ended up relapsing on cocaine the very next day and was never seen again.

While she was M.I.A., Andrew was getting to know many people. A guy he already knew named TQ followed him over from Twin Town about a week later. They grew much closer. TQ knew of a guy that lived two houses down that sold synthetic marijuana. They didn't exactly test for this at the treatment facility so Andrew felt lucky. This connection was responsible for getting half the treatment center high. It must have been a gold mine for him.

During the weeks that followed, Andrew still visited with Journey at a park nearby. Andrew even got visiting passes where he could leave for multiple hours. He would reluctantly go to his parents' house. Journey knew that Andrew despised his family but she wanted them to mend their relationship. One day out on a visit, Andrew went on bragging that he was still able to get high on K2. This was very stupid of him. Andrew just turned a roaring 23 and his mother still wanted control. Tanya informed Journey that she had called Andrew's probation officer but denied it to Andrew's face. Next thing you know Andrew is getting a call from his puppet master saying he had gotten a tip from someone that he was using this synthetic drug. Unfortunately, they DID actually have a test for K2. It wasn't a standard test. It was specialized just for people like Andrew. It wouldn't matter if he took a standard or a special test because he had smoked meth with the boys the night before anyway.

Andrew hung up on his P.O. in defiance and was pulled aside by the staff at the rehab regarding their concerns over him using again. They lectured him for a half-hour and told him he had to immediately go to the testing facility to get his urine examined. Andrew swore at them and went to his room to pack his crap. He then hit the road. After missing the deadline to take his urine analysis, probation called and left a voicemail telling Andrew to turn himself in to corrections. Andrew wasn't planning on going away that quickly. He was going to enjoy a day or two before he did just that. He called Journey and she picked him up at a gas station. They rented a hotel and spent their first night together. They even made love for the first time.

The next day Andrew was dropped off at the jailhouse. The couple had now made it official that they were in a relationship. It was kind of topsy turvy what the status was weeks prior but now it was set in stone. Instead of walking into the jail, Andrew turned around and hopped on the light rail to go see Theo. Journey was aware of this and was blowing up Andrew's phone. In the meantime, he was drinking and getting high with his uncle. Theo and Andrew had so much history that it was hard for Andrew to stay mad at him.

Finally, Andrew got sick of his phone ringing so he answered it to be berated on handing himself over. Andrew gave in to Journey and decided it would be better to turn himself over sooner than later before he was accused of more criminal charges. It was time to suck it up and take the short vacay to get off the tight leash of the government. He kept telling himself that it was only another 2 months and he would be free again.

Shortly after the phone call, Andrew actually turned himself in. He was then transferred to the workhouse. The place had been an old prison back in the day. Supposedly Al Capone and Bugsy Segal had spent a duration of time there. Being a workhouse, the ironic thing was that he had no job so he sat in a cell in block B where the worst of the inmates were placed. They never got to leave the cell besides to go to eat, take meds, shower, and an hour a day recess. They must have spent at least 20 hours contained in a six-by-eight cell.

Block B had 3 tiers separated into two sections by a cage where the guards would keep watch. Each cell was only composed of rolled steel bars and cinder blocks. It was hard to get sleep. The inmates were always yapping and obnoxiously talking shit to each other just about all day every day, shouting from cell to cell. Andrew couldn't take the bullshit anymore. He applied for a job and was transferred to Block A which moved him up a class.

He had gotten a job deburring these thick steel objects that were cut with a laser. He made a dollar an hour working full time. His hours were from 10 pm to 6:30 am. The big thing about having a job was that you were able to smoke. The hours sucked however there came a time when Andrew snuck into Journey's car on his cigarette break. He went inside Olympic Steel (his workplace) afterward and bragged to the other workhouse inmates that he got to see his woman. They all cracked jokes and made assumptions. Maybe working the night shift had its benefits.

After work when they got back to the workhouse the group was strip-searched then directed to the cafeteria to eat with block B. Andrew would eat then go to his cell to sleep. At lunchtime, the barred doors slid open for grub again. By then he was still fast asleep but food was important. Many days a nice negro would wake him up to get his fixings. Andrew would thank him but stay in bed on most occasions as he was still getting used to the graveyard shift.

Andrew found a solution to this problem. He worked with a guy named Taylor who was heavy into narcotics like any typical person Andrew vibed with. They were transferred in the same van to their worksites. On certain occasions, Andrew was flat-out given free meth by him. Taylor asked for nothing in return. They had become pretty cool. In fact, all the inmates in that transport van were cool. Andrew, however, was the only other one out of all of them that was plugged. The meth helped Andrew stay awake at night. He snorted some one night in his cell before his shift. He arrived to work tweaked out of his mind. He was running laps around the other employees and was drenched in sweat. Marquis, an inmate worker who looked like a male Whoopi Goldberg with a missing tooth, asked Andrew if he was ok.

"I'm tweaking balls man!" Andrew panted. His shirt was soaked.

Marquis burst out laughing. "Damn bro! I gotta get myself some of that shit!"

"Sorry man. I'm all out," Andrew retorted.

The Witch's Hat

"Dayum! That's tight!" Marquis replied.

Andrew wasn't at all interested in dealing drugs. He didn't think the guy who gave it to him was either. Besides, what would he trade for? Food? Commissary? It's not like he would be getting any money. He wasn't going to be locked up that long, right? Additionally, only so much could be snuck into the prison at once. It depends on how much you can stick up your ass. Kinda gross when you think about it, but hey, an addict does what an addict does.

Andrew was getting irritated being locked up. He wanted to do more than work, sleep, and eat. It wasn't like he had dope all the time to numb his madness. He was losing his mind. He needed to see Journey. She was afraid to get Andrew in trouble by seeing him while he was at work. It was against the rules and could extend his time. They got into arguments regularly from all the strain the blossoming relationship withheld. Andrew hung up the phone on her numerous times. He was furious. Each phone call cost 15 bucks. She paid it each day. For Andrew to waste her money was disrespectful.

Andrew called her one day and was ignored. He called again and she answered. He heard a man in the background.

"Who's that?" Andrew asked.

"Just a friend," Journey replied.

They argued and Andrew hung up the phone. He called back later on recess on the rec yard's phone booth outside. She said the asshole had picked her up off her feet, which was probably by her ass, and set her on his kitchen counter. They never kissed or anything but Andrew was heated. He was dead jealous.

"I thought we were dating," mentioned Andrew.

"We are. I didn't know he was going to lift me onto the counter," Journey replied in weak defense.

"Yeah but you let him. That's a bitch move. How could you do that to me? I'm going crazy in here. You are the only one that I have."

"I'm sorry," Journey stated. "It's just that it has been so rocky lately between you and I. We were just hanging out. Halsey was with me. We didn't do anything. You have been yelling at me and hanging up on me

229

the whole time you have been in there. I pay 15 bucks a day, sometimes multiple times a day just so I can talk to you and that's what you do? I'm sorry I won't hang out with him again."

"I really hope not or else we are through," said Andrew. "I'm going nutty. I need to get out of here..."

The call ran out of minutes and was brought to an end. Andrew walked inside and back to his cell. He read to try to keep his rattled mind from freaking out. He overheard some inmates walking by saying someone had jumped off the tier in block B. The guy had been transported to the nearest hospital in critical condition. Andrew was sure this institute would try to cover up this one too and just keep it on the hush. I mean who cares right? Happens all the time. Suicide in prison or treatment is everyday real shit. Why would anyone care? Bunch of lowlifes right?

As time inched by, Journey and Andrew slowly worked on mending their wounds. Andrew forgave her and he told her how much he missed her and couldn't wait to be discharged to get back to normal life. He didn't know where he was going to live. Journey said she had put an offer on a townhouse so Andrew would have a place to stay. Andrew was stunned. This was better than great. He would have a home again. She could have had another man, but instead cared for this current bum she had fallen for.

During breakfast one day while Andrew was eating, about midway through his sentence with Taylor, he saw his buddy Samson across the cafeteria. What a coincidence. Andrew waved but wasn't recognized. Samson worked in the kitchen. He made even less than Andrew did. After Samson finished his kitchen duty he went and sat with his people, the Natives. Andrew approached him and they reconnected a short bit. They didn't talk too much. Andrew felt weird because the cafeteria tables seemed to always be separated by race. They said their farewells and carried on with their day.

With his free time, Andrew had another calendar made so he could count down the days. They sure seemed to go slow. It was like he was trapped in perpetual motion. There was no T.V. so he had no idea of what was going on in the outside world. What he did know was that

The Witch's Hat

the movie *Either Which Way* was premiering and he wasn't there to see it. His mother, James, Strat, and Justin were all in Albuquerque at a film festival. Strat sat next to Robert Redford along with Redford's wife during the showing. During the part of the movie where Andrew was getting interviewed, the wife leaned towards Strat and confidently said, "That young man has something to say and he is going to say it."

Andrew was unaware of these details while he was incarcerated. He hadn't even seen the movie. It was moments like this that would drive you nuts from wonder. You had to keep your mind sidetracked. Focusing on studying or creating things is what you should do. The whole time Andrew was locked up he took notes of everything. Or at least anything that meant something to him. He wasn't sure what the purpose was. His mind would slip into a dark place. Was life going to always be this bad? He had an assortment of emotions throughout the day. Such an active thinker was to bounce to and fro from each. Push-ups helped. 100 push-ups a day to rest his mind for a few short minutes. Eventually, time passed as usual and he was released and picked up by Journey and her mother. Andrew walked by Samson's cell upon his departure and gave him all of his remaining commissary. It was the least he could do at the time for giving him a place to live. With his workhouse job, Andrew left the jail $200 richer.

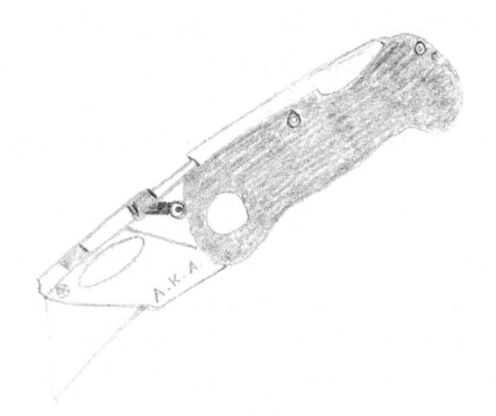

CHAPTER 35
The Real-Life

HIS MONEY WENT to court fees. Journey paid the remainder. For the time being Andrew went and lived with Journey's parents. He stayed in the playhouse in their backyard which was basically a shed with electricity which he shared with her. It was a nice cozy home for the time being. They played doctor from day to day as they awaited the closing date for the townhome she bid on and had gotten. The date was creeping up quickly to what Andrew had grown accustomed to.

Journey had been faithful to Andrew the whole 60 days at the workhouse. She proved it with a token of love. She proved it to him with a home. It would have never been home without her. Some say home is where the heart is. Journey was Andrew's heart. It was something about her that seemed so pure. Andrew loved that she had the same first initial as his brother Josh. It's like the two of them had set an agreement to assist Andrew in his lifetime. Sometime before birth, God had collected the souls and gave them all a life purpose. The double J team were Andrew's guardian Angels but that didn't keep Andrew from his destructive path. It was a path well-protected of which he would learn from. It didn't mean there would be an end

The Witch's Hat

to his suffering but perhaps led to the realization he can do something with his pain for the better.

There is a reasoning for everything. Even for senseless suffering. Andrew's struggle with addiction had left a mark on his image. He was no longer trusted. He would continue to drink in excess and his anger would build within him. They had moved into the townhouse and Journey had done what she could to try to stop Andrew. He just wanted to drink as an outlet from the many things that bothered him. Journey like most people may not have understood or looked at it the same way as Andrew did. He was still a newbie and needed to manage better control of his consumption. They would get into arguments while Andrew was drunk. Andrew tried to establish dominance by throwing a computer down the stairs. All it did was make Journey cry. She would shake and tremble to the floor. Andrew had a demon within him that got satisfaction from someone suffering the same as he did. Transforming this bad energy and expelling the darkness from within himself would be quite the process.

Andrew continued being a drunk and work would come and go. He started off well through a temp agency but would get let go as soon as a company wanted to hire him. He would get fired for failing the UAs for pot. Eventually, he got a job as a printer. They didn't care if he smoked. Andrew told them he would pass the urine analysis with fake pee which he did to his success. He stayed busy printing signs and posters. With the scraps, he would print all sorts of cool things and give them to the father of his girlfriend.

After work hours he continued to buy liquor and drank away his worries. Journey was getting sick of Andrew's lashing anger and snappiness so one day she grabbed all his beer and dumped it down the drain. Andrew started screaming at her to the point she hid in her room. She locked herself in. Andrew was in red mode and ran into the door using his body weight to bust it open to witness her laying in bed crying.

"Please leave me alone!" she said, sobbing. "I can't handle any more! Please!"

Andrew looked into Journey's teary eyes and watched as her mascara dripped down her face. He got right into her bubble and yelled, "You did this to me! All I wanted to do was have a drink. You're gonna regret this!"

Journey tried to get up and run. Andrew grabbed her and pushed her back onto the bed. He went to his nightstand and grabbed his red box cutting knife. The knife blade was brand new and extremely sharp. He screamed, "You want to watch me die? I'll kill myself and it will be all your fault!"

"No! Please don't!" Journey stammered. Her voice was partially inaudible as she struggled to breathe. She was hyperventilating. She got up to try to stop Andrew but fell to her knees. Andrew unfolded the blade so it was in the open position. He put it up to his throat. His adrenaline was spiraling out of control. The terror in Journey's face was very real. She got up again and lunged for Andrew. Andrew dodged her, ran to the bathroom, and locked himself away.

"This is all your fault! You will never forget this! If you want to touch my beer you get to suffer the consequences!" Andrew shouted from behind the door.

"I'm calling 9-1-1!" Journey cried.

"If you do. It will be to pick up my dead body!" Andrew returned.

He opened the door to make sure she wasn't calling the police. She held the phone in her hand but hadn't called. Andrew then rolled up his pajama pants to expose his left thigh. He held the knife in his right hand.

"Take another step and I'll leave blood all over this floor," said Andrew with an evil smirk. The demon had risen. He knew he couldn't go back. He said he was going to cut himself. He had to stick to his word if she went against his request.

"Andrew! Please! Please! Please! Don't!" Journey sobbed.

She ended up reaching for the knife. Andrew quickly, without hesitation, used a fair amount of force to drag the knife across his upper leg. It cut through like butter. Blood started spilling to the floor. He cut at least an inch into his leg fat. The folds of skin had separated

The Witch's Hat

enough to fit the width of two fingers. His inner fat tissue looked like pink cottage cheese.

Andrew had slit his leg because he knew it wouldn't be as lethal as cutting his throat. His motive was to show people he wasn't fucking around and not to test him. Presently, Journey ran and grabbed one of Andrew's wife beaters. She wrapped it around his leg. The muscle tee absorbed the blood like a rag until Andrew got out to the car. Once they started driving he could feel a warm trickle down his leg and into his shoe. Luckily Journey sped through traffic and arrived at the E.R. in no time. She parked the car and helped Andrew into the hospital.

Andrew knew for a fact that he needed stitches. It didn't take a doctor to know that. It was fairly obvious. When he was questioned by a male nurse, Andrew fed him a story about how he was walking through the park and a drunk guy stabbed him. He didn't really think it through too much as he was himself the drunk one. They questioned his girlfriend and she told them the real story. After they stitched him up they brought him face to face with Journey to let him know that he had been found out. Andrew still denied the accusations because he didn't want to be committed to the hospital, but they knew. They gave him some paperwork on what they called a self-inflicted wound and included the suicide hotline number. Next, Andrew was then released after only a few hours.

"You realize they could have locked me up, right? It would have all been your fault. Then I really would have checked myself out. Don't do that again!" Andrew told Journey on the way home.

She cried until they arrived at the townhouse and even when they went to bed. By then the liquor had mostly worn off. Andrew held her close and tried to comfort her. She fell asleep in his arms.

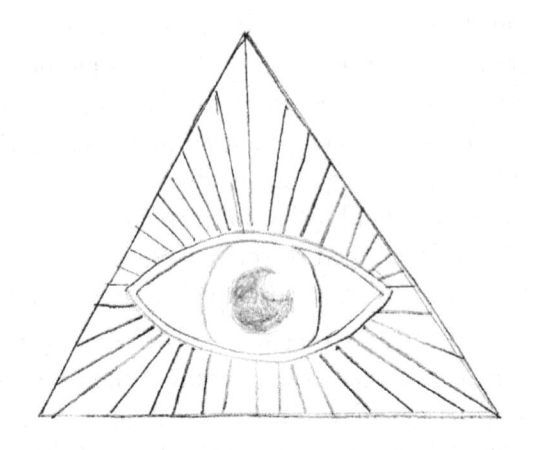

CHAPTER 36
The Medium

JOURNEY AND ANDREW had gotten some shitty neighbors. It was 2016, a year later from when they moved into the townhouse and it was time to leave. They needed to save money. Just so happened Journey's brother, Jarred, was in need of a place. Journey rented out her home to him and the couple moved back to her parents' house. This time Andrew was allowed to stay inside. The kind parents were more comfortable with him now. Andrew was lucky that they even put up with all his bs. They saw potential in him and would try to coach him.

Living was smooth aside from Tanya shutting down the organization named after Josh. There were not enough people participating in the events. The world continued to spin just the same as people stop caring. It was a sad time but Andrew figured if anything, he could start his own society of some sort in the future. He laid this thought to rest for the time being to concentrate on the steps he had right before him.

Soon enough October came along and Journey had bought tickets for Theresa Caputo from the show *Long Island Medium*. She presented them to Tanya and Andrew as a surprise. They were ecstatic, hoping to get a message from Josh. The three of them took the drive down to Rochester, MN at the end of the month and walked into Mayo Civic Center not knowing what to expect. They found their seats before the show commenced. Journey got up to use the bathroom. While she was gone Tanya slipped Andrew some Xanax. It was like she wanted him to slip into his old ways. She needed him to need her.

As soon as Journey got back from the restroom everyone was instructed to shut off their cell phones. Then Theresa took the stage. She said she was going to go around the room and try to give everyone a fair chance at a reading.

Andrew was a believer yet skeptical at the same time. He sat and watched her give readings to some other audience members at random but wondered if they had been staged. After her previous reading, she came walking in their direction. "I feel a tightening in my throat. Like I'm suffocating," she said gently while holding her windpipe. She pointed in Journey, Tanya, and Andrew's vicinity. "It's coming in this direction."

Aww shit! It sounded like it could have been Josh. Andrew's mom stood up. Journey and Andrew followed her lead shortly after.

Tanya blurted, "My son hung himself. Could it be him?"

"Let's see," Theresa responded. "I'm getting a symbol of a stuffed animal made of his t-shirt? Is this relevant?"

"Yes! One of Josh's friends made a stuffed animal with one of his shirts shortly after he died," Tanya replied, choking up a bit.

"He wants to let you know he appreciates that token of remembrance. He also says he loves his memorial that you guys had put on his final resting place. He loves all the decorations that were placed around it too. He also mentioned something about a piercing..." Theresa revealed.

"Oh wow! Josh's loved ones chipped in to have a bench put at his grave. Also, I told him he could get an industrial piercing a few weeks before he died and he was so excited," Tanya said, bursting into tears.

"By the way, I'm sorry for your loss. Josh says he apologizes that you had to find him the way you did. He wants you to know that you don't have to carry any guilt. He appreciates all that you have done in his honor and not to beat yourself up over a decision you made recently. Also, what's an industrial piercing?" Theresa asked.

"It's a bar that goes through your upper ear," Tanya sniveled.

"Oh, I think my daughter has one of those. I believe what is important is that Josh is okay and has served his life's purpose," said Theresa with enthusiasm. She looked at Andrew. "I want to switch over to this man standing over here. I feel like you need a message more than anyone in this room."

"Oh, really?" questioned Andrew nervously. He wasn't comfortable being put on the spot in front of so many people in a live audience but he was wondering what his brother had to say to him.

"Yes. He told me he's sick of following you around," she chuckled. "He's only kidding. It sounds like you have had it rough. He wants to warn you that you will be in an accident very soon that will change your life forever. He wants you to know that he will be right by your side."

"Oh, wow!" Andrew said in amazement. His stomach dropped. He didn't really know how to reply. "I guess I have had quite a few near-death experiences in the past few years. It definitely was tough." Within Andrew's mind, he wondered what accident he would be involved in. He was kinda weary and creeped out.

"Just know everything will be okay," she replied.

"OK," voiced Andrew.

"Also, he mentions another thing made from his shirt. I see a pillow," Theresa stated.

Andrew went blank. He was in his own world thinking about the previous message she had just given him. He didn't even hear what she had just said. He grew paranoid. What was this accident she was talking about?

Theresa repeated herself again about the pillow. No one answered and Andrew was in outer space. She eventually gave up and went to the next reading. The threesome watched the remaining readings until the very end. After it ended Tanya mentioned something about the pillow as they walked out the door heading back to the car to leave.

"I wonder what the pillow thing was all about," Tanya remarked.

"What do you mean pillow?" Andrew asked.

"I don't know. She mentioned something about a pillow made from his shirt," she responded.

"Pillow? No, that was the teddy bear, wasn't it? I didn't hear that but yeah, I've been planning on getting a pillow made from his t-shirt," Andrew said.

"Well, why didn't you say anything?" Tanya retorted.

"I don't know. I kinda spaced out."

"Oh well. I had a great time. Thank you Journey for the gift," Tanya said smiling at her son's lover.

Even with those words, deep down Tanya took this occasion for granted. She felt like it was owed to her. Journey did whatever she could to please her and would bend over backward. She believed Andrew's parents were model citizens. She even started a second job being a personal care aide for Andrew's siblings. Tanya hadn't a job and barely ever had to watch them. She sat back and collected her adoption funds from the state. Even with that in mind, Tanya and Journey had a pretty close relationship. All in all, Journey did a good job reconnecting Andrew with his family as well, even though she would later regret it.

"You're welcome," acknowledged Journey.

The three then hopped in the car and cruised on home.

CHAPTER 37
The Beer Belly Man

It wasn't much more than a month later when on a Friday night the couple took a friend to a bar called Beer Belly's for some drinks as it was her birthday. They sat at a table and conversed. Andrew had worked from 5:30 that morning until 6:30 in the evening doing his printing job. It was a long week and he was plum tired. He finished two beers then he crossed his arms and laid his head down on the table. He was taking a little catnap. Sure it was rude but he didn't care. He wanted to go home but felt he hadn't much of a choice in the matter as the two women talked.

Minutes prior to his catnap, Journey pointed out that one of the bouncers had had a crush on her in high school and he kept staring at the table. Andrew didn't let it bother him until the bouncer came over and told him he couldn't sleep in the bar. Andrew got defensive and said he was just waiting for the women to finish their drinks. He told the bouncer he wasn't sleeping and that he was just resting his eyes. The bouncer held firm that this kind of activity wasn't allowed at the bar. Then he went back to his corner stool and stared some more.

The Witch's Hat

Was he just trying to show off his machismo? Did he think he was Mr. Big, Bad and Tough? If Andrew hadn't the knowledge that this turd had tried getting with his woman before he wouldn't have taken such offense. However, Andrew felt wildly humiliated. He walked over to the bouncer fuming. The fat piece of shit had to be almost twice Andrew's size but Andrew didn't care.

He pulled up to about a foot away from the man and raised the tone of his voice towards him, "I just want to tell you to fuck off asshole! I'm here paying money to visit this dump and you have to antagonize me for resting my eyes? Fuck you man!"

Andrew turned around and speed-walked over to the register to pay his tab. "Can you please hurry and ring me up?" he urged. "I'm getting out of this shit hole and never coming back."

Andrew retrieved his debit card from the bartender and did a 180 to notice the bouncer right on his ass. "So your gonna fucking follow me now?" Andrew barked. "Do you not have anything better to do? You can't see I'm fucking leaving? Fuck off!"

Andrew walked towards the table where his girlfriend and friend sat with his antagonist in hot pursuit. "Babe let's go! Fuck this place! Let's go!" he shouted. Andrew wasn't anywhere near drunk. He was just getting loud because he was irritated. He became especially fired up when the bouncer stood in between him and his party.

Andrew stood toe to toe with him. "What are you gonna do man? I ain't doing shit. Oh, wait! I see! You want to party huh?" Andrew shouted as he started dancing and dry humping the air right in front of the bouncer. He continued egging the guy on. "See, you ain't gonna do shit. C'mon babe! Let's go!"

Andrew then turned his back on the guard and proceeded towards the door. He had made it to the entryway and just as he went to push the door open he was clobbered from behind and lifted from his feet. The bouncer slammed Andrew into and out the door and if that wasn't enough, he even threw him face-first down the stoop outside. He hit the cement using his hands to somewhat brace the impact of his head. Immediately upon thereafter, he was laid on top of by the same guy.

The man weighed maybe about 250 pounds. Suddenly the bar door sprung open again from behind and 1 more security guard along with the owner came pouring out as well as some of the customers and Andrew's distraught girlfriend. It looked like she had seen a ghost.

"Get off him!" she screamed.

"Not gonna happen. We called the cops. This bastard is going to jail," commented the owner standing on the sidelines. He was even heavier than the one Andrew was tangling with. This must have been where the bar name "Beer Belly's" had come from. Why they needed so many assailant security captors in a small bar was bizarre. Andrew tried with all his might to break free but couldn't.

Next off, Mr. Beer Belly himself told the man to get off Andrew. Then the 400 plus pound beer man quickly pounced to lay on top of him. He was so big that Andrew was not able to move a muscle, he could barely even breathe at that.

"Help!" cried out Andrew in a muffled voice.

There were a bunch of bystanders watching. A few were even taking videos with their phones.

"Stop fucking videotaping!" the birthday girl said to them. She then turned to Mr. Beer Belly. "Get off of him! Get off!"

Then Journey chimed in with tears streaming down her face, "Please get off of him! Please! Please!"

"I can't breathe," Andrew said in a cloaked voice. "Help!"

"Can't you hear him? He can't breathe! Please get off of him!" Journey pleaded in hysteria.

The man didn't budge. "He is going to jail," he said zealously. "If he is talking, he is breathing."

As Andrew lay there, he tried his hardest to not pass out. His lungs were being compressed and he could barely intake any air. All of a sudden he had a surge of energy for survival. He screamed bloody murder. He screamed and screamed and screamed and screamed. This action kept him breathing until he finally gave up.

"Please!" Andrew wailed. Then he went silent. His eyes rolled to

The Witch's Hat

the back of his head. About 30 seconds later the police showed up. They weren't located too far away.

"Get off of him!" shouted one of the officers. "Everyone back up! We are going to handle this."

The obese man finally got his fat ass off of Andrew. He came to after a few seconds when the oxygen replenished his body. His soul had wandered like a boomerang and he felt like he was in a trance. His adrenaline was still flowing through his veins. He was fired up but dropped to his knees while tears ran from his face as he gasped for air. He had realized he could have died. He had also scarred his lover for life. Journey would never forget this day. It would have been even more traumatic if he would have suffocated to bring an end to his existence as we know it.

"You are not being arrested," the officer told Andrew.

The beer belly man was upset. He told the story of what Andrew had done but the police didn't care much for it. They figured he had suffered enough. It was just the wrong place at the wrong time. It wasn't like Andrew had killed anybody or even harmed them. He may have been guilty of egging the man on, but it was all in innocence.

After some tears flowed from Andrew's face for a second or two he strongly got to his feet and floated to Journey to give her a great big hug.

In short, after a report was established an officer looked upon Andrew and his crew and said, "You guys are free to go."

The three of them walked to the car and went home. Andrew struggled to sleep that night. He maybe got 3 hours of slumber at the most. The next morning came by and he was still furious. He had also become very embarrassed as he was informed a video of him struggling for his life was posted on Facebook. It went viral and had gotten thousands of views. This caused Andrew shame and deteriorated his mental health. His ego wouldn't let the bar owner get the best of him. He turned his negative feelings into the construction of strength and courage. At this point, Andrew was still levitating, as he would be for a long time.

Andrew had the bright idea to seek revenge on the man. He didn't give up that easily. He felt like the business had gone too far so he went to the police station with his girlfriend and filed charges. Andrew filed criminal charges as well as a civil lawsuit and scheduled a visit for an investigation. A cop called Andrew after he left and informed him that the city's cameras were turned off in the parking lot so there was no footage of Andrew being thrown onto the pavement. The bar owner wouldn't give up his footage either. Andrew thought this was kind of fishy. But it didn't matter. There was still footage on Facebook. It angered a lot of people and they were super upset with the bar owner. A lot of people vowed never to go there again.

Eventually, a woman sought out Andrew over the weekend and stated she had been assaulted at the bar too. They pushed her down the stoop as well. They had to be pretty low bouncers to pick on a woman. It was probably over something petty like Andrew's situation. She shared that there were three others that were assaulted as well. She even showed a picture of a guy she knew of that had swollen black eyes and a broken jaw. He had to get wires to get it back in working order. It almost seemed as if the bar security didn't care for the well-being of a percentage of customers and would eagerly wait for the next person to even scarcely step out of line. They hunted individuals for sport.

Andrew wanted to avenge the victims and he was on a mission to do so. He felt on top of the world, like nothing could stop him. The following Monday after work Andrew went back to the precinct to give a more in-depth statement and brought a recording device with him to record all the conversations with the officer. He also used an app called tape-a-call as well to record phone conversations. He felt like he was in a movie. He got so caught up in everything that he couldn't get himself out of hyperdrive. He would stay up with minimal sleep during the night, plotting his next move.

Soon enough, Strativarious had seen the video circulating on social media and texted Andrew asking if he was ok. Andrew told him things were crazy and that they should chat on the phone. Strat called that night and Andrew went outside on the deck at Journey's parents to chew the fat with him. It had just begun to snow lightly. Andrew paced

The Witch's Hat

back and forth. He told Strat the story and how he was in the process of pushing charges. Strat sympathized with Andrew, then they got on the topic of Strat's career as a rockstar cello player.

During mid-conversation, Andrew heard a rattle of a chain-link fence and looked up to see 3 guys with ski masks hopping it. They started creeping towards him.

Andrew immediately without delay yelled as loud as he could, "Hey! Get the fuck out of here!"

One of the guys in the ski mask fell from the fence onto his ass. The other two had gotten startled and started running with the clumsy guy following in last place. They skirted down the driveway and across the street through the neighbor's yard. The neighbor was outside and they ran right around him.

"Hey man, I got to go!" Andrew said to Strat over the phone. Strat was surprised and concerned when the call ended.

Just then, Andrew's girlfriend's father swung open the door to the garage he hangs in. "What's going on?" he asked.

"A bunch of niggers jumped into the yard. I scared them off!" Andrew replied.

Andrew phoned the police to report the incident as he thought it could have been tied in with his court case. Had the bar owner hired a group of thugs to beat, scare or kill Andrew? An elderly man had just been murdered in his home down the street by a gang member recently. There had been an influx of low-income folks coming from Chicago for Minnesota's benefits system, with this came crime. Perhaps this incident was entirely a fluke but Andrew never doubted the bar owner's involvement in sending this group of individuals after him.

A few minutes passed and the police arrived at the property. Red, white, and blues lit up the neighborhood. Andrew told the officer what had happened and said he thought it was related to the bar incident. The police officer then took the time to search the area.

"I don't see any footprints in the snow," he said. "Are you sure you saw them?"

"It just started snowing. There is barely any snow on the ground," postulated Andrew in a defensive manner. "What... Do you think I made this up?"

"I'm just saying I don't see any evidence that anyone was here," the man answered.

The police officer wrote in his report what they had talked about. Probably said it was some kind of delusion. Due to what the officer said, Journey began to worry about Andrew. She claimed he was seeing things. No one believed him. He felt super alone and in danger.

Andrew waved goodbye to the officer as he launched from the curb. Then he turned to Journey and mumbled in defeat, "If I get murdered it's because you didn't take this seriously."

Sadly, his words didn't get him anywhere. That night, Andrew's sleeping pattern was thrown off even more. He got up at 4:30 in the morning every weekday. He lived upstairs next to Journey's parents' room. He would stay up until 2:00 A.M or later if he even slept at all. One neighboring night thereafter as he laid in bed, he scoped out his room while Journey slept. He was paranoid. His eyes locked upon the closet. He saw a shadow cross in front of him dimming the light from the T.V. There was a window in this second-story room but there was nothing outside to illuminate it and besides the window was covered with a curtain so it couldn't have been a bat or a bird flying by. So what did he just observe?

His instincts geared him into looking at the clock. The time was 11:11 pm. Tanya may have been crazy but she did teach him one thing. She introduced Andrew to angel numbers and Andrew used this to guide his path through life. Anytime something strange would happen he would check the time. Andrew was in the spirit world. He felt like his brother was watching over him as the medium said. His fears had been momentarily relieved, he let his ambitions and feelings of euphoria take over.

Stirred into the mix, while Andrew continued to work the next few days he began to have panic attacks. His heart would start racing and he felt on the verge of snapping. He was still traumatized. When he had these panic attacks it felt in a way like he was all alone with

The Witch's Hat

the weight of the world on his shoulders. He could not give up. It wasn't just his reputation on the line but he had to give the other bar victims the satisfaction of watching the assailant be punished for his wrongdoings. Unfortunately, there wasn't even a court date scheduled. From what it looked like it would be over a month to even see a judge. This was what boosted the anxiety Andrew had. If they had sent thugs after him within a week from the incident, then what could happen in that month-long period? The time it takes to see a judge, unfortunately, puts victims at risk during the duration. They could be blackmailed, assaulted, or even killed. Andrew did what he could to stay near cameras and people. He felt less likely to be ambushed if he was in the proximity of others.

Andrew sat down at home one day all alone after an early work departure and examined the comments on the Facebook video. It had been a little over a week since it was recorded. Most of the comments were in his defense but there were a few derogatory comments aimed at him as well. It was the unpleasant comments that bugged him and the fact that thousands of people watched the video. However, the publicity was good because it made it more likely to give the bar a bad name. Andrew read and read through the comments. Some people called him a "drunk pussy" and that he was lying about not being able to breathe because he was faintly speaking and screaming in the video.

After the comment read, Andrew got upset and began pacing around the house. How will he make this right? He didn't have the patience to wait. He needed to complete his mission but there was no rushing the court system. His body began to tremble. Journey walked in the side door of the home from work. He gave her a big hug and a smooch to welcome her. She said something to him but it went in one ear and out the other.

"Are you ok?" she repeated.

"Huh? Yeah. I'm fine." Andrew said in a daze. It was like he had the 4 Non-Blondes song in his head wondering what was going on. After a long day pacing on his feet, Andrew sat down with the family to eat. They tried speaking to him but he didn't reply. He was too busy lost in his own mind. His eyes skirted away from any eye contact with others.

He instead chose to stare at his food and pretended to examine it to seem like he was physically occupied.

He was snuck up on and felt a tap on his shoulder which got his attention. "There is honestly something wrong with you Andrew. We really want you to drop the charges and check yourself into the hospital. We don't think you can handle all this," Journey said.

"Yeah. Not gonna happen," replied Andrew.

Then her mom cut in. "We have all been paying really close attention to you and you haven't been yourself. We are growing more and more concerned."

The family continued talking to him to do their best to persuade him. He responded with, "Well I mean I guess I can go to the hospital if they can help me out. I mean, I feel fine. I just don't want to be put on a cocktail of medicine. As for the charges, I'm not dropping them."

The family respected his decision. After dinner, Andrew was dropped off at Mercy Medical Center where he spent 3 days in the psychiatric unit. He figured all this jazz was related to the bar event so he made sure to make it known. He shared his story which was overlooked. They thought he was paranoid and having delusions of people coming after him when in reality it was very real to Andrew. As a result, they prescribed him a hefty dose of loxapine.

Andrew didn't really notice any difference after taking it. He just vibed out with whoever and whatever he was doing. He saw the movie "One Flew Over the Cuckoo's Nest" for the first time in there. The part where Jack Nicholson received electroshock therapy gave Andrew the heebie-jeebies. He never wanted to experience such a thing. When Andrew wasn't watching movies he was reading a book called *Common Sense* by Thomas Paine. Instead of independence from Great Britain as Paine advocates in the book, Andrew wanted independence from the chains of this so-called land of the free. The land of the greedy of those who work their lives on by to MAYBE reach a day when they wouldn't have to anymore. But even then, you are still a victim to society's manipulations. Andrew wondered what Paine would have thought of today's tax laws. Essentially everything is taxed. How can you be free in a land where nothing is free? The rich grow richer while the working class blames the poor for not pulling their fair share when in reality we should be targeting the wealthy whales. Andrew put some thought into Paine's book and knew that there was a better way for people to achieve happiness without being exploited. Could life not be a paradise for everyone?

Whatever the case, Andrew knew with technology we should have more free time but why do we stay working 40 plus hours a week? Life should get easier and more laid back. Why is this an issue? Are we made to stay busy to boost the economy, and pay taxes to support war? Are we supposed to be stuck in this never-ending cycle and remain below? Andrew was going through a rant in his head but decided to set the issue aside. He was only one man and strength comes in numbers. This yearning for existentialism had become apparent within Andrew.

Andrew's mind started slowing down. His thoughts had decelerated which in turn hindered his motor skills. The doctor felt like Andrew could manage in the outside world and released him after the third day. He referred Andrew to a psychiatrist. Andrew hated being prescribed drugs. He didn't like the fact that they manipulated you into being something that you are not. If you were to ask him about street drugs that get you high he may have had another point of view. He liked getting high because it made him happy but at this point, he was doped up on an antipsychotic which he didn't like.

The day Andrew was released from the hospital he partook in some Mary Jane. Shortly after, he managed to walk and sit in the garage with his girlfriend's father to watch television while they listened to music. Leopold had recently started playing inspirational music by Bob Dylan, John Lennon, Ted Nugent, and many more. These songs molded Andrew into someone he could be proud of. They hit him hard, deep within his soul. He became obsessed.

Midway through the first song Andrew started to feel his muscles act up. They were locking up from the loxapine. Andrew began to worry. His head was stuck at a tilt and his arms went up like Frankenstein. Every time he tried to put them back in place they moved right back into the Frankenstein position.

"Something isn't right!" Andrew asserted.

"What's wrong? Why is your head like that?" Leopold asked.

"I don't know. My frickin arms are locked into place too!" Andrew said in a panic. "I better get inside before I can't move any more!"

Andrew used his legs and his body momentum to lift himself from the chair as his arms were useless. He exited the garage then crossed the backyard to make it inside the house. Next, he shouted for Journey. Andrew did his best to explain his problem but he really didn't have to. She could see his cocked head and lifted arms. Andrew's legs started to give out in the kitchen and he started falling to the floor. Journey helped him up and guided him into the living room to sit down on the couch. Afterward, she called the ambulance.

When the rescue squad showed up, they came inside and burst into laughter. Both men were ex-military.

"I'm not gonna be stuck like this forever am I?" queried Andrew.

"No, you are experiencing a dystonic reaction," chuckled the young ambulance man. "You will be alright. It will fade away. We will get you to the hospital to check you out. This is one of the reasons why I don't take medications myself."

"Yeah, no kidding. I don't want to take this shit either. They said I had to in order to leave the hospital. Fuckin bullshit!"

"I'm so sorry to hear that man! That sucks. Once we bring you to the hospital I'm sure they will take you off of this," the man responded. "You ready?"

"Yeah. One sec," Andrew said as he took a failed attempt to get up from the couch. "Goddamnit! I'll need help getting up!"

The man helped Andrew up and they loaded him on a gurney outside the front door. Andrew hated ambulance rides. Upon entry, he could smell death inside of it. Other than that the ride wasn't actually that bad. He and the medics cracked jokes as he was being hooked up to an IV. Once they arrived at the hospital Andrew was given a muscle relaxer and placed in a room with Journey sitting alongside him until he got better. They told him he didn't have to continue taking the medication anymore but that he had to make sure to follow up

The Witch's Hat

with a psychiatrist urgently. Shortly before he was discharged the staff scheduled an appointment a few days away but he canceled it. He told his girlfriend he didn't need meds.

The family was worried for Andrew after he got home med-free from the hospital. What would stop him from acting the way he did? He was supercharged again. He felt like a machine in another dimension. He continued to stay awake at night with an eye open. He would go into a somnolent meditative state as he lay staring at the ceiling absorbing his surroundings. He was tired and revved up at the same time. As he lay he heard noises and brushed them off. He had thoughts of someone breaking in. He felt as if he needed a gun to protect himself. He was forbidden to apply for one and felt like a sitting duck.

CHAPTER 38
King of the Ring

It had been nearly three weeks since the night at the bar and it was just a few days before Christmas. Journey and Andrew went to the mall and visited Santa Claus. They made small talk with him and Andrew mentioned he was disturbed due to being assaulted recently. Andrew shared with Santa that all he wanted was to settle his court case. Lo and behold, Santa had the number to a high-class lawyer. Andrew called and the attorney was intrigued to hear from him for the mere fact that he had received the number from Santa. The lawyer said he would contact Andrew back to see if he could take on his case pro bono as Andrew had asked for. Andrew felt like he was on the right path. The lawyer called him within a day and said he could take on the case. The two spoke on and off from here on out regarding the suit.

Finally, Christmas Eve came along which was quite joyous for Journey's family. It gave them hope. Andrew couldn't recall much of it as he was zoning out, but he sure went through the motions. He had to devise a scheme.

A couple days after Christmas, Journey and Andrew took a trip to Las Vegas. They had planned it months prior. It was her first time on an airplane which was exciting. Above all the excitement, Andrew was flying. His mind was racing at all times. Due to Andrew's bar ordeal, he learned that life is precious. It can be taken from you at any point

The Witch's Hat

in time. He had to do something big in Sin City. He needed a ring. He was going to propose. He had failed at making it a surprise. He had no clue what ring to get and wanted to get Journey something she loved. A day after they arrived in Nevada they went to Kay Jewelers and Andrew asked her to pick out a wedding ring. Even though he took away the shock factor, she at least enjoyed the search. Andrew bought the ring and then they roamed for a tobacco shop via Uber.

Andrew mentioned that he was searching for bud to the Uber driver. The guy said it was Andrew's lucky day as he had some. Andrew bought an eighth. It was fire like the man had said. Some of the best weed Andrew had ever smoked. It transported him to a "G-world" of paranoia and heightened sensitivity. It kept him more secure than not and aware of his surroundings while brawling with his anxiety.

They had arrived at a tobacco shop where Andrew was in search of cigarettes and a bowl to smoke up while he was at it. Moments before they arrived a homeless man had tried to rob the store. He was sitting outside with a knife waiting for the police to arrive. As Journey waited in the Uber, Andrew walked past him and went inside to see loose change all over the floor. The owner was a middle eastern man. He had a shotgun in his hand.

"What happened? Did you get robbed?" Andrew asked.

"He tried to," the man said with a thick accent. "He is just a homeless man committing crime to go to jail where they are provided with shelter and food. That's why he is waiting for the police outside. He did this on purpose."

Andrew bobbed his head up and down as he walked to the counter to pay for the merch. He did his best to avoid the broken shards of glass on the ground. He paused during his check-out. He looked into the broken glass display and pointed out a knife to the clerk. He figured he needed to buy one in case the homeless dude tried something funny on his way out. After the purchase, Andrew palmed the knife in his hand to avoid detection as he walked out the door. He nodded to the vagrant. He seemed like he may have been a tweaker swaying back and forth in his noggin between re tapping into his superpowers or making the smart decision of seeking shelter. It was too bad for him,

Andrew thought as he resumed his walk to the Uber car. The love birds were then dropped off at Fremont Street where they had a grand time shopping and being entertained for the night. Eventually, they became tired and headed back to the hotel to sleep. Or at least try.

Journey and Andrew spent the next few days going to shows and gambling. They continued taking Uber's all around the city. They saw Criss Angel which was amazing and even visited the Pawn Stars shop from the television show. Near the pawnshop, they walked down the street to visit some antique stores. Andrew had bought a cool John Lennon poster of the day that he was shot. What a hero that guy was. If Andrew could make a change in the world and be shot down, as a result, he would rest easy. If and only if he was able to live a somewhat full life with children and his loving woman. It was better than dying of COPD, cancer, or a heart attack from smoking. Of course, Andrew wanted to live forever but unfortunately, everyone meets their demise. Knowing this, Andrew adopted the motto of what Neil Young said, "It's better to burn out than to fade away."

After the couple finished shopping, they sat on the curb near Pawn Stars to wait for their ride. The bouncer from the famous pawn shop said they couldn't sit there and that they looked out of place. The ride never came and the man felt bad for their predicament. He offered them a lift to the hotel since he was taking a dinner break, so they took off. After they got to Palace Station, the guy gave Andrew his number in case they ran into any more trouble. The lesson is that not all security guards are bad. The couple then got into their hotel room, relaxed a few hours, and after a little bit of sundown gambling, they called it a day.

New Year's Eve came around and Andrew, still jolted, was having thoughts going a million miles a minute. The lovers took a relaxing walk along the strip where Andrew bought a bottle of UV Blue to boost up his spirit and slow down his mind. Eventually, they looped back to the hotel to get ready for the ball drop. Marijuana would soon be legal in Vegas in just a few hours and Andrew was ready to celebrate. Andrew lit up a bowl which stunk up the whole hotel room plus the hallway. He heard people gossip about it as they went by. Andrew sprayed the hotel room and continued his sesh outside. On the way back inside, a group of young black men were getting hassled in the hallway for strolling around with a bottle of grog sauce. Andrew stopped and confronted the staff lady who was trying to confiscate their bottle.

"It's New Year's Eve and we're in Vegas! Leave them alone! Jesus Christ!" Andrew jeered. The lady did just that, and the men carried on with their night.

Once Andrew got back to the hotel room he went and tried to sneakily grab the wedding ring from the nightstand drawer while Journey watched T.V. Next, he paced the room until it was minutes away from the new year. He pounded down shot after shot until he was plastered. Finally, it was down to the last seconds and Andrew took out his phone to record his proposal. He hit play. The event was sloppy as Andrew struggled to get the words out. It wasn't the greatest at all. He finished popping the question and even through the shitty proposal, Journey still opted to say yes and gladly did so. The ball had dropped and she was now his fiancé.

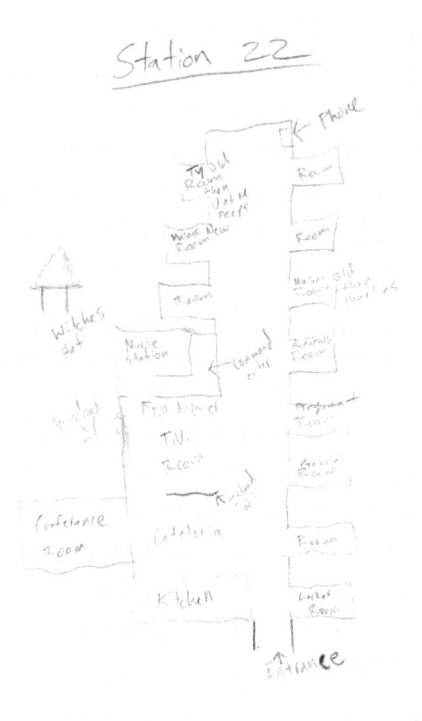

CHAPTER 39
The Circus Retreat

THE PAIR FLEW back to Minnesota and settled back into the soon-to-be in-laws' house. The whole world had been notified via social media that Andrew had proposed. Andrew was also blowing up Facebook with all sorts of crazy stuff like how the Bible was written by kings to basically lead the masses like sheep. He shared music of all sorts of whatever mood he was in. He shared pictures from movies like *Mississippi Burning* or *The Shooter* starring Mark Wahlberg. Most of all, he started getting obsessed with aliens and numbers. He let the numbers guide him and he embraced them. He felt like it would lead him to his higher purpose. He looked at things in multiples of 11 and it grew from there. Pairs, threesomes, and quadruplets were significant when looking at the clock. Such times as 11:11 or 1:11. The

The Witch's Hat

constant repetition and synchronization of it all was amazing. Andrew tried to figure out a pattern. Whatever he thought about at that exact moment when realized was grown upon. He ended up researching more and more into angel numbers. He believed he was in communication with the universe. He believed that we are all wired to a complicated system that we don't quite understand and was confident that there was some sort of purpose behind it. In short, Andrew was getting more and more into thinking that we are all part of some human DNA splicing program brought upon by extraterrestrials. He essentially started to believe that aliens are behind the creation of the human race.

Andrew sat in the garage (man cave) with Leopold one day and went on a tangent about a theory that life was specifically a trial to be positioned into a role for some galactic space battle. Leopold got weirded out and texted inside the house to the women to get Andrew inside and out of the garage. Andrew was deranged as ever and couldn't snap out of it. He had had an epiphany that aliens were absolutely real but what was the purpose? Are we part of some experiment? Is this a test? Is heaven on earth and we had to work to achieve it? Are we slaves? Andrew had tons of questions about extraterrestrials. He knew he was on to something. He felt like his sense of spirituality as well as being out of his mind was related to something special. Was he part alien himself?

Andrew went back into the garage the next day and Leopold shared the same songs he made known and that struck a chord within Andrew. The same songs that played over and over in Andrew's head. The songs were "Masters of War" by Bob Dylan and "Working Class Hero" by John Lennon. He even played some Pink Floyd and talked about the guy in the band who went mad nuts. His name was Syd Barrett. What was most important, however, was that Andrew grew from these songs. They were the water and sunlight to his seed to help him grow into the man he was supposed to be. Leopold then went on to reintroduce the song called "Fred Bear" by Ted Nugent. Andrew was mystified by this song. Who was Fred Bear? Andrew would carry on listening to these songs over and over to gain inspiration. With this newfound energy, he went inside the house to think of his goals and what he wanted to accomplish. Even though some of the goals were enormous, he would be a fool not to take the steps to get there. All in all, Andrew didn't sleep that night.

He grew extra paranoid the next few days. There was so much going on. He was fueled with the excitement of getting married. He was also flustered from the bar incident and still felt like a target. He sat inside the print shop at his desk one of these days to mark his jobs completed. He was still posting all over Facebook. One of the things he came across was a video one of his friends had made. Or maybe he should refer to him as a homie. He was gang affiliated and connected to the underworld. It was Chet, Andrew's old drug dealer. The one that robbed him to be exact. He had long paid his debt and the two were on good terms again.

The video clip was of a gun being racked, loading a round into the chamber. After he cocked the gun he turned it around and pointed it at the camera like "I'm gonna get you!" Chet was a felon and probably shouldn't have been sharing the video. Andrew didn't think of that and decided to flex, sharing the video as well. He now thought all he had to do was pay a drug addict to kill the bar owner. Then things would be settled. Andrew put that thought on the back burner in case things heated up.

Andrew made a separate Facebook post of what was on his mind. The text said the words "I wanna disappear". He was referring to running away into the woods and being alone. He would survive in the wilderness until this court case was settled. Then he would come back and marry his fiancé if she would wait for him. This post alerted people. They had thought he was suicidal. It was coincidental that he had just posted a video of a gun minutes prior. People got the wrong impression. Perhaps not everyone, but his mom was all over it. She made "poor me" posts about how she doesn't want to lose another kid to suicide and to pray for Andrew. It was really none of her business to share but she got the attention that she felt she needed.

While Andrew was sitting in his office chair he didn't think twice to light up a cigarette to calm his nerves. Unfortunately, he was inside his place of business in a warehouse. After a couple of drags, Andrew

The Witch's Hat

realized he shouldn't have been doing what he was doing and put the cigarette out. Then his dumbass went on Facebook and posted "Holy shit! I must be losing my mind! I just lit a cigarette inside my work!"

His mother had seen it and grew even more concerned and didn't hesitate to jump on the situation. She called Journey and shared her worry about Andrew. Her bitch ass told Journey to call the cops to show up at Andrew's work. She even told Journey what to say. Tanya wanted Andrew put away.

Journey texted Andrew saying that she was gonna show up at his work to visit him. Andrew was very cheerful that she was coming. He went outside to wait for her and two squad cars pulled up. An officer drew a gun on him and told him to put his hands up. Andrew did as told.

"You have a gun on you?" interrogated the pig.

"No, I don't! I don't even own one," Andrew answered.

The man searched Andrew up and down then directed him into the back of the squad car. Andrew wasn't cuffed at all. The officer wanted to talk to him.

The man in blue opened his mouth saying, "We had gotten a tip from some people who are concerned about you. We were told you were showing a recent interest in guns and maybe possibly suicidal. Anything that I should know about?"

"Well I'm not suicidal and I'm completely fine," Andrew replied calmly. He knew he didn't do anything wrong. Most importantly, he didn't hurt anybody. He may have had brief thoughts of doing so but they were only visions.

"My name is G. I'd like to hear your full side of the story so I can make a decision of what to do here. Go right ahead when you're ready," the cop told Andrew.

"I was assaulted at a bar about a month ago. I'm working through it. I shared a video of a gun because I thought it was cool. I have no intent of hurting myself or anyone else. It was just a video of a gun," explained Andrew. "So what? I can't post shit on Facebook without being singled out?"

"The thing with Facebook is that it is out there for everyone to see. The fact you have currently been dealing with trauma then go about sharing a gun video, raises a red flag," the officer told Andrew. He then radioed through his walkie to send an ambulance.

"Well that's all I know," said Andrew. "Can I go now?"

"Actually, we are taking you to a psychiatric unit to get checked out. Trust me, you will benefit from this. They will help you work through your problems. Do you have a specific hospital you prefer?" asked the officer.

"I'll take Fairview Riverside I guess…" Andrew replied with little to no resistance.

He knew at this point he had no choice of being detained in an institution again. It was insane what this bar incident led to. The beer belly man owed him. Andrew wanted to collect his money for all the bullshit he had and was about to be put through. The ambulance arrived the same time that Journey pulled up in her SUV. The police spoke with her a few short minutes and then Andrew was allowed out of the squad.

"I'm so sorry!" his fiancé sweetly shouted from near her car. "Your mom told me to do this."

"Well, what the fuck!? Don't listen to her. Now I have to go to the hospital when all I was trying to do was work," Andrew said irritably.

"We are all so worried. We want the best for you. I hope you know that," Journey said with watery eyes. Andrew knew she felt bad. He could see it. She felt like she was doing the right thing but had fallen for Doctor Tanya's trap. This was yet another thing for the mom to brag about to her friends and family. Andrew was super pissed. He was given permission to give Journey a hug before taking his next voyage. He swallowed his emotions for the moment but still felt anger pulsing through his vibrations. He felt super betrayed. After giving Journey a resentful hug he hopped on yet another gurney and was wheeled into the back of the hospital wagon. Along the way to the sanatorium, Andrew was told that he was awarded the last open bed. They said he was lucky…

The Witch's Hat

22 minutes passed and they arrived at the hospital where Andrew was escorted upstairs to Station 22 psychiatric unit. He thought this was cool because it was a multiple of 11. He didn't know it at the time but 22 is also the number of the dreamer. Means your life has purpose and that your dreams will become reality. This place would be the start of his new life. He was then buzzed through secure doors to face a small cafeteria on the left and a living area with a television beyond that on the same side behind an island wall. Straight ahead of him, alongside the right of the cafeteria and living space led an 8-foot wide walkway leading into a hallway with a dead-end that had multiple doorways for patient quarters among each. Butted up to the living area was an L-shaped counter. This was where the staff hung out. Where the counter ended, behind each wall cradled nurse territory.

Andrew took in his surroundings as his top was ready to explode. He presented himself calmly but spewed words toward the staff to try and smooth talk his way out the door. He told them he didn't belong there. They just ignored him. An African man named Abdalla brought Andrew into a locker room where he was told to change into scrubs. His belongings were taken and locked away.

Andrew then waited in the cafeteria at a table facing the island wall in the direction of the L-shaped command center. Abdalla brought Andrew a paper to sign stating he was going to be on a three-day hold and to follow through with any requirements. His signature represented that he understood what was going on or something of the sort. Andrew believed this was a trick. He wasn't going to comply with something he didn't feel was necessary. Maybe instead of coming after him, they should be arresting the bar owner for all the people he has hurt and would carry on doing so. It would maybe have given Andrew some peace of mind. Instead, Andrew was disturbed. He grabbed the paper from the table, crumpled it up, and threw it at Abdalla.

"What the hell is your problem?" said Abdalla with an angry African accent.

"Isn't that your job to figure out? I know what my problem is but you guys won't listen to me!" shouted Andrew boldly. "You guys can't just hold me here. It's violating my rights! I mean seriously!"

"I'm not dealing with this," Abdalla said while shaking his head. "I'll give you a minute to cool down."

"I'm not gonna fucking cool down until I get out of here!" snapped Andrew.

Abdalla had a funny-looking grumpy face as he turned and walked away. Abdalla's frown was transformed into a smile as he strode away with his back to Andrew. He had a bit of warrior in his blood as well and an understanding of where Andrew was coming from but felt like it wasn't in his power to do anything. It was ultimately up to the doctor to decide Andrew's fate.

"We got a lively one!" reported Abdalla to the nurse who stood in the pill dispensary room. "Are you ready for his intake?"

"Sure am. Give me just a minute," said Patricia as she pulled a strand of her gray parted hair from her face and adjusted her glasses.

Meanwhile, Andrew still sat at the table in the dining room. He had missed dinner. He noticed that there was still a small group of patients sitting, watching a movie in front of the T.V. Andrew hadn't a clue what they were watching but he didn't so much care. He had food on his mind. His stomach was growling but he sucked it up for the moment.

Abdalla approached Andrew and escorted him to the nurse who then escorted him to her office down the hall. She questioned him about his situation. He told her the whole story. How a bar incident sent him spiraling into some hypersensitive mode. He told her he had struggled with sleep but played it off as it wasn't serious. He told her he was receiving messages by deciphering numbers and also about the medium he had recently seen who paved the way for his spiritual journey. He mentioned something about being related to extraterrestrials and that we were all connected by the mind, possibly telepathically.

She thought all this was interesting as she took notes. You could tell she was a good person. She never meant any harm. She even shared some stories about herself and Andrew listened intently. It was completely casual. She reminded him of a sweet grandmother. She then proceeded to ask Andrew about any drug use and allergies. He told her he didn't use drugs but that he smoked pot. She kind of chuckled while Andrew went on to say that he stopped taking the medications he had been prescribed because they fucked him up. Then he told her of his sulfa allergies. Afterward, he gave his emergency contacts which were his fiancé and mother. Following that, they shared some kind words and Andrew was taken back to Abdalla to be assigned his room.

Abdalla took Andrew to a room about midway down the hall. It was right across from the L-shaped command center where the staff associates sat and watched things unravel. There was already a name tag on the outside of the door that said "Andrew L." Andrew and the existing patient had the same names so the staff put a sticker on each of their name tags that read "name alert". This was an extra precaution so the two wouldn't get confused by the employees.

Andrew walked in and did his best to make himself at home. He chatted with his new roommate. His last name was Leery which was exactly how Andrew felt in this institution so far. The two got a feel for each other. Group was all finished for the day so they were getting ready for bed. As Andrew was brushing his teeth a staff lady named Karen intruded and harassed him for his signature again on the paper but Andrew's battery was not yet dead. He refused yet again. They would repeatedly threaten that if he didn't sign the paperwork they would keep him longer.

At some point, it turned out the staff had called Andrew's fiancé through his emergency contact list to make her persuade Andrew for his John Hancock. He had no idea that they had reached out to her. It almost seemed like one big prank. In the meantime, Andrew laid his head to rest. He lay in bed in a meditative state. His mind wandered from aliens and their existence, then it vetted to plotting his escape. He knew he was being talked about among the staff as he was kind of a kook. Perhaps they would take him seriously, perhaps not. All Andrew knew was that he didn't belong where he was at.

He had gotten so irritated with his situation that he got up from his bed and wandered to the hallway to the phone. They had forgotten to shut it off that night. They watched as Andrew paved his way to the phone booth.

"What are you doing?" asked Karen from behind command center. "Phones are shut off at 10 pm."

Andrew lifted the phone and heard the dial tone. "Looks like it is on to me," he stated. "I have an important phone call to make! It's only 10:30. My fiancé will be up. I need to tell her to come visit me tomorrow."

Karen rolled her eyes and said, "OK, make it quick."

Andrew held the phone to his ear and dialed 9-1-1. A man answered the phone asking what the emergency was.

"Help me," Andrew whispered. "They are holding me prisoner beyond my will and won't release me."

"What's your location sir?" the man asked.

Andrew's voice grew excited. "I'm in Station 22 psychiatric unit at Fairview…" Then the line clicked. It went dead. Andrew looked over his shoulder to see a disgruntled Karen. She stood out from the crowd with her bleach blonde hair complimented with wrinkly skin.

She gave Andrew the evil eye. "You cannot call 9-1-1 unless it's an emergency. Phones are now shut off for the night. Get to bed!"

Andrew walked to the front counter. He looked up at the wall behind it and saw a classification T.V. screen. They had the patients labeled into different groups. One was team blue which was labeled B. The other was labeled G for green. So there was team blue and green. Andrew saw he was on team G. Each group had different staff. He wondered if there was some kind of characteristic the patients shared to be assembled into these groups.

Andrew looked back to Karen. "You guys will pay for this. And by the way, I can't fall asleep, but whatever, goodnight!" Andrew then turned to go to his room and lay down. He didn't sleep. He just lay there trying to devise more plots on his escape.

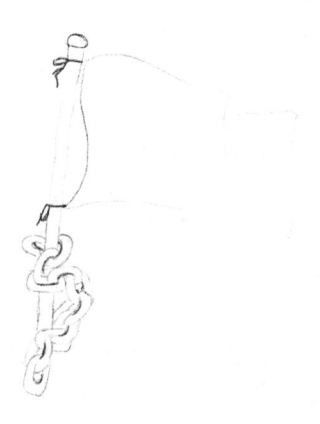

CHAPTER 40
Surrender?

THE NEXT MORNING Andrew was woken up. He was directed to the cafe and given a tray of food for breakfast. Abdalla handed him a menu to choose what he wanted for the rest of the week. Andrew chose scrambled eggs and bacon for every single morning's breakfast. He figured the more scrambled his brains were the more money (bacon) he would collect. He chose the meals for lunch and dinner as well but he wasn't too picky about deciding.

After breakfast, group started. Instead of attending group, Andrew was pulled aside by a doctor. He was an old man. Very robotic and to the point. Who knew who he really worked for? The doc and his assistant pestered Andrew with questions. He tried to answer them as normally as he could but they had too much background info on him and circumstantial observations from his arrival. They took notes of everything. The doctor prescribed him Depakote and sleeping pills along with some other stuff. Andrew felt like he was being lured into some sort of experiment. He wasn't having it. He told the doctor he was not going to take the medications and that they do nothing for him. Andrew told him he wanted the holistic route. He said he needed therapy and possibly some tools he could use to relieve stress like exercise and yoga. Andrew's issue was that he was on a mission and didn't want to die. His energy radiated and he wasn't going to fade away that easily. He didn't want his mind to be clouded with unnecessary drugs.

After Andrew visited with the doctor he skipped the next groups and lay in his room. Every now and then the staff would notify him when the next group started. Andrew denied participation and would only leave his room to eat. But even then he took his tray back to his area to avoid other people. He was pissed off and confused that he was trapped in a cage and used as some science experiment. Again, they would constantly tell him that if he didn't sign his paper, take his medication and go to group he would be in there a long time. They insisted on Andrew to comply with their threats. This was very unethical and unfair. A person should have an open choice to choose if they should be on medication or not. This is what they do in today's world. Seems as if everyone has a problem and supposedly it's in their brain and has nothing to do with how society is set up. Sure some people may need medication but some people just need a role model to give them hope and the drive to move forward. By now Andrew hated hospitals with a passion. Who is this doctor to tell him what he needs by talking to him for 10 minutes anyway? He didn't know him. There is so much wrong with this system. Andrew wanted to shut it down.

After dinner, Andrew finally left his room for a longer period of time when he got a visit from his fiancé. His mother tagged along with her. Andrew didn't know why he put his mother on his visiting list. Tanya's only concern was to bug Andrew about the medications he was prescribed.

"That's all you care about is these fucking medications! Do you ever think I don't need them? There is nothing wrong with me!" Andrew grumbled.

She then went on a rant on how she wanted the best for him. She even suggested what meds he should take from whatever research she did online. Andrew ignored her and carried on his conversation with Journey. After an argument, she convinced Andrew to do everything that the staff told him to do. "Just do everything they tell you to the best you can and you will be out before you know it," she advised.

The Witch's Hat

"I don't trust these people. They better let me out soon. I didn't do anything. I'm also still mad at you guys for calling the cops on me. I don't know who to trust anymore. I'm all alone. But ok, I'll take the pills and everything else. Just understand I don't like what is going on here," Andrew returned.

The visit came to an end. Journey had left Andrew snacks. She seemed to always make the stay more comfortable at every place he went. However, this visit left a sour taste in Andrew's mouth. Even so, he ended up following orders and went to the pill dispenser counter to take his dose of medication with reluctance.

Andrew wasn't scared to speak his mind. "This is bullshit," he spewed at the man behind the counter before he swallowed his pills. The man's name was Tony who was a staff member on team G. They talked a little bit and Andrew thought he had made an ally.

The day was winding to an end and Andrew gave in and signed the 3-day hold paper for whatever it meant. It didn't matter anymore. He felt like he was losing all his battles. After he turned the paper in he was awarded with some headphones. It was a little AM/FM headset. The device looked as if it was about 20 years old and the tuner didn't work very well. Andrew had to tap the headset in order to tune in to different stations. He felt like each station that was tuned in was meant to be heard. Andrew gobbled up information and devoured the music that was shared. The world was going nuts as Trump only had about a week and a half before he took office. People were literally losing their minds. Andrew briefly listened to some of the news. He would tune into a station by chance that was called The Current and rode with the vibes. He was now introduced to his happy place. Music had never meant more to him than this moment here and now. He listened to new songs of local artists, classics, and a little philosophy. He was now tuned in to the world and these sounds made him feel a way he had never felt before.

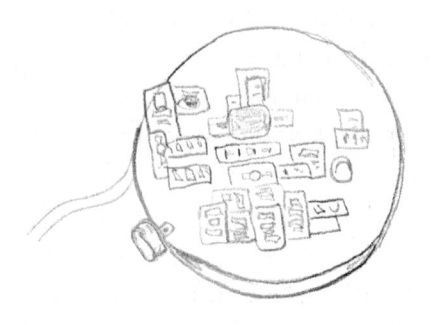

CHAPTER 41
Settling In

THAT NIGHT ANDREW laid in bed adjusting the stations, soaking everything in. After a while, he realized he still couldn't sleep. He then got back up and went to the counter to hassle the staff.

"I still can't sleep. Some medication you have here..." Andrew told them. In all reality, his mind was slowing down but still ran so fast he managed to break the barriers the medication began to construct in his mind. He had just started taking it. It wasn't to the point where he was overpowered. So he kept chugging along at lightning speed.

As a result of complaining to the staff, they gave him more sleeping medication. Afterward, he noticed a man walking up and down the hall with his headphones. He had the new-age ones. They lit up and changed colors as if they reflected your emotions or read your mind. An array of rainbow colors crossed Andrew's path as the man walked down the hall. Andrew was intrigued. He quickly noticed the white man's squeaky clean bald head and long gray beard. He looked like a biker. He had a tattoo of a tiny cross on his right wrist. His hands were tightly clenched and held to his side. He seemed frustrated. He was working off his steam with a brisk walk. Andrew decided to join him and this became one of his nightly routines.

Andrew did a medium-speed walk to keep up with the man going the opposite way. It was harmonized. They would reach the reverse side

The Witch's Hat

of the hallway and turn around at around the same time. Then they steadily and fiercely passed each other in the middle. They elegantly contained their fighting outburst which wasn't at all directed at each other. Andrew had been stirring the pot with the staff since he had gotten there and this man recognized the injustice. They were marching in protest. By looking, you could tell this man went through some struggles. He reminded Andrew of Ragnar from the show *Vikings*. Andrew felt strongly that this man was from the same tribe back in the motherland of Scandinavia.

Andrew had the idea to continue his walk with his palms extended and pointed to the ceiling. He was absorbing every bit of energy that he could. He barely even had his eyes open. He was pushing back his anger and wandering mind with calming music from his headphones. He didn't go anywhere without them. Then on one of the laps around, Andrew bowed in front of the Viking upon his left knee and extended his right wrist before him with his elbow bent at a right angle. On his wrist read a bracelet that said: "no hate" which Andrew rested his head-on. Andrew did this out of respect for the man. The Viking bared his cross on his wrist to Andrew. The clan no longer hailed Odin. Most everyone worshiped a monotheistic God in this present day. That's always what Andrew was used to anyway. Was there really a God? After the two had had their moment Andrew got up and continued a dozen more laps before heading to his room and clunking his head down to the pillow to envelope himself into a half-conscious sleep.

The sleep sucked so he got up and walked to the front desk again to harass the staff of the station. "Let me out of here! This isn't doing me any good!" he shouted. "I couldn't sleep out there and I can't sleep in here! Fuckin trazodone ain't working!"

Then Andrew went on yet again about how they were violating his rights. He had made this a constant routine the first few nights. He was sure everyone in the station heard him. A black man stood by his doorway with his chest puffed out, mean-mugging Andrew. He went by the name Tyrone. Andrew stepped away from the counter and walked back to his room. Along the way, he stared at Ty. Andrew nodded and said, "What up?"

Tyrone just glared at him. The Hispanic in the room next door was watching and laughing. He had a demonic cackle. Once Andrew was in his room he laid down to calm his head. Within a few minutes, he heard shouting in the hallway. Tyrone was arguing with the staff just as well. Andrew changed the station on his headphones and took a 3-hour nap. At some point during the night, he heard a painful scream from down the hall. Andrew learned the cry was from a patient named Gabriel releasing his frustration in the questionably tolerable comfortability of his room in which he never left. The place wasn't anywhere near homey but at least it had heat to protect from the Minnesota winter and was a whole lot better than jail. In the meantime, the angry screams continued to resonate through Station 22 for about twenty minutes, and then there was silence. It seemed as if Tyrone and Gabriel had gone to bed. Andrew did his best to try to stay asleep.

The next morning Andrew was wide awake, bright, and early. He ate breakfast and attended group for the first time. He carried with him a folder in which he noted every group he would attend for record in case he was ever told he didn't go. He even went as far as to get signatures from the staff leaders to place in his files to provide evidence. The staff was getting a little irritated with Andrew as he was with them. The group went in a circle with everyone sharing what they are grateful for. Andrew was given an introduction worksheet to present later that morning. After group ended, he was out in the dayroom and felt an immense urge to pick up one of the chairs and throw it through the large glass window to escape.

He never followed through with it. It would have been a struggle, because outside of the glass was a tall barbed-wire fence to keep in the crazies. Andrew stepped up to the window and looked straight down to notice a big metal covering to a hole about 5 feet in diameter. Andrew imagined that with how old the building was, that back in the day they would throw deceased bodies into it. The river was only a couple hundred feet from the building if that. Andrew figured the hole led to the river where the bodies would be washed down the Mississippi. This was just a thought that came to mind and he actually took it very seriously. He wouldn't have doubted that they had done tests at this

The Witch's Hat

university that had killed the less fortunate. Possibly people who were poor and hadn't any families to miss them when they vanished from society. Suddenly, an overwhelming sick feeling came over Andrew and he had to sit.

During the next group, Andrew was made to introduce himself. He shared with the others of why he was there. The doctor sat in the corner and eavesdropped on the discussion. Andrew went on to tell the group they were all part extraterrestrial and that he felt there was some kind of telepathic capability we humans shared. He wanted everyone to know. The doc took an array of notes of Andrew's speech. After his storytelling, Andrew really opened up to the other patients. He truly wanted to help them. He told them that we are all made the way we are and that there was no need for medication. He told them to do things that are healthy and good for the mind. A pill wasn't going to be just some magical remedy the way they made it seem.

The doctor noticed Andrew's irritability being expressed around with loving advice to the patients. He called Andrew aside to his office. "I noticed you seemed a little forceful with your words out there. I also see you're still talking about extraterrestrials. What has you so worked up?" the doc asked.

"If I told you you would think I'm crazy..."

"Look at where you are at. I'm here to help you."

"I'm not crazy for something I believe in. You guys might see it that way." Andrew's eyes raced back and forth. "I shouldn't even be here. I just had an epiphany that we may be part of some experiment and that we ourselves could be extraterrestrial. We got alien blood in our veins!"

"What proof do you have?" said the evil doctor.

"Well, I have none. Just with all that has happened, I feel very strange like I've had adrenaline running through me for weeks," Andrew replied as he fidgeted his hands and tapped his legs in his chair.

"I think we need to increase your dose of Depakote as I started you out on a low dose. Also, I'm seeing signs of schizophrenia as well. I'm going to suggest an antipsychotic. I'll give you a prescription for a drug called risperidone which I advise you to take one tablet each night before bed. And then of course the trazodone for sleep. I'm going to monitor you the next few days and take blood samples to test the drug levels," the doc insisted.

"Schizophrenia? I don't have schizophrenia!" Andrew said in a raised tone.

"You are suffering from delusions," the doctor said nonchalantly, "I mean you called the cops on three men you thought jumped a fence onto your girlfriend's parents' property when no trace was left in the snow."

"It's fiancé and it had just started snowing," Andrew said in defense. Meanwhile, the doctor just sat in silence.

Andrew put his hands to his face and screamed. He quickly regained his composure and asked, "If I continue to take the pills then I can leave this place right?"

"No, not quite. That is up to the judge to decide," the doctor said.

"What? What the fuck? I thought I got to leave here tomorrow. It will be three days!" replied Andrew furiously.

"Well I'm recommending longer and due to the severity of your case you will be tried in mental health court first," the doctor said with a smug look on his face. "The better you comply now the better you will look to the judge. So I highly recommend taking the medication or else you will be here a long time."

Andrew knew that he had to follow the doctor's orders or stay locked up. "I'll take the goddamn pills but later I'm taking you guys down!"

That concluded the meeting and of course, the doctor ordered more supervision on Andrew. About an hour later, a guy entered the station with a backpack full of tools and who knows what. He went to Andrew's room and messed with the furnace which was working completely fine. He took off the furnace cover and put a device on the inside of it facing out. Andrew watched from the hallway as the man did his work. He was convinced the man had put a recording device in his room to hear what he and his roommate spoke about. Andrew was extremely paranoid. He didn't know who to trust and he was as angry as ever.

When the man finished in the bedroom he went to the meeting room which was camera-free. This time he opened up the light fixture on the ceiling. He put the same device into it as the furnace. Now they were recording what they talked about in their group meetings too. Andrew felt like this was some kind of lab examination. After the man finished, Andrew paced up and down the halls to reduce his anxiety while he jammed to some music. A few minutes later Andrew was asked to take his vitals. He was taken to his bedroom where they checked his pulse and drew his sacred blood from his body. Andrew hated the feeling of being a specimen. On top of all that he knew he was going to get a large hospital bill for all the helpful work the hospital said they were doing when really they were just studying medications and whatever else. In the meantime, Andrew's mind still kept slowing down but he kept fighting. He had to keep telling himself he wasn't gonna turn into a zombie.

Mr. Leery came into the room after vitals and Andrew told him about the bug that was planted. He also informed him that it was getting harder to function the way he wanted to and that he felt like these meds were a tactic to silence them. Then they went on to speak in code. They used creative terms and lingo at the spur of the moment to go around the subject. The words they used were vague but they understood each other. They felt like mice in a maze controlled by what we may consider the government through institutions of this brainwashed society.

All of a sudden a staff member called out that it was lunchtime. It was about 11:30 a.m. After they consumed their food, group started again. This was just a community group discussion. They did trivia. Andrew actually did pretty well. The questions were pretty easy although some were difficult.

"What is the fastest land mammal on the planet?" a black-haired staff woman named Lindsey asked Andrew as it was his turn.

To the right of him sat Tyrone. He had taken a liking to Andrew from his rebellious attitude and story from earlier that morning. He had just gotten out of prison after serving 3 years. He later shared that that place makes you gay. Tyrone didn't seem gay but I guess you do what you gotta do when behind bars. Anyhow, Tyrone whispered the answer to Andrew. "Cheetah," he said.

Andrew looked up at the lady and responded with the same answer Tyrone had provided. It sounded like he said the word "cheater" in a way. Andrew knew the answer to the question but it was nice to know that someone had his side. His answer was of course right. He gave Tyrone a nod.

They continued on, switching up the meeting to an open discussion. Andrew looked at the bald-headed biker dude and asked, "Are you Viking?"

The man's eyes grew wide, as did Andrew's. "Why yes, I'm a Norseman."

"Wow! I felt like I could just tell. I'm Viking too! I feel like I need to get back in touch with myself. Start from the ground up, ya know? My name is Andrew by the way," Andrew said with his eyelids still peeled as far back towards his brain as they could go.

"My name is Brodric," the man said. The two had an understanding. Andrew could see it in Brodric's eyes, which were the windows of his soul.

"Pleasure to meet you," Andrew replied.

"Likewise," said Brodric.

After gaining a new friend, group came to an end and Andrew continued to talk to other patients who were suffering from issues. He noticed that most of all they needed was someone to talk and listen to them. They needed to be directed in the right direction. There was a woman from India named Ramya who was suffering. She was on team B. She opened up and shared that she was placed in Station 22 with her sister, but was left behind when her sister was discharged. She looked like she had seen a ghost. She told Andrew she had been raped, with watery eyes, and that she was struggling with suicidal thoughts. The doctor had made an appointment for her to get electroconvulsive therapy the following day to rid her of her terrible memories. She was terrified.

Andrew tried to calm her down. She shared with him that she wanted to be a doctor. How could people trapped like criminals in a cage have such a good heart? She desired to help people. Andrew knew she could do it and he told her just that. She got a smile on her face and thanked him. Someone who looked so desperate and broken minutes earlier was now as happy as can be. This just proved Andrew's point. Many of the patients didn't need the drugs they were prescribed to. They just needed to realize how to deal with their feelings and know that they are worth it.

Andrew gave her his number in case she needed it. He signed below it in cursive. He had realized the seriousness of the situation. He decided he was going to sue the hospital too! Meanwhile, he sympathized with her and told her to not go through with the ECT. He said that shit will change you forever and that there are other ways. He said the doctor was a bastard and that she could do a much better job than him. She seemed to listen to Andrew's advice and said she would cancel the ECT session. The rest of the day she got more connected with the group and seemed to always have a joyous look on her face. All she needed was someone to believe in her so she could believe in herself. Her feelings from the rape were real but we as humans are subject to emotions that we sometimes have to work through. Andrew knew this from the experience of losing his brother.

After the two had finished their convo, Andrew was approached by an old lady with dark wiry hair. She resembled something like a witch of some sort. She had some of the biggest illuminated eyes Andrew had seen in his life. Maybe her glasses made them look bigger. She looked like she had a lot on her mind with something important to say.

"You know you're an empath right?" she asked as she examined Andrew. "I'm an empath as well. We have the power to help the people in here."

"Wow! Really? An empath huh?" voiced Andrew.

"Yeah I've been around a long time and I can spot an empath a mile away. I see the way you talk to people with concern. It's almost as if you feel their pain," she spoke.

"Well, I do feel their pain. I'm pissed off. We all have to get on the same team. That is what I'm trying to do. Help everyone out," Andrew said proudly.

"I know. I can read the people in here. I can tell the good from the bad. I will also tell you that I feel bad energy in the air. It's almost hard to breathe. Something horrible is happening. I feel like you bring a ray of sunshine to us all, as well as hope. They don't want us to know what we know."

"Oh, I know! I can only imagine the horrible things that have happened in this hospital and that will continue to happen. Thank you for the heads up! I'll keep connecting and try to make the best of this stay. Hopefully, help some people out along the way," Andrew responded.

The old lady smiled and said, "So sweet." She gave him a pat on the back and walked away. Her hair looked staticky as Andrew watched her carry herself towards the window to gaze.

Andrew continued to chill in the lounge area getting to know people. The Hispanic guy from the room next door sat in a chair near the corner of the room. He kicked back and laughed. His name was Mason. He was Andrew's enemy. Andrew felt it. Mason was whisper-talking to himself. It was almost like he was putting a hex on Andrew. This guy may have had a different God from him. Maybe he believed in aliens too. Whether the case, Andrew imagined the digits "666" tattooed on Mason's forehead. All Andrew knew was that he got bad vibes from him. The dude would never participate in group or even talk to anyone.

Finally, after all the awkwardness of Mason staring Andrew down, the next scheduled group kicked off. The chairs were maneuvered to face towards the big screen T.V. They had it hooked up to YouTube. It was a mood disorder group. They shared bipolar and schizophrenia videos of individuals who suffered from the condition. Perhaps they were victims of circumstance too. Andrew sat and listened intently to

The Witch's Hat

their stories. They talked about the medication they were on and how great it was. Andrew was far from a medication pusher. The videos actually kind of freaked him out. He took the medication subject with a grain of salt as he had planned to quit taking his when he was released.

With a foot on an office chair in a Captain Morgan-type pose was a staff member playing guitar behind Andrew. He had the guitar rested on his knee for support. The man had black hair with a matching goatee. He strummed some chords and kept playing. Andrew recognized the tune. It was "Master of Puppets" by Metallica. Andrew felt like the puppet but maybe he was a master at the same time, just down the tier. In this new home, the doctor seemed to be the headmaster. It was boiling down to who was going to eliminate who. The video Andrew was currently watching was just proof that they were trying to convince him he had all these mood disorders when in all reality he felt perfectly fine. He was done explaining himself to them.

The videos wound to an end and the patients were minutes away from visitation hours. Again, both Journey and Tanya showed up. Tanya was of course talking about meds so Andrew told her she was being taken off of his visiting list from here on out. Tanya's grin went to a frown.

"I was just curious if they did anything to change your meds. I think I know something that will work," said Tanya.

"I don't think anything will work. I have to work through this on my own. My medication is none of your business. I'm on the fucked up ones! That is all that matters!" Andrew yelled. "You guys need to leave!" he added as he stormed away to seek shelter in his room.

It was about 4 o'clock now and Andrew had forgotten to go to the pill counter to get his afternoon pills. The nurse ended up coming to find him. She came to the pair of Andrews' shared bedroom to dispense the protagonist's medication. Then after a half an hour went by, Andrew decided to go back into the lounge room.

Andrew then began to feel very on edge. He paid the nurse another visit. "Do you have any Ativan?" Andrew asked. "I feel like my skin is crawling and that I'm about to freak out!"

Andrew stood there squirming. His nerves felt like they were going to burst. The nurse looked at him and replied, "I'm sorry I can't do that. You have a history of drug abuse. I can only give it if I feel you need it."

"Ok, whatever," snarled Andrew.

He walked towards his room and along the way fell to the floor. He was sprawling from left to right and doing complete rolls with his body. He was screaming in horror.

"Ahhhhhhh! Noooo! No! No!" Andrew bellowed. He sounded like a mad man with some issues. Some of the patients were completely terrified. Some stood in shock. Others went into their rooms. Andrew was sure Mason was somewhere laughing like usual.

"Uh oh, time to save Private Ryan," voiced an ally patient on team G while Andrew screeched, rolling to and fro violently, crashing into a chair in the process.

Suddenly, three staff members leaped onto his body and held him down. They called for backup and a big buff guy entered the station. All four each grabbed a limb and lifted Andrew up. He stared at the ceiling as he thrashed side to side. The staff struggled to hold his limbs as Andrew was trying to break free. He propelled his legs back and forth and managed to kick the buff guy in the nuts. The guy crouched over but didn't release him. A woman struggled with Andrew's other leg and let go. He now had one foot on the ground. He tried catapulting himself but was unsuccessful.

The staff ended up getting a good hold on Andrew and hence made it to his bedroom without dropping him. They threw him onto the bed and forcefully rolled him onto his belly. Then the heavy buff guy pushed Andrew's face into the pillow and put his knee on his back. The others grabbed each one of Andrew's wrists and cuffed them with restraints which were then attached to the corners of the bed frame. They repeated the same process with his feet. Now he couldn't move and felt claustrophobic. The man got off Andrew which unmuffled his hollering.

"You gave me the wrong fucking medication!" he shouted. "You

The Witch's Hat

probably gave me the other Andrew's meds! Otherwise, it's that fucked up shit you put me on. Fuck all of you! Ahhhhhh!!!!"

They laughed at him and the room was spinning. They then pulled down his pants. Andrew went from having flashbacks from the bar to thinking he was going to get raped. Why else would they pin him belly down on a mattress? Whether the case, Andrew imagined them taking turns on him. He pulled on the restraints to break free to no avail. He screamed and shouted. Finally, one of the nurses pulled out a syringe and stabbed it into Andrew's ass cheek. They had finally given him the Ativan he asked for. Within a minute he calmed down. They watched him lay there for the next twenty minutes. In a calm manner, Andrew warned them that they need to double-check the medication that they gave him from now on. They had insisted that they didn't make any mistakes as they proceeded to undo the restraints. Andrew was now as free as can be physically at that moment, although his mental freedom could have been improved upon. He went to the dining room to sit in shame as he waited for his dinner grub.

His fiancé just so happened to come visit again that day after dinner. She apologized for his mother who didn't tag along this time. She felt like she had to see Andrew again. She didn't mind paying a fortune for parking to see her lover. It was well worth it for her. Andrew took her to the conference/meeting room where the recording device was planted. He sat at a table with her and talked about the incident that happened earlier with the restraints. He then whispered into her ear that the room was bugged. She didn't believe him. Andrew got angry and became silent for a moment.

Then he went on saying, "Just get me out of here! Please! They are fucking me up! I feel like I'm gonna die in here!"

"Andrew, there is nothing to worry about. You really need the help. Just keep doing what you're supposed to," she responded.

"You are just like them. It's because you listened to my mom, that's why I'm here. I just wanna go home!"

"Yeah... I maybe shouldn't have listened to her. Like I told you before, I just want the best for you. You aren't the same Andrew I first fell in love with. I just want you to get better," she said with concern.

"Goddamnit! I'm fine!" Andrew said in a hefty tone. "I'm just gonna do what I have to do to get out of here!"

The two visited for the whole available time. She would show up almost the very minute from when visitation started all the way until the last second. It was very nice to have such a loving companion to talk to, but eventually, the visit came to an end.

Andrew took his vitals before bed. His blood pressure was 130 over 74 which wasn't too bad. He had a pulse of 74 which was good. Late that night at around ten o'clock a new guy entered the station. Mason was transferred from the room next door into a single-person room as he freaked people out. The new guy went into the fresh vacancy and hid away. Andrew heard noises outside of his room and decided to do some snooping. He carried on with his nightly musical meditation cruise down the hallway.

Andrew walked by the new guy's room on one of his laps and saw him staring out the window of his closed door. The new arrival had his eyes fixated on him. As Andrew walked, he had his arms outstretched with his palms up soaking in the energy again. He nodded to the guy. The dude had to have been around thirty. He observed Andrew for a second then slowly nodded back. Andrew glanced at the name tag beside his door. It said Charlie just like they called the Vietcong. From the way he looked, he seemed like a professional of some sort. He stood there and continued to watch Andrew and the Viking go back and forth, back and forth. Charlie never left his room and finally, Andrew had had enough walking. He went to the counter and hassled the staff for a little bit then went to his room the rest of the night. He laid down and stared at the ceiling.

CHAPTER 42
The Mysterious Men

THE NEXT DAY started with breakfast, then group. Group was titled Occupational Therapy. They came up with a list of things they were grateful for. Andrew put Journey as number one. Charlie skipped sharing his list with the group and they kept moving along.

Lunch came and went. At 2:30 pm visitation started. Of course, right away his fiancé showed up. She had brought her mother as well. They all sat in the conference room.

"So what's this I hear about people listening to you?" Andrew's future mother-in-law asked.

"Because they are. They are listening to us right now," Andrew said in a quiet voice.

"There is nothing to be paranoid about. Your mind just needs some time to settle down," she replied. She held out a piece of paper with lyrics on it. "Here I brought you something. It's a song. I printed out the lyrics."

Andrew looked at the paper and saw the title was "Unwell" by Matchbox Twenty. "Awwwww thanks! I love this song!"

"I don't think you're crazy. I think your mind is worn out and playing tricks on you. Journey and I are just hoping you get better. We want the old Andrew back."

"I'm still here. It's me," Andrew said, pointing to the title on the paper. "You see? I'm just unwell"

"That's right. Everything's gonna be okay. We won't let you be in here forever," she returned.

All three had talked for the next hour until visitation had wrapped up. Andrew went to his room to eat his snacks Journey had brought until community group started. Charlie opened up a little more than from earlier that morning. His "opening up" was still very vague. He basically said he had a lot going on and checked himself in to get his mind right. He was smart for not sharing too much about himself. After group, Andrew and Charlie shook hands. They sat down and ate dinner together and got to know each other a small bit. Afterward, they got up to roam. They continued conversing for a short while.

"Hope you can get your mind situated," Andrew told him. "Let me know if you need anything."

"Thanks," Charlie added. Then the two parted ways.

Andrew observed the wiry-haired empath lady walking around giving people advice again. You can tell she was getting drained. Andrew joined in with her and channeled the emotions of the room and went to the person who needed it most. He went to Mason to say "Hey" for the first time. He just laughed and said something in Spanish. Then he laughed again hysterically. Andrew didn't know if this guy could be helped. The Latino put up his hands in fists and said something else in Spanish. He was in a fighting stance. Andrew backed up, turned, and walked away. Mason laughed his evil laugh and then started mumbling jargon to himself. It was clear he wanted nothing to do with Andrew.

Journey came to another visit from 6:30 to 8 that evening which included even more snacks. This time she brought her cousin, Brittany who seemed interested in what Andrew had to say. He shared that all the meds he was being given were a bunch of bullshit due to a system that is always pushing pharmaceuticals. He said they were experimenting on them and the room that they were in was bugged and they were being listened to at any given moment. Honestly, it kind of creeped the high schooler out. She told Andrew that he reminded her

The Witch's Hat

of Hyde from *That '70s Show* which Andrew took as a compliment. Once visitation concluded, the night came to an end and Andrew sought refuge in his room. He lay in bed thinking of the "Unwell" song. He closely watched shadows dance upon the crease of the wall and ceiling as people walked by in the hallway. He replayed the song over and over in his head. He read and reread the lyrics and made it really sink in. Tony, the staff nurse then peered into the room. He was a thinner middle-aged man with gray streaks in his hair.

"Hey," saluted Andrew.

"You doing ok?" asked Tony with a gaping stare.

"As good as I'll ever be," Andrew stated.

"Good," said the nurse who then turned around and closed the door to where it was cracked a bit. The man knew of Andrew's situation and had a great deal of compassion. It seemed like he knew something was up.

Next, Andrew got up to use the bathroom and noticed two men sitting in metal chairs behind a small table they had moved to the middle of the hallway. On the table rested a laptop. Andrew wondered why they were there. He took a closer look at the two of them as he departed his room and walked to the exercise bike. One of the men was athletic and bald-headed. He had on tan cargo pants and a white t-shirt. His phone case displayed an American flag. The other guy was more buff and looked like Bradley Cooper from *American Sniper* except with a much longer beard. Andrew had some weird suspicion that these guys were military personnel. What was strange, was that there were plaques for all the staff members on the wall and these two were never included within them. Who were they, and what were they doing?

After trying to peddle as fast as he could on the bike, Andrew discontinued and asked them if they would help him out. He told them he was being treated as if he was guilty of something before proven so. He thought the saying was innocent until proven guilty. Overall, the guys refused to lend a hand so Andrew raised his voice towards them and said the place was a battleground between heaven and hell.

"This is bullshit! It isn't right. I'm basically a prisoner right now! You stripped us of our rights. I keep telling you all that," repeated Andrew. He was representing everyone there beyond their will. Everyone knew he represented the people. The two stern dudes just brushed Andrew off so he gave them the finger and withdrew to his room.

About 10 or 15 minutes later Andrew heard a woman scream in agony. "Help!" she cried. Andrew immediately got up to investigate. He opened the door to see the two men and nurse still sitting on their asses.

"Aren't you going to help her?" Andrew asked with good intentions concernedly.

"She is doing it for attention," the bald-headed guy replied. "There is nothing wrong with her."

"Are you sure? She is pregnant! What if she is having a miscarriage from the stress this place brings you! Get off your ass and help her!" Andrew shouted.

The man looked at the nurse who was fresh from shift change. She got up from the counter to go check on the woman. Minutes later Andrew witnessed the lady being wheeled out to the emergency room. Andrew wondered if her meth use had affected the baby.

"There, you happy now?" said the bearded man. It was obvious the two had each other's back. Who was really in charge here?

"Yeah, I feel better. Don't know what you guys get paid for. You're fired!" Andrew rendered loudly before slamming his door.

His headphones tuned in to the public radio station and he listened as he lay in bed. He was yet again going with the flow. The radio played some very interesting stuff.

An eerie voice versed the following, "There is a guy imprisoned for no reason. He is dreaming of a utopia. He is trying to find a way out of his situation while being a man of the people. He is trying to do good and is testing the waters. When he is released there is no way to bring him to his knees. He will never forget..." The man began talking about secret spies then reverted, "He is imprisoned with surveillance monitoring him. I cannot share who this person is but I know you are listening right now. We wish the best for you. One thing I will say is that Gabriel will sound his horn so listen for it. You are a godsend".

The guy talked in a monotone voice. Very crisp but plain. Andrew figured that it was a very good radio voice. The channel turned into a commercial and when it resumed, another guy was on air talking about the troubled king paired with the troubled times in an interview. Andrew listened and out of nowhere he heard Gabriel scream from down the hall. Poor guy. Andrew finished the radio show which he connected with on another level and felt like his engine was refueled. He laid down half asleep, overhearing and watching over his domain. Andrew was staying in touch with his surroundings like never before.

CHAPTER 43
The Warning

Martin Luther King day came around. The date was now January 16th of 2017. At 10 am was Focus Group. Andrew made up his goals and determined his mind with no other choice but to go forward. How would he do it? With his mind or with a crosshair? He would let the road determine. Andrew listened to others as they shared their own goals. After reviewing them, they went on to talk about Martin Luther King Jr. They passed around a piece of paper with a photo of him. When group was over Andrew put the picture in his folder as it was important to him. He wanted to become a politician himself. Andrew shared some interesting stuff during group regarding this and the succeeding group as well. He visited with others during break. Most of all, he spoke with Tyrone.

"I would never do that. Politicians get shot, bro!" Tyrone raved.

"I don't care about that. I'll take the risk. Things need to change, man. That's for damn sure," Andrew responded.

"Be careful bro," Ty said. Then he proceeded to say, "You have a great woman by your side. I saw her during your visit last night.

The Witch's Hat

You can probably achieve anything with her. That makes me want to connect with my family as well bro. It's been so long."

"Yeah, do that man," Andrew replied.

"I'm gonna call my brother," Tyrone said, turning to walk towards the phone booth. "I haven't spoken to him in years! Thanks, ma dude!"

The patients were told lunch was running late for some reason so the next group started at 11:15. Creative Expression was the name. They sat in the conference room and did artwork. Spiritual music was playing with no words. Just the sound of instruments and nature. Ocean waves filled the air with a flock of squawking seagulls. It was calming music of course to keep them at peace as they drew their pictures. All Andrew did was grab some paint and a piece of a large construction paper and let the creators of the music take control. He splashed paint on the paper. He drew squiggles and shapes of all sorts. He didn't have a pattern but perhaps somewhere deep within he did. Finally, he completed it, and to him, it was a work of art. Some others in the group were working on intricate designs. Andrew was the only one that made a mess. He looked at all the different shapes he made while others continued drawing. He tried to decipher different objects. Animals. People. Signs of any sort. The ones he caught all slid into his mind and had a significant meaning.

Soon enough, even this group came to an end. The witch lady came to Andrew and gave him her drawing. It was a very good sketch of a slanted tree running diagonally across the page. The tree had no leaves. Andrew wished it had green leaves. He loved springtime. Green was Journey's favorite color. Instead, along each branch was a child. Some were sitting. Some were climbing. One had fallen from the tree with a ring around his head like Saturn which resembled stars.

There was also a rope ladder tied to one of the top branches and three children were climbing up it at once. Everyone wanted to make it to the top. One thing to devour into your mind was that all the children were sketched in black pencil with no color. It had a white background. There was, however, one child on the bottom of the trunk taking the tough way up. Unlike the others, he actually had some tincture to himself. With blonde hair and a light hue of orangish-pinkish-tannish but mostly whitish skin. He had on a blue shirt with black pants. He was barefoot while the others weren't. Did this represent Andrew making the climb to the top where he would have a better quality of life? Maybe.

In the background of the sketch at the top was a word by the name of "Pean." There was a space after the word like she pressed the spacebar on a keyboard. After the space was the letter "a" written in with a comma following it and then a "b" following that. What did "Pean a,b" mean? Andrew did his research and found that "Pean" means a formal expression of phrase. Then it read that in Ancient Greece it was especially a song sung to invoke or thank a deity. So was this woman Greek? Perhaps she was getting back in touch with her roots like Andrew. He had seen her in Bible group. So what God did she believe in? She had to obviously be Christian. Was she just expelling knowledge and wisdom? Or was it something deeper than that? Andrew supposed so. We are all learning on our spiritual journey. Maybe life is just whatever you believe in. Or maybe it is run and controlled by extraterrestrial beings in cahoots with the government for some higher purpose. Andrew had no idea but he wanted to find out.

She went on to give Andrew a message. "Watch out for that Mason. He has a whole different set of beliefs," she stuttered.

Andrew was well aware. "Yeah, I felt a little weird around him. I'll stay clear. Thanks for the picture by the way"

"You're welcome sweetheart. Just please, please, please be careful. Something isn't right," she shakily said as she turned and left to seek out what more was a-brewing.

Andrew was approached by Tyrone with a jittery warning, "She's a witch. She will put a hex on you." Maybe he was just paranoid.

Charlie stood and observed the show from the middle of the lounge room. He crept and listened but did and said nothing. Andrew pointed out to himself that there wasn't anything wrong with his connection to this lady. There happened to be something about her that just drew him in. She seemed coherent enough and very wise.

That night after Andrew's usual visit with Journey he did his hall

The Witch's Hat

walk a little early. Charlie stood at the window of his own faintly cracked open doorway and continued to study Andrew. What the hell was wrong with him? Did he want something? Andrew went to the phone booth to call his fiancé's cell.

"Hey!" he whispered with heightened energy. "This new guy is making me feel uncomfortable. He has been keeping a close eye on me. Please get me out of here. Something is off and I'm creeped out."

"Babe. It's all in your head," she said. "I've been told by the hospital staff that you haven't been sleeping. That's probably the reason why you are feeling the way you are"

"Well, what the fuck? Aren't I supposed to be better by now? That's why I'm here ain't it? They aren't helping me. I might as well go home."

"Andrew, just be patient. There isn't really anything I can do. They won't release you just because I tell them to. It's up to them now. I have no power," Journey replied. She was struggling. She missed Andrew and wanted him home, but wanted him better at the same time. What she was confused about was that Andrew needed a situational change and time to heal. All the ward wanted was money and a subject to commit to studies. Andrew wasn't falling for it.

The two argued until Andrew realized the conversation wasn't getting anywhere. "Well, I love you. Wish you would help me out. Looks like I'll be in here forever," Andrew murmured. "But they are about to shut off the phones. I got to go." He didn't wait for a response. Instead, he just hung up the phone.

Afterward, he walked to his bedroom and of course, the gentleman was still keeping an eye on him. Andrew said, "Fuck this," and turned around to head to the phone booth outside of Tyrone's door to openly confide in him. Tyrone was laying down and ready for his slumber. The night was wrapping up for the remainder of the patients in the day room as the movie they were watching came to an end. Andrew picked up the phone.

"Hey, T-dog! You there bro?" Andrew said into the receiver.

"Whaddup G?" Tyrone's voice echoed out his bedroom door.

"Bro! Something is going on. We need to band together as one race. They are watching us. They are listening."

"I know this dog. This isn't my first rodeo! I know all that!" he said back.

"We got to do something," Andrew protested.

"I know man. I'm with you all the way. This shit is corrupt!"

The two chatted in fuzzy lingo until Andrew felt suffice that the call had come to a conclusion. Andrew had some words with the staff on his way to his room and in the meantime, Tyrone started spitting it real to them so Andrew turned around to rejoin. They were belligerent with words. They pointed out being coerced into taking meds. They told them they better stop pushing buttons and that it only takes one lawyer and some faulty moves for shit to hit the fan. They provoked them to pick a side.

The militaristic men came in around 10:00 pm usually. It was getting close to that time. Tyrone and Andrew threw the heat at ground control for about another 15 minutes until the bald and bearded man walked into the pod. The two wise guys withdrew into their rooms to avoid confrontation. The two intruding men then sat outside of Andrew and Charlie's door again. Andrew laid down to listen to his headset. The night was at its closing time. It was strange sensing Gabriel's screams but never seeing the guy.

The next day was uneventful. They had a baking group and that's about it. Andrew made it through the whole day without too much of a problem but his mind was getting more clouded from the meds. He did his best to keep his head above the water and help others out. When night finally came, Gabriel didn't scream. Andrew wondered what was on his mind. Andrew imagined what Gabe looked like as he waited for morning to come. He was beyond tired and his eyes grew heavy. He finally had fallen into a much-needed sleep.

CHAPTER 44
The Folder

It was now the 18th of January. Andrew's deep sleep from the night before had made him miss his roommate's departure. Andrew woke up to his roommate along with all his roommate's belongings gone. He had lost his twin and close companion. Andrew asked the staff where he had gone and was told he was discharged. What the hell, Andrew thought. He didn't even say goodbye. Andrew hopped in the shower and cleaned himself up. He actually took a lot of showers in the hospital because the water was somewhat warm. When he got back to his room he decided to do his laundry.

He went into his paper bag of dirty clothes and noticed some interesting attire in there. For one, there was a woman's thong in it. Next, there was a red women's shirt that said: "Play the field". Finally, there was a shirt with Batman on it. It was Mr. Leery's. Andrew understood the meaning of this. It was all set up to happen. Andrew had a choice. He could choose any of the options. He could wear the panties and be a wuss throughout his life or he could wear the women's shirt and play the field. Andrew threw away the thong and the "play the field" shirt he threw in the donated clothes pile in the laundry room. What Andrew really wanted was to be Batman. Batman makes his own respectable rules. It was very very interesting to Andrew. Did the doctor tell his twin to do this or was it just out of nowhere? Andrew believed it was an act of God.

After Andrew put his clothes in the washer he was pulled aside afterward to get his blood drawn and vitals taken again. Why did they need so much blood? Andrew felt violated that they were taking from him what he believed was sacred. Andrew was giving a part of himself to the hospital. He knew they would study it. I mean it was a university. Overall, Andrew's vitals were elevated but not too bad.

After the nurse took his blood Andrew went to the medication education group at 10 am. Afterwards, the doctor called him for a meeting. Instead of meeting in his office, they sat down in the dining room.

"Hey, we came to a conclusion. Due to your delusions, we decided we would recommend ECT. It's a very good treatment for people suffering from schizophrenia and other mood disorders. We believe it will help you out," the doctor said with a smirk on his face.

Andrew felt like the doctor was trying to bring him down. Exterminate him. Andrew didn't want his memories to be lost. This shit was wrong. He was scared and wanted to contact Strat and his lawyer.

"There is no way I'm going to consent to ECT or any kind of shock therapy. There is no fucking way!" Andrew said. He had a shaky but stern voice. His adrenaline started flowing at a higher level than it already was.

The doctor spent a few minutes trying to persuade Andrew to do the treatment. Andrew kept saying no but the doctor was enjoying himself. "It's going to look bad to the judge that you are not compliant. It will be up to him if you get committed. In that case, you will be forced to do the ECT treatment. In any case, I would also suggest you stay away from the marijuana."

"Whatever. I'm not going to quit smoking pot. Nor am I doing the treatment, even if the judge says so," Andrew asserted.

"I guess we will see what happens. I'll be increasing your dosage on both your medications. I don't think it's gotten the full effect. Also, I will begin administering this medication by needle from now on since you are at risk for skipping out on them. It's a once a month type deal. You will get your first shot before you leave."

The doc closed his folder and concluded the meeting. Andrew walked away frustrated and freaked out. He had no clue what his fate would be but he would not give up. He was a fighter. They weren't going to silence him.

As the doctor walked away to the exit, Andrew shouted, "I'm gonna sue the shit out of you guys for all the stress and fucked up shit you are causing to me. I'm not ever going to forget this!"

The doctor looked at Andrew and shook his head then stared at the ground as he exited the station. Andrew took a stroll to the lounge room and looked out the window. To his surprise, he saw hundreds of crows. Maybe over a thousand in the nearby trees. The trees were almost totally black. Every stable branch was covered. It was the most crows he had ever seen at once. Andrew believed at the time that a murder of crows signified something bad is going to happen or happening in your life. Impending death? Did they come because someone wished him ill or even to fry his brain? Or were they there for protection and warmth? Did the witch lady call upon them?

Andrew noticed three new patients entering the station. An Asian woman with glasses, a chunky Hawaiian dude, and another bigger woman. They seemed completely normal compared to the rest of the group but Andrew thought nothing of it. The witch lady walked up behind him and startled him. She was trying to interpret the crow situation. "They have been there all morning. I feel something bad is near. I'd be very careful Andrew. They are scared of you because you are a blue-eyed blonde-haired white man. Just try to keep it together."

After lunch, Andrew noticed there were only a couple of staff members in the pod at that time. A little while later the whole staff team stormed into the station wearing street clothes. There were bikers with leather jackets with patches on them and even guys in military uniform. They all went into the back room behind the counter where all the files were stored. They scurried and put all the files in the paper shredder. Andrew watched in awe. Jesus Christ! What were they hiding? They must have taken Andrew seriously about contacting his lawyer because Andrew knew indefinitely that what they were doing was wrong. He had notes of everything. Never ever would he forget.

"What the hell are you doing? You guys have something to hide?" Andrew shouted.

They ignored him. Then Andrew yelled out, "You slimy assholes!" Then he went to seek shelter in his room. While he was in his room he noticed a blue button-up shirt that Andrew number two had left behind on his shelf. It looked like a prison shirt from *Shawshank Redemption*. Next, Andrew went to the lounge area and grabbed a blue and green marker. He wrote "Change" on the back of the shirt with blue and green every other letter with capitals and lowercase letters spread out randomly to symbolize equality in all of our differences and uniqueness. He was uniting the teams. Team blue were the lost souls and team green were the enlightened ones. The sheep needed to be led in the right direction instead of following the crowd like a group of zombies.

Andrew paraded down the hallway with his new shirt in defiance. He made sure the cameras saw it for whoever was watching. Andrew wasn't a deadhead. He was actually very smart. He noticed a guy enter the station and went through the welcoming process of getting his belongings taken away. He met with the nurse and was assigned to Andrew's room as his new roommate. The guy looked like he did a lot of drugs. Especially meth. Andrew never got the chance to meet him quite yet, but from the looks of him, he didn't think he could trust him. The doctor brought him to Andrew's room for whatever reason. This was the first time Andrew had seen a doctor go into a room. The two were having a discussion.

Come to think of it, Andrew had left his folder on his nightstand. Everyone knew he had a folder. It had all sorts of scribbles in it. A notebook had all the notes of all the experiences he had had. Phone numbers from his fellow patients and drawings he had received from them were included. He had notes of everything, even the times of

The Witch's Hat

events that happened. Names of pronounced people. He kept doing this until his brain started malfunctioning and he could no longer think to keep record. He was trapped in his head but was still somewhat present. He was very worried. He felt like he had no chance to beat this ECT procedure. He just kept pacing up and down the halls with his new beloved shirt.

Finally, his anxiety took control and he went into his room to check up on his folder to see if it was still there. The doctor asked him to leave so Andrew didn't grab it for safekeeping. Moments later the doctor finished his meeting with the drug addict and left the room with his briefcase. Andrew still took his time pacing up and down the hall muttering to himself. Shortly later, he went to his room. His folder was gone. He went nuts.

He marched to the staff counter and roared, "Where is my fucking folder? You guys fucking took it!"

"We know nothing of that. Are you sure you didn't lose it?" said Abdalla, the man from his intake day.

"No, I didn't. It went missing after that doctor went into my room!" Andrew yelled. He paced back and forth and threw his hands in the air. "If I don't get it back I'm seriously going to lose my shit. That is my personal property. It is meant to be private!"

"We will see what we can do," Abdalla replied with determination.

Both Abdalla and Lindsey started making phone calls around the building with no success. Finally, they got a hold of somebody. Andrew didn't know who but they had found it.

After a half-hour of freaking out, a Mexican custodial lady came into the room and said Andrew had left it under one of the chairs in the lounge room. She then gave Andrew the folder.

"Well, why didn't you give it back to me? It had my name on it! You could have given it to the nurse. I didn't even see you come in here! I've been walking up and down the hallway the whole time!"

The lady's eyes wandered back and forth like she was looking for an answer. "Lo siento," she said meekly.

Andrew turned around and stomped back to his room. "Hey, did the doctor take my folder when he was in here?"

"I know nothing man," said his new roommate.

"Are you sure? It was sitting right there when I left!" Andrew said as he pointed at the cubby on the nightstand. "I saw it when you guys were in here and then it just disappeared!"

"I'm sorry. I know nothing dude," replied the tweaker. Andrew did not trust him at all. They probably prescribed him some good drugs for his treachery. Andrew was heated and was very amped up. Everything started speeding up again. He was kicking it into overdrive. He felt his blood pressure go up.

Luckily they had yoga group at 3 o'clock. They moved the tables in the conference room and got to work. Andrew did his stretches before starting. They had an instructor who led the way. She was doing beginner-level warrior poses. She was trying to build the patients' confidence and motivation. Andrew enjoyed it. He felt the growth each and every day. He was totally down for natural ways to reduce stress and anxiety instead of pill-popping.

Andrew was unhappy as many Americans are. The best days of his life were as a kid. And even then he felt like some sort of puppet. What he was doing now was learning how to use the tools to manage. Tools in which he would take advantage of. He wanted to write but they didn't teach that. They gave you a notebook and the rest was up to you. You either knew how to write or you didn't. That was where Andrew found his niche. A niche they wanted to have control over.

The last pose that they did was the mountain pose. The next hour was for leisure time. Then it was dinner. Dinner lasted about a half-hour. Afterward, most of the patients sat in front of the T.V. Andrew was on his usual cruise when they called for room checks. A pair of staff members went down the line and snooped through everyone's bedroom. It was pathetic. First off, they took a hat out of the first patient's room. When they exited the room they held it up for everyone to see. In the next room, they found a pair of sunglasses and held it up for a show and tell as everyone watched. When they got to

The Witch's Hat

Charlie's room they had found nothing. Andrew's room was next. They dug around in the room and came out with scissors. They stood by the entrance of the door and looked up at the surveillance camera. They opened and closed the scissors as if they were cutting the air.

"Goddamnit," Andrew muttered to himself as he stood in the hallway where he had stopped to watch.

He had a couple different thoughts in his mind. Either his new roommate had stashed scissors for protection or to even kill Andrew, which was unlikely because they didn't even know each other. Besides, how would he have gotten it? He had just arrived and they didn't have an art group that day. The more suitable explanation that Andrew had come to was that they were setting him up before his court date the next day. A pair of scissors is a big deal in the psych ward. The staff is supposed to keep a good eye and count them. Among all this, they didn't even say a word to Andrew. They just made sure the camera had a good shot of it.

Andrew knew he was fucked. They knew it too. Andrew was playing the game in their territory. "You know that isn't mine right?" Andrew said very worriedly. He knew they had set him up.

The lady who was conducting the search told Andrew she had found it under his mattress. What a fucking liar. Or maybe she wasn't lying and the doctor had put it there. He must have inconspicuously ordered a room search. It could be that the lady knew nothing of who and where it came from. It was all speculation. All Andrew knew was that it wasn't his. He began shaking frantically. All he could think of was the movie *One Flew Over the Cuckoo's Nest*. The volts pulsating through his brain. He was trembling very badly. He started to blow up on the staff then looked up at the camera and realized he better keep his cool. Whatever is said out of anger can and will be used against you. He wanted that doctor to suffer a painful death. He wanted him to be eaten inside out like a paralyzed victim of a cockroach wasp. However, in reality, it is the people (the patients) who endure this suffering. The doctor seemed to get off easily.

CHAPTER 45
Court Date

THE NEXT DAY was unlike any typical day this January. It was the day of Andrew's court case and also the day before Donald Trump's inauguration. What was strange about this day was that Gabriel left his room. It was the first time in weeks. His name meant "God is my strength" in Hebrew. It looked like he hadn't showered in months. This shaggy young man was now sitting in the dining room eating breakfast in silence. Was this considered the point that Gabriel sounded his horn? It is said that Gabriel's horn does not emit a sound. This signifies that the Lord (the Creator) has returned. Andrew felt God's presence. It was invigorating. This was what his warped radio had been trying to get through to him, what they told him to watch for. He needed all the help he could get in court. It was a great day to bring the presence of God. Andrew sat next to him and the two of them never said a word. They had a mutual understanding.

After breakfast, Andrew participated in the community meeting. Gabriel went back to his hermitage. In group Andrew shared his greatest ambition was to dominate this court case but he knew he had to pursue this smartly. The sanctity of his mind was on the line. Once the group had finished sharing their goals it ended. Andrew then approached the witch lady and the Viking just before they engaged in Bible study. He talked to them about Gabriel leaving his room.

"'I thought he would never step out of his room. He's been in there since he arrived nearly a month ago," said the Viking man.

"Yeah, it's strange because I overheard this stuff on the radio about the current times. It focused on a story about a guy who was locked up and to look out for Gabriel sounding his horn. I felt like it resembled this place we are in. Well, it happened. He finally sounded his horn. It just so happens to be hours before my court appearance. That's strange ain't it?" said Andrew in astonishment.

The Viking man stuck out his arm for a handshake. Instead of shaking with the hands, they grabbed each other's forearms in a forearm handshake. In a wide-eyed gaze, he said, "Welcome to our world brother. I knew you were special when you came in here. Check out the book of Timothy in the Bible. You are Andrew the fisherman. The fisher of men. Keep your eyes wide and have faith in the Lord. He is here beside you."

He told Andrew a Bible verse he was supposed to read. Andrew told him to hold on as he ran to his room to grab the "change" shirt. Andrew wrote the verse title on the breast pocket on his upper left side where his heart is. He threw the shirt over his back and buttoned it up. He ran back to the guys in the hallway with a Bible in his hands. He flipped to the page and read. He found some interesting stuff. In the Orthodox tradition, Saint Andrew was referred to as the "first called". It just so happened that due to Andrew's full name he was always called first. Anywhere and everywhere he went, if it was based on the last name there was no doubt he was at the front of the line. This constructed preparedness and gave him a Devine opportunity to lead.

Saint Andrew also was one of four disciples who visited Jesus on Mount of Olives to ask about the signs of Jesus's return and the "end of age". Andrew felt like it was the age in the current times. It is said Jesus will return with his saints to reign on earth. Andrew felt symbolically that "Andrew the fisherman" had returned. He felt like he had things he was supposed to do for the greater man. Focusing on the quality of human life. He knew happiness was achievable. What worried Andrew was that Saint Andrew was crucified on a saltire. He felt like he was unworthy to be crucified the same way as Jesus Christ. His brother

Simon Peter was crucified upside down for the same reason. It was to Andrew's understanding that Saint Andrew was crucified before Simon Peter. This didn't match his life story. Andrew's brother was crucified before him in the manner that he was criticized unrelentingly. He was picked on for being gay and told he would go to hell. Andrew felt his God would not determine Josh to be a terrible sinner for being homosexual. He believed as long as there is no harm, there is no foul. All Josh wanted was love. He never desired to hurt a single soul.

"You will be perfectly fine," said the witch lady. "Have faith."

"I will do my best," replied Andrew.

Up next was music group. They all sat down in the good old conference room. They drew pictures and took turns playing songs. Some people didn't participate at all. Andrew took advantage by playing his music. He hadn't had a chance to listen to his tunes by choice for a while. He played the songs that inspired him most. He played "Masters of War" by Bob Dylan. Then he went on to play "Working Class Hero" by John Lennon. He played "My Name Is Human" by Highly Suspect in memory of his former roommate. Then of course he played "Unwell" by Matchbox 20. The last song he chose was "Wish You Were Here" by Pink Floyd for his dead brother's respect. When the song finished a lady from team G named Martha told Andrew to play "Brain Damage" by Floyd. It was the first time Andrew had heard the song. It seemed like a good song for their current situation. Andrew loved the lyrics, "got to keep the loonies on the path." "I'll see you on the dark side of the moon" was another verse that stood out. During this song, the doctor walked into the room to get Andrew for court.

"I know this song. I've been to the dark side of the moon a few times myself," the doc said casually.

That guy pissed Andrew off. He was the one responsible for distorting people's minds and making them someone who they weren't. Anyway, Andrew was called away and got up from his seat, it was time for the decision of his fate. It was up to the state whether he would be caged longer or not. Andrew was nervous, but excited. He was taken to the locker room to grab a few belongings from his locker. The lady that

The Witch's Hat

escorted him slipped Andrew a cig in his lunch bag. She knew it would calm his nerves. She also knew how bad Andrew was craving one.

Andrew was released from the station and put into a correctional transport van. They then drove to the mental health court downtown. They parked inside an underground ramp. Andrew got out of the vehicle and put his cigarette in his mouth. He was mindful enough to ask the two officers if he could smoke it quickly. One of them, the younger one, said it was fine. The other gentleman who was middle-aged said absolutely not. The negative chief's decision outweighed the one of the nice officer. The older man took Andrew's cigarette as well as his lighter. The guy didn't know who Andrew was but was still treating him like a criminal. He should have just sparked up the cig with no questions asked. Fuck that man's authority.

They walked to an elevator at one end of the parking ramp and went up. They finally reached the floor where the mental health court was held. Andrew was placed into a room to wait all alone. The walls were bright white. He reached out to the officers through the speaker on the wall and asked to use the bathroom. After using the bathroom he preached to the officers and said that he was caged for no reason at all. An old wise officer who was on the brink of retirement actually had compassion. He saw Andrew's "change" shirt and knew Andrew was different from the standard lunatic you may think of. He was driven. The two talked for a short minute then Andrew was put back into the room to wait for his public defender.

"You're a rockstar, man," the perceptive officer said before he closed the door and locked it.

By the time his public defender had arrived, Andrew had eaten his food and was somewhat replenished. He thought the lady seemed kind of ditsy and like she didn't know how to do her job well.

"So this is an all or nothing type of deal," she said. "You can fight the case but if you lose you will be placed in one of the state's mental health hospitals for the next 6 months where you must follow through with all recommendations given by the doctors. If you win you will be able to go home and leave all this in the past."

"So what do you think I should do?" Andrew asked.

"Well, what do you think the judge will say?"

"I feel like this is all rigged and I will be locked away," Andrew said. "Can you give me a minute to decide?"

The lady left the room to allow Andrew to ponder his decision. She came back a few moments later and introduced Andrew to a deal she had discussed with the judge and the doctor. Andrew would have to plead guilty to whatever he did in exchange to be placed on a voluntary commitment for 6 months. If he was successful they wouldn't put the commitment information on his record. It sounded sweet at first but there were stipulations he had to follow. He could go home but he couldn't smoke weed and had to take pills. He also needed to connect with a psychiatrist, a therapist, and a caseworker on a regular basis and would be monitored.

Andrew didn't want to do none of this. He had planned to quit taking the meds as soon as he left the hospital because it slowed down his thinking too much. He didn't want to be anything other than himself. But he figured he would have a better chance of completing the voluntary commitment than being judged. Especially with all the notes the doctor took that the judge would see.

If the supposed wrongdoing was posting a video of a gun on Facebook he would be guilty, but how is that a crime? Andrew didn't know. The post didn't have a description so they couldn't rightfully accuse him that he was homicidal or suicidal. However, they sure are good at twisting things. Were they trying to commit him because he believed humans were partly extraterrestrial? Many would agree it seemed as if Andrew had a mental breakdown. Andrew kinda looked at it as his mind was in some sort of rebirth. It had been overloaded with trauma, fear for his life, and enlightenment. With all this taken into account, he acted accordingly. He had a new outlook on life. He would never be the same again and nothing the doctors would say or do could change that.

The lady came back and snapped her finger in Andrew's face. "Hey, you there? You figure out what you are going to do yet?"

The Witch's Hat

Andrew wasn't going to take the chance of getting his brain forcibly electrocuted. "I'll take the plea deal," he said.

"Okay. Sounds great! Let's go pay a visit to the judge then. Follow me."

Andrew got up from the chair. He threw on a sweatshirt over his "change" shirt. He refused to completely take it off because it was what he stood for. He would just make like a chameleon and blend in just in case anyone tried any funny business against him because of it.

Andrew saw his fiancé when he walked into the courtroom. He also saw her mother. Moments later Andrew made it to the stand. He threw away his pride as he stood in front of the judge and agreed to the terms of this phony ass voluntary commitment. It seemed more like a pressured-upon commitment to Andrew. It was not like they really cared if he was guilty or not. Anyhow, after the judge concluded court, Andrew had the chance to give his fiancé and soon-to-be mother-in-law a hug before he had to go back to the psychiatric ward. It was Thursday and Andrew wasn't allowed to go home permanently until Monday. However, he was given a day pass that Saturday as a test to see how he could stand the outside world again. Andrew thought of it as they more or less wanted to see if he would run, which would most likely be used to his disadvantage.

Andrew left the courtroom with the sheriff and was pulled aside by his public defender to sign some papers. "Just an FYI, the doctor said he doesn't think you are going to be able to complete this voluntary commitment you have agreed to. He says he expects to see you back here," she said. "It's up to you to prove him wrong."

That fucking bastard, Andrew thought. This info didn't surprise him because of the vibes he felt when he was in the doctor's presence. Andrew wouldn't let it bother him. He knew he wasn't an idiot and would bestow it upon himself to do what he had to do to make it through the commitment. What the doctor thought was irrelevant.

After signing the papers, Andrew was transported back to the looney bin. The place was loopy when Andrew entered due to the upcoming inauguration. It seemed like the whole world went nuts.

Andrew Aaberg

Just so happened the unlucky ones were locked behind closed doors for the time being. Andrew would find a way out and make his way. He had to find his own path.

CHAPTER 46
The Watchtower

A<small>NDREW ATE DINNER</small>, then had his usual visit with his fiancé. Afterward, he was questioned by the new Asian lady. She asked why Andrew was shivering and he replied that he was cold. "It's not cold in here," she said. "Seems like the U of M has treated you really nice. I am actually a student here."

"So, are you pretending to be crazy?" Andrew asked.

"No, I just had a mental breakdown from my studies and had to check myself in. I'm curious to know more about you. Seems like a lot of the patients have taken a liking to you!"

"Probably because I've pointed out that this damn place and the whole system is corrupt," Andrew replied.

"Have you ever thought that you are the problem?" she questioned.

"Well, I'm not," Andrew said angrily. He turned away from her and walked to his room to lay down.

As he lay in bed, his mind retraced to the past and he asked his roommate why he had had a pair of scissors.

"Those weren't my scissors… They were either yours or your old roomies."

"That's fucking sketchy. They weren't mine," Andrew replied. "But alrighty then, I'm gonna try to get some sleep."

After an hour in bed, Andrew got up to do his rant with the staff. He noticed the soldiers outside his room as normal, which wasn't surprising. What surprised him was that the Asian lady and the Hawaiian dude were behind the counter where patients were not supposed to be allowed. They were discussing something with the nurse and the Asian was on the computer. Were they letting her do her homework? But what was the Hawaiian guy doing? Did they know each other? Did they both go to the U of M? Andrew didn't know if he could trust them so he veered away. For all Andrew knew they were actors or visiting the ward for a school project. Andrew didn't have the energy to interrogate, so instead he went about his business.

He walked by them and sniffed out the chunky staff member in the dining room. He was indulging himself in some snacks. "Hey, can I take a shower?" Andrew asked.

"It's a bit late, but I suppose. Let me grab the keys," he replied. He retrieved the keys and unlocked the shower room.

"Thanks," Andrew said as he walked in. He shut the door and turned on the faucet. The water came out blood red. Andrew thought the fucking apocalypse had finally come. This was it. It was now past midnight. It was the day Trump would become president, essentially 12 hours exactly from midnight to be precise.

Andrew reopened the door. He was slightly shaking. "Dude the water is red! This damn place is giving me the heebie-jeebies. What's going on?"

"What? Really? I'll check into it. It's probably rust being flushed out. Don't worry," responded the chunkster.

This didn't calm Andrew's nerves one bit. The synchronization with everything going on tripped him out. Although mentally he threw his fears aside. "Looks like I'll be taking a bath in blood tonight," Andrew said to the fat man. He was determined not to let fear conquer him.

The Witch's Hat

He closed the bathroom door and put a plug in the drain. He let the water rain down from the heavens. He lay down in the tub and soaked in every square inch of his ancestry into his rebirthing soul.

Andrew felt like he was in a nightmare. Was he imagining his senses to be compliant like in reality? It wasn't so much his senses but his understanding of the situation. He knew hell on earth was about to begin. The question was when. He saw the way people were acting. Andrew voted for Trump because he was a businessman. He knew Trump offended people but you had to respect he kept it real and was somewhat funny. Andrew was even on the frontlines as a Trump supporter. He printed thousands of Trump yard signs at his current job as a printer. He even brought one home for his soon-to-be father-in-law. Andrew had faith Trump had his back. Trump's America would pardon Andrew from this commitment, or at least he hoped.

To be brutally honest, Andrew didn't know what Donald's overall true intentions were as he was super-wealthy. Would he only be looking out for the man upstairs or is he looking out for the paupers? Would it be so bad to have an ordinary man take power? What other options did the people of this "so-called" democracy have otherwise? Maybe they should have banded together and elected their own POTUS. If only. If only. Andrew did, however, know that one day the people would rise up. It was in his gut. He wasn't the only one who felt the way he did. He imagined riots during Trump's term but the fact of the matter was that time would only tell when total anarchy would explode into the streets.

After Andrew finished with his bathroom meditation he clothed himself and put on his handy dandy headphones. With the flick of a finger, the static brought into focus the beginning of the "All Along the Watchtower" song by Jimi Hendricks. A light illuminated in Andrew's mind. He was going to go to the window to check out the Witch's Hat. He left the bathroom to gaze outside. It was foggy. Andrew saw the moon partly casting light upon the low-hanging clouds. It was in a waning crescent stage. Andrew spotted the tower through the haziness and stared for the entirety of the song while putting the pieces together. Up in the sky, he could barely make out the culmination of the Lynx constellation. He figured this could have been the wildcat growling in the song. The two riders approaching were Trump and Pence. Andrew was the joker. Andrew's roommate was the thief. Charlie was the businessman and the plowman was Strativarious as that was what his last name stood for. If you did the research you would know. Perhaps he didn't piece things together properly but as shown before, the synchronization of everything was remarkable.

In the meantime, the light flickered in the tower. It was calling him. Each stair step to the top was a different stage of his life. He couldn't let his ambition towards success make him into a bad person. He didn't know what he was doing at this point. One thing he knew was that something shady was going on and that he had to pursue this lawsuit to avenge the victims of Beer Belly's. Could he do it? He wanted to, but time was weighing upon him. He wanted it over and done with. As of right now, he was living an adventure.

After the song finished Andrew went on a walk to his room. The walk was interrupted when one of the staff members asked him for his headphones. He was told that they weren't allowed in the bedrooms at night. This made things really hard for Andrew as music guided his life. He was lost without them but still swam in the light. He gave them the headphones and went to lay down. He had a premonition that night. He saw the city burning. He didn't think much of it because he was so anxious for the inauguration and didn't sleep one bit. Instead, he listened to Gabriel scream his lungs out from down the hall. Andrew had no music to draw out the calamity and felt Gabriel's pain. They suffered together that night.

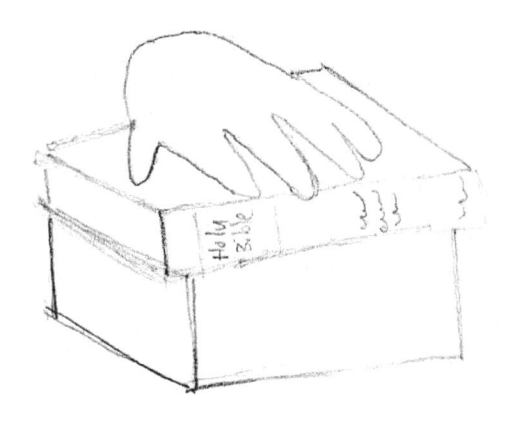

CHAPTER 47
The Inauguration

FINALLY, MORNING CAME. Andrew arose from bed for breakfast. He had the usual scrambled eggs and bacon. This was the last day that Andrew took intensive notes during his experience as he was close to losing his mind. Anyhow, 11:00 am rolled around and the T.V was tuned in to the news. It wasn't long until lunch came. Most of everybody grabbed their trays and sat in the lounge room. After scarfing their food, Charlie and Andrew stood and stared out the lounge room window for the longest. There wasn't a single soul in the foggy streets. No cars, pedestrians, or much of any movement besides the three crows in the tree.

"Looks dead out there, doesn't it?" Andrew asked Charlie.

"I was thinking the EXACT same thing," Charlie verbalized.

"I don't know man… There is something different about this election. I feel Armageddon in the air," Andrew said at a reasonable level so no one else could hear.

Charlie had his arms folded. "You would be amazed," he replied. The room then got louder with intensified energy. They turned towards the television. "Here it is," Charlie added.

Andrew stood in front and to the side of the T.V. giving view to the other crazies who had nothing better to do than to plop down and watch. Given the importance of the date, there were no group meetings that day. Watching the commander in chief being sworn in was a big deal. Andrew paid attention intensively. It was the beginning of a new reign. The crazies began retreating during the short speech. It seemed they couldn't handle the excitement. The ones that remained after the 16-minute inaugural address were trembling. Andrew felt the pivot of power and was anticipating a drastic change.

"PC! PC! PC! PC!!!!" shrieked the witch lady. She was going crazy about this "PC" thing. Ramya looked like she was petrified. Tyrone was tapping his foot while sitting in his chair. He was trying to contain himself but he was tripping out as his eyes skirted from wall to wall. Eventually, everyone left but Charlie and Andrew. Charlie approached Andrew as if he had something to say.

"Hey, you doing good?" he asked.

"Yeah I'm fine," Andrew replied.

"Let's take a walk," instructed Charlie.

They both slowly made their way around the kitchen area and into the hallway. "I manage 13 states," he said to Andrew. "Wisconsin, Minnesota, New York, New Jersey, Maryland, Virginia, Massachusetts, and the list goes on. Consider yourself on a 'watch list'. Here, come here. Let me show you something."

Andrew didn't know if he was joking around or what. Why would Andrew be on a "watch list"? What did he do? Is it because he wanted a revolution? Was it because he mentioned stuff about extraterrestrials to simply raise the topic? Who knows? Andrew was interested and kind of freaked out at the same time. He followed Charlie to the table in the T.V. room from where he grabbed a newspaper. He placed the newspaper on one of the cushioned chairs and opened it.

"Here, listen. I'm going to teach you something." Charlie then proceeded to show Andrew stock numbers and a passage that revealed some sort of secret knowledge. "Invest in everyday things that people use. Imagine if you were stuck only living from home what you would

The Witch's Hat

buy," he said while continuing to list a few things. "You will thank me in a few years."

Who was this guy? Andrew had his suspicions. His heart rate had increased. What did this guy know that Andrew didn't... Andrew was on a trip. The meds made him slow to talk but he was still there. "I don't have the money to invest. I don't even do the bills," Andrew replied.

"My advice to you is to lose the woman," Charlie stated. "They become a distraction and a barrier at times."

"Yeah, that's not happening. I'm going to be getting married," Andrew said back defensively.

"Not a good decision," Charlie contended, shaking his head as he walked away.

Andrew sat down in front of the T.V. and pondered what this guy's objective was. Was he trying to help him? Why? Andrew was amused. This moment in time was very intense. Andrew watched a little bit more of the news until he got overwhelmed and went to his room for the next hour or so. Eventually, he exited and went back to the television. Charlie tapped Andrew on the shoulder and pointed at the countertop between the lounge and the cafe.

Andrew went over to the counter and picked up a piece of paper. It read "!be thoughtful please pick up! (after yourself) not your mother." Listed was "OG name" with Charlie's line posted. The rest was code. Underneath the paper was a JFK book. It was a story of the president's life including, of course, his assassination. Andrew was into conspiracy theories. He understood what Charlie was getting at. Was Andrew willing to put his life on the line?

Andrew paged through the book and looked at the pictures. He didn't read it. He had the idea already in his head. It all became very real. Some way or another Andrew would aspire to build himself to where he could be in a position of power. Whether it be behind the scenes or in the spotlight, being king is a big responsibility. Like in the "Viva La Vida" song Strativarious recorded with Coldplay, the words "Who would ever want to be king?" stood out to Andrew. If Andrew ever was, he would want to significantly change everything. Hopefully, peacefully. As a citizen, he wanted to shut down and revamp the system. Andrew understood the message Charlie was trying to send him to a good extent.

Andrew looked up from the counter to see Ramya and the witch lady being wheeled in by wheelchair. Aww fuck, Andrew thought. They had done it to them. The two women had a vegetable look on their faces, looking super dumb happy. They had gotten the ECT. Andrew was super glad that he had avoided it. Who knows if these two had the decision to do so or not. It was quite sad. These two were unhappy for a reason. Both were societal problems. There was nothing wrong with them. The witch lady may have seemed crazy but she was just a troubled woman, frustrated with the world in the present day. Ramya was troubled in a different way. In her case it was more justifiable to rid her brain of her rape memories. Whether ECT could work for PTSD or not wasn't the question. What the question was, was how fine-tuned this procedure was at this point? Andrew guessed they would learn a thing or two from Ramya's study. But still, it didn't seem right to Andrew. They now lacked drive. They both had exponential room to grow but it was halted. Now they would comply and not be a burden.

On Andrew's walk to his room, a large red-headed lady in a walker that seemed to have schizo symptoms called Andrew the devil. She said it in a whisper like she was talking to herself. Andrew thought that if anyone needed ECT it would be her, so she didn't seem so possessed. Andrew made it past her and laid down in his room to think. Eventually, the nurse got his vitals. His blood pressure was 138/97. He was in hypertension mode. Next, dinner came and went and visiting hours were on the horizon. Journey was the first one there as usual. They went into the meeting room with the unusual device planted amongst the ceiling. Andrew tried to contain himself. He was itching to go home.

They sat by the window in the meeting room that overlooked the cafe and the hallway. At the corner of Andrew's eye, he saw an older gentleman walk towards the front counter for check-in. He looked like an executive. Andrew didn't get too good of a look at him as he was walking quickly. Andrew did notice he had a fedora on. He ended up

The Witch's Hat

checking in under Charlie's name as his father. Who knows if they were actually really related. Or perhaps they were and they were part of some family spy ring.

Andrew's heartbeat was going rapidly. He felt like he had something important to say but no one would listen. Everyone thought he was crazy. He felt like he should have kept his mouth shut from the get-go but needed a companion to confide in. He leaned over across the table with his hands cupping his mouth. Karen, the nurse from team B was watching and staring Andrew down from ground control.

"Hey, I have to tell you something but you have to believe me," Andrew whispered. He didn't want the bug in the room to hear him.

Journey looked at him and said in a normal volume voice, "Why is that guy over there staring at us?"

It was Charlie peeping around the corner looking into the room, being a creep.

Andrew leaned back over to Journey and said in a hushed voice, "That's what I want to tell you about. Will you listen?"

"He looks like a rapist," she commented.

"Don't worry about him," Andrew replied softly but impatiently. "I'm gonna tell you something in secret. Will you listen? This place is bugged so I have to be quiet. They don't want you to know what's going on."

"Andrew! There is nothing to panic about. You will get to come home tomorrow for a short bit, then by Monday you will leave all this behind. Tell me about whatever that is on your mind at any time. I will listen."

Andrew wanted Journey on his side but he didn't know if she could handle the truth. He decided to lean back over the table and spoke directly into her ear. "That guy that is staring over there is part of the C....."

Just then he had gotten a tap on the shoulder and his sentence was cut short. "You can't whisper in here. It makes the other patients uncomfortable," instructed the nosy Karen. Goddamnit Andrew thought. He felt like he was on lockdown and part of some movie scene.

313

It wasn't too long after the B nurse turned away to go back to the L-shaped counter, that the doors to the station exploded open. It was the Asian girl on a gurney. She looked dead-on at Andrew while flailing her arms. "Heeeeeeeeyyyyyyyyyy! Aaaaaahhhhhhhhh!" she screamed as she shook her head in disapproval violently. She yelled the whole way down the hall. "Stop! Stop! Stop!"

Where the hell had she come from? And why were they bringing a person back on a gurney in worse condition than what she was when he had just seen her earlier that day? Andrew hadn't even noticed she had left the station. Was she listening to the recording? Andrew was sketched out as never before. He knew he had fucked up. He messed up his trust with the conspirators. Such a taboo word, Andrew thought.

Andrew came upon a bright idea to apologize at that very moment. He knew that there was a board game called "Sorry" out near the counter space between the cafeteria and the T.V. room where he had gotten his note from Charlie. Andrew had a guilty feeling wrenching in his stomach. He told Journey he would be right back. He approached the counter and searched for the game in the cupboard below. He pulled it out and looked at Charlie and his "dad" who sat in the T.V. room. He held it up high to make it plain and obvious he was trying to send a message. This was his way of apologizing for what he tried to expose. He still wasn't getting a good look at Charlie's "father". For whatever reason, the man had his hand covering his face intentionally so Andrew couldn't see it. He was masking his identity. But why exactly? This just gave credit to Andrew's suspicions. He had a feeling he had figured out what was going on. The feeling was intense.

As Andrew walked back to the conference room he was followed by the walking corpse of the witch lady. The smile on her face seemed bewildered and over excessive.

"Hey can I play?" she asked.

"Yeah sure. I don't mind. I'll introduce you to my fiancé," Andrew replied.

They opened the cracked door to the room and put it back in just that position upon entering. Andrew stood in front of Journey with

The Witch's Hat

the lady beside him. "Hey Journey this is Priscilla and Priscilla this is my fiancé Journey," Andrew said to establish a first impression among the two.

The witch lady clapped her hands in excitement. "Oh, how wonderful!" she cheered. The two greeted each other fantastically.

Andrew stepped away from the table. "Hey, guys let's get away from this window and go into the corner over here," Andrew advocated as he began his walk while the two women followed him. He pulled the chair for his fiancé. The three sat and Andrew arranged the board quickly and neatly onto the table. They all picked colors and went on the run. The witch lady seemed strange with her sudden flamboyance. She really didn't seem to care who won. She was out of it but you could see that there was still a piece of her buried within. It had been rattled with bursts of neurogenesis.

She looked at the couple. "You guys will be ok. I know you will! I already see it now...." she voiced as she looked at Andrew. "You are the king!" She then turned to Journey. "And you are the queen. You both will be just fine. You are royalty."

Andrew was the color blue on the board. Journey was green and the witch lady was yellow. Journey won the first two games. On the third Andrew took the lead. He was less than half of a lap to the end with his last pawn. Suddenly, the same staff lady that interrupted Andrew earlier came and did it again. Visitation was over and so was the game.

They went into the cafeteria to say their goodbyes. Charlie and his dad were on the other side of the island wall where the counter was so Andrew couldn't see them. He gave Journey a hug. A man entered the station as Andrew had his arms wrapped around her. The man gave Andrew a captivating vibe. He had no emotion at all and walked very rigidly. He reminded Andrew of someone with higher intelligence. Maybe a doctor of sorts or maybe even a man in black? What was hair-raising about this man was not just his presence but that he was carrying a suitcase with electrical wires protruding from it. This totally mind-boggled Andrew. He completely froze. He could barely think. Was this the spy equipment they used to listen to Andrew remotely? Was it ECT wires? Was it something else? Journey hadn't seen a thing.

Her back was to the hallway. Andrew wanted to share his excitement. It took everything within himself to keep his mouth shut. It was a test. They were assessing Andrew's trust or just messing with him. Andrew almost gave them away telling his fiancé about the CIA earlier. He should have known better. If his thoughts on this circulated he would get the electrodes for sure. Andrew saw it as one big conspiracy as he withdrew from the hug after planting a kiss upon Journey's lips.

"Hey babe, on the way here I saw somebody wrote the word "trap" on their mailbox. I thought that you would find that interesting," Journey sweetly said.

At that moment Charlie's "dad" along with the man with the wired suitcase walked side by side to depart from the station. The man with the briefcase blocked the vision to Charlie's "father" so Andrew had no face to put to him. Andrew had no recollection of whether or not the suitcase man even still had it or not, but it WAS a trap. Question was, who was doing the trapping?

Andrew looked Journey square in the eyes. "I do find that interesting," Andrew replied rapidly, "Please be careful when you leave. There are bad people out there. It's very dark. They could come out of nowhere. I don't want you to get hurt."

"I'll do my best," responded Journey.

"Sounds good. Hey, give me a sec," Andrew said.

Andrew ran over to the front counter and asked Abdalla if he would be willing to escort his fiancé to her car because he was worried about her safety. He made up a story about how there was a rapist loose on campus which persuaded Abdalla to agree to walk her down. Andrew said his final goodbye and watched the love of his life walk out of the station.

Charlie snuck up on Andrew and looked at him with calm alertness. "Hey, was that your sister?" he joked. He knew who it was. He was just using words to try to deter Andrew from being "strapped down."

Andrew needed to settle down. He had dreams he wanted to accomplish. He could achieve them with Journey by his side. He wanted to enjoy life and felt like she was the right one to do it with. He didn't want

The Witch's Hat

to die alone and liked the fact he could rely on someone at all times. Andrew had a sense of higher purpose to bring about issues in society. His brother was a victim of the struggle and Andrew could imagine that there are many others just like him who take their lives every day. Whether it be mental health, bullying, plainly trying to work through emotions, or whatever it may be. On another note, somewhat related is that some people even die on their drive to work, trying to serve society, spending their whole lives trying to jump the hump but never making it. People who die before retirement is devastating. Andrew could rant on and on.

Andrew moved to a position closer to Charlie. Andrew's face was facing the wall. He was annoyed. He looked out of the right corner of his eyes and said, "That is not my sister! That is my fiancé!"

Andrew left and walked to his room. His nerves were rocking around in his body. He laid down and stared at the ceiling for a good 20 minutes. He thought deeply about things until finally, he snapped. He cried out for help. He didn't know if he could stand it any longer.

Andrew screamed aloud, "Josh where are you!? Help me! Help!! Please! Where are you?"

Andrew kept going and going. He was hysterical. The whole station must have heard him.

"Help me!" Andrew shrieked. "J-man?"

A lady from team G ran to the room to give Andrew some pills. The military men weren't around yet to hold Andrew down. Besides, Andrew wasn't flailing around violently. Just desperate calls for help to the beyond.

"Here take these!" said the staff woman. She was the one who helped Abdalla to make phone calls to get Andrew's folder back. "I included 2mg of Ativan as well. It will make you feel better!"

Andrew was in tears. "Noooo! Josh!" he cried out broken heartedly.

As Andrew reached his hands out for the pills and water, he heard someone spazzing out. It was almost an imitation of Andrew's present outburst but in a totally different direction. It sounded like Charlie's voice coming from the room next door. He was having a breakdown.

"Nooooooo!" he shouted violently. "He knows everything!"

Charlie kept up with this scene until the staff came to calm him down. Andrew heard them whisper back and forth.

Andrew's lack of sleep was so he wouldn't forget. He didn't want to. Andrew's mind had to chew on all this information. And that is just what he did. Apparently, he knew something. This made Andrew feel like a target. He thanked the nurse and laid down. He was paranoid for his life to sleep that night yet again. This magnified it. Andrew became drowsy and went into a half-awake, half-sleep coma until morning when he had his visitation pass.

CHAPTER 48
Home Visitation

It was close to three weeks in the ward. Andrew woke up. He did his morning vitals then did the usual breakfast with scrambled eggs and bacon. After that, he waited for Journey to take him home. Lunch came and went. Andrew still waited. Finally, 2 o'clock rolled around and she had arrived at the arranged time. Andrew only had until 6 pm which was only four hours, a pretty short day pass he thought, but he would make the most of it.

They departed from the station after Andrew signed out. He wanted to run, but held his urges. He was hungry for something that wasn't hospital food. Ironically, the hospital had a Subway. So technically, still hospital food? He ordered his steak sandwich and sat down to eat. He suddenly came upon the idea to visit his old house with some of the most freeing moments of his past. Andrew reminisced on all his old foster brothers and sisters. He found out one had come out as transgender. Another had moved out west. Andrew wished he would attempt to visit them someday. He knew how rough it is on your own. He felt a little guilty and wished the best for them.

The biggest reason why Andrew wanted to go visit the old home was to relive and embrace his memories. Especially all the recollections of Josh. Andrew finished his sandwich and told Journey what he wanted to do and they were on their way. About a 35-minute drive and they were there. They parked at the Lake Itasca trails across from Andrew's old home, the temperature was in the mid-'30s and they decided to go on a walk on the trail. Andrew appreciated the beauty more than ever before. He spent the time in his memory bank and talked to Journey in some of the meantime but was mostly spacing out in his own world. He was still trapped deep in his mind, which would take some getting used to.

They spent a good 45 minutes on the walk. The time was about 3:20 pm when they took off toward Journey's parents. The sky was still lit and Andrew went to hang in the garage with Leopold upon arrival. They were watching *American Pickers* on the History Channel. Andrew felt like he could relate. He wanted to be on the road, totally free from any boundaries and containment. Leopold put on some music in the background with his old-school 3-way stereo system. It blended in quite well. One of the songs was "Run to the Hills" by Iron Maiden. They snacked and enjoyed each other's silence while chain-smoking cigarettes.

Finally, Leopold asked if Andrew wanted to play a song.

"Sure," Andrew replied. "Play 'Rape Me' by Nirvana."

"Ok. I got that," Leopold said. He skimmed through all his alphabetically shelved CD cases aligned in rows above his counter. He pulled out Nirvana's *In Utero* album and skipped to track four. The music begins to play...

"Man some bad stuff happened in there," Andrew revealed crazily, as he imagined getting raped by a bunch of demons while in restraints. "I really don't want to go back!" he added.

"I wouldn't do anything stupid! They will put you away for sure!" Leopold replied.

"Yeah, I know. I won't be dumb about it. I'll go back." In reality, Andrew was itching to grab a bag of belongings and boogy. He actually thought of a plan he cared not to share.

It wasn't long before Leopold and Andrew were called into the house for dinner by the women inside. Journey's mother had whipped together some tater tot hotdish, Andrew's favorite, to celebrate the special occasion. After eating, it was already time for Andrew to head back to the hospital. He overcame his urge to run. He knew he probably wouldn't have a life with Journey if he did so. It was about 5:15 pm when they left her parents house. The sun had set and the temp was still in the mid-'30s which was pretty warm for a Minnesota January evening.

The couple made it back to the hospital's parking ramp. They still had ten minutes and spent some quality time together talking in the car. Andrew was zoning in and out as he feared for his life for whatever reason that was on his mind.

"I just want to get away from all this with you babe! Can we move out to the woods?" Andrew asked.

"I don't think I can be away from my family. I would be ok if we got a cabin," Journey replied.

"We can't afford that. I don't want to be strapped down to a job all day every day for the rest of my life. We need a miracle! I want to get far away from the city," declared Andrew.

"Let's just focus on working hard for the time being and see where life leads us. We will eventually get there one day. I would actually consider moving further away when we retire," Journey responded.

"I just want peace and tranquility," said Andrew. "I want to get in touch with nature. I need to hit the road and travel. I feel like I'm giving away my whole life to this nonsense. I want to enjoy it. I mean my uncle, Malcolm moved to California and is flying planes. I want to follow a dream too! Just don't know how to get there. I'm worried. I'm frustrated and impatient due to limited time."

"Andrew, don't worry. We will get there. Everything you want in life will be achieved due to hard work," she answered.

"It's bullshit. I don't know how much longer I have to live," Andrew chimed.

"Andrew, stop it! It will be ok!" asserted Journey. "It's the way life is."

Andrew tried his best to calm his nerves. He kept staring and zoning, thinking of another way to go about things so he wasn't a working-class slave. He knew he wasn't better than anyone else. He wanted better for mankind. There had to be another way where humankind wasn't so exploited and could enjoy life to its full extent. He would ponder this but he needed help. Maybe somewhere down the line, he would find it.

Journey and Andrew's chat came to an end. It was time for Andrew to be caged up again. They stepped out of the car and walked out of the parking ramp. As they crossed the street to the hospital it began to rain. To Andrew, these raindrops signified his tears in a sense of hopelessness. He was about to reenter the devil's playground to swim, yet again in the light. He couldn't give up the fight. But was he really prepared?

The raindrops continued to fall from the kingdom above. Andrew couldn't waste his life sleeping. He had to get to where he needed to go and he would try to pursue it to his full capacity while keeping his mental health in check. It was his mission. Maybe some of the raindrops were God's tears as well as he wept for the wounded souls. The raindrops would echo through time. One day things will be brighter when the sun shines so very bright up in the deep blue sky.

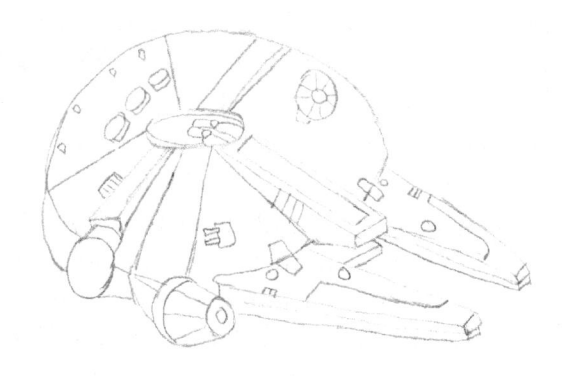

CHAPTER 49
Star Wars

ANDREW ARRIVED INSIDE Station 22 and said goodbye to his lady love then retreated to his room for a few hours. Suddenly he heard excitement in the lounge room. It was going to be a special night. The facility was playing one of the *Star Wars* movies and Andrew was down to watch. This was certainly something he could get into. It seemed as if they had just catered to his mentality. He decided to take a break from his meditations to join in on the fun.

He sat down in the lounge room. He had just requested his headphones back; the very same weird ones as before, to be particular. He valued them for their secret revelations. He watched the movie from a chair to the side of the T.V. at a weird angle. Tony, the male nurse, came and sat next to him. Andrew had a weird feeling. He was fidgety, bouncing his leg up and down. For whatever reason, his uneasiness continued to build. He was putting out unwanted energy. He couldn't get his mind off of how badly he wanted to be released.

The staff nurse got up from his chair and waved his hand in front of his nose as if he was trying to rid the smell of a fart. Then he said something but Andrew couldn't hear because he had his headphones on. He thought Tony might have said Andrew had stunk. This would have been strange because Andrew showered every day and he didn't just fart; maybe it was the lack of deodorant. Tony walked away and Charlie sat in the man's former chair. Andrew took off his headphones partially and they chatted. They ended up coming up with an idea to reenact *Star Wars* themselves, Andrew didn't know exactly which character everyone was but they went along with it.

They battled in the hallway with their fake lightsabers. Another patient from team B joined in on the action and played for a few minutes. He was a white Mexican, unlike Mason. Andrew and this new Hispanic guy shared the same skin color but were still from different tribes although Andrew loved the unity within the game. When Andrew started getting serious and crawling on the ground to sneak up on people is when the Mexican quit. Andrew looked up at the staff and saw them watching him while they took notes. Andrew knew he was on camera too. He figured he better quit. He was only a monkey puppet and the strings took control. He quit playing because he felt like they would threaten to take away his release date for some stupid reason.

Andrew crawled back to his seat near the T.V. He looked over at command center and started tripping out. All the staff behind the counter was a character in the movie. There were some different characters but they all resembled something out of this world. The military men walked into the room to stand guard. They were the stormtroopers, Charlie was Darth Vader, Andrew was Luke Skywalker, and Jabba the Hutt was Karen at the pill dispenser. Andrew closed his eyes to shake off the scariest of them all. He was in the mood to go to bed. Forget the movie. He went up to Jabba the Hutt and took his pills.

"Make sure you get the right ones this time," Andrew instructed with madness. He had lost his mind. "Boy do I love to take pills. Gosh, you guys are the best. I want to be like you when I grow up."

Andrew went about finding the light in things with his sarcasm. He gave a tense face to Jabba who dropped the pills on the ground and had to get more. This would be his last dose of risperidone in pill form in the ward. Jabba kept a close eye on Andrew to make sure he wasn't cheeking them. Andrew could have attempted to do this his whole stay but decided to make the choice of taking whatever pill or shot was given. Whatever happened to him would have to be dealt with later on. Whatever brain damage Andrew went through was just more suffering to testify in court. Andrew was still determined at this point. Very determined but clouded. He took his pills and stuck out his tongue for Jabba and went to rest on his mattress for the night. The bitch followed and took his headphones and that was that.

CHAPTER 50
The Patriot

THE NEXT DAY was just like any other day but filled with tons of jitteriness for it was the day before Andrew got to go home. At least the facility was more laid back on Sundays. During reflection that morning Andrew pointed out that he was going to finish this so-called "voluntary commitment". He kept it plain and simple; he bid everyone an early farewell. But it wasn't over yet.

Lunch and dinner passed and finally, the AFC championship started playing in the T.V. room. It was the Pittsburgh Steelers versus the New England Patriots. Charlie had come out of his room with his Patriots shirt on. Andrew was pacing up and down the hall taking glimpses of the television as he walked by. Charlie pulled his right sweatpant cuff up. Or perhaps it was his left. He for sure had a blue shirt on. He stomped around the playroom like he was royalty. He definitely seemed like a gang banger type but more of a professional leadership role. The right side cuff rolled up could have signified he was a member of the Crips. Crips wore blue which was his shirt color. The left meant Bloods which were also known as the "Crip-Killers". They wore red. Suppose he wasn't part of either, but some higher management. Andrew didn't know.

He walked up to Andrew and divulged, "If you want to make money, bet on the Patriots. They are a for sure win. I have a lot of money down on them guys. They are gonna win it all."

"Oh really? Ok..." Andrew replied.

"I have close connections to that team. I manage a few of the players as well. Like I told you before, I manage many states. Be careful what you do or say, because you will be sought out."

"No way," Andrew said. But in reality, he was very fearful and paranoid. He turned away and started pacing up and down the halls again. He requested his headphones, which they gave him. The song "Hall of Fame" by The Script tuned in. It was on some random channel. Andrew was disgruntled about what was going on and the power that this guy had. Andrew made it to the T.V. area to watch the game shortly. He had pulled down one side of his headphones so he could hear better.

In the meantime, Charlie was standing with an African American staff member who looked of Somali descent. He was another additional mystery member missing from the wall of associates. Andrew didn't know why he was there. Maybe he was just a new member of the staff. Charlie and the man watched the room of crazies who were lost in their minds. A lot of what was going on was built up throughout the whole stay. It is hard to describe the feelings that they all felt at that moment. Andrew overheard the two exchange words. They were standing cool, calm, and collected unlike everyone else. Their talk was easygoing.

Charlie looked upon the staff and said, "Man, we are kings in here! This has really become a command center."

"Damn right! We are running this shit!" replied the young Somalian man.

It was all just so crazy. The patients were going nutty and Andrew was fed up. He walked down the hallway to the phone and made a call to his fiancé.

Andrew's mind was racing, "Hey babe! Call DA and DE! I need help! Get me out of here! They're going to kill me!"

"Andrew, I don't know what you're talking about. You only got one more day! You will be fine!" Journey conveyed.

"But it won't be over! They will still have me by a leash with this bullshit voluntary commitment shit! They can find whatever reason to take me back here if they want! Then they can do whatever they want to me!" Andrew said angrily. "Fuck it! I can do this! I can defeat them!"

He thought of all the outcomes. Journey did her best to cool him down but Andrew knew he had fucked up by calling her for help. He thought he had gotten himself even more on Charlie's bad side. Andrew felt like this was all some secret society. Some conspiracy. All he wanted was for the truth to be told.

Andrew looked over and saw Charlie staring from down the hall. "Hey, babe! I gotta go!" he said to Journey quickly.

They concluded the call and Andrew didn't much want to but he sat down in the living area to watch the Patriots again. He felt like there was some truth to what Charlie was saying but Andrew was still skeptical. Even so, he rooted for the Patriots as well because he thought it was a good time to be one.

After a few moments, Andrew was pulled aside. It was time for his shot. He thought of J.F.K. taking a bullet for the country. Andrew had no choice but to comply in order to leave, so he followed Tony's evil commands. They went to Andrew's room where he had to flash his butt cheek and got stuck by a needle. The trigger was pushed and he was injected with a foreign fluid.

"You will be alright. Just leave the room like this and don't say anything," Tony instructed as he rubbed the side of his own ass cheek. "By the way, I wouldn't piss off Charlie's dad. He is not one you want to mess with."

"Okay," Andrew replied. He understood very clearly. He walked out of the room rubbing his right butt cheek and sat back down. Then he blurted out loud, "The bastards shot me!"

Now all Andrew could think about was death until the game had finished. The Patriots really did end up winning. They were now going to the Super Bowl. Andrew got up to go to his room. Charlie said farewell to the Somalian man and followed.

"Hey!" shouted Charlie. "I need to talk to you! I have a question!" He seemed a little concerned. Maybe even worried. His chest was puffed out.

The Witch's Hat

"What's up?" questioned Andrew after he had turned around.

"Do you know Michael Sullivan?" chuckled Charlie evilly.

Andrew shook his head as if saying no but in all actuality, he did know of a Michael Sullivan. He was one of his uncle's childhood friends growing up. A typical thug. What was going on? Charlie turned his back to Andrew and laughed sadistically. Andrew grew very paranoid, but it was time for bed. He laid down but didn't even bother going to sleep that night because he knew he would be discharged the next day and could hopefully look forward to sleeping at a place he called home, in a nice comfy bed.

Luckily he was awake because he came upon a scheme. Some of the patients in the hall were coming up to the army men sitting outside his door and asking for cheese.

"Ok I'll put you down," the bald man would answer repeatedly after a total of five patients consecutively went up to them. Of course, of the five, consisted Charlie and the university kids. All of them were put on whatever list this guy was taking. Andrew noticed from the linguistics that something fishy was going on here. He thought that they were asking for money to be paid off for their work. Andrew left his room to ask for his cut. They had better give it to him if they wanted him to keep his mouth shut.

"Hey, can I get some cheese as well?" Andrew asked the army men. "I'm starving!"

He watched the bald man tune into his laptop to do a search on a chart. It read of codes. What code names were and for what. It also had patients' names with categories and notes beside them.

"I'm sorry, I can't get you any cheese," said Mr. Clean.

"C'mon, I'm hungry. Are you going to let me starve?"

"Ok fine. Talk to Jack over there." said the man pointing to the snack-loving staff member sitting at the cafeteria table.

This was not what Andrew meant by the term cheese. He figured it was in the books that he shouldn't have his cut and nothing he could do or say could change that in their eyes. Plus he was still trying to be undercover to a degree to not give them a reason to keep him. Andrew would get them back. He would unleash his fury upon them for something greater. He would seek to uncover divine secrecy and bring the light to others. Maybe he would even take up the task of becoming a leader. Who knows?

Andrew walked over to Jack who was eating as usual. He was more than willing to give Andrew some cheese sticks as he jostled up a bunch of food for himself as well from the locked kitchen. Andrew received the mistaken cheese he asked for and was grateful for the food. He took it and went to his room to do some thinking.

CHAPTER 51
Discharge

Andrew got out of bed to get his vitals taken in the cafeteria the following morning. He was anxious to leave. Find out his blood pressure was elevated. Charlie got his vitals next while Andrew grabbed his breakfast and sat at a table nearby. The staff member taking the vitals was another military person aside from his hospital job. The man wrapped the cuff around Charlie's arm and initiated the machine. He looked down upon the sitting "patient" and said, "Looks like a burn notice."

Andrew had an idea of what they meant from watching the show in jail. He must have been banned from the secret organization but why? Was he at risk of spilling information? Did they think Andrew was making things up? Either way, he was to be disavowed. This didn't change the fact that Andrew wanted to see things turn the corner. He didn't need them.

Andrew got out of his seat and walked up to the vital man. "When can I leave?" he asked.

"We still have to contact your fiancé. We are backed up at the moment," the man answered.

Andrew felt like this was a test because he was about to explode. He was literally pulling his hair. "So she doesn't even know when to pick me up yet? I need to get the hell out of here!"

"Just be patient. The moment will come," the man replied as he removed the cuff from Charlie's arm.

Andrew marched away cussing to himself. They were testing his patience. It is hard to define how close to the brink of snapping he was. He practiced and maintained self-control. Andrew considered himself passive-aggressive. How much passivity will Andrew handle before he had had enough? It would only be so long before he took a shot back. He surely picked and chose his battles. There are moments in life where you can walk away and fight another day.

Andrew caused a commotion in morning group. He threw his arms up in the air and stormed away. He wasn't going to participate today. Instead, he began to pester the staff at the counter. He gave them a fierce attitude. When he got going, he really got going. He wouldn't stop.

"Call my fiancé now! I want out of here!" Andrew yelled. In return, they just fed him some more bullshit. Andrew continued, "Just let me leave! I can wait outside for my ride! My grandma lives in Prospect Park. I can walk there if I have to. Just let me go!"

"We can't let you leave without a ride," said the lady across the counter of command center. The staff members began to circle Andrew. His fists were clenched as he turned to do a full 180 to head to his room to rest and refrain from getting into any trouble. When he got to his room he was approached by his roommate.

"Hey bro. I have a gift for you," the roommate said as he held a brand new leather Bible in one hand and a fancy leather journal in the other. "Here, pick one. This is the King James Version of the Bible, otherwise, there is this journal for you to write. You can pick one to bring home with you."

"Oh cool," Andrew responded as his roommate handed him each of the belongings to examine. "I'll take the journal if you don't mind."

"It's all yours," replied the roommate.

The Witch's Hat

"Thanks, man," Andrew concluded.

Andrew took the journal and set it on the room's heater vent near the window. His roommate left the room. Andrew opened up the first page of the journal and scribbled in chicken scratch was the phrase "No Hitler." What the hell did that mean? Just then, Jabba the Hutt entered the room.

"We've contacted your wife and she is on her way," she said.

"Thank God! Fuck this place! I'm ready to go!" Andrew said sternly.

Jabba left the room. Andrew sat down on his bed a minute then went to do his daily pacing in the hallway to calm his nerves. It felt similar to being released from jail. The restlessness and anxiety. He thought about being caged and compared it to dogs being trapped in a kennel or any creature for that matter. What a sad life he thought. Andrew skipped lunch and continued pacing the halls ranting until he was called for a meeting with his doctor. As Andrew was walking towards the cafeteria to where the doctor and his assistant sat he was pulled aside by Charlie.

"Hey, do you have that paper I gave you?" he asked.

Andrew brought forward the folder with the worn-out spine from his sweaty hands. He pulled out the folded note from within and handed it to Charlie. Charlie set it on the counter between the T.V. room and the cafeteria and drew a couple symbols on it. It was the dollar symbol along with the cents symbol. He handed it back to Andrew and nodded toward the doctor. Seemed as if he was still trying to help him out.

Andrew grabbed the note and proceeded to sit down with the doctor and his colleague.

"I'm not taking another shot of that stuff," Andrew told them. He set the paper on the table and slid it in front of the doctor with Charlie's recent scribbles facing up. "I highly advise you to consider this if you don't want trouble."

The doctor and his colleague laughed. "All your appointments are already scheduled. If you don't follow through with the recommendations I expect to see you back here," the doctor said. He looked to his predecessor. "We have nothing to worry about. Business will carry on as usual."

Andrew pulled the paper back towards himself and placed it back in his folder. Shortly after, Journey ended up entering the station. She spoke to the doctor for a few minutes. Andrew didn't hesitate to get to his feet as the doctor explained to Journey all the stipulations he must follow. She agreed that she will keep him on the right track. The two then went to the counter to sign the release papers. Andrew was more than ready to go. He signed them and left Journey at the counter as she discussed more with the staff. Jabba escorted Andrew to the locker room and unlocked his stuff. Andrew gathered all his belongings. He was looking forward to a cigarette.

He stepped out of the locker room fully coated and noticed Mason the devilish Hispanic in the corner near the pill dispensing station speaking gibberish. Andrew didn't know what was going on if Mason was speaking in tongue or what? Andrew felt like he was going to put a hex on him. Mason stared at Andrew the whole time and started laughing hysterically going back and forth from his verbal nonsense and his laughs. Andrew was uncomfortable. He had the urge to give Mason the finger.

"Just let it be," said Jabba. "It's not worth it."

"Well, he's got a staring problem," Andrew sneered.

Journey approached from command center and they were on their way. The secured doors leading to freedom were keyed open. Andrew took a step out holding his fiancé's hand and took birth into a new life. Andrew didn't wait to get outside. He departed the hospital into the frigid cold. He took a deep breath. So this was what it was like to be a freak on a leash. Andrew's future was uncertain at this point. He just knew the battle wasn't over. This puzzle is not yet complete and it would be in Andrew's best interest to play his cards safe.

Sincerely,

The Andy Ward Experience

About the Author

I have the feeling that you all have an idea of who I am. I wish you safe travels through your journey.
Godspeed!

Made in the USA
Coppell, TX
07 June 2024

33210448R10193